HALSEY FAMILY TREE

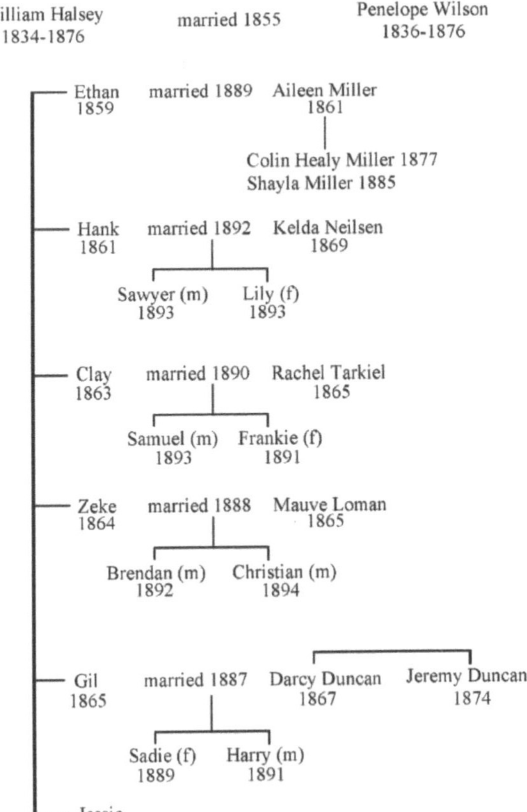

Halsey Homecoming Series

Laying Claim
Staking Claim
Claiming a Heart

LAYING CLAIM

Halsey Homecoming Series

by
Paty Jager

Windtree Press
Hillsboro, OR

LAYING CLAIM

Contact Information: info@windtreepress.com
Windtree Press
Oregon
Visit us at http://windtreepress.com

Cover Art by Covers by Karen
First Edition November 2013

Published in the United States of America

ISBN 13: 978-1-94006-445-1

Special Thanks

To my husband who took me on an Alaskan Cruise which set the scene for this book after we visited Skagway and rode the train up the White Pass.
And
To my awesome critique partners who keep me true to the characters and the story. Danita Cahill and Lauri Robinson, you two are the best!

Chapter One

January 1898
Skagway, Alaska

Clara Bixbee hadn't prepared herself for the mass of bodies and fervor that carried her along the Skagway dock. The crowded conditions on the boat she'd traveled on from Seattle should have hinted at what to expect. If two men hadn't been in a hurry to disembark and practically lifted her off the boat, setting her on the dock, she would still be trying to capture the layers of her skirts to descend the plank. She swat at the men's hands.

A man, well more than one, was the reason she had to endure the ship and was now alone in a sea of bodies and destined to cross the Chilkoot trail.

Crushed among the moving bodies, Clara was propelled toward the rustic town set back from the shoreline. The swarm stepped off the pier. Most of the men moved to the right where loaded row boats were shoved onto the shore and added to the growing pile of goods and trunks that had been stowed below deck on the ship.

Clara stopped to scan the pile for her trunk. Someone ran into her from behind, knocking her into the back of a man. Hands fumbled about her wool coat. Having grown up in Seattle, she knew when her pockets were being picked.

She jabbed her ever-present umbrella into her accoster's belly. Air whooshed from the man's mouth as he doubled over, withdrawing his hand from her pocket along with her pocket book. The very pocket book that held half of the money she'd brought with her.

"I'll take back what's mine." Clara retrieved her pocket book from the man's hand and decided it would be best to find a room and send someone for her trunk. The trip on the boat had been harrowing enough with so many men, bawdy women, and not a moment's peace. If they weren't all talking about how they would find gold, they were gambling, drinking, and carrying on all hours of the night. She'd complained to the captain, but he'd been in the midst of the rabble-rousing.

Shoving the pocket book into an inside coat pocket, she continued out of the throng of bodies, poking them with the point of her umbrella to move them out of her way. Once she put space between herself and the new arrivals, Clara stood in the middle of a muddy street. The mountains rising up beyond the town were white with snow, yet the streets of Skagway were muddy and the air not much different than she would have encountered in Seattle had she been out exploring the city with friends.

"Outta the way!"

Clara returned her attention to the street and found her feet stuck in the mud as a team of horses pulled a wagon loaded with goods up from the dock and straight at her. The mud sucked tighter around her ankles as she jammed the point of her umbrella in the muck and tried to pull her feet free. Her heart raced as the brace of animals continued forward.

Frantic, she waved her arms and shouted, "Stop, I'm stuck. Stop!"

The horses tossed their heads and their eyes widened, but the man in the wagon continued to lash out at them with a whip.

The thud of the large hooves and wooden wheels vibrated the ground under her feet. Heat from the horses' breath touch her cheeks.

"He—" Her cry for help was cut short as an arm wrapped around her middle and pulled her out of the mud and onto a rider's lap.

"Miss, you really need to stay to the board-walks this time of year."

The male voice warmed the shell of her ear. The arm about her middle held firm but didn't feel invasive.

Before she could offer there were no sidewalks from the dock to town, the arm released her. She slid to the board walkway. When her balance was restored, she spun to thank her rescuer, but all she saw was a gray Stetson, a wool coat stretched be-tween wide shoulders, and the backside of a black horse before the man and horse were swallowed up in the bodies and conveyances in the street.

She glared at the man's back. *I don't need a man to rescue me. Quite the contrary, I'm here to do the rescuing.*

Clara stomped the mud from her boots with more force than was necessary. Six days on the ship and her anger over being considered unfit to run the family business still rankled. Her mother, who hadn't a lick of business sense, has always bowed to the superior male. The mud plopped onto the wooden walkway revealing her boots. Thankfully, she'd worn her oldest pair for this trip. She shook the mud off the bottom of her brown traveling skirt.

Glancing at the building behind her, she immediately hustled along the boardwalk. *Men.* Not only had the man plopped her down in front of a saloon, but reading the signs across the street, there were two more. She didn't mind a glass of sherry now and then, but the way men sauntered in and staggered out of the buildings, she made a note to stay far away.

A sign caught her eye. *Telegraph.* That would be the fastest way to let her mother and family know she'd arrived safely. She hurried to the door under the sign and went in. Not only would she get a message off to Mother but she'd locate a respectable hotel as well.

A thin man with a mustache and close-set eyes stood up. "Can I help ya, Miss?"

"Yes, I'd like to send a telegraph to Seattle, for Mrs. Randolph Bixbee. 1113 State Street." She dug her pocket book from inside her coat. "Have it say, in Skagway."

"That'll be five dollars." The man held his hand out palm up.

"Five Dollars? That's outrageous. I only asked you to send two words." She clutched her pocket book to her chest as if the man would snatch it away and stared at him.

"Miss, you'll find the prices up here are a lot different than you're used to." He nodded to his hand. "Why a bed is going to cost you a dollar here and two-fifty on the other side of the pass. Meals is a dollar."

Clara continued to stare at the man as she calculated the money she'd brought with her and how far it would go if she had to pay the outlandish prices. It would save her mother a lot of worry if she received a telegraph today rather than a letter in a month. She turned her back on the man and dug in her pocket book for a five-dollar note. With her pocket book back in the folds of her coat, and the currency in her hand, she turned back to the telegraph operator.

"Could you direct me to a respectable hotel, please?"

He took the note and pointed to the door. "Go back out and continue into town. Take a left on Bond Street. You can't miss St. James Hotel."

"Thank you." Clara tucked her umbrella under her arm and headed back out into the street. It was barely three in the afternoon and the sky was beginning to darken. Randy's letters stated the nights were long in the winter and short in the summer, but she hadn't conceived it would grow dark so early. The streets were still crowded with men. She didn't wish to be on the streets after dark.

Traveling on the ship had opened her eyes to a rougher world than she'd ever experienced. There had been lewd comments tossed her way along with groping hands when she'd dared to catch a breath of fresh air on the deck. She'd never thought her parents coddled her, since they'd allowed her and her sisters and brothers to travel about Seattle as they wished. But this journey showed her she *had* lived a coddled life. If her mother knew the conditions, she would have never sent her oldest daughter alone to find her son, and as of their father's death, heir to the family business.

I shouldn't have to be here looking for my older brother. She still fumed over the fact that no one felt her capable of running the family business because she was female. Yet, it was a man, a crooked manager, who, after the death of her father, was running the business into debt. *If they would have given me the chance, I could have changed things. We don't need Randy.*

She turned the corner and spotted the large building with the placard "St. James Hotel."

A steady stream of people entered and left the building. *Please, let there be a room available.* She trudged across the street and, using her umbrella, poked her way through the men standing on the walkway.

"Well, what have we here?" A tall thin man with a black beard grasped her arm.

"Unhand me, this instant!" Clara smacked his arm with her umbrella while yanking out of his grasp.

He laughed. "Only checking out the new scenery." The man's eyes roved up and down her person making her cringe.

Huffing and ignoring the other men's laughter, she shoved open the hotel door and entered. Stuffy warm air wrapped around her, thawing her nose. A line of five people, all men, stood at the counter inquiring about rooms. To her left she noticed an opening to a restaurant. The stench of unwashed, sour bodies overpowered the aroma of roasting meat.

"I'm sorry. That boat that just came in filled me up, boys. You'll have to go looking somewhere else." The clerk closed the large book on the counter and shook his head.

Clara elbowed her way through the stream of men walking her way. At the counter, she stopped the clerk from leaving by clearing her throat.

"Yes, Miss?"

"I would like a room, please." Clara drew her pocket book from inside her coat.

"I don't have a room, but I do have a bed. You'd be bunking with Mrs. Eiderly."

"A married woman?" *That would be better than no room at all.* "Where is her husband?"

"She's a widow. Been up here a month waiting out the winter to go back in and work her claim."

"I'll take it." She could use the advice of someone who had been over the pass. And maybe this Mrs. Eiderly had run into Randy and could tell her exactly where to find him.

"How long you staying for?" He turned the book on the counter and handed her a pen to sign her name.

"Only until I can get supplies and a guide. Two, maybe three days." She signed with a flourish and smiled at the clerk. She'd get out of this male dominant town as soon as possible. Perhaps on the trip back, she could convince Randy how helpful she'd be with the family business.

The man shook his head. "If you didn't bring supplies it could take you longer than you think to round them up unless the last ship brought more supplies in. Which pass you going over?"

"Chilkoot. It's the fastest."

His gaze skimmed her from head to toe, and then he shook his head. "Miss, you don't look strong enough to handle that pass. You best set your sights on the White."

"It takes longer to cross the White Pass. I don't have the luxury of time." She placed another five-dollar note on the counter. "Use this for my room and to send someone to the dock to pick up my trunk, please."

Holding out her hand, she asked, "Do I get a key, and what number is my room?"

"You'll find room twenty-seven at the top of the stairs to the right." He slid a key across the counter. "You best chat up Mrs. Eiderly. She'll set you straight."

Clara picked up the key and headed to the room she would share with a stranger. At least on the ship she'd had a small cabin to herself. From the congestion of people and boisterous atmosphere, this room may be her peaceful retreat as was the cabin on the ship.

At the room, she knocked on the door. No point in scaring the woman by unlocking it and barging in. No answer. She unlocked the door and stared into a dark room.

Once her eyes adjusted to the darkness, using the dim light from the hall, she noticed a light bulb, like those dangling in the hallway, in the middle of the room. The light was, of course, up high enough no one would hit it with their head. Stretching on her toes, her finger tips didn't even touch the bulb. She scanned the room and found a chair hidden under a pile of clothes. Clara dumped the clothes on a bed and dragged the chair under the light.

Standing on the chair, her fingers found the turnkey. The light clicked on. From her perch on the chair, she was pleased to find two single beds in the room. The thought of sleeping with a woman she didn't know had sent her mind into worrying if the woman was large or small, well groomed or not so well groomed.

Her mind stopped mid-thought. The clothes strewn about the room were mostly men's. *Did I enter the wrong room?* She stepped off the chair and back out into the hall to reread the number twenty-seven. It was, indeed, the right room.

She closed the door, unbuttoned her coat, and hung it and her hat on the hook by the door. To keep busy while waiting for her trunk to arrive, she cleaned off the bed that looked the least used. Clara picked up and folded the clothing on the bed and placed them on the other bed with rumpled covers.

Once her bed was cleared, she kicked the other belongings away to make a path from the door to the window. The glow of light through establishment's windows and open doorways were the only shafts of light in the dark streets.

Where was her roommate and when would her trunk arrive?

Chapter Two

Jeremy Duncan sat in the back corner of the Mascot Saloon reading the last letter he'd received from his sister. The letters filled with all the Halsey's lives usually cheered him up, but for some reason this time, it gnawed at him like a beaver whittling away at a tree. He was missing out on his nieces and nephews birthdays and watching his big sister be a mother. And he had to admit, even though he'd lived with mostly men the last five years, he missed Gil, Ethan, Hank, Zeke, and Clay. The five Halsey brothers had taught him what it was to be a man and treated him like a blood brother, not just a brother-in-law.

Loud laughter caught his attention, and he glanced around the packed saloon. This was his favorite place to get a whiskey at the end of a day before he wandered to the livery. A livery wasn't much of a home, but it was his since gold was found in the Klondike and he brought his pack string over White Pass to hire out.

He'd learned his first year up at Circle City he wasn't a miner. He smiled remembering the sorry lot he and Darcy had made trying to mine in Galena all those years ago. The best thing that came of that was her falling in love with Gil Halsey. He snorted. *Fat chance I could fall in love here surrounded by men.*

The few women he'd met up here so far were either married, actresses, didn't want a man, or weren't the kind you took home to your family. He'd yet to come across one that would be strong and feisty enough to fit in with the Halsey wives. She'd have to love him unconditionally, be a good mother, get along with his sister and her family, and be a good cook. He wanted a woman strong in her beliefs but who could also compromise.

He refolded the letter and tucked it inside his jacket pocket. The load of freight he had to get to Dawson before March was his last. That is if he handed the shipment over to Brightly on time. The man had offered to pay twice the going rate for the early delivery. That payment in hand, he'd sell the horses and equipment and return home. With that and what he'd sent to Darcy to bank for him over the years, he could start up any business he wanted and live anywhere he wanted. And he wanted to live in Sumpter. Close to his family.

The first six months in Circle City he'd learned the hard way you didn't keep money or gold no matter how well you thought it was hidden. There was always a mole around watching your every move and telling the other ruffians how to find it. Every time a mail boat left Dyea, it had a package for Darcy.

A commotion by the bar drew him out of his reveries. Two men who'd come in on the ship today were arguing about the best route to the interior. Jeremy tossed back the last of his whiskey and stood. He could hold his own in a fight but preferred not to. From the growing noise, it would be a brawl soon enough.

Keeping to the wall to avoid the men surging forward to take sides, he made it to the door just as the first fist was thrown.

Outside, he pulled the sheepskin collar of his coat up around his neck and ears, shoved his Stetson tighter on his head, and hunkered into the coat as he strode down the boardwalk toward his livery on the outskirts of town. Lights bobbed in the direction of the dock. They were too low to come from a ship. Jeremy changed direction and jogged toward the dock. There shouldn't be anyone on the shoreline after dark.

When he was close enough to make out shapes, he saw two men, pulling women's clothing out of a trunk sitting on the shore.

"Hey! What are you doing?" he called and ran towards the two men.

They took off, lights and all. Using the sliver of moonlight, Jeremy picked up the scattered belongings and closed the lid of the trunk. He'd have to pack it to the livery and see if he could find any identification inside to get it to the rightful owner.

He heaved it up onto his shoulder and headed for the livery. If he was lucky, the woman who owned the trunk was staying in a hotel. Trying to find her if she was staying in the tents or had gone on to Dyea would be next to impossible.

At the livery, he dropped the trunk on the packed dirt floor and retrieved his lantern. He opened the trunk. The scent of lavender that wafted out wrapped around him and set his mind to thinking of a soft woman and warm fire. *Soon.* When he returned to Sumpter he could think about finding a wife and settling down.

He moved the garments around, enjoying the flimsy feel of several undergarments. Swallowing, Jeremy forced his thoughts to how worried the woman must be and not to wondering if she was young or old. He found a bible and opened the cover. Looping letters on the first page spelled the name Clara Bixbee. That must be the woman who owned the trunk. He shut the lid with a resounding thunk. He didn't have any place to lock the trunk up. If the two he'd chased away watched from the dark to see what he did with the contents, they'd be lurking around outside the livery.

This was one of the few times he wished he had a partner. He could leave that person here to watch the trunk while he inquired at the hotels for the woman. Packing the trunk all over town while he located the woman didn't set well.

Jeremy stared at the doors on the livery and scanned the interior. A smile tipped up the corners of his mouth, and he nearly chuckled. Wilbur, the mule, wouldn't let anyone but Jeremy in his stall. He picked up the trunk, walked over to Wilbur's stall, and opened the gate.

"You won't let anyone near this will you, you old grump." He set the trunk in the corner farthest from the gate and patted the mule on the neck as he turned to exit. "Take care of that and you might just get an extra treat."

Whistling, Jeremy blew out the lantern and headed back out into the cold night air. He spent nearly an hour walking the boardwalk and inquiring about the woman, Clara Bixbee, at every hotel and boarding house. He had one left. St. James Hotel was always full and probably turned away everyone who came through the doors today, but he'd ruled out all the other possibilities.

"We don't have any rooms," the clerk said wearily.

"I'm not looking for a room. I'm looking for a woman. Clara Bixbee." He leaned on the counter.

"Why are you looking for her?" The man's gaze narrowed.

"That's between me and her. Is she staying here?" Jeremy didn't like the way the man bristled.

The clerk opened the ledger and ran his finger down the list of names. His finger stopped. "Yes, she's here."

"What room?"

"It isn't proper for a man to be asking about a ladies' whereabouts."

Jeremy frowned at him. "This is not the middle of some big city. This is country where formalities could get someone killed."

The man took a step back. "Is this woman a criminal?"

Jeremy shook his head. "No. What's the room number?"

"Twenty-seven."

"Thank you." Jeremy spun on his heel and headed out the door. He jogged back to the livery to stay warm. It was also getting late. The woman would need her things to get ready for bed.

The livery doors had a gap wide enough for a man to enter. Crouching, he put a hand on his pistol and slipped into the barn.

Wilbur's stall gate stood open. A man was sprawled on the floor five feet in front of it and another was smashed between Wilbur's right flank and the stall.

Jeremy couldn't hold back the laugh building in his chest. He let loose, and the man pinned in the stall turned wide, worried eyes his direction.

"Wilbur, old boy, you are the best guard mule I've ever had." Jeremy walked into the stall on the side opposite the squished man and picked up the trunk. He patted Wilbur on the neck. "Good job. Hold him there until I get back."

"You can't leave me like this!" the man wailed.

Jeremy didn't even glance back or comment. He kept a steady pace out of the building and down the streets to the St. James Hotel. A man was exiting the hotel as Jeremy approached.

"Hold that door," he called out and hustled through.

The clerk stood stalk still as Jeremy continued up the stairs. At the door marked twenty-seven, Jeremy knocked and waited, listening to muted sounds behind the door.

"Who's there?" a female voice questioned through the wood barrier.

"I have a trunk for a Clara Bixbee."

The door swung open. A girl stood in the opening.

He blinked.

No. A girl didn't fill out the front of a dress like this one did. But she was small. Tinier even than his sister, and she barely came to his shoulder.

"It's about time you brought my trunk. I've been waiting hours for it to arrive." Her green eyes snapped with anger.

"I don't know who you asked to pick this up, but I found two thieves rummaging through it on the beach and saved it."

She gasped, then her small pink mouth set in a grim line. "I paid the clerk downstairs to have someone bring it to me."

No wonder the man had a startled look on his face when Jeremy hauled the trunk up the stairs. "Where would you like me to put it?"

The woman stepped back, opening the door wider. "I cleared a spot over there. I've yet to meet my roommate but will have a word with her about this mess when she comes back."

Jeremy set the trunk on the floor and turned to the woman. Her blonde hair was pulled up into a working woman's bun, but her clothes, the ones she had on and the ones he'd sifted through in the trunk, were not working-class clothes.

She stood with her hands on her hips, her head tipped back, eyeing him. "How did you know this was my trunk?"

"After I chased the men off, I took it to my livery where I had some light and looked through it until I found the Bible with your name in it. Then I left it in safekeeping and started asking for you at the hotels."

Her smooth, creamy skin flushed a deep pink. "You went through my trunk?"

"Would you rather I left it to the thieves who wouldn't have brought it to you even after they took all they wanted from it?" While the woman was soothing on the eyes, he wasn't keen on her attitude.

She gasped and dropped to her knees in front of the trunk. Her tiny fingers clasped the broken latch where a key had most likely locked the box. She unclasped the other latches and dug down to the bottom of the trunk shoving the clothing, causing them to spill over the sides.

Jeremy watched in fascination as she burrowed into the contents. She pulled out an oilcloth jacket and pushed her hand into a pocket. A smile crept across her face. Her hand reappeared empty. He'd guess she had money stashed in that coat.

He cleared his throat and she jumped. In her urgency to make sure she hadn't been robbed, she'd forgotten he was still in the room.

"Mr…?"

"Jeremy Duncan. Miss…?" He hoped she didn't say she was married. It would be a shame to have rifled through a married woman's unmentionables. It would make fanaticizing about her not near as much fun.

"Bixbee." She frowned. "You know my name. Why are you asking?"

He smiled. "Just figuring out if you're married."

"I am not, and it isn't proper for you to be in my room." She pushed to her feet and stood, again, with her hands on her narrow hips.

Jeremy nodded to the open door. "The door isn't closed so you haven't been compromised."

Chapter Three

Clara couldn't believe the arrogance of the man standing in her room. Yes, having the door open did make it more respectable, but he'd dug through her clothing and now stood over her, with a smirk on his face. Typical male superior behavior. The most disconcerting thing about the man were his eyes. The light gray color had startled her. She'd never witnessed light colored eyes on one with such dark hair. Hair that could use a barber. His whole demeanor spoke of someone who was comfortable outdoors, in the wild.

"Thank you for bringing my trunk to me. I would have hated to send a telegraph to my mother telling her I'd lost my clothing." She mentally slapped her hand with a ruler. That wasn't information this man needed to know.

He tilted his head and peered down at her with those odd but compelling eyes. "You couldn't send a telegraph if you wanted to."

The man is delusional. "Yes, I can. I sent one earlier today from the telegraph office."

Mr. Duncan shook his head and chuckled. "That isn't a working telegraph. Soapy Smith put that up to get gullible people like yourself to put easy money in his pocket."

"No!" Why was this man baiting her with this ludicrous lie?

"You can ask any of the locals. They'll tell you. There aren't any lines from Skagway to any place. Those poles and wires you see leading from the office go nowhere." He spread his hands. "It's a scam, like most of the services you'll be offered if you aren't careful."

Clara didn't want to think she'd been duped so soon or so easily, but if he spoke the truth, the widow would be able to set her straight. She walked over to her coat hanging by the door and slid her hand into the pocket containing her pocketbook. This man deserved something for his trouble.

"Jeremy Duncan what are you doing in my room?" A deep feminine voice boomed from the hallway.

A robust woman with fiery red hair, dressed in men's clothing resembling the wardrobe Clara had found strung about the room, stepped through the door.

"I returned a missing item to your roommate."

"My what?" The woman took another step in and scanned the room.

Her gaze rested on the clothes folded on her bed, then the trunk, and last she peered at Clara.

"No one told me I'd have a roommate." The woman's gaze, again, did a scan, this time of Clara.

"I'm Clara Bixbee. This was the only bed available when I arrived this afternoon." Clara stepped forward, extending her hand.

The other woman grasped her hand and squeezed so hard, tears burned in Clara's eyes.

"Pleased to meet you. I'm Belle Eiderly." Belle scowled up at Mr. Duncan. "What are you doing standing there gawking. Say your good-byes, I want to hear all about the happenings down yonder."

Clara held back a snicker at the man's embarrassment. She held out a silver dollar. "Thank you for retrieving my trunk."

The man stared down at the money in her hand then those unsettling eyes stared into hers.

"Miss, I didn't do it for the money. It was the right thing to do." He stepped into the hall and disappeared.

Clara stared at the open door. He was a most contradictory man. She thought only her brother was that way. It appeared she had a lot to learn about men besides the fact they liked to boss women around.

"So, Clara. Tell me where you came from and what you're doing here?" Belle plopped down on the folded clothes on her bed and stared expectantly at her.

The next half hour was spent with Clara telling Belle about her life in Seattle and the request by her mother to find her older brother to take over the family business since the death of their father. "If he doesn't return and take over, the rest of the family will soon be on the streets. The manager my father hired six months ago is moving the business toward failure. Randy, as the oldest son, is the heir to the business. If not for laws being in the favor of men, I could have ran the business and saved myself and my family all this trouble."

She hated the fact, the only reason she was here, surrounded by more males than she cared to be surrounded by, was because of a male dominant society. She had to find her brother to take over a business she could run. She'd argued with her mother until the only recourse was to come find Randy herself.

"We haven't known how to contact him for several months. He doesn't even know that Father has passed. I have to take the quickest route into the Yukon."

Belle held up her hand. "Do you even know where to look for your brother?"

"His last letter came from Forty Mile. I'll start looking there." That was the best plan she had.

"And how are you going to get there? There aren't any stages or trains up here."

"I'll hire a guide." That was the reason for the money hidden in the coat. To hire a guide.

Belle stared at her so long she began to squirm. The woman finally spoke. "Do you know how to tell when someone is genuine and someone is a cheat?"

She thought of the five dollars she'd spent on a non-existent telegraph service. "No, but I'll check around before I hire anyone." She peered into the woman's face. "I can ask you. Right? You would know who is genuine and who is scamming me."

Belle nodded then tipped her head toward the door. "The man that just walked out the door is the most honest man you're going to run across in these parts. He has a pack string that he uses to carry people and goods over White Pass."

Clara shook her head. "No, I'll go over Chilkoot. It's faster."

Belle raised an eyebrow. "Honey, I've only crossed Chilkoot once. It was the hardest thing I've ever done, and I don't plan on doing again. Take my word for it, you don't want to take that route this time of year. You'll freeze to death if you even make it to the top."

"My guide will see to it that I make it over—"

The woman let loose a harsh laugh. "Girl, there isn't a guide that crosses the Chilkoot would care if you made it. They'd roll your frozen corpse to the side of the trail after they picked your pockets and your belongings clean."

"They wouldn't!"

"Up here there is no law. Why do you think Soapy Smith is running this town and taking gold from miners and money from newcomers?"

"Like the telegraph office?" She hated to admit she'd been duped already, but she had to see if Mr. Duncan was telling the truth.

Belle laughed. "That scam has fleeced more newcomers than anything else he's done."

Clara turned to her trunk and opened the lid. "I'm tired from my travels. I'd like to go to bed." She pulled her nightgown out of her trunk and turned her back to the woman. Belle had given her a lot to think about. Namely, did she want to stick to her original plan and hunt down an honest guide for the Chilkoot or take Belle's word that her best bet was the guide with the unsettling eyes?

<h1 style="text-align:center">Chapter Four</h1>

Jeremy hefted another crate from a wagon of supplies and sundries that had arrived by ship the day before. He scoffed. Probably the same ship that brought the woman he couldn't get out of his mind. What was someone so young and inexperienced doing in Skagway? He had a lot of questions to ask. Questions that kept him tossing and turning most of the night.

When he'd finally fallen into a deep sleep, he heard Felix pull up to the livery with the laden wagon. As Jeremy unloaded the crates, he set the goods in piles to be packed onto his mules and horses for Dawson. Brightly, the owner of a saloon, did his part in ordering the items to get here early enough Jeremy could get them delivered before the March first deadline. Brightly wanted his business up and running before a rival's.

With it being the middle of winter, he'd take

the pack string all the way to Dawson. Usually, he took the goods over the pass and someone else met him at the lake shore to take the goods on into the interior. But this time of year the usual water routes were frozen over. Brightly had been adamant he couldn't wait for the spring thaw. If Jeremy delivered his goods by March he'd pay double.

He'd thought himself too old to get homesick, but the last six months that was all he could think about. Returning to Sumpter and starting a life close to his family.

He heaved a box onto his shoulder and carried it into the livery. He placed the wooden crate next to a pile with another crate. That would even out the load.

"Excuse me."

The words were spoken so quietly he almost didn't hear them. But when he turned around, standing in the doorway was the woman who had kept him up half the night. Miss Bixbee.

"Miss." He tipped his hat and waited.

Her gaze flicked around the building's interior, and she walked three more feet into the building. She cleared her throat. "I've been discussing the prospect of procuring a guide to take me to Forty Mile with Mrs. Eiderly. She suggested you would be the least likely to knock me over the head and take my money."

How had she said that with a straight face? Jeremy peered through the dim lighting at the woman. *Cuz she was dead serious.* Knowing it would only provoke the prim and proper woman, he laughed. Couldn't help himself. The way she'd come out and said it, just tickled.

"Mr. Duncan, I don't see anything funny about my trying to find a guide I can trust."

"That's not what's funny. It's the way you said it." Jeremy dried the tears streaming down his face and walked closer to the woman. "Why do you need to go to Forty Mile? The gold there is starting to peter out and so are the jobs."

"I'm not here for a job or to waste time looking for gold. I'm here to tell my brother our father has passed and the family needs him to return home and run the business." She stood still, her intent gaze on his face.

There wasn't a flicker of sorrow in her eyes. No, it looked more like smoldering fury. Her gloved hand gripped a black umbrella, making an indention in the middle of the fabric.

"Why didn't you just send him a letter? Or send a male relative to collect him?"

She inhaled deep and let it out slow. "We have sent letters, but he hasn't responded. We didn't have a relative to send." Her gaze flashed with annoy- ance. "We believe he may have moved on from Forty Mile and did not wish to send someone else on a goose chase."

"Then why are you going there?"

"Because it is the last place we know he resid- ed. When I arrive there, I'll ask questions and find someone who can point me to his new claim." Her chin pointed up at him, and she peered down her pert nose.

He laughed, this time not from merriment but from the foolhardiness of this woman. "You think you'll get some old sourdoughs to tell you where your brother is? You'll either end up dead or working in one of the camps as who knows what."

Her foot stomped, and she glared at him. Had she been older and stouter that glare would have put a little fear in him. But she was small, frail looking, and couldn't be much out of school. And that was the reason he grit his teeth and glared back at her. She had no business being up here talking of traipsing all over the interior looking for a brother that could be dead. Chances were if he hadn't answered his mail he was no longer able to.

"You pay me a finder's fee, and I'll go find your brother and give him a letter from you or whatever you want, but you have to get back on the next mail ship out of here." This was the best solution for her problem. It would get her back safe in her mother's care and give him a little extra money in his poke.

"How can I trust you'll even look for my brother? For all I know, you'll take the money, burn the letter and go on your way. We'd never know if you found him." She took two steps closer to him.

"You just asked me to take you to him for a fee because Mrs. Eiderly said I could be trusted." He took a step closer to her. He peered down into her upturned face. Her green eyes were lit with rebellion.

"You could be trusted not to kill me and take my money, but just handing money over to you and betting you'll do the service…" she shook her head. "No. I don't trust you."

He smacked his hat on his thigh making her

jump back a step. "Didn't I save your trunk from thieves and hunt you down last night so I could get your belongings to you?"

The heat in her gaze lessened. "Yes. But you were probably hoping for a *finder's fee.*"

She spit the last two words out as an accusation.

"I didn't take anything from you for bringing your belongings to you."

"Because Mrs. Eiderly arrived. You probably didn't want to spoil your reputation in front of her."

That just about did it. Jeremy took a step toward the infuriating woman. "You need a good paddling and sent back to Seattle. This is no place for someone as young and frail as you. Hasn't the happenings so far sunk into your pretty little head?"

Clara was struck dumbfounded for a moment. *He thinks I'm pretty.* Good sense halted her fancies. *And frail.* That starched her backbone and added to her fury at the man. How dare he think she was frail and not able to take care of herself?

"I am not going back to Seattle without either my brother or proof he is dead. If you won't help me I will find someone who is willing." She had hoped the packer would help her. Belle had sung high praises for the man all the way through their shared breakfast. While she was still unsettled by his light-colored eyes, especially when he was angered, she did believe he would do right by her. She gave him one last chance to offer.

He stared at her, his arms crossed, his stance stating he wasn't budging on his statement.

With a huff, she pivoted and headed back out

into the snow that had started falling. *I hope this doesn't delay my departure.*

She hurried under the closest cover and debated her options. She needed a guide. Her mother would not approve, but Clara had the notion she'd find guides in the saloons. Making sure her wool traveling coat was buttoned to her chin, she strode down the boardwalk. Belle had mentioned most of the saloons were down near the docks. She'd step inside the saloons, state her business, and ask anyone interested to contact her at the hotel. She could meet with them in the lobby, and then ask Belle if they were trustworthy.

The idea formed and settled. Clutching her umbrella in front of her, she headed to the dock.

She'd had only minor altercations at the first three saloons. Once she smacked the first person to grope her with her umbrella, the rest backed off and listened. She stepped into the Jeff Smith Parlor. The first person she spotted was the thin, bearded man who'd grabbed her arm as she entered the hotel yesterday.

She pivoted to head for the door.

His voice rang out, "Stop her."

Two men standing by the door stepped in her path.

"Please move. I see I walked into the wrong establishment." She smiled sweetly, but the men didn't budge. Their eyes raked over her like the tall thin man's had the day before. Nausea bubbled in her stomach.

"Well, now. What are you doing here? Looking

for work? I could use a pretty little thing like you with the rest of the girls." The thin man's deep voice caused her hands to tremble.

"Girls?" Clara glanced around. Scantily clad women sat on men's laps and rubbed up against the men at the bar and tables.

"Oh no! I didn't come here for work." She tried to back up and jumped forward when a hand pushed on her backside. She'd forgotten the men at the door. *They think I'm a loose woman because I entered a saloon.* Why did all men think a woman was only good for one thing?

Panic froze her feet. Clara swallowed the fear clawing up her throat and thought of her family and all the outrages she'd suffered from men. *My family is counting on me. I'll not fall prey to any man.*

The tall man looked down at her. His eyes were black just like his hair and beard. "If you aren't looking for work, did you come here looking for me?" He spread his arms. "I own this parlor."

"No, I definitely did not come here looking for you." His questions stung like a bee and festered like a sliver. Anger starched her courage.

He grasped her arm, pulling her toward him. Clara smacked his hand with her umbrella and used the accessory to push the man to the side. She scanned the room. Everyone watched the exchange between her and Mr. Smith. *This is my opportunity.*

"I'm looking for someone to guide me over either the Chilkoot trail or White Pass. I don't care which. I need to get to Forty Mile. If you are interested, please, come to the St. James lobby at two this afternoon." She nodded her head and turned to leave.

Mr. Smith grabbed her arm. She glared up at him.

"Sweetheart, I have the means to get you to Forty Mile. How much are you willing to spend?"

She peered into his cold black eyes and knew he was fishing to see how much money she had. She'd be no match physically if any one of the men in this establishment robbed her. But she had a very quick mind.

"You would be paid once I meet up with my brother."

"He's the one paying for the trip?" The man's eyes narrowed as his gaze once again roamed up and down her person.

He knows this is a tailored coat. "That is the instruction he gave me." This was a lie. But under the circumstances, her mother would forgive her allowing a falsehood to slip so easily from her tongue. However, Mother would not forgive her keeping company with this ilk of men or soiled doves.

"And he's in Forty Mile?" Again the man's black eyes bore into hers.

She swallowed. "Yes."

He released her arm, but she could tell by his calculating gaze he wasn't truly convinced.

When she turned this time, the men parted and she left the establishment. After that encounter she wasn't going to take any more chances.

Big, wet snowflakes continued to fall as she hurried along the busy streets to the hotel. The muddy streets now glistened in white. A wagon passed and within seconds the tracks filled, leaving no visible trail.

She peered up into the sky. Dark gray clouds hung low and ominous. The mountains she'd seen yesterday completely hidden and perhaps holding the clouds in place. Clara ducked her head and trudged through the snow the two blocks to the hotel. Once inside, she headed for the restaurant. A warm cup of tea and she'd be ready to interview perspective guides. That is if she knew the right questions to ask…

Chapter Five

Jeremy couldn't believe what he'd just over-heard. Two old sourdoughs discussing if the "little gal" that came in the saloon had the money to hire a guide. The "little gal" they talked about had to be Miss Bixbee. She was the only little gal he knew of looking for a guide. The thought of her being at the mercy of any of the greedy men who might offer to take her, tore at his gut like a bear gnawing on a salmon.

He bought a bottle of whiskey and sat down with the sourdoughs. "What exactly did that gal looking for a guide say?"

The one with the longest, dirtiest whiskers peered at him from one squinty eye. "Why? You thinking of helping her?"

Jeremy shrugged. "I don't care to take green-horns over the pass. It's treacherous enough getting my pack team over with all the city folk cluttering the trail. Just curious why she'd be askin'."

"She said she was looking for a guide to take her over either pass and on to Forty Mile. If we're interested we're to meet her in the lobby of St. James today at two o'clock."

At least she'd been smart enough to meet in a public place. No telling what might have happened had she met them in her room. Or been surrounded by no-good men inside a saloon.

That thought shook him from his head to his heels. The girl probably didn't even realize three-fourths of the men she talked to in the saloons would just as soon use brute force to separate her from her money as take her over a pass.

Jeremy left the bottle on the table with the men and walked out of the saloon. He had some heavy thinking to do. Darcy kept popping into his head. She'd want him to do the right thing with the little gal and help her find her brother. His sister believed in family. That's why she did the things she did when he was a kid to keep them together. Miss Bixbee and Darcy were built pretty much the same. He smiled. And held just as much grit and gumption too.

His gut told him this wasn't the smartest move he'd ever made, but it felt like the only thing his conscience would allow. He pointed his feet toward the St. James Hotel.

Clara had questioned half a dozen men who professed to be guides, but so far didn't feel comfortable with any of them. She leaned back in the chair in the dining room and sipped her cool tea.

She'd asked the red-faced clerk to send the men in as they arrived. The clerk had watched her intently as though he expected her to light into him. She knew it probably had to do with the fact Mr. Duncan brought her trunk to her. She wasn't going to say anything, since the clerk was being more than complying with the interviews.

She closed her tired eyes. She and Belle had talked until late, and then the woman had insisted they eat breakfast together. Clara had agreed not realizing Belle ate at five. Two hours before Clara usually was out of bed.

"I heard you're looking for an honest guide."

Her lashes snapped up. Her breath caught at the sight of the man standing in front of her. She narrowed her eyes and stared at him. His silvery-gray, hypnotic eyes held a hint of amusement, wrinkling the skin at the corners. His lips were tipped into a smile. The smile made it hard to remain aloof.

She motioned to the chair across the table from her. "Have a seat." *Why was he here, now, after turning her down earlier?*

The waiter arrived with a cup of coffee and placed it in front of Mr. Duncan.

"Thank you." He picked up the cup and took a sip, watching her over the rim.

"Could you please bring me more hot water?" she asked the waiter. He nodded and as he left she leaned back in her chair. "Why this change of heart, Mr. Duncan?"

He placed the cup on the table. "Call me Jeremy. No one calls me Mr. Duncan."

She nodded. "Jeremy, why are you here? I

clearly heard you say you would not help me when I asked this morning."

"My sister."

That wasn't at all what she'd expected. "Your sister?"

"Yeah. She's about your size and tough and tenacious as a badger. If she knew I'd left you to the likes of these other vultures, she'd sic her husband and his brothers after me." He ran a hand over his face. "I'd like to keep my face lookin' this way and not lose the respect of my family."

"I see." She studied the man. When he talked about his sister and the brothers, the love he felt for all of them was evident in his eyes and the warmth in his voice. "Where do they live? Here in Alaska?"

His expression sobered. "No. They're all in Oregon."

This surprised Clara. "They are that far away, and yet, you are afraid they'll discover you turned me down? How on earth would your family find out?"

His light-gray eyes stared at her. Straight in her face. No drifting up and down her body like the black-haired man in the saloon. His gaze was direct, and she saw conviction staring back at her.

"Because it would have ate away at me, and I'd have had to tell Darcy what I did."

Even if he hadn't been highly recommended by Belle, this one statement told her he was the best man to take her to her brother. His loyalty to his sister and his inner guilt showed he had scruples. Something she'd seen few of since boarding the ship in Seattle. The honesty he'd shown since meeting her was refreshing. Few men in her life had ever been honest with her.

"I see. Well then, it looks like I have a guide."

The waiter returned with her hot water.

"We'll each have steak and spuds," Jeremy told the man.

"I'm not that hungry," Clara said, to the waiter. "Just bring me toasted bread and jam, please." When the waiter left, she peered across the table, stifling a yawn. Now that the worry of finding a guide was over, she felt drained from so many sleepless nights on the ship. She'd rather slip off to her room and sleep than eat. "You don't have to eat with me."

"Miss, I do. We have to discuss your supplies, how strong you are, and what I'm getting for guiding you." Jeremy leaned back in his chair and placed his gray Stetson on the extra chair to his right.

"Please, call me Clara. We're going to be working together to find my brother, and I'm going to get awful tired of hearing you call me Miss." She smiled to shave some of her irritation off. Miss was what a school girl was called. She'd been out of school several years. A yawn escaped before she could cover it.

"My apologies. I didn't want to be too forward. But you don't look old enough to be sent up here alone to find a brother." His eyes remained on her face.

"I'm twenty-two and have been working for the family business the last five years."

"What is the family business?" His tone stayed

neutral, and his gaze remained on her face.

Clara perked up. She knew the family business inside and out thanks to her insistence that she work at the warehouse. Her father finally gave in when he discovered she wasn't going to let up. But he only allowed her to tally and do menial jobs. It was her doggedness to know everything and talking with all the others who worked at the warehouse that taught her about the business.

"We have a warehouse on the docks. We unload ships, then transfer the goods to the respective owners. We are paid for storing the goods and the bookkeeping to route them to the right places." The business had been in her family since the founding of the port city of Seattle.

"I see. Are you one of the people in charge of the bookkeeping or are you part of the labor?" There was a hint of mockery in his tone.

"I oversee the loading of the freight onto the wagons."

He smiled. "That's how come you're so bossy."

"I beg your pardon? I am not bossy." How dare he proclaim her to be bossy after only meeting her a few times?

The smile on his lips lit his eyes and added crinkles at the corners. The sight shaved off a bit of her indignation, but the word continued to echo in her mind. *Bossy.* She could give orders to men. They mostly responded because she was the boss's daughter, not because they respected her. No, that was going to come when she returned with Randy and he kicked the manager out.

The waiter arrived with a plate half covered

with a slab of meat and the other half mounded with fried potatoes. This plate, he placed in front of Jeremy. Her mouth watered at the sight of the food. But until she found Randy, her finances had to keep her alive. With the cost of food and necessities up here, she wasn't sure if the funds would hold, so she'd ordered the least expensive item she could think of.

She stared down at the two slices of toasted bread and dollop of jam on the side. Her stomach grumbled. She hadn't eaten a thing since breakfast and it was nearing dinner time.

"You sure you don't want a steak?" Jeremy watched her with narrowed eyes.

"This will do nicely." She smiled and spread jam on a piece of bread.

He shook his head. "I'm paying for the meal, if you want more all you have to do is say so."

"I couldn't ask—"

"You didn't ask, I offered." Jeremy stared at the young woman. Now that he knew her age it felt wrong to think of her as a girl even if she still looked about sixteen. When she'd ordered toasted bread, he'd figured she was one of those women who eats next to nothing when with a man. But the longing in her eyes when the waiter set the steak in front of him, he decided there was something else going on.

He called the waiter over. "Bring us out another steak please."

The waiter nodded and hustled away.

"Here." He cut his steak in half and placed it on Clara's plate. "If you're going to be hiking the trail you need to have plenty of strength."

"But," she started to protest then her gaze fixed on his. "What do you mean hiking? I thought you had pack horses?"

"I do. And that's what they do, they pack. The trail is too treacherous to ride a horse. If they lose their footing you and the horse are a goner. We lead the horses. If one slips, you let go of the rope. We may lose the goods and several horses but we'll still be alive. I don't take my horses over anything I wouldn't feel comfortable walking over, but there have been a couple instances when I've lost a horse." His mind went back to last fall when a damn greenhorn crowded his string. The last horse had ended up with a broken leg, and he'd had to put it down. He'd given the man a tongue lashing when what he wanted to do was send him barreling over the edge of the trail.

"It's the greenhorns who think if they don't go hell-bent for fury over the pass they'll miss out on the gold. Those are the people you don't want behind you, shoving and tormenting the horses as they pick their way up the trail."

He took a bite of meat and chewed, noticing Clara was doing the same. He swallowed and took a drink of coffee, deciding if he should tell her about the horse carcasses strewn over the trail or wait and let her find out first hand. He'd wait. It was appalling enough to see. He didn't want to put notions in her head.

"If this is so dangerous, why do people take the trails, and why do you take your horses over it?" She sipped her tea, stifled a yawn, and watched him.

"The why of others as far as I can see is greed.

They had nothing where they were due to the economic state of things and set all their hopes on finding a fortune up here. Me, I came up in '93 with another fellow, looking for an adventure and a nest egg to go home with. I wanted to prove to Gil and his brothers I could make it on my own." His mind went back to that tearful departure. He'd hated to leave his sister, Darcy, they'd been all each other had since their parents died, but she was in good hands with her husband and his family. He wanted to prove to himself as much as everyone else that he could make it on his own. He'd gone from Darcy taking care of him to the Halseys. He'd wanted to see if he could take care of himself.

"So you like the adventure of perhaps losing a horse every time you cross this trail?" Her left eyebrow rose.

"No, the adventure seeker in me is gone. This will be my last trip over White Pass. I'm ready to return to Sumpter and my family." With this load and Clara's payment he'd be ready to leave. But in all truth, he didn't need this last load. He was so homesick, if he hadn't already told Brightly he'd deliver his goods, he would have sold the horses and headed home on the next ship. Now, he not only had the load for Brightly, he had to get the bossy woman sitting across the table from him to her brother.

Chapter Six

Clara finished the steak and leaned back in her chair. That was the most food she'd eaten in one meal since leaving Seattle. With the six sleepless nights while on the ship worrying about the drunken men entering her room and her full stomach, she was ready to go to her room and sleep. She hid a yawn behind her hand. Her eyelids felt heavy, and the man across from her blurred.

"Are you awake enough to complete our business?"

Jeremy's voice drifted into her mind, but she was having a hard time keeping her eyes open. She hadn't felt this tired in…she couldn't remember when.

The motion of her chair moving backwards registered. She roused herself enough to push to her feet. Her eyelids felt as heavy as the warehouse doors, but she opened them. Jeremy peered into her face.

"Why are you so sleepy?"

"Not enough sleep on the ship, worry, and now a full stomach, I think."

He wrapped an arm around her shoulders, navigating them through the restaurant and lobby. She walked as if in a dream. The walls and people were a blur, but her feet moved one in front of the other until the stairs.

"Pick your feet up."

Jeremy's frustrated tone was the slap she needed. Her eyes opened and she pointed her nose to the top of the stairs. One by one, she lifted her feet. With her feet moving and Jeremy's arm still around her keeping her moving in a straight line, she made it to the top.

"I'm sorry, I've never…" Her eyelids started drifting down again. Clara fought to keep them open as she dug in her pocket for the key. She grasped the metal object and pulled it from her pocket, leaning against the wall.

"Let me."

The key disappeared from her hand, and her body rose in the air.

This must be a dream. She stopped trying to open her eyes and relaxed into the cradle that rocked. The scent of hay, horses, leather, and—she sniffed— musky male invaded her senses and took her to a dream world she hadn't visited in a long time. A knight on a white horse was whisking her away. She snuggled her face into the soft flannel covering his chest and sighed. Just like the books she'd read as a child, she was being saved by a noble knight.

The scents and fluffy flannels disappeared. She stretched recognizing the give of a mattress under her. She smiled, rolled to her side, and continued the dream.

Jeremy stared at the woman on the bed and couldn't help but smile at the angelic pose. But dang how was he get her over the pass if she fell asleep over a couple nights bad sleep? He didn't like the prospect at all, but he'd already committed to taking her.

She tucked her hands under her cheek like a child. He reached out, pushing a stray strand of her shimmering sunshine-colored hair away from her face and pulled the blanket sides up over her still-clothed body.

He'd come back tomorrow to either finish up their business or talk her out of her fool notion she could travel to the interior. Either way, it set right this was his last trip before heading home.

Jeremy backed out of the room, locked the door, and slid the key under the door. Whistling, he descended the stairs and pulled the collar of his coat up around his neck before stepping out into a blizzard. While he'd been in the hotel a foot of snow had fallen.

He looked in the direction of the pass and could barely see the next building. The heavy, wet snow falling could stop travel over the pass for a week or better. It would be suicide to try it in these conditions. But it would make a good base for when they did strike out.

Clara woke up and struggled with the blanket and clothing that wrapped around her. The room was dark and cold. She stopped and listened. The only breathing was her own. What time was it and where was Belle?

She thrashed around some more before getting loose. Moving her hands back and forth in front of her and out to the side, she felt for the chair. Her right hand smacked into the wood back.

"Ow!" She sucked on the knuckle of her little finger. With her left hand, she grabbed the chair and pulled it to what she thought was the middle of the room. She climbed on the chair and swung her hand around in the air.

Nothing.

She stepped down and moved her hands in front of her until her palm touched a wall.

Leaning right then left, her fingers traveled up and down the wall looking for the door. The cold knob touched her hand and she grasped it. It wouldn't turn. Clara fumbled in her dress pocket.

No key. The dark closed in on her. Her skin tingled as the hair stood up. Think! *Where is the key if not in my pocket?*

Jeremy helped me to the room. I took the key out of my pocket, he opened the door… Did he take the key with him after locking me in? Anger started building. *Leave it to a man to lock up a woman.* What if Belle doesn't return? Am I going to have to pound on the door to get out?

Anger and humiliation tumbled about in her head. If I had locked someone in a room what would I do with the key? A thin light shone at the bottom of the door revealing the hall light.

I'd slip the key under the door!

Clara dropped to her knees and felt the wood floor. Something skidded away from her fingers and into a bit of the light under the door. The key. She scooped it up and stood.

In the dark, she jabbed at the keyhole until the key finally slipped in. A click, and she flung the door open.

Light from the hallway provided enough illumination to see the bulb in her room dangling six feet to the side of the chair. She repositioned the chair and turned on the light. The brightness made her blink several times as she walked over to the door and closed it. She dug into her dress pocket and pulled out her father's pocket watch. Her mother gave it to her for the trip.

"That can't be right." Clara put the watch to her ear and listened. The device ticked along at its usual steady rhythm. "Where could Belle be at eleven o'clock at night?"

She glanced down at her boots and then sat on the chair. "How did I come to be fully dressed and sleeping in my bed?" Clara shoved the wayward strands of hair out of her face and thought.

Jeremy Duncan escorted her to her room, unlocked her door... She popped up off the chair. The meal and so many sleepless nights had made her so sleepy she could barely keep her eyes open. She shot her gaze to the door, then to her bed, and back to the door. The dream of being carried by a knight...that had to be... Her heart raced. *The impropriety! If mother knew, she'd, she'd... oh!* Clara didn't even want to imagine what her mother would think. And what must Jeremy think? *He already thinks I'm too fragile to travel over the pass.*

She groaned at her own frailty. *I should have left the dining room after he agreed to escort me. Then he wouldn't be able to use my falling asleep against me.*

She ran her hands over her clothing and stared at her shoes. *Nothing was amiss just wrinkled. He was a knight in shining armor!* He'd put her to bed. That's all. Nothing more.

Clara closed the door to her room and began undressing. *Where is Belle? What could keep her out this late?* She thought about the men who had tried to steal her money when she first arrived and the ones Jeremy said he chased away from her trunk. *Belle could be laying somewhere hurt.*

"But what could I do? I can't wander the streets looking for her." But the more she thought about it, guilt tugged at her conscience.

Clara stepped back into her dress and buttoned it up. She slipped on her coat, mittens, and warm cap. Leaving the light on in the room, she descended the stairs. The lobby was full of people talking, drinking, and watching the windows.

"Excuse me. Excuse me." She threaded her way through the people to the door.

"Where you going, missy?" A gnarled hand grabbed her coat sleeve.

"To find my friend. She hasn't come back." Clara peered in a wrinkled and whiskered face. The man smelled of body odor and fish.

"Most likely she holed up wherever she was

when the storm hit."

"Storm?" Clara walked to the door and opened it. Snow blew in, and she couldn't see three feet outside. "Oh!" She tugged the door closed.

"See what I told ya." The man tapped the one next to him on the arm. "Fool women can't take a man's word for nothin'."

Clara huffed at the man and scowled. The storm had to be the reason Belle hadn't come back to the room. "Will this hold me up going over the pass?"

Several men laughed. The sound raised her hackles. She didn't like to be laughed at by men.

The smelly man stopped laughing. "This here storm will keep all of us inside for a couple days. Then no one'll go over the pass until the scare of an avalanche is over."

She mentally tallied her traveling money. "How long do you think until the pass is navigable?"

"Till it's what?" The old man scrunched his face.

"How long until we can cross the pass?"

"I'd say a week or two. Depends on the weather." The man's gaze drifted up and down her form. "You don't look big enough to take on the pass."

"I have no choice. I was sent to find my brother and that's what I'll do." She pushed her way back through the men crowding the lobby. "Excuse me. Excuse me."

"You the missy looking for a guide?" The deep quiet question not far from her ear, drew her attention and raised her hackles.

"I was. Why do you ask?"

"You already found someone?" The man speaking had shaggy brown hair, eyebrows, and beard. He stood slightly taller than her but much broader. Like a boulder stood next to her.

"Yes. I did." Scanning the men in the crowd, there wasn't a one of them she'd feel comfortable traveling with.

"Did you already make a deal?" The man moved closer to her.

Clara backed away. A presence of another close behind her prickled the hair on her neck and panic tightened her chest. She fought to keep her face from showing her fear and forced the words, "Yes. Excuse me."

She hurried to the stairs and started up. Halfway, she peered over her shoulder to make sure no one followed. Chills, not from the cold, still rippled up her spine from her encounter with the man. She wondered if the presence she felt behind her was an accomplice. Surely, they wouldn't have tried to rob me in the midst of everyone else?

She looked over her shoulder while opening her door. The hallway was clear. She slipped in the room, closing and locking the door. Her back to the door, she breathed deeply and calmed her jitters. The idea of being cooped up in her room for a week or better would be pure boredom, but she'd do it rather than run into a group like that again.

Chapter Seven

Jeremy woke earlier than usual. Sleep had been as elusive as the gold h'de tried to find in Circle City. Last night, he'd walked straight from the hotel to his livery and tried to sleep. But after holding that bit of a woman in his arms, he'd had a hard time slowing his heart and chasing away his hardness. The last few years he'd stayed away from prostitutes. He wanted more than they offered. He wanted to lie down at night with a woman in his arms and wake with the same person snuggled against him. To whisper secrets in the dark and work out life's problems together. That was why he was headed home. He'd started to crave a wife. It was highly unlikely to find a woman that fit what he wanted in the Alaska wilds. And he missed his family.

He rolled out of his cot and into his clothes not bothering to light a lamp. The flannel shirt and wool pants lay where he'd left them when he undressed.

The animals shifted and gave soft nickers hearing him moving around. He pulled on the knee-high leather boots and stood, inhaling the horse and manure scent that took him back to childhood. He and Darcy had spent many nights in livery stables after their parents died. All to stay one step ahead of their nasty uncle. He shook his head. Best thing that ever happened for the two of them was the day Gil Halsey walked in the marshal's office in Galena and fell in love with Darcy. When Gil married Darcy and brought them into the Halsey family, they finally had a roof over their heads and a sense of security.

To feed, he lit a lantern. Only the hotels and a few other businesses had electric lights. He couldn't see the need in a livery. He doled out the rations of grain he paid a high price for to keep his animals in top shape. When the last one had his portion, Jeremy returned the bucket to the nail and grabbed up his blanket-lined coat, slipping it on and buttoning it up to his chin.

Crunching and an occasional cough came from the stalls as he walked to the door. He'd come back later and clean the stalls. He wanted to survey the outcome of last night's storm. The way the snow came down as he walked home from the hotel, he was curious to see what he would be dealing with.

He opened the door and blinked at the bright white world. The sun wouldn't rise until after nine, but the brightness of the snow made the town glow.

The snow was half way to his knees. Pushing it with his toes rolled it along the ground gathering more. Perfect snowman snow. The dark shape of clouds crowned the top of the pass. Snow was still falling up there. Avalanche snow. That's what the heavy wet stuff was called. He stood in the street calculating how long it would be before they could head over the pass. The horses and mules would get worn out trying to trudge through deep snow.

Barking drew his attention to Buck Reilly and his team of dogs coming down the street. He'd have to keep that idea at the ready. If the snow continued to fall, dogs and sleds would make getting to Dawson a whole lot easier than his pack string.

Right now, he planned to have breakfast with Clara and finish discussing their business.

He opened the hotel door and found men sleeping all over the chairs and floor. From the looks and sour odor, they were miners from the tents on the outskirts of town. With the snow they must have decided the lobby was a warmer, dryer place to stay.

Cautious steps took him through the sleeping bodies and up the stairs. He took off his hat and knocked on room twenty-seven's door. Rustling sounds and hurrying footsteps made him smile.

The door opened far enough for him to see one green eye peering out at him.

"Oh! It's you. Just a moment." The door shut, and he heard scraping and grunting.

The door opened, and Clara stood at the opening with perspiration beading her brow.

"What was that all about?" He stepped into the room and noticed her trunk to the side of the door.

"Belle didn't return last night."

"So you were keeping her out?" He made sure there was a teasing lilt to his tone.

"No!" She glanced at him then shook her head and smiled. "I started to go look for her and ran into a crowd of men in the lobby."

His mouth dried thinking of her in the middle of the group he'd just walked through. "Did they hurt you?" He stepped forward, studying her face and trying to recall if she'd shown any signs of injury when she opened the door.

"No. An old man said the snow would make the pass impossible to cross. Then another man—" she shivered "—asked if I'd found a guide. I told him I had, but he was persistent. It sc-bothered me. I came up here and pushed my trunk in front of the door."

Jeremy didn't like the sound of the persistent man. "What did he look like?"

"My height. Stocky with brown shaggy hair and beard." She wrapped her arms around herself as if warding off cold air.

From her reaction and the description, he'd bet the man was one of Soapy Smith's riffraff. "Your instincts about the man were right. He's one of the men who scams greenhorns. He says he'll guide them, then takes them part way and steals their food, money, and belongings, leaving them stranded."

"Why? That's despicable to leave someone stranded like that."

"He's part of a gang that has taken over this town. They take what they want because there's no law to stop them." If he'd planned to stay around, he would have offered to clean up the gang, but he wasn't going to let the likes of Soapy Smith keep him from getting home.

"There's no law in Skagway?"

"No. The closest is the Northwest Mounted Police who check each person crossing the pass to make sure they have enough supplies to keep them alive while they're in the interior." Jeremy rolled the brim of his hat in his hands. "I came to take you to breakfast and finish our business arrangements." His neck heated thinking of how light and womanly she'd felt as he carried her to her bed the night before. He doused that thought by wondering, again, why she believed she could make the journey to the Yukon. After seeing her vulnerability last night, he had second thoughts about taking her.

"Oh! Yes. I'm sorry I couldn't stay awake last night before we could conclude our business." She braced her feet shoulder width apart and peered into his eyes with a defiant gleam. "I don't usually fall prey to sleepiness. It had to be the fact I slept very little on the ship to Skagway."

"Why didn't you sleep well on the ship? Was it the motion?" Jeremy could tell she wasn't saying everything.

"No, the motion was quite soothing. I didn't like the way some people behaved." Clara took a couple steps backwards. "Will I need a coat or will we eat in the restaurant in the hotel?"

He didn't like the flicker of fear he saw in her eyes while talking about how people behaved, but by not telling him everything she proved she wasn't the type to dwell or go on about something that was over.

"We'll stay in the hotel. There's a foot of new snow out there, and it's still snowing on the pass."

Her legs seemed to crumple as she sat on the chair in the middle of the room. "How long will it be before we can leave for Forty Mile?"

The distress in her eyes triggered his protective instincts. He crouched beside her, one hand on the back of the chair, the other over her clasped hands in her lap. "It's hard to tell." He'd planned to tell her this morning she had no place trying to make the pass. Seeing how distressed she was and having seen her pushy side the day before, he had a feeling leaving her behind would only nag at him. Wondering if she had gone home or was following him, or worse, took off on her own.

"If I can't make it with the pack string, I'll trade the animals for dogs and sleds."

"You'd do that for me?" Her eyes brightened, and her cheeks blushed a deep rose.

"Yes, and for myself. I have freight that's to be delivered to a saloon in Dawson by March first. If we don't get out of here in two weeks, it will be cutting it close to deliver the goods and claim the other half of my payment."

The color faded on her cheeks, and her gaze became less coy and more direct.

"Are you ready to accompany me to breakfast?" He stood and crooked his arm in her direction.

Clara shook off her infernal girlish notion that he was being sweet on her and stood. When he'd blushed about carrying her to her bed, her insides had squiggled like when Marshal Tompkins kissed her at a dance. And his statement he'd trade his horses for dogs, she'd thought he was the chivalrous knight she'd dreamed of. But, as she was quickly learning up here, everyone, even Jeremy Duncan, was motivated by money.

She placed her hand through the crook of his arm and allowed him to escort her out of the room. They stopped, and she pulled the door closed, checking to make sure it was locked. She had the money she would use to pay Jeremy in her trunk. The other money was tucked in a pocket sewn on the outside of one of her underskirts. She'd added the pocket knowing it wasn't a good idea to have her money all in one place while traveling. Her pocketbook with five dollars rested in her skirt pocket along with the room key.

Halfway down the stairs her nose crinkled. Body odor, animal musk, and something she couldn't confirm wafted up the stairs with the heat. Clara placed her handkerchief over her nose as Jeremy led her through the waking bodies of the men who'd filled the lobby last night. They now used the animal skins they wore as clothing as blankets and pillows.

Once they were seated in the restaurant, she cautiously lowered the handkerchief and asked, "Why are those men sleeping in the lobby, and why does the establishment allow it?"

Jeremy glanced over her shoulder to the lobby and shrugged. "They were probably out carousing and saw the snow was coming down fast and furious and decided the lobby was a drier, warmer place to sleep than their tents on the outskirts of town."

She shook her head. "But the hotel could throw them out."

He peered into her eyes. "This land is harsh. Those that have been here a while know you help one another to stay alive."

The waiter poured coffee and took their orders before disappearing through a door. The lot in the lobby were waking and wandering into the restaurant.

"Then why have I been tricked out of five dollars for a telegraph that couldn't be sent, paid for my trunk to be delivered to my room only to have it rummaged through and my things soiled. And every person, besides you, I've talked to about guiding me over the pass has given me the feeling they would knock me over the head and take my money and belongings."

Jeremy smiled and the corners of his twinkling silver eyes crinkled. "That's why this country keeps you on your toes. Some days it's hard to know who is friend and who is foe."

"Do you really like living with the threat of danger every day?" She found the stress exhausting.

"I don't live it every day. Once you're no longer a greenhorn, new to the area, there's less testing by the sourdoughs, the men who have been here for years."

Their food arrived, and so did the shaggy brown-haired man from the night before. He stood next to her chair, emitting an odor that soured her stomach. She tried to scoot her chair over but couldn't get it to budge without actually standing.

The man nodded his head toward Jeremy. "Is this your guide?"

"Yes." She leaned away from the man's narrowed dark eyes.

"He don't know the pass as well as I do." The man's eyes didn't waver when Jeremy started to rise out of his chair.

Clara shot Jeremy a scowl and a slight shake of her head. She returned her gaze to the man. "But he won't kill me in my sleep and take my goods."

The man cursed and walked away.

Having stood up to the nasty man, her appetite was in full force. She wouldn't be a greenhorn for long.

She raised her gaze from her plate to Jeremy. A wide smile graced the lower half of his face and twinkling eyes sparkled from under his dark-brown brows.

"That gumption of yours is going to be a fun thing to see along the trail." Jeremy dug into the food on his plate, his lips still curved in a smile.

His words warmed her chest. Her mother had nearly worried herself sick about sending Clara alone to Alaska. She argued it was not a place for an unchaperoned young woman and worried if Randy wasn't able to contact them, what would happen when Clara was swallowed up in the wilderness.

But they didn't have any other choice. The honest workers at the dock needed to stay there and keep an eye on the crooked manager. They didn't have any relatives who could afford the trip, and they didn't have the funds to pay for someone to go along. It was her gumption, as Jeremy called it, that had convinced her mother she could do this. But her mother had stood on the dock with the children gathered around her and wept as Clara boarded the ship bound for Skagway.

She peered across the table at the man who would take her over the pass to her brother. With his help, she would find Randy, and their family wouldn't end up on the street.

Finishing the last of the eggs, she pushed her plate away and sipped her coffee. She'd slept fitfully after her encounter with the men in the lobby until she'd pushed the trunk in front of the door. Her stomach was full once again, but she wasn't sleepy. No, she was fidgety and anxious to learn when they would leave and how much money Jeremy would charge to take her.

The room was full. The voices of the chatting men was like dunking one's head in a tub of water. She studied Jeremy. He shoved his plate to the center of the table and leaned back in his chair. He frowned and leaned over the table.

"Go get your coat. It's too noisy in here to conduct business." He stood when she did and walked with her to the stairs. "I'll be here when you come down."

She nodded and hurried up the stairs as fast as she could while holding up her skirt. At the room, she dug the key out of her pocket and slipped it in the keyhole. The click registered and she turned the knob. Inside the room, she noted Belle still hadn't returned. *Maybe Jeremy and I should go look for her.*

Clara shoved her arms into her coat and wrapped a scarf around her head and neck. She shoved mittens into her coat pocket and stepped into the hall, locking the door. The key dropped into her coat pocket, and she descended the stairs. Like a sentry, Jeremy stood at the bottom of the stairs, staring out the door.

Her heart did a little flip. She stopped a few steps short of the floor and studied him. He looked more formidable from the back with his leather coat stretched across his wide shoulders. Her glance drifted to the gray Stetson in his hand. *He was the man who pulled me out of the muddy street!* Agreeing to guide her was the third time he came to her rescue. He might prove to be a better man than most she'd come across.

Jeremy rotated and looked up at her. A frown disappeared, replaced by a smile curving his lips.

She drew in a breath and descended the last three stairs, stopping in front of him.

"Put your mittens on. The wind is bitter cold." His gaze dropped to the mittens in her hand.

Dutifully, she slid her hands in and asked, "Where are we going?"

"I figure most everyone will be holing up in all the establishments to stay warm and have company, so the best place is my livery. It's warm and dry, and the only disturbance will be the horses and mules."

Clara nodded and slipped her hand in the crook of his arm. A livery sounded downright peaceful, and she'd take the smell of animals over the ripe bodies of the miners any day.

Chapter Eight

Jeremy stayed to the sheltered areas along the sides of the buildings as he led Clara to his livery. He'd never felt as conscious of a woman on his arm as he did now. What was it about her that made him feel so protective? He'd have to fight that instinct if he planned to get them over the pass alive. If he let his guard down at any point while crossing the pass, one or both of them could end up at the bottom of a crevice or canyon. To make it to the interior, a person had to always be on guard for danger.

He looked down at the scuffed toes of her leather shoes darkening in color from the wet snow. *She's not dressed to go walking through a foot of snow.* Moisture crept up the bottom of her dress leaving a dark, wet ring. If she didn't bring pants with her, she'd have to purchase three pair along with the other supplies the Northwest Mounted Police would require for her to cross into the interior.

They arrived at the livery, and Jeremy opened the smaller man door. He called it a livery because it housed his pack string and once in a while he'd rent a mule to a miner he knew, but he never sold his animals or took care of others.

Clara stepped through the door and waited as he grasped the lantern and lit it. The golden glow softened the bareness of the building. He shut the door to stop the wind that followed them in and walked toward the area where he slept and had his belongings in a trunk.

Jeremy motioned for Clara to sit on the trunk. "I don't have much for furniture," he mumbled and sat on an upturned crate he used as a table when he ate cold beans and biscuits.

She settled on the trunk like a hen settling over a batch of eggs, rearranging her skirt and shifting this way and that before she stopped and her gaze scanned the livery.

"How many horses do you have?" she asked, bringing her attention back to him.

"Five horses and six mules." He looked over his shoulder at the animals relaxing in their stalls. He'd have to take each one out today and stretch their legs.

"Do you use all of them every time you go over the pass?"

"Not all the time, but mostly. That way I can carry smaller loads on each animal and if something happens to one there is less to divide among the rest. This trail is hard on horses. Especially in the spring during the thaw when things are slippery." Jeremy stood up and ran his hands over a pack harness hanging on the wall at the end of his cot. He'd lost two horses the past year. One because of a greenhorn in a hurry, and the other put his hoof in the wrong place and broke a leg.

She waved her hand toward the packs already holding Brightly's merchandise. "Are those filled for the trip?"

"They have the items I'm to deliver in Dawson. You'll have to purchase enough supplies to get you through the Canadian inspection."

Her brow furrowed. "What do you mean?"

"The Northwest Mounted Police are at the boundary for Canada and don't allow anyone to pass into the Yukon without enough supplies for six months and two hundred in cash plus you'll have to pay duty tax."

"But I don't plan to be here for six months. All I need is enough to get to my brother. We'll go home once he hears why I've come for him." Clara's eyes grew wide. "And if I pay for the supplies and your services, I won't have two hundred to show the Northwest Mounted Police."

Her hands squeezed into fists. Her downcast eyes hid her emotions from him.

"I don't have to pack a year's provision because they know I go back and forth. I might be able to persuade them I'm taking you to your brother and they'll let us go, but it won't hurt for you to take plenty of supplies." Jeremy saw the unease slowly slip from her eyes and her body relaxed a bit. "You're also going to have to buy new clothes."

She opened her mouth as if to protest.

"You're going to need wool pants. Those skirts

are going to get in the way. We'll be walking with the pack string. I don't ride, it's too dangerous." He hoped she could take the long uphill trails that led to the summit. If he had to, he could put her on a horse and lead it, but it was too dangerous to trust a horse to find better footing than a person could. "You'll need high leather boots, like these," he tapped one of his boots, "and four pair of wool socks. It's easier to keep your feet warm if you have plenty of dry socks."

"Where will I find the items you recommend?" Her brow furrowed again.

"I'll take you, so they don't try and cheat you. I know the going prices up here. Figure double what you'd pay in Seattle. They see you walk in the door, they'll double 'em again." Jeremy had a feeling he'd be tagging along with Clara until they left on the trail. If too many men caught sight of her and realized she was all alone, they'd try to take advantage of her every way possible.

Clara pulled off her mittens and unwrapped the scarf around her head and neck. Her blonde strands shown like ribbons of sunlight in the lantern's light. She let out a heavy sigh and settled her shoulders back before staring into his eyes.

"How much are you charging and how much do you think I'll need for the clothes and supplies?"

He didn't blink even though looking into her apprehensive gaze he couldn't charge her as much as he wanted. "Two hundred to take you to your brother and it will be close to two hundred for clothing and supplies."

Clara sucked in her breath. *Four hundred dol-*

lars to get to Randy. "You said I wouldn't need six month's supplies if I told the Northwest Mounted Police I was only searching for my brother."

Jeremy shook his head. "I said we could try it, but if they won't allow you to go on without the full supplies, you'd have to find a way back, resupply yourself, and find another guide. Once I'm over the summit, I'm headed to Dawson. I'll collect what Brightly owes me and head home on a ship out of St. Michael."

Clara stared at him as fury swirled in her belly. *The effrontery of the man*! "You'd leave me at the summit with no means to return or go on?" And she'd just started to think the man might be different. But all men dropped what they had when something else better came along.

"I won't leave you there because you'll have the required supplies. Once we get by the check point you can sell supplies and make more money than you paid for them. Everything on the other side of the pass doubles in price." Jeremy shrugged and sat down. "We can buy your clothes and boots today. That way you can get used to wearing the boots and work them in. That way they won't hurt your feet. Seeing as how the weather has turned for the worse, you might want to purchase the supplies now before they run low from all the people stuck here until the trail clears."

He made a good point. All the people mill-ing around town would start using up the supplies quickly. "Where would I store my purchases?"

"You can keep them here. We'll go ahead and load them into the packs so we can load up and get

up the trail at the first sign it's not too treacherous."
Jeremy kicked one of the empty packs at his feet.

"I'm prepared to go purchase the supplies and
clothing now." She stood. She'd get that done and
then barter with the guide.

Jeremy picked up the lantern and headed for
the door. His back threw a shadow across her.
Clara took this moment to lift her skirt and top two
underskirts to search for the hidden pocket in the
underskirt closest to her body. She didn't want to do
this at the store when she purchased her supplies. It
would be improper. To disappear into a room and
return with money, would be a signal to the many
greedy men she'd come across on this trip to try and
look for more.

Her hand encountered the pocket when the light
brightened and she glanced up. Her gaze caught
Jeremy's the moment his scanning eyes left her exposed pantalets and peered into hers. She snatched
the money from the pocket and dropped her skirts,
shaking them to make the fabric lay correctly.

Jeremy's eyes narrowed. "That's not the best
place to keep your money. If anyone but me saw
that you'd find yourself in a heap of trouble."

Clara squared her shoulders. She didn't need
a man, especially this one telling her how to take
care of her money. If he hadn't turned around,
he wouldn't have known where she kept it. Long
strides carried her to the door. "That's why I was
trying to get at it before we went to the store."
She glared at him. "You weren't supposed to turn
around."

He lowered his face to within a few inches

of hers. "If you'd told me what you were doing, I would have given you privacy." His gaze landed on the hand with the money. "Get that deep in a pocket before we walk out the door."

She shoved the money into the inside pocket of her coat, wrapped her scarf back around her head, and pulled the mittens on.

Jeremy looked her over and opened the door. Cold wind blew in and swirled around, chilling her face.

"It can get real cold when the wind blows down here. But this is nothing compared to up on the pass."

Clara forced her eyes to stay open as the icy wind made them sting. The pass was worse? *What am I getting myself into*? It didn't matter. Her stomach could spin and her heart could race with fear but there wasn't a thing she could do about it but find Randy. Without him her family would crumble.

Jeremy slipped Clara's hand through the crook of his arm. Tears from the cold streamed out of her eyes and left frozen rivulets on her face. They moved at a steady, hurried pace along the front of the buildings, until he stopped and opened a door. The warmth from within made her face sting and her eyes water even more. She wiped at the tears with her wool mittens to absorb the wetness and stared through blurry eyes at a vast array of merchandise.

Jeremy put a hand on her back and moved her down the aisles to the back of the store where shelves held wool pants, flannel and wool shirts, socks, and men's under garments. She touched a blue plaid shirt and Jeremy held it up to her.

"Too big." He grabbed another one and held it up. "This size works. You'll need two."

Clara found another blue plaid shirt, and Jeremy tossed a brown wool shirt over the other two.

"Layers help keep you warmer." He picked out four pair of socks and handed them to her. His hand hovered over the shelf of men's long underwear. He plucked out a small pair and placed them on the pile in her arms. "Layers."

His attention turned to stacks of wool trousers. "Try these," he said, picking up a pair and dangling it as if guessing the fit.

Clara shoved the clothes she held into his arms and unbuttoned her coat to reveal her waist. Holding the pants up to her body, the waist was too big but the legs were the right length.

"Belt." He turned and walked to an area with leather belts. Jeremy set the clothing down and walked toward her with the belt. He leaned in, looping the belt around her body inside her coat and buckling it on the last notch. The belt rested on her hips. His face held steady in front of hers as he peered into her eyes. "That's the smallest one. We can add a couple more holes."

His closeness and silver eyes gazing into hers caused her body to warm and her heart to thud in her chest. She couldn't speak, so nodded instead.

"Can I help you?" asked a voice growing nearer.

Jeremy spun toward the voice, leaving her to regain breathing and get her wits back.

"Duncan, it's you. What can I do for you?"

Clara peeked around Jeremy and was rewarded with a jovial smile in a round face. The store owner had a round barrel-shaped body and sturdy limbs.

"Ned Garver, this is Clara Bixbee. I'll be taking her over the summit. She needs outfitted." Jeremy moved to the side, giving the man a clear view of her but not enough room for her to get past Jeremy without touching him.

Clara nodded her head. "Mr. Garver."

The pleased-to-meet-you expression vanished. "Duncan, are you crazy taking a lovely little thing like this over that cussed pass?"

Clara started to open her mouth, but Jeremy jumped in.

"She came here to get to the interior and find her brother. If I don't take her, who do you think will?"

Mr. Garver's face reddened and scrunched into a glare.

"Exactly. Who is she better off with; me or the likes of Ronson?"

"Most definitely you. Miss, if you're set on going over the pass this is the man that'll get you there and not fleece you along the way."

The conviction in Mr. Garver and the praise Belle had bestowed on Jeremy made Clara feel like she was in good hands. "Thank you Mr. Graver. I appreciate knowing that."

Jeremy motioned to the belt around her waist and tossed the other clothing on the counter. "She'll take these, and she needs a pair of boots."

Mr. Graver smiled. "This way, Miss." He led her to a room behind a curtain. Boots much like the pair Jeremy wore sat on two long shelves, starting from a small pair that looked like it might fit her to some much larger than Jeremy's feet.

"Have a seat and remove your boots, please." Mr Graver motioned to a stool and walked over to the shelves.

Clara felt a little self-conscious taking her boots off in front of not only Mr. Garver but Jeremy as well. Her fingers fumbled with the buttons.

"Here, let me help." Jeremy knelt in front of her and grasped her left foot. He placed it on his thigh and used a button hook Mr. Garver handed him to unhook the buttons. The boot slipped off, and he did the same with her right foot. Jeremy then slid a pair of the wool socks over her stockings. Rather than stand and allow Mr. Garver to try the boots on, Jeremy took the first boot from the store owner and slipped her foot inside, then tugged until his fingers were between the boot and the area below her knee. Her face grew warm as his fingers slowly slipped out and his hand ran the length of the boot to her foot. The pressure of his hand sliding along the footwear made her insides flutter.

He picked up her other foot and went through the same ministrations as with the first boot until her heart thudded in her chest and her body simmered.

"Stand, so we can see if your feet have enough room." His voice sounded deeper than usual.

She stood, holding her skirt up, revealing the boots.

Jeremy pushed down on the toes and felt all the sides of her feet. "Walk to the end of the room and back to see if the heels slip."

Clara brushed by Jeremy, glad to have her back to him and clear her senses. How could his hand on the outside of a boot wrapped around her leg make her feel light-headed? She pivoted and walked back toward Jeremy and Mr. Garver.

"Are your feet slipping around inside the boots?" Jeremy asked.

"No. They feel fine." *More than fine*. But she wasn't going to say that to Jeremy or in front of Mr. Garver who had a big smile on his face.

"She'll take this pair." Jeremy picked up her old boots and tucked them under his arm. He motioned for them to go back into the main part of the store.

Jeremy dumped the clothes on the counter and walked to a wall of coats. "Try this."

He handed her a leather, fur-lined coat with a hood. She started to slip her wool coat off.

"No. Leave that on. You'll have several layers under this."

She followed his orders and pulled the coat on over everything. "It's tight in the arms."

He pulled down another coat and four coats later she had one that fit. "Put that on the pile." Jeremy then walked to a table piled with round, duck-cloth bundles. He picked one up and joined her at the counter.

"What's that?" she asked.

"A sleeping bag. You can't just huddle under blankets in the weather around here."

She'd never heard of a sleeping bag before and was anxious to get it back to the hotel and roll it out to see how it was made.

Jeremy placed a hand on the mound of clothing. "Wrap the clothes up for Miss Bixbee to take now and send six months' worth of supplies for one person to get through the Canadian check point to the livery."

Mr. Garver cleared his throat. "Who's paying for this?" His gaze bounced from Jeremy to her to Jeremy and back to her.

"I am. Can you give me a tally?" She slid her hand into her coat to pull out the money. Jeremy stayed her hand with a bump of his arm.

Mr. Garver started writing down figures and adding them up. He glanced up at the two of them once then erased a number and refigured. "Two hundred and forty-five including the supplies I'll send to the livery."

Clara shot a glance at Jeremy and saw him frown. She cleared her throat and said, "That's not the total Mr. Duncan and I figured for supplies." She shifted her body to conceal her face from Garver as she peered into Jeremy's face. "Didn't you tell me the supplies and my clothes would only come to two hundred?"

Chapter Nine

Jeremy had a hard time stopping the smile that tugged at his lips. Clara was playing Garver to get the price of the goods down. This was a side to her that might come in handy.

"Yes, the last person I packed over the trail only paid one hundred-fifty dollars for supplies. You do have clothing to add on but that wouldn't be ninety-five dollars' worth." He slid his gaze to the store owner.

The big man's face glowed red. He slapped the paper he'd been figuring on down on the counter. "These are my prices and my figures."

Clara bumped into Jeremy's arm as they both leaned over to read the numbers. He stayed arm to arm with her sniffing her faint floral scent and trying to make the numbers stop fading in and out as his mind cluttered with thoughts of the woman next to him.

"Hah! Right there!" Clara put her finger on one of the numbers. "And right here." She moved her finger down the list. "Both these places you added wrong. It should be two hundred and twenty five." Her eyes twinkled, and her lips were set in a smug smile.

"Let me see that!" Garver pulled the paper to him and began figuring.

Jeremy winked at Clara. Her face reddened, and her eyelids lowered, hiding her eyes behind blonde lashes. The woman was not only pretty, she had a mind for numbers. Jeremy grasped her elbow, maneuvering them with their backs to the counter and Garver.

"Take out the amount of money you added up on the paper," he said, motioning to her coat.

Clara nodded and pulled out the paper money.

He directed his gaze to the doors, making sure no one walked in and saw her peeling money off the folded wad. When she finished, Clara tucked the rest back in her pocket.

Garver cleared his throat. "I was mistaken the total is two hundred and twenty-five dollars."

They both faced the counter.

"That is the amount I came up with also." Clara set the money on the counter.

Garver grabbed it up and counted it three times before he grunted and shoved it into a small safe. "I'll get these things wrapped up and send the others to Duncan's livery later today."

Jeremy nodded and walked over to a selection of knives. He'd thought about taking a knife back for each of his brothers, but then he'd have to find something for each of their wives and all the nieces and nephews. He grinned. That would take up most of his earnings. Guess they'd all just have to be happy he'd come home.

"Mr. Duncan, would you help me, please?" Clara's sweet voice pulled him out of his reveries. She stood by the counter, her new fur-lined coat over the one she was already wearing, holding the smaller of two brown, paper-wrapped packages. The sleeping bag stood next to the large package on the counter.

He ambled back to the counter. If he hurried to do her bidding, Garver would get the wrong idea about the two of them. The man had been smiling like someone tickled his feet the whole time he and Clara were gathering the clothing.

Jeremy picked up the items Clara had left on the counter and headed for the door.

"You two going to be back by this way after you cross the pass?" Garver's gaze roved back and forth between them.

"Not me, I'm headed home after this trip." Jeremy offered.

"No, thank you. Once I find my brother, I hope to never set foot here again."

Garver smiled. "Good luck to the two of you."

Jeremy couldn't read the expression on the man's face, but it resembled a look his aunt Aileen would get when she listened to Hank swear he didn't have feelings for Kelda, the woman he married.

He shook off the notion and focused on Clara's declaration she didn't want to set foot back here.

She'd only been in Skagway two days and she was ready to leave. How the hell was he to get her over the pass if she dreaded the weather and town?

"Let's drop some of this off at the livery. You only need your boots and a set of clothes for the first day. The rest can be packed." He grasped her elbow, guiding her through the people crowding the streets now that the sun peeked through the clouds.

"Will I be able to take my own things? I'll need them for the trip home." Worry edged her words.

"You can take your clothes, but the trunk will have to stay here. You can sell it and buy a new one before you get on the ship in St. Michael."

"But that takes longer to get home. Once I find Randy, I'm sure he'll want to get home as quickly as possible. We'll come back this way. Probably take the Chilkoot trail since it's faster."

He stopped and stared down into her solemn face. "You haven't crossed the pass once and you're thinking of coming back over?" Jeremy would have ran a hand over his face if both of them weren't holding the woman's packages. "By the time we get to your brother, the easiest and safest route will be to ride the Yukon River on out to St. Michael. Trying to get back this way with the spring thaw would be suicide."

"Oh." Her brows scrunched together in thought.

Jeremy started walking, moving her along faster when he caught sight of sporting ladies hanging out the second-floor windows of a saloon.

"Hey handsome! Come on, you know you want to look up here!"

Out of the corner of his eye, he watched Clara

stare at the women.

"Honey, tell your man he can take a look!"

Clara stopped. "Is she talking to me?"

Jeremy tugged on her arm. "Ignore those women. They'll only get you in trouble."

"Why?" She spun toward him, her eyes wide and questioning.

"You know what they are don't you?" He nodded toward the women still calling out the window, only now, to a handful of miners gathered below them.

"Yes. But why would they call out to me? And to hang out the window like that. They'll catch their death of cold."

He stared at Clara. She peered up at the women as if she truly cared that they could catch a cold. "Respectable women don't speak to those women." Jeremy tugged on her elbow again and this time she started walking.

"Respectable women who don't speak to the likes of the women hanging out the window, should be ashamed of themselves. Many of them aren't lying on their backs and letting men root around on them because they like it."

Jeremy stopped. How did she know what went on with a sporting lady? This wasn't the place to get into a conversation about it. He resumed walking, lengthening his strides to where Clara was nearly running beside him.

"Slow down. We aren't running from a fire are we?" She yanked her elbow from his grasp, breathed deeply a couple of times, and continued at a calmer pace.

He fell into step beside her as the livery came into sight. Once inside, he set his parcels on the ground and lit the lantern. Clara proceeded to the cot and dropped her load onto the mattress.

She had the parcel untied, rummaging through it when he placed the parcel he carried on the cot.

Clara pulled out all the socks and held the men's drawers between her pointer finger and thumb. She'd never touched men's unmentionables before. They had a woman who washed the clothes and did the ironing. Her shoulders slumped. They *had* a woman. Her mother now did the laundry among several other things they had paid servants do before. She stared at the clothing. The few garments had cost twice as much as they would have back in Seattle, using up half of the money she and her mother had scraped up to get her here.

Randy you have to be easy to find. What will I do if I run out of money and can't find him? That wasn't an option, though she'd rather starve to death here than watch her family suffer living in the streets.

"You going to stare at them drawers all day?"

Jeremy's voice jogged her back to the present.

Her face heated, and she tossed the drawers on the socks. She'd wear them the first day under her pantalets and the wool trousers to see if they helped. She added one pair of trousers to the pile and opened the other package, taking out one shirt and adding it to the other items that would be packed.

"When should I bring my items over to pack?" Luckily, she'd only brought minimal clothing and personal items with her. The trunk was a small one.

"And where would be the best place to sell the trunk?" She wasn't going to leave it, she needed every penny she could get. The trunk had been an old thing her mother found in the attic. The container meant nothing to her. But she'd learned the value of every cent.

"The safest would be to see if Garver would buy it. Otherwise you'll have to stand on the dock or on a corner and hock it." Jeremy placed a large empty canvas bag next to the bed. "Put what you want packed in here. This will be your personal pack."

She nodded, folding her clothes and placing them in the bag. The parka was warm. It would be enough for right now. Clara took the parka off and then started unbuttoning her coat.

"What are you doing?" Jeremy's voice kind of squeaked.

"I won't need my wool coat while around here if I use the parka." She slid her arms out and folded the coat, slipping the few dollars she had left from the pocket. After placing it in the bag, she slipped the parka back on and snuggled into the fur lining.

"That was fun watching Garver squirm when you questioned his prices." Jeremy flipped the canvas lid over on the pack.

Clara stared at the man. He thought she made the storekeeper uncomfortable on purpose. She narrowed her eyes and stalked toward him. Mr. Duncan needed to learn a thing about her. She stopped close enough she could poke his chest with her finger. "I was brought up to know the price of the items I intend to purchase so as not to spend a penny more than necessary. I don't know how you grew up, but I have never intentionally hurt a person in my life. I merely wanted to make sure the money my mother and I scraped together to send me here wasn't squandered."

"Sorry. But it was impressive the way you figured the numbers so quickly."

"I'm good with numbers from working in the warehouse adding up crates and shipping costs." And that's how they discovered the manager was stealing from them. Before her father's death there was never a discrepancy in the numbers—all crates matched the loads and all money was accounted for. After his death every other load had missing boxes while the businesses were getting charged for all the boxes. When she told her mother, she reported it to the police. They talked to the manager and he told the police the women were just overwrought over losing the head of the household. And the papers in question came up missing. Businesses started complaining about their lost goods and going elsewhere. Clara tried to fire the manager, but he laughed in her face saying she had no legal right as a woman to run the company. That was when her mother insisted they needed Randy.

"Why are you frowning? There's nothing wrong with a woman knowing numbers." Jeremy stepped closer.

She had to tip her head back to look into his eyes. "I agree. If I hadn't been good with numbers, we wouldn't have learned our manager was stealing from us." Clara dropped her gaze. "I hope it isn't too late by the time Randy and I get back. Mother and the children don't have anywhere to go if the business keeps failing."

Jeremy placed his fingers under her chin, making her look at him. "How old are your brothers and sisters?"

"Grace is eighteen. She's started working in the warehouse, but tends to flirt more than work. Mabel is fourteen, and has two more years of school. Russell is twelve, and George is ten." She watched his eyes grow wider with each sibling she recounted. "As you see, my brother is needed back home, not only for the business, but to help my mother with our younger brothers. They'll need a man's guidance as they grow."

"A strong sister can be as good as a father figure." His words were barely a whisper.

This bit of his past intrigued her. "Did you not have a father growing up?" What had formed this man's integrity if not for a father figure?

"Ma and Pa died from diphtheria when I was ten. We were to live with my ma's brother, but once there he treated me like a slave and sold Darcy to a whore house."

Anger flashed in his eyes. The fingers on her chin flexed, tightening momentarily then relaxing.

Panic caused her to step back. His hand followed her, and his touch lightened. Even knowing she could cause him to become angrier, her curiosity wouldn't let go of his reactions.

"Why did your uncle do such a thing? How did she get out?"

A faint smile crept onto his lips. "Darcy has always been clever. She slipped out of the whore

house and came for me. We were on the run from
our uncle when we landed in Galena and ran into
Gil, who is now Darcy's husband." His hand slid up
her jaw and cupped the back of her head. His eyes
shone like stars in the sky. "Darcy taught me all
about right and wrong and doing for others, but to
never let anyone take advantage of me."

His warm palm against the back of her head,
his eyes peering deep into hers, and his mouth only
inches from hers weakened her knees and set her
heart racing.

"I promise I will get you over the pass and help
you find your brother. I'm a man of my word."

She saw the conviction in his eyes. His actions
up till now had all been honorable. Her gaze flicked
to his mouth. Was he going to seal his promise with
a kiss rather than a handshake? Her lips tingled at
the thought.

A horse snorted and another shifted.

I'm alone in a livery with a man. Heat rose up
her neck and flamed her cheeks.

Jeremy blinked twice, exhaled, and slowly
backed away, breaking the connection.

Clara stumbled back a step when he released
her.

"I'll come get you at the hotel when we can
leave. There's no need for you to come back here
again." His voice was rough as he pivoted away
from her and strode toward the horse stalls.

"I-I thought you wanted my clothes packed
beforehand?" She mentally shook herself. *I stood
there like one of those women who was hanging out
the window, waiting for him to kiss me.* Clara carved

that thought in her memory to keep her from repeating what just happened.

"Sort through them, and I'll pick them up later." He opened a stall and started tossing the soiled bedding into a pile.

The message was clear, he wanted her to leave. She buttoned the parka, slipped on her mittens, and glanced one more time toward Jeremy. He continued tossing manure out of the stall. *What have I done? Was that a test?* Her chest squeezed, making it hard to breathe as she walked out into the cold air. Had he pretended he would kiss her just to see if she was a loose woman? If so, she didn't think she passed his test. Will he still escort me over the pass?

Chapter Ten

Jeremy cleaned the stalls and walked each of the horses and mules, using up most of the day. No matter what he did, he couldn't get his actions this morning out of his head. He'd been about to kiss Clara. Not a good idea given they would be in close contact for two months or longer depending on how easy her brother was to find. He didn't want to give her any ideas. She wasn't the type of woman he was interested in. She was fool-hardy. Coming here expecting to waltz over the pass and find a man who was either dead or hiding. And prickly as a berry bush.

His stomach growled. The snow around town had packed due to all the people milling about. He had a hankering for a meal at the Rookery. Mrs. Otis made the best dried apple pie he'd found since leaving home. Jeremy doused the lantern leaving it by the door and used the muted light from the other businesses to find his way down the streets to the restaurant.

There were two empty tables. One sat closer to the kitchen, the other near the chilly entrance. He walked through the room nodding to the men he knew and sat at the one near the kitchen. After wearing his heavy coat all day, it would be a relief to slip it off while enjoying his meal. An older woman came over with a cup and coffee pot.

"Special today is moose roast with potatoes and bread," she said, filling his cup.

"I'll take that along with a piece of pie." Jeremy's mouth watered just thinking about the pie.

"Be out in a minute." The woman stopped at several tables filling cups as she made her way to the kitchen.

Jeremy sat back and listened to the conversations around him.

"Heard some little gal took one of Soapy's girls to the Methodist preacher, and then shot at Soapy's feet when he tried to enter the church to get his gal."

This conversation caught Jeremy's attention. Who was brash enough to go against Soapy Smith? Jeremy kept listening, hoping to hear a little more, but the two started talking about the weather.

His dinner arrived and he set to eating it. But the men's words kept tumbling around in his head. Whoever the woman was, you could bet Soapy would be out for revenge.

Clara looked over her shoulder at the reverend and the woman standing by the alter watching her. "I don't think he's coming back tonight." She walked down the aisle toward the two. "I think he's learned his lesson."

"Miss Clara you don't know Soapy. He's not going to stop trying for me."

Clara winced. The woman's face was black and blue. There was no telling what the man would have done if Clara hadn't heard the noise in the alley and intervened. No one deserved to be beaten to this extent.

"Lily, when I came upon you, he didn't look like he was going to stop beating on you. I couldn't let that happen." She glanced at the reverend. "Every life is precious."

"Yes, it is Miss Bixbee. I'll do all I can to get Lily on a ship out of here as soon as possible." The reverend threw a glance at the front doors then toward the back of the building. "It wouldn't be safe for any of us to set foot outside tonight. Soapy may have men watching and there wouldn't be anyone around to help."

Clara wasn't excited about sleeping on a wooden pew, but it was better than stepping out and being grabbed by the angry man with black hair, beard, and eyes that she'd run into before—Soapy Smith. She should have put the two together when Jeremy was telling her about the man.

She hadn't set out to put herself in harm's way or to have the most feared man in Skagway out for her, but the whimpering and sound of flesh hitting flesh couldn't be ignored. Queasiness overtook her at the memory of what she'd witnessed. The man had been so intent on his beating, she'd sneaked up behind him, clobbering him in the head with a board. She helped herself to his pistol before half carrying Lily to the nearest church.

She sank to a pew as she realized she'd fired the man's own weapon at his feet when he'd tried to enter the church and get Lily.

"Miss Bixbee?"

She heard the reverend's low voice before she hung her head down in front of her knees and breathed deep long breaths.

Still wondering about the event at the church, Jeremy wandered into Soapy Smith's Saloon. There was one sure way to find out if there was truth behind what the sourdoughs said at the restaurant.

He took a spot at the bar not far from the table where Soapy was sporting a bandaged head and looking meaner than usual. The bartender placed a shot glass of whiskey in front of Jeremy. He sipped the amber liquid and listened with his ears tuned to the owner.

"I want both those women here in the morning. I don't care if you have to kill the preacher. I won't have one of my girls stealing and get away with it and away from me. No do-gooder is going to get away with bashing me in the head." Soapy touched the bandage gingerly. His dark eyes narrowed. "And no one shoots at me with my own pistol!"

Jeremy threw the rest of the whiskey down his throat and headed for the door. Someone better warn the reverend and the two ladies they needed to find some place other than the church to hide. What woman would defy Soapy? Another one of his girls? If that were the case he would have said two girls. No. Whoever was helping his girl had to either be too stupid to know who they were dealing with or plain crazy.

He cut through alleys and did a wide circle of the church to see if Soapy had men watching the doors. Jeremy spotted a man at the front and back entrances. His options were either sneak in unseen or take out one of the men. The latter would work toward getting the reverend and women out to a safer hiding spot.

He stumbled out of the alley toward the man watching the back door. When the man came toward him puffing on a cigarette, Jeremy tripped toward the man, falling into him. Pulling himself up the man's body in an attempt to right himself, he brought the handle of his Colt alongside the man's head, dropping him to his knees. A quick scan of the alley revealed the scuffle hadn't attracted attention.

Hands under the man's armpits, Jeremy dragged him three buildings over, stuck his bandanna in the man's mouth, and tied his hands and feet. Quick, soft footsteps carried him back to the alley behind the church. He stepped onto the stoop and opened the door, creeping through the back and stepping from behind the alter.

Click.

He froze at the sound and peered into the murky candlelight to see who held a gun on him. Slowly, the reverend approached, his face was etched with concern and fear, but his hands didn't hold a weapon.

"If you were sent by Soapy Smith you need to leave. I won't have violence in the house of God."

The reverend waved toward the door Jeremy had just entered.

"I'm not with Soapy Smith—"

"Jeremy?"

The voice registered at the same time Clara came into view. He stepped forward. "What are you doing here?" The moment the words were out he knew who the uppity girl was Soapy had threatened to hurt. *Clara.*

"I saved Lily from Soapy Smith and now we don't know what to do." The gun fell from her hand. Her arms wrapped around his waist.

His arm automatically drew her close and held her tight. He placed his chin on her head and peered at the reverend and red-headed girl with a puffy, black and blue face. She looked about Clara's age. The two cautiously walked closer.

"I heard Soapy say he was going to make the girl who shot at him and his girl pay. I had to warn you that he was coming for you." He untucked Clara's face from his chest and peered into her teary eyes. "I didn't know it was you."

She hiccupped. "I wasn't thinking straight. I saw him beating on Lily and couldn't go for help for fear he'd kill her before I got back."

He hugged her close. "I know. We have to get all of you out of here to a safe place." He started for the back door. "Come on. Reverend, you have a blanket or something to keep Lily warm and hide her dress?"

"I do." The reverend disappeared and returned with a worn, brown blanket and draped it around the soiled dove's shoulders.

"I tied up the man they had watching the back door. We'll go to my livery and make plans from there." Jeremy headed to the door, his arm snugged around Clara's shoulders to keep her next to him. Knowing the nastiest man in Skagway was out to get Clara had his heart banging in his chest and his mind racing with how to get her out of this mess.

Once out in the alley, he continued moving behind the establishments. Groping in the dark with his feet, he moved along as quickly as he could. The reverend and Lily shuffled along behind them.

When they were only a couple blocks from the livery, Jeremy took them toward the main street. They would have to cross and hope no one saw them. He didn't need Soapy Smith and all his gang shooting in the livery and killing not only them, but the horses and mules as well.

The street remained dark and empty. He started forward and continued at a long stride all the way to his door. Clara's skirt flapped around his legs as she moved along beside him. He flung the door open and motioned the two following to enter first. Inside, he opened his arm, allowing Clara to move to the side of the entrance. Jeremy latched the door and lit the lantern.

"It's not much, but no one will come looking for you here." He grasped Clara's hand, leading her over to the trunk she sat on earlier that day. Jeremy noted the trio all had glum faces.

"Reverend, do you have a place you and Lily can stay that will be safe?" Jeremy would keep Clara safe.

"I'd like to put Lily with Captain Moore. He

can get her over to Dyea and on the next ship head-ed out." His face reddened. "But I'd best explain the circumstances to him before I bring Lily along."

"That seems reasonable." Jeremy studied the girl. She appeared eager to do whatever was asked of her. How had someone so young ended up one of Soapy's girls? He turned to the reverend. "Can you go talk with Moore now? It will be easier to move her about in the dark than daylight?"

"Yes, of course." The reverend stood. Lily grasped his arm. "Don't worry, my child. We'll have you on a ship headed home soon." He disengaged her hand from his arm and moved across the build-ing. "I'll knock four times when I return."

Jeremy nodded, impressed with the man's fore-thought that he might meet a gun should he enter without announcing himself. Jeremy turned his attention to Clara.

"We're going to have to leave here as soon as I get the horses traded for dogs and sleds. Sooner or later Smith will learn where you're hiding and I can't hold off all his men."

The color and determined attitude slowly crept onto her face. She straightened her shoulders and nodded. "I figured as much while sitting in the church." Clara stood, walked over to the cot where Lily sat, and put her arm around the other woman. "Lily's going to need proper clothes to travel, and I need my things in the hotel."

"That was my next thought." Jeremy slid his rifle out of the scabbard and handed it to Clara. "I'm going to find Belle. She can gather your things together in a pack, so no one knows your stuff is leaving the hotel and sell your trunk for you." He nodded to the rifle. "If someone comes through that door without knocking four times, pull the trigger."

She pointed the barrel at the floor and heaved a deep sigh. "I will."

He had a notion she'd never killed a person and most likely taking aim at Smith earlier was the first time she'd pulled a trigger. At least he knew she wouldn't be squeamish if she did need to pull the trigger. Jeremy holstered his pistol and slipped out of the livery, leaving the two women huddled on his cot.

Chapter Eleven

Clara hated that she became more and more indebted to Jeremy Duncan. But there was no one else she trusted to keep her alive to find her brother. She sat on the cot exactly where Jeremy had left her when he headed out in search of Belle. Lily had long since stretched out on the cot behind her.

She stared at the young woman's puffy, discolored face. How could a man do that to a woman? She'd heard of beatings before but never experienced the horror of watching it happen. A shudder slithered down her spine. She'd made an enemy of the type of man that had no conscience.

Four soft knocks sounded at the door. That might be the code, but she wasn't taking any chances. Clara placed the stock of the rifle up to her shoulder and aimed at the door as it opened.

Reverend Daily stepped in and shut the door. Feeling guilty for aiming at the reverend, she dropped the barrel and placed the rifle on the cot beside her.

The reverend scanned the interior. "Where's Jeremy?"

"He went to get clothes for Lily and my belongings." Clara pulled out her father's pocket watch. "He left right after you did." An hour ago.

"William is willing to get Lily to Dyea and stay with her until she can board the next ship." The reverend rubbed his hands together. "Is there a stove in here?"

Clara shook her head. "I haven't spotted one."

Four knocks, louder than the reverend's, echoed through the stillness. Being cautious, Clara picked up the rifle and aimed at the door.

"That's—" started Reverend Daily.

"I'm not taking any chances." Clara held her breath as the door opened, and Jeremy's gray Stetson came into view. Letting the breath out slowly, she noted he wasn't smiling as he drew closer to the lantern light.

"What's wrong?" She placed the rifle on the cot and stood.

"I can't find Belle." He peered into her eyes. "Do you have any idea where she's at?"

"No. I haven't talked to her since the first day I arrived. She didn't sleep in the room last night." Clara paced from the nearest stall to the cot. Lily sat up. Her face looked worse than before.

"Bring in a bucket of snow," Clara said, picking up a bucket and handing it to Jeremy.

"Why do you want snow?" he asked.

"The cold snow will reduce the swelling on

Lily's face." *I should have thought of this sooner.*

Jeremy nodded and strode out the door. Clara walked into a shadowed corner and pulled off one of her underskirts. A large square of fabric was ripped from the skirt when Jeremy returned with the snow.

"What are you doing?" he asked, standing in the lantern light, watching.

"Making an ice pack." Clara put two handfuls of snow on the square and folded it into a small pillow shape. "Hold this to your face. When one spot feels cold move it to another." She handed the bundle to Lily.

The girl winced but kept the snow to her bruises.

Clara pulled her scarf over her head.

"Where are you going?" Jeremy grabbed her arm as she walked by him.

"To get my things." She stared at him with what she hoped showed more conviction than she felt inside. Roaming about the streets was a sure way to get caught by Smith, but Lily needed clothes and she needed her belongings. Especially, the money tucked in the oil cloth coat she'd brought.

Jeremy ran a hand over his face. An action she'd come to learn meant he was thinking and not happy with the outcome.

"I talked to William. He can get Lily to Dyea, but like you said, we need to do it before people are up and milling about." The reverend inclined his head toward Clara.

She sent him a thankful smile. "We can't wait for Belle to show up or you to spend the whole night looking for her."

Jeremy peered into her eyes. "We'll go. But you have to listen to me. We can't have anyone telling Soapy they know where you are."

Clara swallowed and nodded.

"What if he has men watching Clara's room?" Worry laced Lily's question.

"I'll do some reconnoitering before we go to the room." Jeremy held out his arm like they were going for a midnight stroll.

Clara slipped her hands into her gloves and slid her hand through his crooked elbow. He led her to the door and out into the night.

Jeremy didn't like walking around town with Clara. Soapy had men everywhere. He also knew if he didn't escort the head-strong woman she'd go on her own. What would have happened if he hadn't come back when he did? Would she have struck out on her own? Most likely the woman was rash and didn't think things through. Like bashing Soapy Smith in the head and taking his girl. Jeremy's gut twisted at the thought of Clara ending up in Soapy's hands. The mess the man made of Lily didn't bode well for what he'd do to the woman who defied him.

Two men who frequented Jeff's Saloon walked toward them. Jeremy swung Clara into his arms and backed her up against the store front.

"What?" Clara shoved at his chest, but he pressed all his weight toward her.

"Shh. Those two coming this way are part of Soapy's gang. Relax. I'm hiding you." He rested his forearms on either side of her head and leaned in. The night hid her expression from him, but her body, pressed to his, revealed her breathing quickened.

"Look at them two lovebirds," a man hollered and pointed.

"If you ain't gonna kiss her I will," said the other man.

A thousand better times and ways for a first kiss came to mind. Jeremy's heart raced and Clara's palms pushed at him, again. It was either follow through with the men's friendly chiding or risk them seeing Clara.

"I'm sorry." He lowered his face toward Clara. His lips grazed her cold, soft cheek. He'd planned to only hover over her mouth and pretend to kiss her, but his lips had their own ideas. Her plump sweet mouth under his made him as drunk as a bottle of whiskey. Just as whiskey made him happy and carefree, so did Clara's kisses.

He angled his head and licked the seam of her lips. She gasped and he took the kiss deeper. Even with their layers of clothes, their bodies pressed together and her hands now wound in the hair at the nape of his neck. Without her hands between them her soft curves registered, driving him to wrap his arms around her and explore what he could.

"Really! There are houses for such things!"

The woman's shrill voice ripped through his horny haze. Shame slammed into his chest like an avalanche. Jeremy pulled out of the kiss but kept Clara sheltered from any onlookers. He peeked right and left and found the men had moved along. A couple dressed in city clothes stood five feet away staring disdainfully.

"Wife, you know better than to get me riled

up," Jeremy said, taking Clara's hand and leading her down the block. As soon as they came to an alley, he pulled her into the darker recesses. He rubbed a hand over his face. What did Clara think of him? He'd shamed her out there, treating her like a soiled dove on the street in plain view. He'd just become lower than a mud fish.

He stood in the darkness, trying to find the words to apologize.

Clara took a step toward him. He stood ready for a slap. He deserved it. Hell, if Darcy were here, she'd give him a lickin' with a lecture that would make him feel like a mud fish.

"We need to get to the hotel before more people start moving about." Her voice was clear but a bit shaky. No recriminations. No accusation.

"Clara, I'm sorry. I only meant to hide you, I don't know—"

She placed a hand on his chest, stopping his words. "I know you're honorable and were only trying to keep me safe. We need to get to the hotel."

Honorable my ass! If I was honorable I would have never kissed you. He tried to see her face and see if she was as shook up. But the darkness, while being their savior, was his own personal enemy.

Jeremy grasped the hand still resting on his chest. "Let's go." He led her down the alleys until they were one block away from the St. James Hotel. "Stay here. I'll go see if there are any of Soapy's men hanging around."

Her hand trembled in his. "You'll be safe. Just stay close to this building and don't move." He started to lean down and kiss her, but caught himself before making that mistake, again. He'd never had the urge to kiss a woman to allay her fears. Clara Bixbee had seeped under his skin. He was going to play heck with the devil escorting her to her brother and keeping his lips to himself. Especially since he wasn't interested in marrying her and that's what kissing a woman all the time led them to believe. Squeezing her hand once and letting go, he moved out of the alley and walked down the boardwalk to the hotel's entrance.

Two of Soapy's men stood across the street. Puffs of cigar smoke curled with steam from their breath. Jeremy entered the hotel and noticed less people sleeping in the lobby tonight. He crossed to the clerk and asked for the second time tonight, "Is Belle Eiderly in?"

"Haven't seen her or her roommate for some time." The clerk swept his gaze toward the street.

He knew Soapy's men were keeping an eye out. That's the problem with a wintered-in town. Nothing to do but gossip.

"Thanks. If you see Belle could you let her know Jeremy is looking for her?"

"Sure will."

"Thanks." Jeremy pulled his collar up around his neck and walked out the door. This time he went two blocks beyond the hotel and ducked down the alley. As he'd figured, there were two men standing at either corner of the hotel in the back alley. He ducked out to the next street and circled back to Clara.

The minute he made out her shape in the dark, he whispered her name. Her body landed against his as her arms wrapped around his waist. He rubbed his hands up and down her back.

"Soapy's men are stationed all around the hotel."

"Then I can't get my things or dresses for Lily?"

The defeat in her voice triggered his anger at the man responsible for everything wrong and corrupt in Skagway. Soapy Smith.

"We'll get your things. I just need to do some more looking around. Give me the key to your room. If I can get in, I'll gather all your stuff and bring it back."

"How will you know what is mine and what is Belle's?" She slipped the key into his hand.

He smiled. She'd forgotten he'd dug through her trunk the night he saved it from thieves. He'd memorized every garment and personal item. Even before he met Clara Bixbee, he'd been intrigued by her.

"You two are different sizes, and she wears men's clothes. I think I can tell the difference. And I'd bet you have nearly everything in the trunk waiting to leave."

Clara giggled. "You're right. It is still packed other than the items we bought at the store today." She sighed. "I can't believe that was just today. This day seems like it has been a year."

It was good to hear the lightness in her voice. "It wasn't today. It was yesterday."

"It is past midnight isn't it?"

He gently grasped her arms. "Do you want to stay here and wait for me or go back to the livery?"

His male pride wanted her to wait for him, but he knew she would be safer at the livery.

She was quiet a moment. "I'll wait here. I can help you carry things."

He rubbed his hands up and down her arms. "Are you cold?"

"I'm fine. This parka is keeping me warm. It's my feet that are getting cold."

Jeremy moved her against the building. "If your legs can take it, squat. That will cover your feet more and add a little more heat." This time he didn't hesitate. He leaned forward and kissed her. "I'll hurry."

"Don't forget my umbrella. It's hanging on a peg by the door."

"There isn't going to be rain this time of year. And you can buy a new one when you get home." Fool woman. There wasn't a need for such a thing during the winter.

"I don't want it for rain." Her tone became defensive.

"That's all they're good for." Why would you want an umbrella if not for rain?

"They also work to keep people a respectful distance from me and provide protection."

He shook his head. Heck if he knew what kind of protection a piece of steel, wood, and cloth could do, but he'd bring her the umbrella. "I'll grab it."

He used the dark alley to work his way toward the back of the neighboring building.

If Soapy's men caught him entering her room, how long would it be before Clara realized he'd been caught and wasn't coming back?

Chapter Twelve

Clara stood in the dark alley watching Jeremy's murky shadow disappear. She was too proud to have told him how scared she'd been when he left her here the first time. A group of laughing, raucous men had passed the end of the alley. She'd covered her mouth to suppress the squeak made from air escaping as her chest constricted.

Pricks of cold stabbed at her toes. She slid down the wall and wrapped her skirt around her feet hoping the bit of extra cover would lessen the pain. For not the first time she wondered at her sanity of defy Soapy Smith. She'd be up in her room huddled under the warm blankets right now if she hadn't charged down that alley unthinking.

To chase away her dismal thoughts, she touched a gloved-fingertip to her lips. Her face heated from the shame of having allowed a man to kiss her so intimately in public. Reliving the kiss, shame disappeared and desire, along with curiosity, inflamed her limbs, bringing relief to her toes and dots of perspiration to her scalp. How could the action of two people pressing their mouths together bring such elation? Was this why the soiled doves like Lily lay with men?

Her mind wrestled with the new emotions from the kiss and how it made her no different from Lily, and she no longer feared being alone in the dark alley.

Jeremy entered the building next to the hotel, took the stairs to the top, and jumped from that roof top to the hotel's roof. His boots slid on the wet shakes, and he landed hard on his chest. He dug his toes into the shakes and stopped sliding. On hands and knees, he crawled to the side of the building with a second story balcony and lowered himself quietly.

He peered over the railing, spotting the two men still smoking and keeping an eye on the hotel door. As long as they kept their eyes riveted to the door, chances were they wouldn't discover he was in the building. Jeremy tried the knob, and the door opened with ease. He peeked down the hall. Empty.

Long strides carried him to room twenty-seven. He inserted the key and stepped in, closing the door quickly behind him. Walking to the middle of the room and stretching his hand over his head, he found the light dangling from the ceiling. He blinked at the brightness and cursed when he saw the window. He'd just signaled to the outside someone was in the room.

Thankfully, Clara traveled light. He scooped everything from her trunk up in his arms and placed it on a bed. Then he quickly found the items bought at the store and the umbrella with a ceramic handle. He tossed them on top of the pile and tied the corners of the blanket together. The light glared into the hall when he flung the door open. Long strides carried him down the hall to the balcony.

He pulled the outside door closed behind him moments before the balcony shook and the pounding of feet echoed in the hall. The men no longer stood across from the hotel. Down was easier than up. Jeremy hurried to the side of the balcony, dropped the bundle to the ground, grabbed the railing, and stepped over. He gripped the railing, suspended in air, and glanced down to see where he'd land. Nothing to hinder his fall. Jeremy let go, dropping to the ground. He missed the pile of clothes and rolled to ease the fall and get to his feet quicker.

His hand latched onto the knot on the top of the bundle, and he ran down the alley, across the street, and into the next alley without stopping to see if anyone saw him. Breathing hard, he stopped and caught his breath before he came to the area he'd left Clara.

With his breathing under control, he strode toward Clara and called out quietly, "Clara?"

"Over here." Her shadow separated from the building.

"Come on. We need to get off the streets." The bundle was slung over his right shoulder. He grabbed her hand with his left and hurried down the alley toward the livery.

"Did they see you?" The quiet words fluttered with fear.

"No. But I didn't think about them noticing the light. Once it came on, they all headed for the room. I made it in and out without being seen, but they're going to wonder what happened. They'll be out searching."

They arrived at the livery. Jeremy banged four times on the door and entered, dragging Clara in behind him. He dropped the bundle and braced the door with a metal bar.

"We were getting worried," Reverend Daily said, stepping forward.

Lily still dutifully held the snow pack to her face. Jeremy had to admit it did seem to be doing some good. Clara approached the two, checked Lily's snow pack, and then turned to him. Her eyes were wary and her cheeks flushed.

Jeremy bent to pick up the bundle and avert his gaze. He would regret kissing Clara until the day he turned her over to her brother. That moment would make the rest of their trip together unbearable for him. Knowing how she tasted and felt in his arms. But he had to ignore his body and use his head. She was paying him to get to her brother. And he had plans to marry when he left here, not before. If her brother discovered Jeremy had kissed her so brazenly in public, there was sure to be a shotgun wedding. His honorable self, the one that couldn't leave her to another dishonest guide, was the same one beating him up over his earlier actions.

He carried the bundle over to the cot and placed

it beside Lily. "I grabbed everything out of your trunk and the things from the store."

"Thank you." Clara had the snow pack in her hand, staring down at it.

"You two ladies do what you need with these things. I'm heading back out to find two dog teams and sleds. If possible, I'd like to be loaded and gone before anyone realizes we've headed to the pass." He continued to avoid eye contact with Clara and strode to the door.

"I'll be ready when you return."

Jeremy glanced over his shoulder. It was ridiculous to head up the trail without a night's sleep, and even more ludicrous to drag a city woman up that trail. The determined look on Clara's face told him she would face anything and trust him. He nodded. The choice was easy. They had to head over the pass. To stay here would mean death for Clara. At least on the pass he could battle forces one man could deal with. He wasn't a match for Soapy Smith and all his men.

After tasting Clara's lips and seeing her strength, he'd do everything within his power to keep her alive and get her to her brother. And try his damnedest to remain honorable in her eyes.

"Reverend, put this back in place when I leave." Jeremy pointed to the metal bar, slipped out into the dark, and hoped Buck Reilly was camped in his usual spot.

Clara avoided the questioning glances of the reverend and only answered direct questions as she pulled an extra set of underclothes and one brown wool dress out of the bundle on the bed. She then split her brush and comb set up, giving Lily the brush. Lily had curly hair that would work best with a brush, and Clara's straight hair would do fine with a comb.

She handed the dress and undergarments to Lily. "Why don't you go change in an empty stall? If you aren't dressed like a soiled dove they will be less likely to take a second look at you."

Lily smiled. "Thank you. For everything." She hugged Clara and carried the clothing to the first stall.

Clara smiled, her chest warmed seeing the other woman walk with more bounce to her step. She didn't know how Lily came to be a soiled dove, but she was willing to help the woman get out.

While Lily changed, Clara left all but one set of undergarments, a dress, and her personal items in the blanket for Lily. She put her personal items and the one set of clothes into the pack Jeremy had said to use for her belongings. She had fewer belongings now. They barely filled the pouch half way. She didn't regret giving her things to Lily. The girl needed to be presentable, both to get her out of Skagway, and while in route on the ship. If she looked like a soiled dove, she'd be treated like one.

Lily returned. They were nearly the same size.

"You look nice dressed proper." Clara put a hand on her arm. "If you dress respectable, and act respectable, no one is going to know your past. When you get to Seattle, go here," Clara handed her a piece of paper with the warehouse address, "And tell them I sent you there to apply for work." She peered into Lily's eyes. "You can read and write?"

"Yes."

Lily's confident tone washed away Clara's doubts about sending her to the warehouse. "Good. And tell my mother you've seen me, I'm well, and heading to the interior to find Randy."

"I will. You be careful, I've heard that trip isn't easy." Lily hugged her. "I'm glad you came to my rescue."

Clara blinked back tears. "Me too." Lily may be a soiled dove, but she was a woman who deserved help and respect just like any other. And quite possibly it was a man, Soapy Smith or some other, who led her down the wrong path. When Clara returned to Seattle, she hoped to start up a real friendship with the woman.

"Lily, we need to get moving. The town will start waking soon." Reverend Daily stood by the cot, the blanket tied back up into a bundle.

Clara held out her wool coat to Lily. "Wear this." Lily slipped her arms in the garment. "And this." Clara placed her wool scarf on Lily's head and wrapped it around her face so only her eyes and bangs were visible. "Keep the scarf wrapped until you are away from Skagway."

"I will."

Lily's muffled reply and tears shimmering in her eyes squeezed Clara's heart. Lily was brave to leave Soapy Smith and head out on a ship alone. Much like her journey to find Randy. The two had a bond over thwarting the vile man and their willingness to brave new trials to make their futures brighter.

"I'll see you soon. Don't forget to tell my mother you saw me." She hugged Lily, again, and then motioned for her and Reverend Daily to go.

Once the two exited and closed the door, Clara hurried to the empty stall and undressed. Cold air wafted around her exposed arms and fluttered under her shift as she stood in the stall deciding if she should tuck the long shift into her pants or cut it off, since she didn't think to bring camisoles for under her corset. Leaving off the corset was out of the question. No respectable woman would be seen without one.

Four loud knocks, dropped her to a crouch in the stall. Crossing her arms and peering at the door through a crack in the stall, Clara mentally chastised herself. *Why didn't I block the door?*

Chapter Thirteen

Jeremy pushed the door open and scanned the inside of the livery. *Where was everyone*? The lantern illuminated the empty bed. Both Lily and the blanket of clothes were gone. In their place sat wool socks and the new pair of boots for Clara. The pack he'd told Clara to use sat at the end of the cot, the top flap open. He didn't see any signs of a struggle.

"Clara?" he asked in a natural tone. He didn't want to yell with Soapy Smith's men prowling the streets.

"I'm over here."

Her voice came from the stalls.

"What are you doing?" He strode that direction.

Her blonde head appeared from her nose up. "Stay there!"

Her hysterical voice froze his feet and his heart. "What's wrong?" He worked hard to keep his voice calm. Why was she hiding in a stall?

"Just stay there. I-I'm changing." Her eyes closed.

Something wasn't right. "Where's Reverend Daily and Lily?"

"They left. I gave Lily all my things except for one set of clothes, and they went to meet the reverend's friend." Her voice was stronger, held more conviction.

"Then you're alone in the stall?"

"Yes!" Her head popped up above the board and her narrowed eyes glared at him.

His gaze traveled downward, glimpsing her creamy neck and round shoulders. He instantly spun, putting his back to her. That's why she was scared. He'd walked in when she was naked. The thought sent his mind and body to holding and kissing her. He had to shift to release tension in his britches. His thoughts couldn't go that direction. Desire and lust weren't good trail companions. He had to stop these reactions to Clara. She wasn't the right woman for him.

"I'll just wait here until you're done." His scratchy voice didn't sound quite like him, but there was nothing he could do. Thoughts of Clara's naked body parched his throat like a dry August day in the high desert. *I've gone too long without bedding a woman.*

A deep sigh met his ears. "That's the problem."

"Pardon?" What did she mean? Dressing was a problem?

"I didn't bring along a chemise and my shift won't tuck into the trousers..." She sighed again. "And I sent my scissors with Lily..."

Her voice trailed off. Jeremy replayed her words and still didn't understand the problem. "What does that have to do with getting dressed?"

"I either have to take off the corset and the shift and have you cut the shift, or have you come in here and cut the shift while I'm wearing it and the corset." Another deep inhale and exhale. "Either way is most improper."

He didn't like the prospect either. Not because he didn't want to see Clara in her unmentionables, in fact, he'd give anything to see her and touch her skin where no one else had. Nope, he wasn't sure he had enough control to not devour her with his gaze and then crush her to him and take another sampling of her kisses.

He groaned. The best way to deal with the shift would be without her in it. His mind hazed over, but that meant she'd be standing in the stall naked. Heat rushed through him and hardened his shaft. Thinking those thoughts weren't good either. He ran a hand over his face.

Now he understood the urges that had Gil and Darcy cavorting on the side of Olive Lake before they'd married. As a twelve-year-old, all he could think was their pa would be highly disappointed in Darcy. As an adult, he recognized, empathized with, and fought the pull of desire.

He cleared his throat. "Which one would you be more comfortable with?"

"Neither. Hand me your knife."

Jeremy faced the stall and swallowed again taking in her messy hair, flushed cheeks, and dainty hand reaching over the stall. He forced his feet to slowly cross the dirt floor. With his height, he could have easily peered over the stall. His conscience wouldn't let him. He stopped at a point where he could hand her the knife but not see down into the stall.

"Sure you won't cut yourself?" he asked, keeping his tone even.

"I'm not worried about cutting myself so much as making a mess of the shift." She disappeared.

He heard fabric tearing.

"Here."

The handle of his knife appeared. "You know, you'll have so many layers of clothes on no one will know if you're wearing a corset."

Her green eyes met his over the stall. "I'll know."

He grabbed the knife and walked over to the pack by the cot. "Buck will be here in an hour with the dogs and sleds. It's a good thing you thought to change your clothes now."

Clara stepped out of the stall dressed in the trousers and a blue flannel shirt. She walked to the pack and folded her dress and skirts before placing them in with her other clothes.

"You might want two pairs of socks," he offered as she sat on the cot and pulled on the socks.

"It will be that cold already?"

"Feet can never be too warm up here."

She shrugged, dug another pair of socks out of the pack, put them on, and pulled on the boots.

"I'll scrounge up some hard tack and beans. That's all there's time for until we've put some distance between us and this town." Jeremy headed to the dark side of the livery to dig through the packs and find something to give them energy for the first push on the trail.

He couldn't believe how easy it had been to deal with Buck. If he didn't know the man hated Soapy, he'd be worried about Smith and his gang storming the livery. Which was a better thing to occupy his mind than visions of Clara in next to nothing.

Clara donned the parka and sat back down on the cot. With Jeremy's back to her, she could watch him and not be embarrassed. The way he'd spun on his heels when he'd realized she was in her unmentionables had her confused. The way he'd kissed her in the street she'd feared his behavior when he walked in on her. Surely, someone who would kiss so boldly in public wouldn't be scared to see her in her unmentionables. Yet, he'd spun so quick she'd felt a draft. That led her to believe she wasn't pleasing to look at.

What was wrong with her? Mother always commented on her pretty hair and her friend Sarah complimented her eyes all the time. *It must be my body.* With the layers of clothing, it was hard to tell whether she was slender or padded. But he'd turned from her when her top half was revealed. Was it her small bosoms?

Pounding on the door brought her out of her miserable thoughts.

Jeremy eased the doors open enough to peek out. Then shoved the large doors open. Cold wind, one, two, three, four, five, six dogs, and three sleds whirled into the livery. The long line of dogs and sleds reached from the stalls to right inside the entrance.

"Close the doors," said the man bundled in a parka like hers, fur boots, and oilskin pants.

The doors closed, and Clara knelt to pet the lead dog who sniffed her. He resembled drawings in a book she'd read about wolves. She peered into his yellow eyes. Was he a wolf?

"Clara Bixbee, this is Buck Reilly. I traded my horses and pack saddles to him for two dog teams and their food." Jeremy shook hands with the man.

Unsure what a dog team consisted of, Clara extended her hand. "I'm pleased to meet you Mr. Reilly." A fur lined mitten engulfed her hand as she stared up into a bearded face with sparkling dark eyes.

"My pleasure ma'am. Anyone who gets the best of Soapy Smith I'll call a friend." Mr. Reilly smiled, showing a large set of teeth hidden behind his beard.

He turned to Jeremy. "Get these loaded, I'll go get the other team. The streets are coming alive, so you need to hurry if you want to get out of here before anyone notices." Mr. Reilly covered the ground to the door in an instant and disappeared.

"What did you mean by dog teams?" Clara stopped petting the dog. The animal moved away to sniff at the dog hitched behind it.

"A dog team is six dogs hitched to three sleds." He took hold of the harness on the lead dog drawing him in a circle and pulling the sleds farther into the livery, closer to the packs.

"Why is he bringing two? Who is going to drive the other one?" She'd never owned a dog and had never driven a buggy.

"We'll need two teams. One will carry your food required by the Northwest Mounted Police and the other will carry the merchandise I will deliver to Dawson. You will be in charge of the second team." Jeremy carried filled pack bags over to the sleds.

"Me? I don't know anything about dogs or making them pull sleds." She stared at Jeremy. "I'm paying you to take me."

"And I will. I'll be in the lead. You'll just walk behind and shout the same instructions to your dogs that I shout to mine."

He finished unloading the first pack and placed one by the first sled. "Unload all of this onto the sled."

"Why can't we just put the packs on the sleds and cover them?" The minute the words escaped she recognized the packs were twice the width of the narrow sleds. She'd guess the sled to be less than two feet wide. The thin wood that made up the frame didn't look like it would hold the weight of the freight. The frame resembled toboggans children played on in the snow. The front runners stuck out a good foot beyond the ten-foot-length of leather that made up the base of the sled.

"They won't fit properly, and I'm trading the horses, mules, and the equipment to Buck. The packs are the equipment."

"It seems like he's getting the better deal." Clara had been in the business world and knew when someone was getting more than was fair.

"I don't need the horses or the packs where I'm going. But we need the dogs and sleds to get you out of here. And up here a dog is worth four hundred dollars." He peered into her eyes. "If we don't leave soon, I'm not sure I could hold off Soapy and all his men."

She saw the regret in his eyes. He would battle to the death to keep her safe. But Jeremy alone against Soapy Smith and all his men wasn't good odds. She nodded and worked twice as fast. There was no way she'd let harm come to him because of her actions.

Pounding on the door jumped her heart and riveted her gaze to the big doors.

Jeremy opened the doors again and another string of six dogs entered followed by three more sleds and Mr. Reilly.

"Hurry. Soapy himself is stomping up and down the streets." Mr. Reilly, pointed at Clara. "It would be best if we hide her on a sled, and I go with you to the first camp. I can hike back down the next day."

She watched Jeremy. He thought on it a moment. "That's a good idea. If the two of us head out, no one will suspect anything. I've told enough people I have a shipment to get to Dawson and taking your dogs will make sense that you're going along." He slapped Mr. Reilly on the back and carried over more items to put on the sleds.

Clara drug the pack over with her clothes. "What about my things I don't have a bag to put them in."

Jeremy picked up the half-filled pack and

placed it on the sled. "We'll take this pack."

"Sit down here so I can pile the goods on the sled in front of you." Jeremy folded up the blankets from the bed and made a pad at the back of the first sled.

Clara stepped onto the sled and sat with her legs crossed.

"Is that going to be comfortable to sit for two hours?" Jeremy asked, his gaze searching hers.

She pulled her knees up to her chest, wrapping her arms around her legs. "I'll have to stay hidden for two hours?"

Mr. Reilly hauled over a box. "You'll need to stay hidden until we get by Ragtown. Otherwise someone could see you and word would get back here fast."

Chapter Fourteen

Jeremy was grateful for Buck's help. They left Skagway as the sun started to cast a golden hue on the town. A few miners hailed them as the dogs pulled the sleds by the camp of tents.

The snow was fresh, wet, and packed easily under their snow shoes, but it required he and Buck take turns walking in front of the dogs to pack the snow and make it slick for the sleds to slide across and not sink.

The snow made the first river crossing easy. The water was frozen and eight feet of snow covered the ice. If he didn't know the river was in the small canyon he would have thought they were traveling on land. As Jeremy trudged ahead of the dogs, packing the snow, he realized starting tomorrow, he'd be the only one to make trail. Clara was too light to do a good job of packing the snow.

Nearly two hours passed when they finally arrived at Ragtown. The area was so called because of the tents with wood frames, now mounds of snow, that housed restaurants, dry goods, and other services men required. The area had been walked, and he could rest his legs as they continued through the settlement, waving at the people who poked their heads out to see who was crazy enough to be tackling the trail so soon after the storm.

Once they were out of sight of Ragtown, Jeremy stopped the dogs and walked to the sled where Clara hid. He untied the rope holding the tarpaulin over the load. Her mittened hands grasped the cover shoving it forward. She drew in great gasps of air and blinked at the sun shining off the white world.

"You can get out and walk now." He held out a hand, helping her to stand.

"Oh!" She grabbed her leg and rubbed. "I don't think I've sat still that long since grammar school." Clara stepped off the sled, and her legs sunk up to her knees into the snow. Her gaze took in the snowshoes on his feet.

Jeremy grasped her under the arms, pulling her up to sit on the tarpaulin covered mound of supplies. "You'll need snowshoes."

Buck brought the pair they'd tied to the top of one of the bundles. "These are going to be big but they're the smallest I had."

Jeremy's gut squeezed at the smile Clara gave Buck. He remembered her looking at him with just such a smile and how it had warmed him. He glanced at Buck. Yep. He was looking moony-eyed too.

"Check the dogs," Jeremy said, snatching the

snowshoes from Buck and bending to put one on Clara's feet. She wasn't his to be ordering another man away from, but the jealousy gurgling gin his gut soured his temperament.

The man stood there a moment before moving off.

"That was rude of you." Clara's voice was barely above a whisper.

He peered up into her questioning eyes. "I'm your guide," he said roughly. "I'll be the only one you need to trust." *And the only one to touch you.*

"What harm would his putting my snowshoes on do?" One blonde eyebrow rose above her merry green eyes.

Jeremy's face heated. Did she see his jealousy?

"It wouldn't be proper for every man who comes along to lay his hands on you."

She scoffed. "And that kiss you gave me *was* proper?" Her hands fluttered about. "And all the times you've touched me, trying on boots, escorting me place to place, and now this."

"It's different. You're my employer. I'm doing my job making sure you get to your brother." Yes, all the things she'd mentioned he had done, but always with the end thought of getting her safely to her brother. *You can try and fool her, but you know you touch her more than is proper.* He mentally pummeled the voice in his head. Her kiss still lingered on his lips. He did crave her nearness. *It has to stop!* But I'm not letting any other man touch her.

Both snowshoes securely in place, he picked her up and sat her on her feet. "Try them out."

She shuffled her feet along the top of the snow.

He laughed at her hesitant stride.

"No. Pick your feet up. Just like walking."

Clara heard Jeremy's laughter and it made her heart thrum in her chest with happiness. He wasn't laughing at her inadequacy but with her silliness as she over exaggerated her steps.

Seldom had a man laughed when she couldn't perform a task. She'd put herself in a mostly male world working at the warehouse. When she couldn't perform a task, they only nodded and hurried off to spread the word the boss's daughter couldn't hack the business, laughing behind her back instead of within earshot.

She took a regular step and another, moving back down the path the men and sleds had made.

"Good! Come back this way. You can follow the teams. It will make the walking easier for you." Jeremy walked on the unpacked snow to the head of the dogs. "Move out!" he shouted to Buck who started walking in front of the lead team.

"Mahsh!" Buck and Jeremy both shouted. The teams strained at the harnesses, slowly pulling the sleds until they moved easily.

Clara walked behind the second set of sleds, realizing she had the best position. Buck walked sideways, packing the snow so the sleds would pull easily. After fifteen minutes, Jeremy moved to the front and started the sideways walking. Buck waited until the second team had passed him, and he fell in step behind her.

It was unnerving to have the big man huffing behind her, catching his breath after packing the trail for the lead team. Eventually, his breathing quieted.

"Duncan didn't say why you need to get to Dawson."

Clara decided if Jeremy didn't mention it, perhaps it wasn't something to mention so she remained quiet.

"The way he ordered me away, I'm thinking you and he are…"

He left it for her to fill in, but she didn't have an answer to that. It would have been easier to say, "I hired him, and therefore, he feels I am much like the supplies he is delivering to Dawson." However, she hadn't seen Jeremy gaze at the supplies like he'd gazed into her eyes every time he touched her. Her insides had gone all warm and fuzzy when he'd ordered Buck to check the dogs. She hadn't had much experience with men, but she knew a possessive look when she saw it.

On one hand the thought he was possessive thrilled the woman in her. But the possessiveness also angered her. She was a possession. She was a person. Something her father and the men at the warehouse seemed to forget too easily.

She looked up and caught Jeremy staring back at them. A scowl brought his brows together above his nose. Clara shook her head, trying to convey to him not to worry.

They were now going nearly straight uphill. The dogs had to dig in with their nails to pull the loads up the incline. Jeremy and Buck helped pull the sleds until the incline became easier.

Jeremy waited on the side, until she stood abreast of him.

Without giving him a chance to talk, she stopped and faced him. "Why didn't you tell Buck I'm paying you to get me to my brother?"

His eyes widened, and he tipped his head just enough to hide his eyes in the shadow of his hat brim. "I figured the less he knew, the less he could blab to others. If certain men, namely of the ilk of Soapy Smith, heard you could afford to hire me to pack you to your brother, they might think you have more valuables worth taking."

She sucked in air. The thought hadn't occurred. Grateful he'd had the good sense, she smiled up at him. "When I didn't fill him in, Buck decided you are bringing me along for entertainment."

"Damn!" Jeremy grabbed her arms. "I would never compromise you."

Her heart bounced around inside her chest. His words sounded like he was denying something he'd already done. "Yes, you have been honorable. And I am grateful—"

"The kiss. I only did that to keep you safe. I wasn't…" He released her arms and ran a hand over his face. He glanced ahead. "We need to catch up or Buck will get suspicious."

His strides were twice the length of hers, catching him up to the second team and leaving her behind to wallow in her thoughts.

Why did he always deny the kiss? The experience had been the most exquisite thing to ever happen to her. How come he kept treating the kiss like he'd violated her? *Because you barely know one another and it was an intimacy that should be kept to a husband and wife's bedroom.* It appeared her guide was more in control of her proprieties than she was.

The remainder of the day was spent slowly climbing up and up, traveling in and out of canyons. At one perilous spot she noticed Jeremy stopped and placed his hat against his chest as if praying.

She caught up to him. "What are you doing?"

He started before turning his gaze on her. His gray eyes held sorrow. "I lost one of my best horses here last fall. Damn greenhorn pushed him too fast and he fell." He swept his hat toward the gully. "Under all this snow are thousands of horse carcasses. I only lost two to this trail but there are men who beat an animal until it can no longer walk and then keep on going until it collapses. Or they push the animal past its comfort and it makes a misstep and falls over the side." Bitterness laced his words. He swiped a hand over his face as if trying to wipe away the memory. "I've seen men crawl over a horse that fell in the trail and rather than stop and put the animal out of its misery, the greedy men following keep crawling over it until the animal is dead and falling to pieces."

Bile rose in Clara's throat. Her stomach pitched, and she pivoted to face the mountain side rather than the canyon below.

Buck stopped up ahead. "It's your turn."

Jeremy slapped his hat on his head and edged his way by the sleds and dogs. Clara's heart lodged in her throat watching him navigate the narrow trail.

After what felt like hours of switchback trails, they stopped. Clara accepted the water canteen Jeremy handed her and followed his hand as he pointed.

A waterfall had frozen. The clear ice shone in the sunshine like a huge diamond.

"It's beautiful!"

"It's a real sight to see in the summer when the water's running." Jeremy waved back down the trail. "We've crossed the river three times and will one more before we stop at Ford for the night."

"I haven't seen water or ice." Clara thought back to the trip and couldn't remember anything that resembled a river.

"They are all frozen and covered with snow." He nodded in the direction Buck was moving with the dogs. "In the interior, in the spring after the thaw, most of the gold seekers float the river to their destinations. We'll travel on the frozen rivers with the dogs."

They traveled three more hours in the gray of dusk before she spotted mounds of snow the size of hay stacks with stove pipes sticking out of them and packed snow. A man walked out of a mound and waved.

Buck was walking beside her.

"What is this?" she asked.

"Ford. There's tents under those humps of snow. This is one of the main stops on the trail." Buck waved and headed to the front of the sleds and dogs.

Clara watched him shake hands with the man who emerged. Jeremy stepped forward, shaking hands with the man and talking. She remained at the back of the teams waiting to see if she was to be acknowledged or remain hidden.

Jeremy nodded to the man, as Buck headed

around the back of the mound with the dogs and sleds following. Jeremy beckoned to her. Clara willed her tired legs to carry her the twenty feet to the two men.

"Clara, this is Red. He runs the establishment we'll be staying in tonight."

Clara held out her hand. "I'm pleased to meet you."

The man squinted as he tried to see her face hidden behind the fur edge of her parka hood. "Likewise, ma'am."

"Go on in with Red and get warm. I'm going to help Buck put the dogs up for the night." Jeremy motioned to the hole in the snow.

Clara studied Jeremy's face. He didn't appear apprehensive or worried about her entering the snow mound with the man. His lack of concern for her safety gave her the confidence to follow Red into the snowy hole. And the smoking stove pipe proved there would be warmth.

The tunnel proved to be steps carved in the snow that led down to a four feet wide flat area in front of a wooden door. Red stopped to unlace his snowshoes. Clara did the same, leaning the webbed footwear up against the snow wall.

Red opened the door. Warm air and mouth-watering aromas swirled into the snow tunnel. He entered what appeared to be a large canvas tent re-enforced with more wooden poles than a normal tent would need. He removed his outerwear and hung it all on a peg by the door. He uncovered a round bald head and stocky body.

"Welcome!" He waved her into a one-room

area with a cookstove, long table and benches, and three rows of bunks along one wall.

The scent of baking filled her nostrils and increased the growl in her belly. Clara removed her mittens and rubbed her hands together. She hadn't realized how cold her fingers were until they started tingling from the heat.

Red waved her over to the stove. "Step up and warm yourself."

Clara scanned the interior. "Is this a hotel?"

"I'm one of three establishments such as this here at Ford. Even though most travelers are only one day from Skagway, after climbing this far they are in need of company, a hot meal, and perhaps some necessities they forgot." He winked. "And I supply all but the company for a price."

The thought of what a warm meal would cost her nearly squelched her appetite. But all the walking she'd done up the mountainside had her stomach rumbling louder than an angry bear.

Stomping and male voices backed her into the stove. It had to be Jeremy and Buck. Red seemed genial enough, but the claustrophobic atmosphere made her edgy.

The door opened and the first face she saw, slowed her breathing and eased the tension. Jeremy's gaze found her the minute the door opened and didn't leave her face until she'd offered a small smile. He dropped two bundles on the floor and turned to the proprietor.

"Red, you have enough supper cooked up for the three of us?" Jeremy unbuttoned his coat and stepped to the stove. "You might want to get your coat off before you start roasting," he whispered to her.

Now her face warmed from the inside out. Clara ducked her head and worked the buttons through the fur-lined holes. Keeping her attention on the task rather than the three men exchanging information and settling down at the long table in the middle of the room.

Once the coat was open, she walked to the pegs by the wall and hung her coat alongside Jeremy's wool coat and oil duster. She'd noticed he didn't dress like the others. He layered in clothes you'd see on men in Seattle. No knitted wool cap or fur-lined parka for him. This made her wonder at his reasoning.

She faced the room. Jeremy glanced her way and patted the bench beside him. The only other option was the bench on Buck's side of the table. Jeremy made her feel safe, and she enjoyed being close to him. She stepped over the bench and sat, keeping a proper distance from him.

Red sat four spoons and deep tin plates on the table. Jeremy passed them out as their host returned to the stove and waddled back carrying a large steaming kettle. Before he sat, Red fetched another tin plate piled high with biscuits. These were the scents that met her at the door.

Once the meal was in place she expected the men to dig in, but was pleasantly surprised when they bowed their heads. Silence followed before each one whispered "Amen" as they each finished their individual blessing. This side of the men pleased her. Especially, knowing Jeremy believed.

Jeremy picked up her plate, and Red ladled stew onto it. The aroma that tickled her nose was as herb infused as any she'd encounter in a top restaurant.

"You'll want a couple of Red's biscuits before Buck eats all of them." Jeremy's voice was low and warm against her ear as he leaned and placed two biscuit's on the side of her plate.

"Thank you." If she turned, their faces would be only inches apart. Her insides squiggled at his nearness. Clara kept her gaze on the stew as she swirled her spoon around, checking out the ingredients.

From the corner of her eye, she watched the men all dig in. She took a small spoonful and tasted. It was as good as it smelled. Clara cleaned the bowl with first her spoon and then a biscuit. The whole meal was delicious.

Feeling as if she should do something, she stood and started to gather the dishes. Jeremy captured her wrist.

"What are you doing?"

"I'm going to help with the dishes." She stared down into his eyes.

"The money he charges for this meal, you don't need to help him with the dishes." Jeremy took the plates out of her hands and set them on the table.

"How much do I owe?" she asked, directing her question to Red.

"Nothing. I'll take care of it." Jeremy's tone was low and ominous.

She stabbed her hands on her hips. "I can pay my own debts."

Chapter Fifteen

Jeremy groaned inwardly. He didn't want to fight with her in front of the two men taking in the whole scene with unabashed glee. Standing, he grasped Clara's arm and led her to the door. "Put your coat on."

She glared up at him. He took the coat down, placed it over her shoulders, and led her out into the small flat area outside the door. He made sure the door was closed tight behind them before he started talking.

"I will take care of all the expenses between here and your brother." She started to open her mouth, and he raised his hand. "They are part of the cost to guide you."

Her face relaxed, and her body shivered. Lord help him, but he couldn't stop his arms from pulling her against him and trying to ward off the cold.

"You're safer if you keep the notion you have

money out of other people's heads."

She leaned into him. "But they'll know you have money. Doesn't that make you a target?"

Her worry for him made him smile and formed a lump in his chest. He hadn't had anyone worry about him in a long while.

"I know everyone on this trail, and they know me." He tipped her head back to peer into her face. "I have a reputation that keeps trouble away."

He saw a flicker of uncertainty and felt her body stiffen.

"W-what kind of reputation?"

"I'm good with a gun and a knife, and they know I have lots of lawmen in the family that will hunt them down."

"Oh." Her body relaxed and she smiled. "Do you have a large family?"

He shivered and drew her closer. "I'll tell you another time when I'm not standing in the cold."

"I'm sorry! Why didn't you grab a coat?" She snuggled closer.

He forgot the cold, inhaling the faint floral scent coming from her hair and feeling her arms hugging his waist. Yep, his body was definitely heating up.

"If we stay out here too long Red and Buck are going to get the wrong idea…" He left the thought for her to fill in.

"Will that keep them from looking at me like I'm a piece of cake?"

He'd noticed their hungry gazes as well. He'd hoped she hadn't. "They're decent men and would stay away from what they thought was mine."

She snuggled closer. "Then let them think what they want. I don't want either of them thinking they can have liberties with me. If I thought that I wouldn't sleep all night for fear."

He'd been wondering about the sleeping arrangements. They'd all be in the one room. He didn't like the idea of Clara on a top or bottom bunk. He wanted her close. Where he could touch her and know she was safe. Red and Buck would both think he was crazy, but the best place for Clara to sleep was by the wall and then his bedding on the other side of her. He'd know if anyone came near her and be there if she needed anything during the night.

"Come on, the dishes should be done and you can get ready for bed." He started for the door but she escaped his arm.

"I need… where does one relieve themselves?" Her pretty face was red as a ripe apple.

He nodded to the snow. "Anywhere out there. Or I'm sure Red has a chamber pot you could use."

She thought a moment then tucked her arms into her coat sleeves and started up the snow steps to the opening. It was dark. She wouldn't be able to see where to go and could end up in an avalanche or stepping into an air pocket around a tree.

"Wait. I need my coat. I don't want you falling and freezing to death." He hurried into the cabin. Both men looked up from a game of checkers.

"You two staying outside tonight?" Buck's eyebrows waggled.

"No. We'll be back in shortly." Jeremy grabbed his wool coat and closed the door soundly. Clara stood at the top of the opening, her back to him. She'd kept up the pace today without complaining or slacking. He'd expected her to ask to get back on the sled and ride once she saw what was ahead of her.

"We'll need our snowshoes."

She returned to the area where the snowshoes all leaned against the wall. He helped put hers on before stepping into and lacing his. "Okay, follow me."

They climbed out into the weak moonlight that shone brighter off the white world. "Remember to always wear your snowshoes when outside unless I tell you differently."

"Why?"

"You saw how you sunk in the snow when you first climbed off the sled. And you see how the snow is over the tents? If you try to walk around up here in this deep snow, you'll either sink and suffocate or break something."

He led her to an area behind most of the mounds. This time of night there was little chance someone would wander out. The locals would use their chamber pots rather than brave the cold wind that constantly chilled the air. He understood Clara's desire to not use one at Red's.

This area was stable without trees to make air pockets. "Use this spot. I'll walk over there." He pointed back toward the tent mounds.

"But how?" She stared down at the snowshoes extending two feet front and back from her body and a foot across.

He knew what she was asking. "It will clean off

on the walk back."

The grimace on her face and shudder of her body told him she understood.

"You'll learn to forget proprieties and make this kind of trip quickly." He walked twenty steps back toward the smoke stacks and curls of smoke and stopped with his back to her.

The sounds carrying on the frigid wind blowing across the top of the mountain made him wish he had a proper outhouse for her to use. She grumbled. He heard clothing rustling, and more grumbling, and he was pretty sure a whimper. Had to be when the icy wind stung her exposed backside.

"Jeremy."

Her plaintive cry spun him around. She stood in place, her face pointed down to her feet. He walked back to her.

"What?"

She tipped her face up. Frozen tears glistened on her cheeks and the mortification on her face tore at his heart. He grasped her face in his hands, using his warm palms to melt the tears.

"Shh. Nothing's so bad we can't fix it. Don't cry. Tears are your enemy in this icy wind." He kissed her cold cheeks.

"My feet are stuck. My…" she hiccupped. "It froze the snowshoes to the snow."

He glanced down and saw yellow ice. "It's okay." He put his arms around her and lifted. He strained, and her snowshoes popped free. She dangled in his arms, the webbed contraptions bumping against his lower legs.

"This has happened to everyone who has ever

crossed this pass in the winter." He set her down, shoved her hands into her parka pockets, and led her back to the entrance with an arm around her shoulders. Their shoes became tangled a couple of times. He laughed, untangled their feet, and continued. By the time they arrived at the snow cave entrance, her spirits had been lifted.

Jeremy helped her out of the snowshoes, leaning her pair and his up against the side. He took her hand and led her into the cabin. The warmth made his face tingle and his ears burn. He should have worn more clothes. Clara winced. She must be feeling the burning sensation as well. He mentally slapped himself. *I should have put more outerwear on both of us.*

"You two were gone a long time…" Buck's gaze moved from Clara to Jeremy and back to Clara.

She kept her head tipped down as she worked out of her parka. Jeremy helped her shrug it off and hung it on a peg.

"We had some talking to do." Jeremy ushered Clara over to the stove to warm up.

"That what they call it?" Red asked, and he and Buck started laughing.

Clara flinched. He touched her shoulder, and she met his gaze then smiled. She'd have to get use to the rawness of the people they would meet on this trip. Buck and Red were acting more civilized than he'd expected.

"Warm up while I set out our beds." Jeremy picked up the bundles he'd dumped by the door. He rolled out the sleeping bag Clara bought next to the front wall and not a foot away, because of the small area, he rolled out his. There wasn't a need for the oil canvas he usually used top and bottom to ward off the wetness. He left it folded and placed it under where his head would rest.

"Ready," Jeremy said, facing the room and seeking Clara's acceptance.

"Why are you two sleeping on the floor when you can see I have bunks available what with the storm that just blowed through." Red squinted at him.

"Yeah, you two are lookin' awful cozy your beds so close together," Buck said, watching them both with a calculating stare. "Or you worried she's gonna run away from you if you get too far away?" Buck laughed.

Jeremy didn't find the man amusing. He knew Clara wouldn't run away from him. She needed him. The man doing the accusing might be helping to get back at Soapy Smith, but he wouldn't be above using a woman for his own pleasure. That was why Jeremy wanted Clara tucked safe between the wall and himself. But to tell the man that, would only start trouble.

"I'm scared of heights and—," Clara drew in a deep breath, her gaze flitting about the tent, "—I have claustrophobia."

Red and Buck stared at her like her eyes had just popped out of her head.

Clara laughed. "It's not a disease. I don't like being in closed in places. Like a bunk over the top of me."

Jeremy caught the glint in her eye and winked

at her. She'd just made a good excuse for them to sleep on the floor. "Now that you know the reason, we've got a lot of trail ahead of us tomorrow." He motioned to the beds he'd made.

A weak smile curved Clara's lips as she walked to a bench and sat down. Her fingers shook grasping her boots and tugging.

Jeremy fisted his hands, fighting the urge to help her, and sat down a couple feet from her to remove his own boots. A sideways glance, caught a glimpse of fear in her eyes. He reached over, squeezing her leg.

She met his gaze.

"You're safe. You need your sleep. Tomorrow the climb gets tougher." He wanted to lean over and kiss the wrinkles on her forehead.

A throat cleared, and he released her leg. Clara stood and walked to the bags, stepping over his. She lay down on the bag and didn't move. *Why wasn't she getting in?*

"You two ready to turn out the light?" he asked, directing his attention to the two men watching Clara.

"Soon as we finish this game," Red said, his gaze never leaving the rigid woman on the sleeping bag.

Jeremy walked to his bag, took off his outer wool shirt, and lay down on his side, facing Clara. She turned her head and wide, questioning eyes peered at him.

He leaned her direction and whispered, "You need to take off some of them clothes or you'll be too hot in the bag."

"I'm not undressing in front of all of you." Her eyes narrowed.

Anger he could deal with. The frightened, timid Clara he didn't know how to handle. If these men scared her, how did she fair working in a warehouse?

"You slip into the bag, then shuck off the outer layer of clothes."

She sat up and slid into the bag. The bag bulged here and there and eventually, she pulled out her britches, then her wool shirt. After much huffing and he was pretty sure a couple words a woman shouldn't say, her flushed face appeared at the top of the bag.

She crooked her finger at him.

Jeremy leaned closer.

"I can't get my corset undone, and I can't sleep with the thing pinching me."

His stomach knotted. "What do you want me to do about it?"

Her face shone a deep crimson. "I need you to help unhook it."

The thought of touching her so intimately hardened a part of him that had no business being inflamed. He licked his lips and stared at her. "I think that would be best to do after the lights are turned out."

She nodded and pointed her nose to the ceiling. Jeremy stayed on his side, knowing it made it harder for the other men to see Clara. He knew a female liked privacy, and she'd already voiced her concern about the men watching her. But why in the world did the fool woman wear her corset if she couldn't get in and out of it herself?

Chapter Sixteen

Clara closed her eyes and steadied her breathing. *Did I really ask Jeremy to help me take off my corset?* The stays dug into her back, but she didn't move. While looking at Jeremy and talking to him, she'd noticed he made a short but comforting wall between her and the other two men. It was his constant consideration of her feelings that had her heart racing thinking about his hands unlacing her corset and setting her free.

To keep her thoughts from heading into dangerous territory, she pulled up resentment for the way he ordered her outside when she'd started to argue with him. Why did men think they could always haul a woman around?

The muffled voices of the men drifted in and out as the long day of walking tugged on her eyelids and her body relaxed. Warmth cocooned her body, chasing away the chill from the trek outside. She nudged aside the memory of the sting of wind on her backside and snuggled deeper into the sheep's wool cushion of the sleeping bag. Her mind floated into a springtime dream.

"Clara? Clara, you awake?" whispered a male voice.

Puffs of air tickled her cheek. She raised a hand to brush the butterfly away. The back of her hand scraped a prickly object. Her eyelids flew up and air filled her lungs as she prepared to scream. A hand covered her mouth as warm air blew across her ear.

"Clara, it's Jeremy. You said you wanted to take your corset off."

His whispered words in her ear and his calloused hand on her lips didn't scare her. No, her body crackled and leapt to life, like kindling.

She turned her face to him and their lips touched, bringing back vivid memories of their kiss on the street. His hand cupped her head, holding her lips to his as he nibbled and kissed and spun her mind, making her dizzy. Clara worked her hands and arms out of the bag and rolled, slipping her arms around his neck and holding on.

Safe.

Jeremy made her feel safe and cared for. The kiss lightened. Her heart returned to a normal beat and her mind cleared, bit by bit. As the haze faded from her mind, she remembered where they were. This behavior was most improper. She drew her arms from around his neck and crossed them across her chest like a shield.

Jeremy released her head. He sucked in air like he'd hiked up a mountain. A stay jabbed her rib making her grimace. Kissing this way was as inappropriate as the request she'd asked of him. Her proprieties warred with her common sense. She needed a good night's sleep if she wanted to keep up with Jeremy and the dogs tomorrow. The stays pressed into her side.

A sigh escaped her lungs as she battled with herself. *He let me go when I pulled back.* While he initiated both kisses, he always allowed her to pull away.

The next step was all about trusting him. He would have his chance to touch her where no man had touched her. She found his hands in the dark before rational thoughts kept her from a good night's sleep.

"Only unhook the corset, no wandering," she whispered.

His head bobbed, and she drew his hands into her sleeping bag, placing them on her corset. The friction of his hands moving up and down the garment tickled. She covered her mouth to stifle her giggle.

His fingers slipped under the top edge of her corset. His knuckles pushed against her breasts and she nearly moaned from the sheer pleasure of his touch. *How could such a thing make her woman parts throb*? He tugged the two sides together, squeezing her ribs, and again, sensations she'd never experienced before fluttered her stomach and pulsed between her legs. The first hook came loose.

His hands moved lower, he tugged, her legs squeezed together, and the hook came free.

Her body quivered, heated, and agonized for

more. But she didn't know what more she wanted.

Jeremy's voice moistened her ear. "Feels like there's only one more to go. Hold still while I get it loose."

She sucked in her belly when his hands pressed into the softness. Her body responded to the touch with another round of quivering. The last hook gave way and she lay still, waiting. Clara wanted him to continue touching her, yet, this was a test to Jeremy's honor. Would he run his hands over her, or would he roll back to his area?

"Does that feel better?" he asked, his breath warming her cheek.

"Yes." The word came out breathy.

"Get a good night's sleep. We'll head out at first light."

His presence was gone. She turned her head and watched his shadow settle into his sleeping bag. As much as she should worry about proprieties, she mourned the loss of his hands and closeness. Clara pulled the corset out from under her and vowed to keep this from happening again. She'd not put the garment on again until she donned a dress. Having Jeremy put his hands on her was thrilling and frightening at the same time. She didn't understand her body's reactions or her feelings of security when with him.

Jeremy lay in his sleeping bag wide awake. He couldn't very well take his problem in hand. Thinking he could help Clara with her corset and not become aroused had to be the stupidest idea he'd ever had. Touching her body, whispering in her ear; all actions that only made him crave her more. The trust she put in him was humbling and scary. She'd kissed him just as hungrily as he'd kissed her. Tonight they had chaperones. What would happen on the nights they were huddled in a tent together with no need to be restrained?

He groaned and rolled to his side, staring in the dark interior of the cabin. If he was going to sleep he had to forget what just happened. Closing his eyes, visions of a blonde-haired, green-eyed woman welcoming him with open arms floated into his dreams and he let her in.

Jeremy woke refreshed. Once he allowed Clara into his dreams, he slept with abandon. The fire crackled in the stove and the lantern was lit. Red stood over the stove stirring something. He didn't see Buck. Rolling, he lay on his side and watched the sleeping bag next to the wall rise and fall.

Would she be shy this morning after the kiss and his hands roaming about her body? *Damn!* He should have left those thoughts alone. Now he was hard and needed to go visit the outdoors. Jeremy crawled out of his sleeping bag, donned all his outwear, and grabbed his boots from beside the stove.

"You're forgetting something," Red said, waving his hot cake turner at Clara's sleeping bag.

"I'll be back. Need to pee." Jeremy snatched his coat from the peg by the door, slid his arms in and opened the door all in one movement. In the snow entrance, he laced on the snow shoes and headed for the area he took Clara the night before. Turning to head back, he spotted Buck hurrying up the trail they'd made the day before.

"I'll get the dogs up!" he shouted, heading for the area where they'd put the dogs and sleds for the night.

"What's the hurry?" Jeremy jogged over to Buck.

"There's a string of miners coming up the path we made yesterday. We broke trail for them lazy bastards." Buck kept walking. "You might want to find a place to hole up and let them break the trail for you from here on out."

"We can just stay here today and tonight and pull into the line tomorrow." Jeremy didn't like being in the middle of the crazy, greed-driven greenhorns, but it beat breaking trail the whole way.

Buck shook his head. "You're only a day away from Skagway. Easy enough for one of Soapy's men to come see if the girl is here."

Jeremy had shoved that piece of memory to the back of his mind. *Damn!* They had to get out of here ahead of the masses. "I appreciate your help." He headed to the cabin and stomped through the door.

Clara sat at the table, her blonde hair hanging straight around her shoulders and down her back. The shiny, sun colored strands reminded him of his hand on the back of her head last night. He shook that memory away and sat on the bench beside her.

"Hurry up. We have to get going. Our taking off must have convinced the others they could hike the trail in the snow. Buck saw a string of miners coming out of Skagway."

"There's no need to hurry off. Let them break trail for your sleds," Red said, placing a plate of hot cakes in front of each of them.

Jeremy spread preserves on his and handed the jar to Clara. "We can't. We need to stay ahead of them."

Red squint one eye and pointed the hot cake turner at one and then the other of them. "There something you ain't tellin' me?"

Jeremy knew Soapy tried to muscle Red out of this outpost and hadn't managed. The gang leader also had men here working scams on the unsuspecting miners as they lingered overnight, drinking and telling stories in the four tent saloons.

"The best thing you can do is when people arrive and ask about me, you only saw me." He inclined his head toward Clara. "I didn't have a woman with me. Buck came this far to show me how to control his dogs."

Red stared at Clara a moment then returned his gaze to Jeremy. "This lady I didn't see. Who she running from? A husband?"

"No husband," Clara chimed in. "Mr. Red, I'm not sure why Jeremy isn't telling you everything, but if he hadn't helped me leave Skagway when he did, I would hate to think what Soapy Smith would have done to me."

Jeremy watched Red's face go from calculating to downright livid.

"If you're running from that dung heap of morality, I ain't never seen you."

"Get your boots and coat on. We need to move." Jeremy finished off his meal and downed a cup of coffee while Clara pulled on her boots and buttoned her coat. "What do I owe you?" he asked, pulling the leather pouch hanging around his neck from inside his shirt.

"You had two meals and place to sleep. That will be three dollars." Red held his hand out.

"That's just mine. For the both of us that would be six." Jeremy started to count out six silver dollars.

"Nope. Just three for you. I never fed nor saw anyone with you." Red winked, took the three dollars and cleared the tables.

"Thank you," Clara said.

Jeremy rolled up their sleeping bags and stuffed them in a bag. He joined Clara at the door.

"Thanks Red. You take care." Jeremy motioned for Clara to exit.

They slipped into their snowshoes and found the dogs and sleds ready to go. Jeremy tucked the sleeping bags into the sled with Clara's belongings.

"Thank you for your help, Buck." Clara held out her hand. The man shook hands and smiled at her.

"You two be careful. I'll hang back here and make sure there ain't any of Soapy's men following." Buck released Clara's hand and grasped Jeremy's outstretched one.

"Thank you. I can't hide where we go with the tracks we have to make, but if it starts snowing, I'll strike out on a different path and hope we throw anyone who might be following off." He slapped Buck on the back. "We appreciate your help."

"Get going."

Jeremy checked to see if Clara was ready. She waved and he started the dogs in motion. "Mahsh!"

He walked ahead, once again breaking trail. Today he wouldn't have someone to spell him. They'd be lucky if they made it to the summit before dark.

151

Chapter Seventeen

Clara didn't think she could move another step. The ascent right after leaving Ford was so steep they had to push the sleds while the dogs pulled. Then the narrow ridge they walked along not only took exact foot placement but she had to keep her racing heart and rapid breathing from causing her to faint. The back third of the sleds hung over the edge of several curves, causing her heart to lodge in her throat with worry the sled would fall, pulling all the sleds and the dogs to their deaths.

They traveled in switchback fashion down and back up crossing the deep gorge. Nearing the top Clara stopped to catch her breath and give her wobbly legs a break. In the distance she spotted a red and white flag and little curls of smoke escaping snow mounds.

"The summit is there, where you see the flag," Jeremy said, also stopping to rest. "Once we pass this check point, we don't have to worry about Soapy Smith or one of his gang. The Canadian Mounties don't allow Soapy or his gang over the summit."

Knowing they no longer had to fear Mr. Smith's retaliation, eased a knot that had resided in her stomach since leaving Skagway.

Clara studied Jeremy. He wouldn't have to push so hard now, that the threat was gone. His legs had to be twice as tired as hers from all the stomping he did to break trail. Guilt ate at her for not being able to help clear the path for the dogs and sleds. She held the canteen of water out to him.

"Thanks." He gulped three times and wiped his mouth quickly so any lingering drops wouldn't freeze to his face.

"I wish I could help you with the trail." She scoffed. "Handing you water seems trivial."

His gloved hand cupped her chin. Tilting her face to look into his, Jeremy said, "This is the first trip in a while that I'm enjoying the company."

Heat scorched her cheeks. *Was he talking about the kisses?* She couldn't speak for the racing of her heart. Searching his eyes, she looked for a clue.

"You've kept up and haven't complained. You wouldn't believe the dandies I've hauled in here that didn't hold up as well as you are." His hand dropped away, and he walked to the head of the whining dogs who all shoved to their feet as he walked by. The animals knew they would soon rest and be fed.

Clara stood in the snow watching the dogs, sleds, and Jeremy approach the summit. *He enjoys my company because I don't complain.* He initiated the first kiss and took over the second kiss once she initiated it. Did he truly enjoy her company solely because she didn't complain and allowed him privileges—she thought of his hands touching her intimately as he unhooked her corset.

Does he believe I'm a loose woman? Mortification swept through Clara, jabbing her belly like a knife. She clutched her waist and bent. Bile rose in her throat, burning and spilling to the ground. She retched until tears froze on her cheeks and her body shook from the exertion.

Jeremy peered over his shoulder. Clara was bent over heaving. "Whoa!" he shouted to the dogs and scrambled back along the line to the spot he'd left Clara only minutes before. Why hadn't she told him she didn't feel well? *Because you were complimenting her on her sturdiness.*

He stopped beside her, averting his gaze from the yellowish substance freezing on the front of her snowshoes. "Sweetheart, why didn't you tell me you weren't feeling well?" He wrapped an arm around her shoulders, making her lean against him. "Come on. You can ride on the sled the rest of the way."

"No. I'm fine." She tried to push out of his arm.

"No, you aren't fine. Look at your snowshoes." The moment the words came out he groaned. She glanced down and her body shuddered.

"Never mind." He scooped her up in his arms and packed her to the sled she'd hid in the day before, only this time he placed her on the top of the tarpaulin. "Ride," he ordered and then hurried to the lead dog of the first team. He packed the snow ten feet ahead of the dog then gave the command to move. New energy pushed his feet faster. Clara was ill and needed a warm place to rest. He didn't care if the others caught up to them. They'd stay over a day at the summit. A mile later he stopped at the tent housing the Northwest Mounted Police.

"Hello!" he shouted.

A dark-haired head stuck out of the snow at the entrance of the wooden shack. "We didn't expect anyone for several more days. Hold on." The head disappeared.

Jeremy walked back to the sled carrying Clara. Her pale face and downcast eyes worried him. He scooped her up into his arms.

"Put me down!" She shoved against his chest.

"Not until you're in a warm tent and being tended to." He carried her back to the front of the first team as two Mounties appeared. "You can start inspecting if you want, I'm taking Clara to Bertha's." He nodded to the vomit on Clara's snowshoes and the men backed away.

"Come right back. We'll need to know what you're hauling and declare the woman's goods," said the dark-haired Mountie.

Jeremy nodded. Half the establishments were covered in snow and the sides away from the continual wind were bare other than an overhang of snow that blew over the top and froze like an ocean wave. He found Bertha's boarding house and pushed the door open.

"What'ch you carryin' young Jeremy?" Bertha, a large black woman, crossed from the chair she sat in to the door quicker than a cougar pouncing on dinner.

"Bertha, this is Clara. She's exhausted and needs someone to look after her while I make the Mounties happy." He marched to the center of the wood and canvas structure, setting Clara on the nearest bench. He knelt to remove her soiled snow-shoes.

"Don't!" She protested, trying to stop him with her hands.

He batted her hands away and quickly pulled the shoes off her boots. "Bertha will take good care of you. I'll be back soon." He pushed her parka back and kissed the top of her head. Glancing at Bertha, he saw the glint in her eye and couldn't help but smile and wink at her. She shushed him out the door and shut it behind him.

Jeremy banged the snowshoes together dislodg-ing the frozen vomit then leaned them up against the tent wall. Bertha was a strong woman who was fair. He'd found an ally in the woman his first trip over the pass. She'd confided her husband died trying to get them to the Yukon and make them rich. She stopped once she reached the summit. Too tired to go on, and nothing to go back to, she was happy to stay here, boarding the men and women who made it to the summit.

Nearing the sleds, he found the Mounties tally-ing the goods for Clara.

"I'm taking Miss Bixbee inland to meet her brother, but knew you wouldn't let us through without her having the proper rations." He stopped beside the sled they were inspecting.

"And the items on that team?" The Mountie pointed to the items he was delivering to Dawson.

"That's freight for Brightly in Dawson."

"We're surprised you are trying this trip so soon after the last storm." The shorter of the two Mounties stared at him.

"It didn't look like the weather was going to let up and Brightly promised me extra if I delivered his goods by March first. When the last storm stopped, I set out." He propped a foot on the sled and stared back at the man.

"And Miss Bixbee. Why would she risk her life to leave so soon?"

"Her family needs her brother back home right away. She was hiring anyone who could get her to the interior quickly. Since I was in a hurry, I was the right person." He didn't like the man asking so many questions about Clara.

"Yet, it appears you have threatened her health, no?"

The short Mountie was picking at Jeremy's patience.

"She didn't tell me she was ill. As soon as I saw how sick she was I made her ride and got here as fast as I could with the conditions being what they are."

The dark-haired Mountie held out a slip of paper. "Give this to Miss Bixbee, it's her duty on the goods. And this," he handed a paper to Jeremy, "is the duty on your goods."

He didn't look at the numbers. He knew they'd be high. The Canadians were making good money off the people traveling to the Yukon and beyond.

"Put your sleds behind the shack. You'll get them back when you pay the duties."

The short Mountie needed knocked off the high horse he thought he sat on.

Jeremy tightened the roped on the tarpaulins and directed the dogs to the back side of the Mountie Shack. There was a window that looked out at the area. Crisscrossing ropes through the rungs and around the bundles, he tied the sleds together in a fashion that would take a person a long time to unravel or cut.

He grabbed a bundle of frozen fish. The right rations for a meal for the dogs and led them over behind Bertha's. He staked the dogs out to the side of the establishment and fed chunks of fish. When the dogs all curled up covering their noses and feet with their tails, he headed for the front.

Clara had looked awful pale when he left her. What caused her stomach to be upset? The exertion of the trail? Something they ate? He knew she wasn't going to be strong enough for this trip. What was he thinking when he agreed to guide her? With his thoughts colliding, he left his snowshoes by Clara's and entered Bertha's.

His gaze sought Clara the moment the door opened. She sat wrapped in a blanket in Bertha's chair next to the cookstove. Her small hands clutched a steaming tin cup. Her downcast gaze didn't raise to watch his entrance.

Jeremy glanced at Bertha. The woman shrugged and turned to the pan sizzling on the stove.

He hung his coat and hat by the door and

crossed to the chair. Crouching beside Clara, he cleared his throat, unsure what to say. "Are you feeling better?"

She nodded but still kept her gaze averted. Had retching on her snowshoes embarrassed her that much?

"Look at me." He waited what seemed like hours before her face came into view. Her lashes remained lowered, shielding her eyes. "Show me those pretty green eyes."

Just when his patience had run out, she raised her lashes and the hurt he saw in their green depths was like a sucker punch to his gut.

He wrapped his arms around her, embracing her. "Sweetheart, where do you hurt? Did you hurt yourself on the trail?" Jeremy peered over her head at Bertha. "Did you check her over?"

"There's nothin' wrong with her body a little rest and good food won't fix." Bertha lumbered over to the table, placing three plates and utensils on the cloth she'd spread while he was waiting out Clara.

"Clara." he tipped her face up to his. "I can stay here as long as you need to get rested. We still have a long but not so rugged trip ahead of us."

"No. I don't need rest. I need to get to my brother. We don't need to rest here." The anxious movement of her eyes and her stiff body wasn't the Clara he knew.

What had her so anxious? So wary? He released her and stood, running a hand over his face. "I'm going to get our sleeping bags and belongings." He tipped his head toward Clara when Bertha looked up. She smiled and nodded. With his coat and hat back on, he watched Clara a moment before slipping out the door. Maybe Bertha would find out what had caused the change in Clara. He couldn't continue on if every night he had to deal with her retching and being distant.

Chapter Eighteen

Clara felt childish avoiding Jeremy, but she had to decipher his actions and her feelings. She couldn't do that when he was smothering her. Which was something else she didn't understand. Why did he call her sweetheart and kiss the top of her head if he only thought of her as a loose woman and a bother?

Once he disappeared out the door, she relaxed and pondered all his actions and words since they met.

"Miss Clara, it ain't none of my business 'bout you and Jeremy, but I'm seein' a side to him he ain't showed before." Bertha pulled one of the benches from the table over in front of the chair Clara occupied.

Clara stared into the woman's eyes. Caring and concern glimmered in their chocolate depths.

"I've never been on my own like this before."

She wound the blanket around her fisted hands. "This trip has had a lot of firsts, and I still have a long way to go to find my brother."

Bertha's gaze slipped to the door then back to her. "Is one o' them firsts the man takin' you to your brother?"

Clara bit her bottom lip. Was this a woman she could confide in? Bertha reminded her of their Negro maid, Serendipity, who they had to let go when Father died. The maid had been easy to talk with. Clara took a deep breath, releasing it slowly, building up the courage to spill her concerns.

"Jeremy's a good man. He'd never do nothin' to harm you. And I seen the way he looks at you. He ain't goin' to let no one else hurt you." Bertha nodded her round head and the short kinky black hair with silver streaks bobbed.

"Do you really think he likes me?" Clara had thought so from the kisses, but then he did things that made her think she'd put too much store into his actions.

"Child, he is smitten!" The woman nodded and smiled. "I ain't never seen him so smilin'."

Clara's cheeks heated thinking Jeremy Duncan had the same thoughts about her she had about him. "That's what I thought after the first kiss. He sent shivers all over my body and my legs could barely hold me up. But not two seconds later, he acted like nothing happened. And last night. He came to my rescue so many times, then kissed me making my body throb, and when he helped with my corset—"

Bertha stood nearly knocking the bench over. "Landsakes, child, you and he better be seein' a preacher!”

"No! It's not like that. See, I had to get un-dressed in the sleeping bag. Red and Buck were in the tent too, and I couldn't get the hooks loose on my corset—"

"Child you don't need one of them contraptions up here. Look at all them layers of clothes you have on."

"Yes, I've learned that lesson. No more corset with all these clothes. But last night I needed his help and he kissed me...." Her body heated at the memory of his knuckles pressing against her. "Then this morning he was distant and on the trail he said he enjoyed my company because I didn't complain. That was it. Nothing about our kisses or our conver-sations. That put the notion in my head he thought I was a loose woman." She grabbed Bertha's hands. "I'm not a loose woman. I've never kissed anyone before this trip, and I couldn't sleep with the cor-set. I knew if I didn't get sleep I wouldn't be able to keep up today." Clara swallowed her pride and continued. "So when I couldn't get the corset unfas-tened while trussed up in the sleeping bag, I trusted Jeremy would help and not take liberties."

Bertha sat back down, a wide smile curving on her face. "Trust. You gotta have that. Uh-huh. Me and my Clarence had it. That's why I came with him to Alaska. I trusted he knew what was best for us." Her face fell and a tear slipped from her eye. "But he didn't make it to the summit. Lost him at Dead Horse Gulch along with the pack horse he was lea-din'." She closed her eyes. Her large bosom moved up and down as she collected herself. She opened her eyes and smiled.

"I'd say you and Jeremy will be plannin' a summer weddin'." Bertha winked and stood. "I need to finish dinner before that man comes back and wonders what we been doin'."

Clara shook her head at the notion of a summer wedding or any wedding. Her happiness came after she found Randy and the business was back making a profit. Not before. And she wasn't tying herself to a man. She saw how miserable most women were and saw the way their husbands squashed their freedom.

The fact Bertha thought Jeremy was sweet on her, helped ease the idea he might think she was a loose woman. She smiled. He had done sweet things, like kissing her on the head, taking off the nasty snowshoes, and making sure she had a trustworthy guide. Not to mention putting himself and his freight at risk by getting her out of Skagway before Soapy found her.

The warmth inside her body now equaled the warmth radiating from the stove. Jeremy did care for her. It was in all the little things he did. And she'd acted like a child. *No more*. He'd been willing to talk with her about everything that had come along, there was no reason why she couldn't sit down and let him know why she had acted so strange.

The door banged open. A pack and sleeping bags came into view before she spotted Jeremy's Stetson and head peeking over the top. She jumped out of the chair and hurried to help him.

Jeremy didn't know what put the bounce back

into Clara, but he wasn't complaining. She helped him put their belongings on a set of bunks in the back of the establishment, and then helped Bertha with the meal.

During the meal, Bertha asked him about his family. He noticed Clara listening intently. Once in a while she asked a question. He had a hard time giving Bertha his proper attention when answering her questions. His gaze wandered to Clara, wondering over the change in her. Finally, he couldn't stand it any longer. "Bertha, what did you give Clara?"

The woman smiled and her eyes twinkled. "All we did was talk. Sometimes what's on your mind is as afflictin' as a disease."

He nodded but wasn't sure what could have made Clara so sick that needed talked out.

Clara peered into his eyes. "After the meal, we need to have a talk."

Why did her little declaration send his stomach into a tornado and his mind tripping over itself? He tipped his head in acknowledgement but couldn't stop the apprehension squeezing his chest. What could they need to talk about? Especially, that had her so upset?

Waiting for the meal to end had the same effect on him as when he was small and knew Darcy would get him back for a joke he'd played on her, but he didn't know where or when.

Bertha stood, picking up dishes. "I'll do the dishes if you two want to go yonder and talk." She nudged her chin toward the row of triple bunks on the back wall of her place.

If they stayed over a day or two those bunks

would soon be full of the men following the trail they broke.

Clara tugged on his shirt sleeve, drawing his attention to her. She stood and headed to the corner farthest away from the woman moving dishes to the stove. He'd hauled in several buckets of snow for Bertha to melt in kettles on the stove for dishwater.

With feet heavy as the huge boulders along the trail, he followed Clara. What did she want to talk about? Did she feel his concern was overly attentive? Hell, he couldn't help it. She was a little mite of a thing and brought out his protectiveness.

She sat on a bottom bunk and patted the criss-crossed ropes next to her.

He cleared his throat and sat, keeping his body from touching any of hers, which was a feat, considering the sagging rope made his section lower and she could practically roll into his lap.

Clara stared at her hands nervously picking at the weave in her trousers. "I want to apologize for my childish behavior earlier."

Jeremy shook his head. *Childish*? "Getting sick isn't childish. Anyone can have a case of a sickly stomach."

"No, I'm not talking about getting sick, though that is connected." She twined her fingers together, placing her hands in her lap. Her gaze remained on her knotted hands. "When you said I was good company because I didn't complain, I had thoughts that made me ill."

Jeremy's heart pounded in his chest. How could his words make her sick? The last thing he wanted to do was cause her pain. "How could—"

"Just let me finish," she butted in. She drew in a gulp of air and swallowed.

The hesitancy on her part gave him the jitters. *What was so darned scary she couldn't say it?*

"Because you made the comment, I thought you believed me to be a loose woman. Someone who would allow a man to kiss her and touch her." Her wide green eyes stared into his.

What was she talking about? "Why would I think you're a loose woman just because I gave you a compliment?" His head hurt from the frown bunching the skin on his forehead.

"I had expected you to say you enjoyed my company for the conversations and the shared moments of intimacy…" Her lashes dropped, shielding her thoughts from him.

He didn't have to be hit by a sledgehammer to understand. She took the kisses to mean…Oh hell, she was fishing for a marriage proposal. He liked her. But marriage? He wasn't ready. Wasn't going home with a bride from Alaska. Especially, not this one. While he did have a problem keeping his body under control around her, she wouldn't fit in with the Halsey wives. She was bossy, rash, and fool-hardy.

Jeremy stood, smacking the top of his head into the bunk above. The impact sat him back down hard. His head buzzed. He rubbed the injured scalp, and gradually, he heard her talking.

"…I know my actions since meeting you haven't been proper, but I've been scared and you have been so supportive and…" She put a hand on his arm. "You're the first male, besides my family, that

I trust."

Her touch and the glint in her eyes, heated parts of him that had no business coming to life. He collected his thoughts. She watched him, her gaze steady and her hand gently squeezing his arm. That right there made it hard for him to figure out what words to say. Like the night before when he'd helped her with her corset. Knowing there was only thin fabric between his hand and her skin had him close to shooting in his drawers.

Jeremy picked up her hand to move it off his arm. His body had its own mind. Instead of placing her hand back in her lap, his fingers laced with hers. *Traitorous body*!

"Clara, I don't know what you're trying to say." Keeping her talking would give him more time to collect his answer.

Her cheeks darkened. "Are you helping me strictly for my payment or do you like me?"

Blunt and to the point. Jeremy shook his head, trying to make sense of the whole conversation.

A mind-numbing smile brightened her face. "I knew you thought more of me than a customer."

That smile and her hand twined with his made it hard to say the words he knew needed to be said. Jeremy cleared his throat, squeezed her hand, and then released. "Clara, you are a beautiful, intelligent woman. In some ways you remind me a lot of my sister."

Clara's smile dimmed and her gaze became distant.

He took another fortifying breath. "I did enjoy our kisses and you're a good companion on the trail.

It was my protectiveness that made me agree to take you to your brother. I didn't want to see some tragedy befall you. Yes, you are paying me. Yes, I'm doing this for the money."

Her lips tipped into a frown and her shoulders sagged.

"I'm also doing this because you stressed how important this is to your family. I have a strong bond with my family and know how you feel. My plan before you came along was to deliver this load to Dawson, continue on to St. Michael, and return to my family. That is still my plan once I deliver you to your brother." There. He'd plainly told her there wasn't going to be any wedding between the two of them.

"You're right. Family does mean everything to me." She stood. "I'm glad we had this talk. I have only one condition that needs to be said."

He nodded for her to speak.

"There will be no more kisses or intimate touching." Her eyes bore into his.

The slight rise of her right eyebrow made him take the statement more as a challenge than a condition. "I agree." He held out his hand to shake on the deal.

Confusion swept through her green eyes before her lids lowered and she grasped his hand, giving it one solid pump and releasing.

"Glad we have that cleared up." Jeremy dropped his hand, wondering when she'd break her own stipulation.

She walked over to their bunks, spread her sleeping bag on the bottom one, and lay down on top of the bag.

Jeremy wandered to the stove, plucked a tin cup off a hook, and poured a cup of coffee. How in the hell was he going to keep his mind off of touching and kissing her for the next month when they would be spending so much time in close quarters? She was right. He had not right to be doing either when he had no intention of marrying her. He hated admitting her stipulation was probably a good thing to have considering how his lips and hands tended to wander her direction.

Chapter Nineteen

Clara didn't want Jeremy to have to keep breaking trail, but she agreed with him when he suggested they take off and keep ahead of the miners. Thinking of Jeremy trying to keep her safe from so many men didn't set well. There was no need for him to be hurt defending her. Not that any of them would be interested in a skinny, small-bosomed woman like her. They had gold on their minds. But her mother had taught her, there were few men who could control their physical needs. How her mother knew such things they'd yet to discuss, but she'd witnessed the disillusion in her mother's eyes when she told Clara to be careful and avoid being alone with men.

Clara laughed. She *was* alone with a man. Had been for days, and he was staying true to her stipulation. He'd only called her Sweetheart once the last two days and kept his hands to himself. Leaving the scraggly timber, she spotted a multitude of smoke spirals and white dots around the half-frozen lake. Lake Bennett proved to be a tent settlement as large as a city.

They arrived as dusk turned the world into grays. Men milled about the structures with wood frames and doors, and canvas walls and roofs. Half a dozen wooden structures stood closer to the tree line. Along the shore of the lake, piles of logs and planks lay beside wooden structures as tall as a man.

Jeremy stopped the dogs, and she hurried up beside him. "What are those things by the lake?"

"They're platforms used to place logs on to whipsaw them into planks." He motioned toward a row of half-built boats. "The men and women spending the winter here are building boats to take them down river to Dawson when the rivers thaw."

"We aren't staying until the rivers thaw are we?" She didn't want to be away from the business any longer than necessary. It could be months before the rivers were navigable.

"That's why we have the dogs. We'll travel alongside the rivers or if they are frozen enough on them." He put a gloved hand on her arm. "Stay close to me. There are a lot of lonely men spending the winter here."

Clara shivered and nodded. This was what her mother had been fearful of when they discussed her traveling alone. She peered into Jeremy's eyes. But she wasn't alone, and the man she'd put her faith in wouldn't let anything happen to her.

They found a smaller establishment with a cot

for her and room on the floor for Jeremy. Behind the large tent structure stood a lean-to where the sleds and dogs could be kept. The proprietor was anxious for news and listened intently as Clara told him all she knew from two weeks ago as the man prepared the evening meal.

Jeremy placed their sleeping bags on the cot nearest the stove and then shoved the cot closer to the stove to make room for him to sleep on the floor and not be stepped on by the persons occupying the bunk bed next to them.

Clara wrapped her arms around herself. Only she, Jeremy, and the proprietor where here now. Later a dozen other men who were wintering in the structure would arrive. While the tent was a large one, she knew when more males arrived it would feel very small.

Jeremy called her over to the cot. He sat and drew her down beside him. "I know you set conditions back at Bertha's." He spoke low, only for her to hear. "To keep you safe, I'm going to have to ask you to forget them. Snooker Pete figures us for a married couple."

Warmth tinged her cheeks as Clara peered into Jeremy's earnest eyes. He was as attentive as a husband most of the time. But allowing him such liberties wasn't a good idea. It led to her wanting more kisses and him bossing her around.

He continued. "We need the other men who are staying here to think the same. No man will bother you if they know you're already spoken for."

Clara nodded. *That made sense. If only they didn't have to touch.*

"So don't get huffy or reprimand me if I put a hand on your back or help you. It's what they'll expect with us being married." His silver eyes scanned her face.

Allowing Jeremy to treat her like a wife would be easy. She'd missed his touches since proclaiming her conditions for the trip. *But don't get used to it.* Her always practical mind wouldn't allow her to take his actions to heart. They would both go their separate ways once they found Randy.

"I agree it is the best way for me to get to Randy with an untarnished reputation." Clara saw a brief flinch on Jeremy's face.

He captured her hand in his and smiled. "We'll leave here tomorrow morning. You'll only have to endure this for one night." Jeremy stood, helping her to her feet and leading her to the long wooden table. He placed her at the end of the bench and sat beside her.

The door opened. Two men bundled in scarves and coats lumbered in, shed their outer wear, placing it on a set of bunks, and took seats at the table.

She shivered when their gazes roamed over her like hungry wolves looking at a carcass.

Jeremy squeezed her hand.

Snooker Pete started placing food on the table. "Walter and Fred, this here is Mr. and Mrs. Duncan. They're only here for the night."

The two men glanced at Jeremy, grunted and started filling their plates. The other men straggled in. Each time Snooker Pete introduced she and Jeremy as Mr. and Mrs. Duncan the men would shoot a gaze at Jeremy, and then fall to eating.

Clara relaxed seeing Jeremy had been right about the men retreating when they discovered she was taken. *I'd hate to be a single woman among this many men.* No doubt, most would be civil. She had a feeling the three who shot her hooded glances would have pressed advances if not for Jeremy.

She scooted closer to Jeremy. Touching him thigh to thigh made her feel more secure. His hard muscles proved his strength. He could protect her from any man. Knowing his honor, he would keep her safe. The thought fluttered her insides. Few men in her life had shown they cared for her safety. His caring was evident in the way he sheltered her from the others.

Jeremy glanced at her sideways and winked. She smiled back and dug into the food on her plate. She'd come to learn beans, sourdough biscuits, canned fruit, and, if you were lucky, moose or caribou stew were the only menu items at the remote settlements.

The grizzled old man who ran the place wasn't much of a cook, but the food was warm, and he had a jovial attitude for someone living so remote. He continued to question her about everything happening outside of Alaska while the other men at the table remained quiet. She could tell they listened because the noise of spoons clanging the tin plates lessened when she talked.

"Do you ever leave here?" Clara asked.

"Not since I landed here and started my business. I will when the idjits quit coming over the pass." He chuckled and leaned close to whisper in her ear. "I can afford to move anywhere I want and not have to work another day once the gold runs out in the Yukon."

In the same conspiratorial tone she whispered back, "I guess a few years alone is worth it if you can live how you please later." Clara glanced at Jeremy. Was that why he was in Alaska? Working far from his family to be able to spend the rest of his life with them? Jeremy caught her studying him. Instead of avoiding his gaze, she held it. His silvery eyes didn't sparkle with humor like they usually did when she was bold. *What was he thinking*?

"Yep." Snooker Pete's voice yanked her thoughts back to the table of men.

She smiled at the white-haired man. He winked back, stood, and picked up her empty plate, moving to the large kettle he'd set to warming before he sat down to eat.

The men, one by one, rose, put their plates in the kettle, and either went to their bunks or sat back down at the table. Clara sat on the end of the bench waiting for the men to get settled before she slipped into her sleeping bag. This many men in the same room where she slept had her already feeling it would be a long night.

Jeremy had watched each man as they studied Clara. Three of the men didn't douse the desire in their eyes at the mention she was already taken. Those three he'd watch closely. He swiveled his body to face Clara.

"Would you like me to escort you outside?" He kept his voice low knowing talk of such things as a privy in mixed company made womenfolk embarrassed.

"Please." Clara rose from the bench.

Jeremy extended his hand. Clara placed hers in it without hesitation. He didn't like the circumstances that made her so compliant. But he'd missed connecting to her physically while following her request they not touch or kiss. They walked to the cot with their belongings. Jeremy helped Clara into her parka. She wrapped a wool scarf around her head and pulled the parka hood up. He pulled on his coat and snugged his hat onto his head. He motioned for her to head for the door.

Three lanterns sat on a shelf by the door. Jeremy lit one with a match from a box also sitting on the shelf. He took the lantern down and opened the door. Out of the corner of his eye, he saw half the heads in the room watch their exit.

The lantern illuminated the packed snow from the many feet walking through the settlement. Clara's body sagged the moment the door closed. He'd known being surrounded by so many men would make her uncomfortable. One more reason to stay close and give her support.

A path wide enough for one person to walk in the three feet of snow trailed behind the establishment and straight to the privy.

"Take your time, I'll check on the dogs in the lean-to." He stopped ten feet from the small wood building and stepped sideways so Clara could pass. Holding out the lantern for her to see, he waited until she'd settled inside the outhouse before backtracking to the lean-to. Dark, furry mounds covered the ground in front of the sleds. Wolf, the lead dog, raised his head and sniffed. Recognizing Jeremy, he settled his head back down, covering his eyes and nose with the end of his tail.

Jeremy counted the fur balls. A dozen. He walked through the middle of the dogs and held the lantern high, scanning the sleds. All the ropes looked in place. There were so many people in this stop-over he didn't like leaving his goods unattended, but he couldn't leave Clara inside alone, and he didn't want to make her sleep outside when there was a warm place for her to stay.

He left the lean-to and noticed a shadow lurking at the corner of the nearest tent. Tensing, preparing for action, he returned to the privy.

"Clara, sweetheart, are you ready to go back in?" The volume of his question should have carried it to whoever stood in the shadows.

The door opened and Clara emerged. She pulled on her mittens, but kept her gaze downcast. Her embarrassment was endearing. Jeremy wrapped an arm around her waist, pulling her close to his side, so they could walk side by side on the path. She snuggled into him, and his heart expanded two-fold. Since meeting her, there had been several times when Clara's actions made him feel like a victor. This was one of them.

Her trust in him overwhelmed him and at the same time made him feel ten feet tall. He continued to the door of Snooker Pete's hugging Clara to his side. No one was taking her away or harming her as long as he was breathing. At the door, Jeremy doused the lantern and faced Clara, putting both hands around her waist and drawing her close.

He leaned his face close to hers inside the hood

of her parka. His hat slid back on his head. "Someone has been watching us," he whispered, his nose touching hers. "Just making this look like we're taking a private moment before heading into the cabin."

Her breath puffed against his mouth, and he couldn't stop his actions. He brushed her lips with his, softly, only a brief touch. Clara pressed her mouth to his, and he accepted the invitation. Angling his head to get a better connection and tease Clara's lips until they parted. His tongue slipped in, savoring the sweetness and silk.

Raucous laughter on the other side of the door reminded Jeremy where they were. He slowly drew out of the kiss. Their foreheads touched as they both caught their breath.

"Sweetheart, thank you for that kiss. It will keep me warm tonight while I'm sleeping on the floor." He released her, catching her by the elbow when she wobbled a bit. A smug smile tipped his lips. She might set up conditions, but the way she initiated the kiss, he'd bet those conditions were to keep her in check.

Chapter Twenty

I kissed Jeremy. Clara couldn't look at him. Embarrassment over her bawdy action kept her gaze directed to the ground. She had to keep a better rein on her body and actions. If someone had seen the way she initiated the kiss… Or if he took it to mean she was falling for him… She didn't need a man. But his kisses made her want more.

Jeremy opened the door, ushering Clara inside. The odor of so many unwashed male bodies, deep voices in discussion, and raucous discord reminded her they weren't alone. She refrained from pressing against Jeremy and grabbing a fistful of his coat as he replaced the lantern.

He smiled at her, crinkling the skin by his eyes and making her feel like the only person in the room. His arm draped around her shoulders. The weight of it and his body pressed to hers gave her courage.

At the cot, they both took off their coats, gloves, and hats. Jeremy helped spread out her sleeping bag on the cot. He shuffled their gear around on the floor, rolling out his sleeping bag.

"Thank you," Clara muttered to Jeremy when she sat on her bed to take off her boots.

"You're welcome. Want help with those?" he asked, his voice low.

She was so tired her arms barely had any energy in them, but she didn't want him to think she couldn't take off her own boots. "I can do it." Her arms wobbled, and she strained, trying to pull the wet boot from her foot.

Jeremy knelt in front of her and took her booted foot in his hands. "Hang on and point your toe." His gaze held hers for several moments before he cleared his throat and tugged on her boot.

She held onto the cot and braced the other foot against his thigh as he pulled and worked her foot free.

"You might want to wear one less pair of socks." He wrapped a hand around her toes, his fingers didn't touch.

She nodded and held up her other foot. The same process released her foot from that boot.

"Thank you," she muttered, again, and took off the three outside pairs of socks, leaving one pair on to keep her feet from getting cold during the night. Clara undressed down to one layer of outer clothes over her union suit. A man's clothing item she never thought she'd wear. But they proved a warmer layer than her cotton shift and flannel pantaloons, though a bit trickier when relieving herself. Once inside the bag, she shed the outer layer of clothes and snuggled her union suit-clad body into her warm bed.

The sound of rustling clothes and clanging tin plates lulled her to sleep. She was safe. Jeremy was on the other side of her, and she trusted him.

Jeremy sat on the floor beside Clara's cot arguing with himself. He wanted to mingle with the group to see if there was any word of the weather conditions toward Dawson, but he didn't want to leave Clara's side. It was highly unlikely anyone would be foolish enough to try anything with him and the other dozen men in the tent, but there always seemed to be one man who lacked good judgment.

Snooker Pete stopped at the end of the cot. "You need me to keep an eye on your wife while you visit?

The older man had taken to Clara like a grandfather. Jeremy held no distrust of the man.

"Thank you. I doubt there will be any trouble. But with this many men and few women around there might be someone who's stupid." Jeremy stood. He clasped the man on the shoulder. "I'll pull your chair over for you."

Jeremy set the only chair in the establishment at the end of Clara's cot. He noted half a dozen men watching. If they needed a release, he knew of two tents that had women who would gladly take their money to service their needs. They could all stay a good distance from his Clara.

His Clara. When had he started thinking of her as his? *The moment I decided to be her guide.*

He stopped the grin starting to spread across his face. Those kind of thoughts had to be quelled. She wasn't his and he didn't want her to be. Clara was a duty. A job. Nothing more. He groaned internally. *Then I have to stop kissing her.*

To keep the group at the table from noticing his agitation, he turned to the stove and poured a cup of coffee.

With his sensibilities back in order and the cup in hand, Jeremy settled at the end of the bench. "Did you all come from Skagway?"

Most heads bobbed up and down.

"Anyone come from Dawson lately?" He took a sip of coffee and watched the seven men seated at the table. Two of them were Walter and Fred. They'd watched Clara more intently than Jeremy liked.

"We came from there a couple weeks ago." Walter nodded to Fred. "Before the last big storm. They're runnin' out of supplies in Dawson cuz the ships didn't make it up before the rivers froze."

"Then none of the rivers are open?"

"Naw, we snowshoed," Fred volunteered, his dark, bearded face only revealing his bulbous nose, full pink lips, and shiny dark eyes.

"How much snow was there before the storm?" Jeremy wanted to determine how much trail breaking he'd have to do the next five-hundred miles.

"You know Dawson. They don't get much there along the river but it was cold enough to freeze your eyeballs shut." Walter narrowed his eyes. "Why do you want to know about the snow?"

"My wife and I have freight to deliver to Dawson." Jeremy couldn't control the happiness in his voice when he said wife. He liked saying the word. He stopped himself from looking at the cot where Clara slept. *She's not the woman for me.*

"You're goin' to take a woman into that wilderness in the middle of winter?" Fred's eyes opened wide and his lower lip dropped, showing off brown, stained teeth. "They're's people starvin' all along the rivers."

"She's tough. We have plenty of provisions, and I've traveled the route before with horses. The dog teams I have will make it even easier."

Walter shook his dark-brown, bearded face. "Don't seem right taking a woman out like that." He stared straight at Jeremy. "She should stay here, wait for you to come back."

A couple other men at the table agreed.

"I'm not leaving my wife here. She wants to go and if anyone tries to stop her, you'll have your hands full." Satisfied he had all he'd get from the men, Jeremy finished his coffee, put the cup in the kettle of warm water, and returned to his spot on the floor.

"Thank you," he said to Snooker Pete, startling the man awake.

The older man nodded, pulled his chair back to the stove, and settled on his cot on the opposite side of the stove.

Jeremy undressed down to his union suit and slipped into his sleeping bag. He had an urge to kiss Clara goodnight just to show the men he wasn't leaving her behind, but didn't want to startle her.

He snickered. He'd like to see any of these men

try to keep Clara from continuing. She was hell bent on getting to her brother. Her family depended on her. He understood that sense of loyalty. That was the spark that had him heading home. He missed seeing all the families growing. He may have joined the Halsey family through his sister's marriage but they were his family, too.

Someone roughly shook Clara. She shoved her arms out of her sleeping bag and opened her eyes. The lanterns were glowing, backlighting the dark, furry head so close she could smell his sour breath.

"Get away from me!" she said loudly. *Where is Jeremy*? She shot a glance to the floor. His sleeping bag was empty.

"What have you done with Jeremy?" She sat up, forcing the body looming over her to have to back up.

"We decided you ain't goin' with him."

She stared at the man in front of her. It was one of the first men they'd been introduced to. And one of the men who'd made her nervous the way he stared at her.

"You have no say over what I can and can't do." Inside her body quivered and her stomach squeezed with fear. Outside, she scowled and clenched her fists. Working at the warehouse, she'd learned to be strong on the outside no matter what she felt on the inside. Men always thought they could bully her.

Clara dropped her arm over the side of the cot and groped the floor for something to use as a weapon. Her trusty umbrella was packed in one of the sleds.

"It ain't right for a young thing like you to be goin' into the wilderness. You could get ate by a bear or worse." The man nodded his head.

Several voices behind him agreed. She looked beyond the man in her space and spotted four more. Panic clamped her jaw shut. *Jeremy, where are you*?

Her hand found something long, round, and cold. She grasped it and pulled Jeremy's rifle onto her lap. Before the man could move to take it from her, she swung the business end toward him.

"Back off!" She glared at all of them. "All of you. Get back."

They all backed up, apologizing and glaring at the back of the man she held the rifle on.

"Where is Jeremy? Did you do something to him?" She quickly scanned the room. "Where's Snooker Pete?" She clicked the pointy thing on the top of the rifle just like she'd watched Jeremy do when he prepared to shoot a rabbit on the trail.

"Don't go shooting me. They're both fine." The bearded man's eyes moved in his head like bubbles in a pot of boiling water.

Clara nodded to the others. "Bring Pete and Jeremy here, or in five minutes I'm going to shoot this man in the foot." She let the end of the barrel drop enough to see the man's big boot.

They others scattered out of the tent, leaving her with the rifle aimed at the man's foot.

"There's no reason to be so ornery," the man said, his voice shaking.

"There was no reason for you to meddle in my life. That's one thing I don't take kindly to— men meddling in my affairs." She glared at the man and hoped Jeremy arrived soon. She didn't know how to keep the gun from firing.

Chapter Twenty-One

Jeremy couldn't believe he'd been jumped coming out of the privy. The five men, including Walter and Fred who gave orders, tied him up and stashed him alongside his sleds. The dogs had growled and jumped to their feet like they'd take the men, but Jeremy calmed the animals down before a gag was shoved in his mouth. He didn't want the dogs harmed. They'd need every last one to get to Dawson.

The reason behind stashing him in the lean-to had to be Clara. If they wanted his sleds and goods, they could have made off with them earlier. Clara wouldn't believe he left her. Or would she? But what would they do to her until he could get loose to help her? That ate at his mind. He flexed his arms and legs trying to loosen the ropes.

Five minutes passed, and they dumped a trussed up Snooker Pete beside him. The old man also had his mouth gagged and his hands and feet tied. Clara didn't have anyone to protect her now. Anger rallied his strength, and he worked harder at his bindings.

Jeremy had barely worked up a sweat fighting his bindings when he heard voices and footsteps.

"Do you believe the spit in that kitty?"

Fred and the other three men appeared in the lean-to. Jeremy glared at the men. If he didn't have the gag he'd have given them a cussin'.

"Don't go throwin' no blows. We're goin' to untie you. Your wife is crazy," Fred said, leaning down with a large blade knife and slicing the ropes binding Jeremy.

Jeremy pulled the gag out of his mouth, shoved to his feet, and took a swing at Fred. Two others, caught him by the arms, holding him back.

"Don't waste time gettin' back at me. You better come fast, your wife is gonna shoot Walter," Fred said, stepping aside.

Where did Clara get a gun? Did she even know how to use it? Fear for Clara kicked his muscles into action. Jeremy shoved the men out of the way and ran to the front of the establishment and slammed through the door.

He stopped at the threshold.

He'd never seen a more beautiful sight. Clara sat on the cot with her sleeping bag pooled around her waist, her upper body clad in a bright red union suit, her small, firm breasts pushing at the flannel. Ribbons of sunshine-colored hair shimmered about her shoulders. Her dainty face tipped to the side as she glared down the barrel of his rifle, sent his heart beating like the hooves of a racing horse.

Her gaze shifted from Walter to Jeremy. The glare disappeared. Her eyes widened, her cheeks flushed, and her lips curved into a saucy smile, just for him. His heart did a double flip.

Clara mouthed the words, "Come here."

Jeremy walked around the man standing four feet from the end of the cot and stood next to her.

"I don't know how to make this not shoot," she whispered and smiled sheepishly.

His heart did a flip. He tried to ignore the happiness tumbling in his chest. This woman was what he'd pictured as his wife. All her fool-hardy beliefs and rash behaviors wasn't the type of woman he needed. But darn if his head and heart weren't having a tug of war.

He sat behind her on the bed, placed his hands over hers, and showed her how to release the cocked hammer. Her body sagged into his. He hoped she couldn't feel the racing of his heart. Jeremy set the gun on the bed and hugged her tight, kissing the top of her head.

The man at the end of the cot shuffled his feet. Jeremy started to reprimand the man, but Snooker Pete came up behind Walter and smacked him in the back of the head with the flat of his hand.

"You idjit!" Snooker Pete stood in front of Walter. "I knowed you wasn't all there in the head, but this is the dumbest, durnedest thing you've ever done. You do something like this again and you and your brother are goin' to have to find another place to winter."

Jeremy ignored the men and spun Clara to face

him. "How did you get my rifle?"

"When that smelly man said I had to stay here, I panicked. All I could think of was getting away from him and to you. I hung my arm over the cot to try and find something to hit him with. I came up with the rifle and pointed it at him." She leaned close and whispered, "He didn't know I didn't have a clue how to use it."

Her eyes glistened with tears. "When I didn't see you, I thought they'd hurt you."

He pulled her to his chest. "Shhh, they jumped me when I came out of the privy. Had me and Snooker Pete tied up in the lean-to." He hadn't a clue what the men had planned to do with either of them. Gauging from the intelligence of Walter, they probably hadn't thought that far ahead.

"He said I shouldn't go into the wilderness. What did he mean by that?" Her words were muffled against his chest, but he didn't want to let her go.

"After you went to sleep last night, I asked around about the condition of the trail to Dawson. Walter got it in his head, that it was too hard of a journey for you." After witnessing her holding a rifle on Walter, Jeremy released all his doubts about taking Clara to Dawson. She'd proved over and over again that she was a lot tougher than she looked.

She pushed away from his chest. He let her lean back but kept his hands linked, holding her in the circle of his arms. Now that he was seeing her differently, he couldn't get his mind to overrule his body's actions.

"Is the trail going to be harder than what we've come over so far?" Her big green eyes peered into his.

"No. The traveling will be easier, but it will be colder and long. It's going to take us twenty-five days to get to Dawson, if we don't have to hole up for a storm." He pushed the soft strands of her pale yellow hair out of her face. "There won't be a settlement every night. We'll be in a tent. Alone." He wanted to lean in and kiss her.

His hand on her back felt the tremor in her body. *Was she afraid to be alone with him*?

"Ahem."

Jeremy glanced up. Snooker Pete stood at the end of the cot with a blanket draped over his arm.

"Hold this up so's your wife can get dressed. I think the sooner you get out of here the better, considering how knuckleheaded Walter is." Snooker Pete handed him the blanket. "I'll have vittles ready by the time she's dressed."

Jeremy ran his hand over Clara's red flannel back. The only thing between his hand and her back was the cloth. The thought triggered blood racing to his loins. He kissed her cheek and stood.

"Get dressed behind this." He grasped a corner of the blanket in each hand and held it up, making a screen for her to hide behind and dress. This position hid his desire from Clara and gave him time to deflate.

Rustling of clothing, and the creak of the cot, sent his mind whirling with thoughts of the two of them snuggled in her sleeping bag.

Stop! He directed his mind. That kind of thinking didn't help the state he was in.

"Done." Clara pulled the blanket out of his hands and folded it, placing it on the end of the cot.

She was just as desirable in her layers of clothes as in the union suit. "Go eat. I'm going to get our things ready to go." Jeremy waited for her to move by him to the table before he started rolling up the sleeping bags and stuffing all their belongings other than their outerwear, into the canvas pack.

By the time he finished, Clara was in a discussion with Snooker Pete about the different establishments at the lake.

"If there are two or three houses of soiled doves, why were the men so set on me staying? I don't want anything to do with them." Clara bit on a biscuit.

Jeremy held his tongue waiting to see what Snooker Pete had to say to that. He took a spot on the bench next to Clara and filled his plate with biscuits and poured the thin watery gravy over the top. He couldn't wait to get back home to fresh milk, eggs, and vegetables.

"Well, to my line of thinkin', Walter had it in his head that as soon as your husband wasn't around to take care of you, you'd need protectin' and he'd be the one." Snooker Pete shook his head. "He wasn't lookin' for no favors other than havin' someone pretty to take care of."

Clara's cheeks reddened, and she dipped her head.

Jeremy found the fact Clara didn't see herself as beautiful an endearing trait. She was the prettiest thing he'd ever set eyes on. "Don't worry. We'll be headed around the lake in an hour and you can put all this behind you." Jeremy wanted to kiss her cheek, but held back. Show her he would take care of her because she was special to him. He ran his hand over his face. *I really need to stop these feelings, I'm going to end up hitched.*

"It won't be too soon for me." She smiled pleasantly at Snooker Pete. "Except, I'll miss our conversations. It was a pleasure meeting you Mr. Pete."

"When you and your man come back through you can bet I'll make room for you." Snooker Pete smiled, showing off half a mouth of teeth.

"Oh, I—"

"We won't be coming back by. Once we drop off the freight in Dawson we're headed on out to St. Michael and leaving Alaska." Jeremy cut Clara off before she blurted out more than this man or any of the others hanging around the establishment needed to hear.

"Are you done eating?" He stood, waiting patiently for Clara to finish her biscuit and wash it down with coffee.

She pat her lips with the tail of her wool shirt. "Now, I'm ready."

Clara stood, smiling at Snooker Pete. She walked to the cot and picked up her coat. By the time Jeremy caught up to her, all the pleasantness she bestowed on Snooker Pete had disappeared from her face.

"Why did you cut me off?" She whispered and shoved her arms into her parka.

"We need to keep our stories similar. If you'd said you were searching for your brother, then that would have got the old man wondering why you were searching and not me. Then he'd ask questions." Jeremy wrapped his wool scarf around his neck, pulled on his wool coat, and buttoned it up. He slapped his hat on his head and pulled on his moose-hide gloves. "Let's go." Snatching the canvas bag off the floor, he headed for the door.

He didn't need to look back to make sure Clara followed. Even though she wasn't happy with him at the moment, she wouldn't lag behind. The woman had enough sense to know she was safest with him.

Clara shot a quick glare at Jeremy's back then stood in front of Snooker Pete. "Thank you for everything. When you leave here and return to Feddersville, I hope you find everything you want."

"It's been a pleasure meetin' you girl. That's a good man you have there. Don't do nothin' to make him leave ya." Snooker Pete patted her head.

She nodded, not sure what she was nodding about, but it seemed the thing to do. Clara walked out the door, and Snooker Pete closed it behind her. She followed Jeremy's broad back to the lean-to. The cold air prickled her skin. She pulled her scarf up over her chin and nose.

Jeremy shoved the canvas pack under the tarpaulin on the last sled and untied the ropes lashing the sleds together.

The wind whistled through the lean-to. It was going to be a cold day for traveling. She shivered and glanced at the privy. This was going to be her last chance to have a small bit of privacy.

"I'm going to the privy," she said and headed that direction. Jeremy didn't even grunt, so she assumed he didn't care. The small building smelled, but she was out of the wind and didn't have to squat. She struggled with all her layers of clothing and finally sat on the cold wood.

She finished her business and opened the door. Freezing wind hit her like an icy wall, shoving her back into the building. The door slammed shut, and she wiped at the tears flowing down her cheeks.

The door opened, and Jeremy barred the opening. "Are you all right?"

"Yes. That wind is cold and strong." She stepped forward and noticed his arms braced him from plunging through the door.

"I'm going to turn around. Grab my coat," he instructed and turned his back to her.

Clara grasped his coat in her fists and followed as he slowly moved forward, his head tipped forward.

A gust hit Jeremy, stopping him and leaning him back. Clara pushed on his back, helping him stay standing. How were they supposed to travel in wind like this?

Jeremy stopped at a sled. He had all the sleds and dogs hooked up and ready to go.

"How are we going to travel in this?" she shouted, so he could hear her above the howling wind.

"Once we get around the lake, we'll be sheltered in a canyon." Jeremy smiled. "And the wind will be at our backs. We'll be able to stand on the sleds and let the wind push us, making less work for the dogs."

Clara pointed to the snow shoes tied to the sled. "No snow shoes?"

"Not while we're on this side of the lake. The men have the snow pretty well packed from cutting and dragging in trees from along the lake's edge." He pointed to the two small runners sticking out the back of the sled. "Put your feet on there and hang onto these." He placed her hands on the sled back.

He leaned into her parka, pulled down her scarf, and kissed her lips. "Just holler out what I do and the dogs will be fine."

Clara stared at Jeremy as he walked to his sled and stepped onto the runners.

They no longer needed to pretend they were married. *Why did he kiss me*?

"*Mahsh!*" Jeremy shouted, and his dogs pulled on their harnesses and the sleds gradually picked up speed.

Clara shook herself and hollered, "*Mahsh!*" Her dogs responded, digging in and soon the sleds with her riding the runners, sailed across the snow. This was more exhilarating than the arduous climbing they'd had to do to get up the summit and down to the lake. The dogs trotted along as if they weren't pulling a thing. The cold wind had a double bite to it with the speed they were moving. She clenched the sled tighter with one hand and pulled her scarf up clear to her eyes. Only a narrow line of sight was teamed on Jeremy.

Gliding along the snow, she could let her mind roam. Seeing Jeremy rushing through the door had sped her already racing heart. The look on his face of fear and then the desire that sparked had rippled goose bumps across her flesh. He held her so tight, she believed he was happy nothing had happened to her. Every time she needed help he was there. His kind, gentle demeanor was lowering her defenses.

Soon her hands were numb from the cold and her feet started to tingle. She'd have to ask Jeremy about a second pair of gloves. They continued for two hours before, the dogs slowed to a walk. Clara stepped off the runners and walked to move her feet and hands and warm them up. While riding was easier, she found walking kept her warmer.

Two hours later, the lake was no longer on their left. The wide expanse of water turned into a narrow white path.

Jeremy stopped, dug into his sled, and walked back to her. "We'll take a break here before we start down the river."

Clara stared at the white road. "Are we traveling on the frozen river?" A shiver slithered down her back.

"I'll check it for thickness, but as cold as it is, I'm pretty sure there is a thick layer of ice." He stared at the trees on either side of the river. "And it will be the easiest route."

She took the canteen he offered and drank the sweet, cold water.

Jeremy handed her three long strips of dried meat. "Eat these when you get hungry. I don't plan to stop until complete dark. We need to put in as many miles each day as we can."

"That's fine with me. Are we walking or riding?" She shoved one of the strips of meat in her mouth and the other two in her coat pocket.

"It will depend on how level and easy a pull it is. Why?" He peered into her eyes.

"My hands and feet get colder when I ride than when I walk."

Jeremy went to the first sled in her string, untied the rope and dug under the canvas. He pulled out a pair of moose-hide gloves like he wore. "Put these on under your mittens. We can't do anything about your feet until tomorrow. I guess your four pair of socks might make your boots hard to get on and off, but they'll keep your feet warmer."

He helped her pull the mittens over the gloves. She enjoyed his attention. More than she cared to admit. Clara studied his face as he worked her second mitten on. The concentration on his face and concern in his eyes, made her feel special. The mitten was on. His gaze met hers. And slowly, his head lowered, until his face was inside her parka hood.

"I know you set conditions, but Sweetheart when you look at me like that, I have to kiss you."

His lips touched hers and she forgot conditions. His embrace, drew her tight against him. She wrapped her arms around his neck and opened her mouth, allowing his tongue to dance with hers and send heat radiating to her toes.

Chapter Twenty-Two

Jeremy knew better than to kiss her again. But the adoration and longing in her eyes after he'd helped her with her gloves had driven him to pull her into his arms and kiss her. She clung to him, returning the kiss with innocent abandon.

He eased away. That innocence had to be kept intact until they found her brother. *And I can figure out what I'm really feeling.*

Clara groaned but lowered her arms.

"I could kiss you all day, but we need to move on. I know of a sheltered spot we can spend the night. It's still a good lick away." Jeremy stared into her dazed eyes. A smile curled his lips. "You're hard to resist."

"Really?" Her beautiful eyes widened with wonder and her kissable lips remained slightly parted.

He wanted to kiss her again, but groaned instead and walked back to his team of dogs. Standing at his sleds, he called back to her. "Yes! And that's why I'm keeping my distance!" Jeremy grabbed a pick from the sled with their equipment and headed down the white channel of the river.

Rustling and footsteps behind him halted his steps. Sure enough, Clara was following his footsteps. "Go back! Wait by the sleds. If it is thin ice and I fall in, I'll need you to get me out. If we both fall in we'll freeze to death."

She stopped. "Be careful!"

"I will. Go back to the sleds."

Jeremy tapped the pick on the ice every four or five feet listening and seeing if it cracked. The ice appeared to be a good foot or more thick. It would be an excellent road to travel on. Though it would be in their best interests to check it every mile or so. He walked back to his team confident they could travel this way for some distance.

"*Mahsh*!" he shouted and stepped onto the runners of the last sled. Glancing over his shoulder, he watched Clara step onto her runners and give the command to her team.

The woman was smart, a quick learner, and not afraid of anything. Too bad she'd also shone she was prone to not thinking things through. He might be seeing her in a new way, but he'd keep his desires tamped down. They still had a long way to go and he wasn't going to let emotions or sentiment cloud his thinking.

An hour down the river a tree blocked their path. The large cottonwood had snapped at the base, falling across the river. Jeremy studied the limbs frozen to the ice and the gap between the trunk and the river.

"Wait here," he told Clara when she walked up to him. "I'm going to climb over and see what it looks like on the other side. That will determine if we cut through or go around."

She nodded and sat on the first sled.

Jeremy climbed over the trunk using the limbs as handles. On top of the tree, he surveyed the amount of work it would take to make an opening. The time it would take to saw or hack through the girth of the tree, they could try going around it. He followed the trunk of the tree to its base. A path around the stump looked more appealing than cutting through the tree.

He jumped down into the snow. It was several feet deep. He'd have to don the snowshoes and pack the snow, but that would still take less time and effort than clearing the river path.

Back at the sleds, he grabbed his snowshoes.

"What are we doing?" Clara asked. She'd sat on the sled, watching Jeremy as he searched for a new route.

"We'll take the sleds around that end of the tree, but I'll have to pack the snow first. Eat the jerky I gave you." He squeezed her shoulder and laced his snowshoes.

Patting her coat pocket, she felt for the dried meat. Jeremy worked up from the edge of the river, taking small steps and smashing the snow. If she followed his path it would help save time.

Clara leaned against the sled, donned her snowshoes, and rummaged under the tarpaulin for her umbrella. Tromping across the icy river, she glanced up. Jeremy was watching her. Would he make her go back and sit down? He smiled, shook his head, and continued smashing the snow.

A glow started in her chest. For the first time on this journey she felt like a partner instead of a burden. Helping Jeremy was instinctive. She wanted to lessen his loads and help where she could. Clara stepped up onto the river bank. Taking small steps and using her umbrella like a cane, she leaned all her weight on each foot, helping to pack the snow. Rounding the tree stump she glanced ahead. Jeremy had his head down watching where he put his feet. Beyond him on the opposite side of the river stood three wolves.

Her voice lodged in her throat as fear iced her insides. Would the wolves attack? Jeremy's rifle leaned against one of the sleds on the other side of the downed tree. Forcing air out of her lungs, she finally managed an odd sounding squawk.

Jeremy glanced over his shoulder. Clara lifted her arm and pointed to the wolves. She knew the minute he saw the creatures. His hand went to the top of his boot before his body seemed to grow larger. He stood tall, his shoulders broad, and his arms outstretched. A wide, wicked looking knife glinted in his right hand.

He couldn't take on all three of the wolves. Unsure what to do, but knowing she couldn't run back to the sleds for the gun and leave him alone, she moved slowly up behind Jeremy.

"You should be going the other way," he said, not glancing behind him.

"I'm not leaving you." She wanted to grasp his coat. To have a way to connect with him. But her clinging to him would hinder his movements.

"You should go to the sleds and get the rifle." His tone wasn't an order.

Clara two steps to his left side and opened her umbrella. Mimicking him, she widened her stance and raised her arms, swinging the big round circle of cloth.

"You're a quick learner. If we make ourselves look bigger they are less likely to attack."

The pride in Jeremy's voice warmed Clara. She didn't care for the wolves staring at them with their tongues hanging out, but this trip was, so far, the most thrilling and invigorating thing she'd ever done. Her umbrella caught their attention.

"Should we yell or something?" Of all the things her mother warned her to be careful of, wolves was not one of them.

"I'd hoped showing them we weren't running would move them along. We can yell and see what happens."

Clara drew in a large breath and yelled. So did Jeremy. The wolves jumped and streaked into the trees on the other side of the river.

Jeremy wrapped his weaponless arm around her, drawing her flush against his body.

"The next time a wild animal is around, get my gun, don't follow me into trouble with your umbrella." He kissed her temple. "Come on. We're losing daylight." He replaced the knife in his boot.

Clara twirled her umbrella before closing it. "I thought it more prudent to stand beside you than run back for a gun I don't know how to use." Clara followed behind him, smiling at the way he'd held her and spoken so gently. If he'd really been upset he would have yelled. She knew all about the anger of a male. Her father, though he never laid a hand on her, had used angry words to hurt and tear down her self-worth.

Back at the sleds, they roused the dogs and quickly worked their way around the tree stump and were back on the river and headed north.

The wind didn't blow as harsh in the river canyon, but as the sun set, the cold settled deeper into her bones. In the gray of the evening, she watched the edge of the river hoping to glimpse the area Jeremy said they would stop.

Her eyelids grew heavy, and she no longer felt her hands and feet. *Tired. I just want to sleep.*

Jeremy glanced back to tell Clara they would stop soon. The dogs and sleds were following but he didn't see Clara.

"Whoa!"

The dogs had barely stopped when he ran back down the river. Fifty feet back from the last sled he found Clara curled into a ball. Her blue lips and eyelashes covered with frost brought on the fiercest bout of recrimination he'd ever had.

Jeremy cussed his stupidity for not listening and doing more when she said riding on the sled made her colder. He cuddled Clara against his chest, carrying her back to his sled. He placed her under the tarpaulin.

"*Mahsh!*" he shouted, driving the dogs as fast as he could to the outcropping of rocks where they would spend the night.

At the spot, he ran the dogs into the sheltered area. He urged the two lead dogs to lay under the tarpaulin with Clara to keep her warm while he collected sticks and larger limbs. When the fire raged, sprouting rippling shadows on the rock cliff behind them, he pulled out the coffeepot and filled it with snow. Clara would need warmth inside and out. He unrolled both sleeping bags, spreading his on the ground as close to the fire as he dared and placing Clara's on top of his.

Once he had the bed ready, he uncovered Clara. Her skin was even paler than usual. He kissed Clara's cold cheek and removed her boots, before sliding her into her sleeping bag. Once she was sheathed in the bag, Jeremy spooned coffee into the pot. Waiting for the drink to boil, he pulled Clara's hands out one at a time and massaged them through the glove and mitten to get the blood moving and warm her up.

"Sweetheart, come on. You're a tough one. You can't give up now. We have a lot of days ahead of us to get to your brother." He leaned down, kissing her cheek.

Here eyelids fluttered up and her teeth chattered. "I-I-I'm-m-m s-s-s-o-o-o c-c-c-o-o-o-l-l-l-d-d-d."

"I know. The coffee's ready. You need to drink some to warm you up on the inside." Jeremy left her only long enough to pour a cup of coffee. He knelt beside her, raising her head, and holding the steaming cup to her lips.

Elation expanded his chest as she drank half the

cup. "That a girl. How about the rest?"

She barely shook her head.

"I'll give you a couple minutes." He tucked the sleeping bag around her with only her eyes and nose peeking out and went about the chores of unhooking and feeding the dogs. Once the animals were settled for the night, he returned to Clara's side.

Jeremy tossed the cold coffee out into the night and poured a new cup. He returned to her side. "Come on, a little more coffee and I'll make up some broth." With his hand under her head, he picked up her head and slid his leg under her shoulders, giving her more stability to drink. He held the cup to her lips, and again, she stopped at half a cup.

He stroked her lips. The blue was slowly fading. Her cheek didn't feel quite as cold when he kissed it, but her body shivered in the sleeping bag.

Jeremy laid her back down and started two pieces of dried meat steeping in a small pot of water. He added more wood to the fire and paced. He was only one day from the lake. He could take her back, make her stay with Snooker Pete. He could go on and find her brother and bring him back to her. Risking Clara's life was out of the question. *I won't take her any farther*. It was going to be this cold all the way to Dawson. He didn't know how to keep her from freezing every day.

Pacing, he worried over all the arguments he knew Clara would throw at him. He glanced down. The broth was ready. Once again, he tossed out the cold coffee and filled the cup with the broth. He resumed his position with her head on his lap.

"Clara, Sweetheart, drink this broth." He held

the cup to her lips, and she drank. This time emptying the cup. He kissed her forehead. She was still cold and shivering. But her teeth didn't chatter quite as much.

There was a method he'd been told where body heat from another helped to warm the afflicted person. He stared down at Clara's white face and shivering form. Surely, she would understand the grave danger she was in.

Jeremy knelt beside her. "Clara. The best way for you to get warm is if I get inside with you. But we need to take off some of your layers for my heat to penetrate to your body."

Her eyelids rose and the green eyes that stilled his heart peered into his. "S-s-s-o-o-o c-c-c-o-o-o-l-l-l-d-d-d."

That pushed past his objections to climbing in the bag with her. She pulled off her gloves and mittens. Jeremy pushed the front of the bag down enough to unbutton her coat, her wool shirt, and flannel shirt, drawing them off her arms and out of the sleeping bag. He reached down to unbutton her wool trousers. Her hand stopped his.

"You'll have the union suit and whatever else you have on, but the wool will keep my heat from penetrating to you."

Her gaze remained locked to his as she nodded slightly.

He unfastened the trousers and slid them down. Her legs worked them loose. They could stay at the bottom of the bag. It would make the garment warmer when she put them on tomorrow.

She was ready.

Jeremy tucked the sleeping bag around her while he took off his coat, hat, and outer clothes. He was down to his union suit when he slid into the bag.

Two bodies in the sleeping bag was a tight fit, but holding her shivering form in his arms and cradling her against his body felt like heaven. As his body registered each curve shivering against him it heated from the inside out.

"Y-y-y-ou-u-u w-w-w-on't-t-t t-t-t-ell-l-l a-a-any-o-o-one," she whispered.

"That we slept together?" he asked, kissing the back of her head.

She nodded.

"Nope. The only people who matter are right here in this sleeping bag." He rubbed his hands up and down her thighs and arms. Wrapping his socked feet with hers, he rubbed hoping to restore heat to her ice cold feet. His actions were to warm her. With each stroke he gained intimate knowledge of her body. His concern for her health overrode his desires. He forced his hands not to stray to areas that would take him beyond his control.

Warming her was his priority. Their first day traveling the interior and Clara was close to freezing to death. *Why'd I let this slip of a woman talk me into bringing her?* Because if you hadn't she would have found someone who would let her freeze to death. Or climbed in her sleeping bag for all the wrong reasons.

He cursed the cold Yukon winter and continued rubbing her limbs.

Clara grabbed his hands, lacing their fingers

and pulled his arms around her body like a blanket as she snuggled her backside even tighter against his length and her back pressed into his chest. It was going to be a long, torturous night warming her and praying she was ready to travel in the morning.

Chapter Twenty-Three

Clara gradually floated from deep sleep into a half-awake half-asleep state. Her sleeping bag felt tight and twisted around her. She tried to stretch and realized her legs were wound around…she moved her foot up and down. *Another leg*! The warmth and security hugging her were muscular arms. She wiggled back against a hard, hot body. Her mind came fully alert. She'd given Jeremy permission to sleep with her to stop her shivering.

His hand cupped her breast. The warmth and gentle squeeze caught her by surprise.

Her heart raced.

She shouldn't be lying here allowing him such liberties, but her body was shouting out for more. More of what she hadn't a clue, but they were clothed, if only in union suits. It was nearly the same as bundling. Her mother had shared the story of how she and Clara's father had to share a bed when they were courting. Clara's grandmother had wound Clara's mother up in a blanket and put her in one side of the bed while Clara's father had slept in the other.

Her heart fluttered. She and Jeremy weren't betrothed. If they were this would not be so scandalous. But it was the scandalous nature of it that heightened Clara's awareness of Jeremy's hand, now kneading her breast and his warm, moist breath on her neck.

His soft lips kissed behind her ear. She shivered but not from cold. It was anticipation. *What would he do if I turned in his arms*? Not waiting to wonder, she used her feet to spin, until her breasts were pressed against his hard chest, and she snuggled her nose into the crook of his neck, inhaling his outdoorsy, male scent.

His hands slid to her backside, gliding up and down over the curves. The light touch triggered sensations low in her body. She sucked in a breath. He kissed her cheek and nudged her face out of her hiding place.

Jeremy placed his lips on hers. With his tongue, he traced the seam of her lips, tickling and teasing her mouth open. His tongue slipped between her lips. His entrance and seductive exploration, shot heat to her toes and unleashed a yearning she didn't know how to appease.

Her mind was dizzy with the sensations his kiss and hands stirred in her. He slowly withdrew his tongue and nipped at her lips. When the kiss ended, she realized the flap on her union suit was open, and his hands were touching her bare backside. The realization both embarrassed and excited her.

"Sweetheart, either we get up and get ready for the day, or you go back to sleep and stop me from doing something that we'll regret later."

His husky voice sent another wave of heat through her body.

"Why would we regret kissing?" Her own husky tone surprised her. She nipped at his chin and wiggled closer. That's when she noticed the stick in between them. Clara pressed her bottom into Jeremy's hands to give her room to move the stick. She grabbed the offending hardness and discovered it was inside Jeremy's union suit. He groaned and she tightened her grip.

"Clara." He moaned and grasped her hand.

But she tightened her grip on the stick.

"Let go, you're killing me."

The pain in his voice scared her. Clara opened her hand. "What is that?"

"It's the part of a man that procreates." Jeremy's voice was low and husky. "Sweetheart, you don't touch a man there unless you want him to make love to you."

Clara tried to find a recollection where this had been talked about. She couldn't come up with a thing. "I don't understand?" She snuck her hand back down to the area and touched the hard long shaft through the union suit.

He grabbed her wrist again. "Don't touch me. I don't think I can keep from spilling my seed."

She used the light of the waning fire to peer into his face. She saw pain. "Oh dear! Did I hurt you?" Clara wrapped her arms around his body and hugged him. The hard shaft pressed against her belly. Her woman parts responded with a throbbing ache.

Make love. It dawned on her what he meant. She'd witnessed animals mating. That hard shaft was inserted…she squeezed her legs together and the throbbing grew in intensity. *What have I done*?

Jeremy's hands moved up her body to capture her head. He rubbed his thumbs back and forth on her cheeks. "Clara, I've never wanted a woman as deeply as I want you right now. But I won't tarnish your reputation." He kissed the tip of her nose. Then he started to shove out of the sleeping bag.

She clung to his waist with her arms, pressing his hard shaft between her breasts. "You don't have to get up. It's still early."

He went still in her arms. She peered up his body. The heated expression in his eyes melted her to her toes.

His fingers sifted through her hair as he drew in a deep breath. "You don't understand what I would want if I slipped back in that bag." He released her hair and removed her arms from his waist. "You deserve to be loved in a big bed with soft coverlets by the man you plan to spend the rest of your life with." He stood and dressed.

A shiver slithered down Clara's back. She slid deeper into the bag. It felt cold and lonely without Jeremy. His words sunk in. She knew he was headed home and she was headed to Seattle when they found Randy. But somehow having him say out loud they would be parting, disappointment sloshed into her thoughts. She grit her teeth against the feeling of abandonment. *I don't want a man mess-ing up my life. I want to keep things friendly, not be smothered by emotions.* She nodded at her uplifting thoughts.

She heard Jeremy moving about. Pots clanged and the dogs jingled their harnesses, growled and crunched their morning meal. It was still dark. She didn't know what time it was, but she'd try to sleep until he rousted her out of the sleeping bag.

Jeremy made noise as he prepared breakfast of sourdough biscuits, dried meat, and coffee. He'd known crawling in that sleeping bag with Clara was a bad idea before he even had her clothes off. But he'd also known it was the quickest way to warm her.

His body flamed at the memory of waking with her in his arms. She hadn't minded his hands wandering. The feel of her silky skin on that sweet round backside…His cock was hardening again at the memory. And when she grabbed him. Lord, he'd about spouted like a damn whale. But her actions only showed him she was as innocent as he'd believed. She hadn't a clue about making love or the parts of a man. You would have thought with a father and an older brother she would have a bit of a clue.

Shoot, he knew all about woman parts at a young age. He'd seen things most children his age hadn't, but that was only because he and Darcy were out on their own and living off the goodness of others. Some of those people had been prosti-tutes. Several nights, he and Darcy had slept next to rooms where the ladies conducted business on the other side of the wall. One of them had a hole in the wall, and he'd watched until Darcy caught him. He smiled. That was where he learned a couple things that he'd discovered over the years women liked.

But that didn't help him with his predicament right now. In fact, he needed to get rid of all those kinds of thoughts before he did something he'd regret later. He wouldn't sully Clara. She'd want to go to the man she married as an unsoiled bride. And he didn't need an angry brother chasing him to Sumpter. But remembering her sweet backside in his palms and the way she'd grabbed him…He groaned and snapped his thoughts back to cooking and getting on the trail.

He harnessed the dogs as the gray dawn filtered into the canyon. Clara still hadn't emerged from the sleeping bag. Had sleeping with him embarrassed her so much? She hadn't acted embarrassed. She'd been clinging to him like she wanted him to make love to her. *Damn, there I go again thinking of things I shouldn't.*

He walked over to the sleeping bag. "Sleeping beauty, you need to get dressed and eat, and I need to finish loading the sleds."

Mumbling came from within the bag. Her blonde head emerged. Her big eyes blinked several times, and then she smiled. The smile melted his heart and hardened the part of his body he'd been trying to ignore.

"Good morning." She disappeared back into the bag.

From the lumps moving around in the bag, he figured out she found her trousers at the bottom of the bag and was pulling them on. He turned to the fire where he'd been warming her shirts and coat and retrieved them.

Her head once again emerged along with her red-clad shoulders. She shoved the sleeping bag to her lap when she reached for her shirts. He hadn't meant for his gaze to leave her face, but it did, and he watched in fascination as her nipples peaked and protruded under the thin flannel union suit.

He pivoted to the fire and squat, placing biscuits and jerky on a plate beside a steaming cup of coffee. After groping her earlier, he didn't want to let her see him ogling her breasts.

A hand rested on his shoulder.

"Thank you for getting me warm and taking such good care of me. I'm sorry I've become such a burden."

He peered up into her sincere face. "You're welcome." He motioned for her to sit on a log he'd placed on the other side of the fire.

She sat and he handed her the plate and cup. She stared at the plate and sighed loudly. "I…you… I'm pretty sure what happened this morning…"

Jeremy mentally smacked himself. "Will not happen again."

Her sad gaze contradicted the resolute nod and breathy, "Good."

Jeremy went to work rolling up the sleeping bags and storing them on the sled. He'd been wrong to let temptation get the better of him. And now, he had to tell her they were going back to Bennett Lake, and she'd have to wait there. Because she wasn't going to like the arrangement, he'd decided to wait until the last minute to tell her.

Clara finished eating. She helped clean up the dishes and store the rest of their belongings in the sleds.

When he either had to head to Bennett Lake or tell her what he was doing, he swallowed his fear and strode up to Clara.

"Clara, we're heading back to Bennett Lake."

Chapter Twenty-Four

"Why?" Clara shoved her hands onto her hips and glared at Jeremy. There was no way she was going back to Bennett Lake. The memory of the men who tried to separate them and the fact it would take that much longer for her to find Randy set her mind to making Jeremy see they needed to keep going. Why would he change his mind? *Was it because we slept together*? That had to be it. He thought she *was* a loose woman and didn't want to deal with her.

"Was it because I allowed you into my sleeping bag?"

Jeremy held up his hands. "No, it isn't because you allowed me in your sleeping bag. If I hadn't crawled in with you, you may not be here arguing with me. That's what I don't want to happen. Clara, I don't want you to freeze to death before we find your brother."

"I won't. From now on when I feel my feet

and hands getting numb, I'll get off and walk. If they're cold and we're walking, I'll let you know. I'll stop trying to be tough and let you know when I'm cold or hurt or hungry." She stepped up to him, pressing her hands against his chest. This morning had shown her she had more leverage with him than she'd thought.

Clara rose up on her tiptoes. "Please. I don't want to stay at Bennett Lake without you." She said the last sentence with sincerity. She didn't want to be left at Bennett Lake alone. The men there had scared her. And she'd become accustom to Jeremy's presence. *And his kisses.*

Jeremy peered into her eyes. She could see he battled with what he felt he should do and what he wanted.

Clara rested her head on his chest. "Please don't make me go back."

A groan vibrated under her face pressed to his chest.

Jeremy held her out, peering into her eyes. "Only if you promise to tell me everything that is bothering you and make me stop when you need to stop."

Her heart danced inside her ribs. "I promise."

"I hope I don't regret this." His statement whispered between his lips as he continued to stare into her eyes.

The dogs growled.

Jeremy swung her behind him in one swift movement. His hand grabbed the rifle, pointing the barrel to the opening of the outcropping.

Two wolves stood at the entrance.

"They must have smelled the cooking." Jeremy walked toward the entrance.

"Don't!" Clara started to follow.

"Stay. They aren't going to be trouble." Jeremy waved his hands and the gun. The two animals spun and raced across the river and into the trees.

Jeremy placed his rifle in the sheath on his sled and doused the lantern, placing it on the top of the sled.

"Let's go. Mahsh!" The lead dog started Jeremy's team in motion.

Clara waited until the first team was outside before giving the command for her dogs to move. Out of the shelter, the gray diffused light proved it was morning, but she'd come to learn it would be several more hours before the sun would be up and shining.

Two hours later, the light bouncing off the white world made Clara's eyes water. The sunshine was misleading. While the light was bright and cheery, it gave off little heat.

Clara hopped off the runners and walked behind her team. The only problem, the team was trotting. She trotted behind them for a while but was soon winded and had to slow to a walk. Jeremy and his team were still in sight but getting smaller by the minute. She called to her lead dog to whoa. They did and she caught up to them and hopped on the runners.

"Mahsh!" she called as Jeremy disappeared around a bend in the river. Clara's team was just about to the bend when a boom echoed through the canyon. She shrieked and urged the dogs to go faster. They raced around the bend and found Jeremy bent over a medium-sized antlered animal.

"Whoa!" she stopped the dogs.

Jeremy smiled and stood. "We'll have fresh meat. This caribou will feed us for a week. The cold will help keep it fresh." He handed the rifle to her. "Stand guard, the smell of a fresh kill could bring out the wolves."

Clara took the rifle but wasn't sure why. She didn't know how to shoot. Watching Jeremy skin and clean the animal, she forgot to watch for wolves. Growling from the pack of dogs reminded her of her job.

Scanning the riversides, she found what the dogs saw. Three wolves; two silver and one black, paced back and forth along the river's edge.

"They'll wait until we're gone." Jeremy pulled out a canvas bag and shoved the largest hunks of meat into the bag. He cut the long strip of meat along the backbone and put it in the bag. He washed his knife and hands with snow and pulled on his gloves, taking the rifle from her.

"Let's go. The wolves can have the rest." He stepped onto the runners and waved Clara forward. "You go first. I want to make sure they don't follow."

The idea wolves could have been following them sent a shiver up Clara's spine. She'd been walking behind her team not even worrying about a wolf. She'd stay with her team from now on. No more lagging behind.

"Mahsh!" she commanded, and the dogs set off down the frozen river. While it was fun feeling like the leader, yet knowing she only had to follow the river, she glanced over her shoulder often to make sure Jeremy was behind her.

They once again traveled until full darkness prevented them from seeing where they were going. Jeremy set up a tent for them to sleep in before cooking up thin steaks. The meat tasted like the best steak she'd ever eaten. She was sure it wasn't that the meat was that good, but that she hadn't had a full meal in several days.

Clara glanced over at Jeremy when they entered the tent to retire for the night. She knew their sharing a sleeping bag the night before had been to keep her warm, but her body wanted it to happen again. Only to voice her thoughts would make Jeremy think she wasn't as proper as she'd been acting. And could make him think she was weak.

She sighed, plopped on her sleeping bag and tugged, trying to get her boots off. She'd added the four pairs of socks that morning, once again, making her boots hard to remove.

"Let me help." Jeremy scooted to sit on his sleeping bag in front of her and grasped her foot.

She pressed her other foot into the ground to keep from being pulled onto Jeremy's lap. Finally, the boot worked loose.

He placed her sock-covered foot against his middle and held out his hands. She placed the other booted foot in them. Another struggle and the boot finally came loose. Jeremy caught her foot before she pulled away. His eyes twinkled in the lantern light. He massaged her foot, warming her toes and sending heat up her leg.

This was the kind of actions that would land them in a sleeping bag together. As much as she was interested, she didn't want him to know that. She pulled her foot back and took off three layers of socks, ignoring him.

"I'm going to turn the lantern out. Get un-dressed and get in your sleeping bag." Jeremy said, kneeling and stretching his hand out to the lantern hanging from a hook by the entrance.

The tent went dark. Clara hurried to get out of her outer clothes and down to her union suit before she became too cold. She slid into the cold bag and shivered until her body heat warmed the linen lining. Pulling the opening tight around her face, she peered in the direction of Jeremy. She couldn't see a thing but heard him moving. Closing her eyes she drifted to sleep.

The routine remained the same for two weeks. They rose during the gray early hours before the sun fully lit the sky and started out. If they waited for the sun, they would only have a few hours of day-light to travel in. Instead, they traveled half the time by the gray dawn and dusk and occasionally, when clouds made the usually gray hours dark by the light of the lantern. Each evening after a warm meal they would both crawl into their sleeping bags and sleep until they rose in the morning and started all over again.

Jeremy was unusually cheerful one morning. Clara didn't mind the cheerfulness, but she didn't see where this day was any different from the past sixteen days.

"Why are you so happy this morning?" She tightened the ropes on the sled where she'd just stored the dishes.

Jeremy put his hands on her shoulders and leaned down, his silver eyes were lit with merriment. "We will sleep in beds tonight and eat something we didn't cook ourselves."

Clara couldn't believe what she heard. "We'll be in Dawson?" They'd get rid of the freight and head out to find Randy.

"No. Fort Selkirk. We're still about a week from Dawson." Jeremy watched her intently.

She tried to hide the disappointment. "It will be nice to sleep in a bed and take a bath. Can we stay long enough I can wash these clothes?"

"We'll send our clothes to the laundry while we soak in tubs of hot water."

Clara stared at Jeremy. "I heard prices over here are outlandish. How can we afford that?" Jeremy hadn't asked for his payment yet, but she had to make sure it was there when they found Randy.

Jeremy smiled and his eyes twinkled. "It will be my treat."

She pushed out of his arms. "I can't keep taking favors or treats from you. It's not right." Clara crossed her arms not sure why it upset her to have him paying for all the extras she wouldn't pay for herself.

"Nothing about this whole set up is right. Any other respectable woman wouldn't have pranced into Skagway saloons and proclaimed she needed a guide." He arched an eyebrow and stared at her.

Clara sputtered and glared back at him. "What

are you accusing me of?"

"Nothing. I'm just saying taking 'treats and favors' from me doesn't mean you have to pay me back. Not like some men would have led you to believe had you taken the offer of the first man that said he'd guide you." He moved to his sled. "And there isn't another man in Skagway who would have headed out with you knowing Soapy Smith wanted you."

Jeremy stepped onto the runners of his sled and ordered, "Mahsh!"

Clara stared at his back, huffed, and stepped onto her runners. "Mahsh!"

She wanted to stay mad at Jeremy, but he had a point. He was the only man to come to her rescue without even knowing her. Both when she was bogged in the mud in the street and when her trunk was being pillaged and he brought it to her not looking for a reward. Those two acts had shown his true nature. She couldn't have landed in the hands of a better guide. *But that doesn't give him the right to accuse me of being foolish.*

Chapter Twenty-Five

Jeremy saw the curls of smoke coming from Ft. Selkirk before he actually saw the open meadow where the town sat. Today, he'd kept the sleds along the edge of the river on the thickest ice where there was less chance for an accident. In the middle of the wide river thin ice and open spots revealed the fast moving water underneath.

When they'd stopped for a break, Clara had been less hostile and more like the determined but jolly woman he'd come to know. The more time he spent with her the more he wanted to learn about her. He had a decision to make. Tell the Harpers they were married, even though they probably wouldn't care one way or the other, or have Clara stay with the couple in their cabin while he pitched the tent? That idea didn't set well. He trusted the Harpers, but he didn't want to be away from Clara. And he had his mind set on sleeping in a bed, not the hard ground.

The tiny dots of several log buildings and a scattering of tents along the river came into sight. He glanced over his shoulder, caught Clara's attention and pointed. She smiled and nodded.

She had to be ready for a hot bath. His head was itchy, and he could smell himself. Women liked to be clean. He remembered a few times when Darcy got downright cranky when they'd gone a week without a dip in a river or a hot bath from a good Samaritan.

Their arrival at Ft. Selkirk was heralded by a team of dogs tied up in front of the store. Between the team, some loose dogs, and the excited barking of their two teams, Jeremy had to walk next to Clara and talk loud into her ear.

"The Harpers are a nice couple. I'm sure they'll put us up in one of the cabins. I'll introduce you then put the dogs and sleds up."

Clara smiled and nodded. "I'll need my things. A dress to put on after my bath."

The longing in her voice made Jeremy smile. *I was right about the bath.* He untied the tarpaulin on the sled carrying the canvas pack with all her belongings. He grasped the pack in one hand and placed his other hand on the small of her back as he escorted her into the store.

A small, dehydrated-looking man sat behind the glass counter of knives, needles, and thread. "All I have to sell is condensed milk at a dollar a can."

Jeremy had met the store keeper before. J.J. Pitts was a melancholy man who talked people out of buying supplies rather than selling them items they didn't need.

"Where are the Harpers?" Jeremy watched Clara wander over and check out the native fur boots.

"They went outside for the winter." Pitts didn't get up.

"I was hoping my wife and I could use a cabin for the night and take a hot bath." Jeremy felt Clara stiffen at his statement. He knew she'd bristle at still playing his wife, but he didn't want word getting out there was an eligible woman in the settlement. At the sight of all the tents there was no telling who was holing up here. He didn't feel like fighting off the lonely men hunkered down here for the winter.

"You can use the Harper's cabin. They won't mind. But you'll have to heat your own water." Pitts stood, slowly donned his coat and a fur cap.

Clara returned to him and whispered, "Why did you say we were married?"

Jeremy shook his head. "We'll discuss it in the cabin."

Pitts went out through the front door. "You can put your dogs and belongings in the lean-to on the cabin."

"Thank you." Jeremy motioned to Clara. They led the lead dogs and the sleds in line behind the man. He walked faster out in the cold air. He stopped at a cabin behind the warehouse.

"This is the Harper's. Leave it clean, you can use provisions, but don't take nothing else," Pitts said, opening the door and moving inside. He lit a kerosene lantern and knelt at the small wood stove, starting a fire.

"Thank you," Clara said, standing just inside the door.

Jeremy noted they would need their sleeping bags for the two-person bed in the corner of the one room cabin.

"Is the bathing tub in the lean-to?" Jeremy asked. Thinking about Clara in a tub with bubbles had him antsy.

"Yes. Pack in snow, melt it, and there is your water." Pitts nodded to Clara and left them alone in the cabin.

Jeremy closed the door as Clara hung her parka on a peg on the wall and spun in a circle taking in the room.

"I said we were married to be able to stay near you. If word spread there was an eligible woman here, it could end up like it was in Bennett Lake." He pulled off his hat and ran a hand through his hair. "The bed's big. Once we lay the sleeping bags on the mattress, it won't be any different than sleeping side by side in the tent."

Clara stood warming her hands at the stove. She stared at him over her shoulder. Her green eyes held the same heat he felt in the depths of his loins. He either had to find another place to stay tonight or they would end up making love.

"I'm going to put the dogs and sleds up." He pivoted and left the room, pulling the door tight behind him. *What were you thinking*? Staying in a cabin just the two of them would be like being husband and wife. With that came certain conjugal liberties. He shook his whole body like a dog trying to shed the images of making love to Clara from his mind.

Clara stared at the closed door and her insides quivered. She and Jeremy would be in this bed together tonight. If she asked right, perhaps even in the same sleeping bag. It thrilled and scared her. The idea of being held in his arms again thrilled her. What scared her was not knowing what more would happen. He'd talked about making love the last time they'd shared a sleeping bag. She'd overheard conversations of young women at parties talking about how wonderful it was to be thoroughly loved by their husbands, but would it be good when you weren't married? And what exactly was it?

Clara scanned the room again. It was warm, cozy in a simple way. There was a small window on either end of the building. A crude plank table with two logs for chairs. *Jeremy will bring the bath tub in from the lean to. I can start the snow melting.* She picked up two buckets by the stove and trudged outside, tamping the snow tight into the buckets to get as much water as possible.

Back in the cabin, she placed the metal buckets on the stove and dug through her pack for clean clothes. From what she saw of this place, she'd be washing their laundry.

Jeremy stomped into the cabin carrying their camp supplies. Clara crossed the room and helped him unload.

"That's the food and sleeping bags. I'll get the tub next and see if one of the local women is willing to wash our clothes."

He disappeared back out the door before she could offer to do the laundry.

Within minutes, the door banged open. The tub

wasn't a large one but she would be able to soak off the sweat she'd accumulated over the past weeks.

"Thank you. I can do the laundry. We don't have to bother anyone."

Jeremy stilled her movements and caught her gaze. "You're tired and it will get done faster if I take it to a local woman. Several women will work together to melt the snow and have the laundry done faster than you would have time to melt the snow."

Clara saw the logic. She dumped the melted buckets into the tub and handed the empty buckets to Jeremy. "I see that getting enough water for the bath is going to take a while. Having to melt it for laundry would take me all night."

He grinned and exited to get more snow.

Clara tested the water with her hand. The next ones would need to be near boiling to stay warm while more buckets were being melted. She sighed. *I might as well make a nice supper while I wait for there to be enough water for a bath.*

She rummaged in the pack with their food. Pulling out the flour and last of the meat, she diced the meat, found an onion in the small box of provisions by the stove, and set about making meat pies. The small cookstove had an oven. After placing the pies in the oven, she stirred together soda bread for the trail. It would be nice to have fresh bread with each meal for a while. Next, she pulled out a can of peaches and made a cobbler topping with butter and sugar. The small tin fit beside the meat pies in the oven.

While she cooked, Jeremy continued melting snow, dumping pails of snow in the tub and pouring boiling water into the tub.

"Mmm. That smells wonderful whatever you're making." He stopped between trips to sniff deeply.

"Since I had a stove, I wanted to cook something different."

The meat pies and cobbler were cooked. Clara pulled them out of the oven and set the pans of soda bread in.

"Our bath is ready." Jeremy stood at the end of the steaming tub.

"Our bath?" She studied his expression. He had to be joking. There was no way they would both fit in that tub.

"You first, me second. I'll fill the buckets with snow to warm up the water when it's my turn." Jeremy headed toward the door with the buckets in his hands.

"Where are you going to be while I'm bathing?" The thought of him being in the cabin while she bathed made her nervous and excited.

"I'll go visit with Pitts at the store."

Clara nodded and waited until Jeremy had deposited the buckets of snow on the stove and pulled the door tight behind him before loosening one button. She quickly shed the dirty clothes, picked up her lavender scented soap, and stepped into the tub.

The water was warmer than she'd thought it would be. The heat was a shock after so much exposure to the cold. Perspiration beaded her forehead as she slowly slid down, crossing her legs and getting her body into the wonderful heat. The water sluiced around her body. *It was heavenly!* The heat worked out the kinks from sleeping on the hard ground.

She dunked her head and lathered her hands with the soap, working it through her hair. The scent took her back home, to the enamel tub with faucets she bathed in once a week. She'd never gone this long without a bath. Her skin had begun to itch.

The sound of the door creaking open sent her mind into panic. She grabbed at the blanket she'd placed by the tub to use to dry and stood, hiding behind the woven fabric.

"You don't look like you're done washing your hair."

Jeremy's voice erased some of the fear pounding in her head. At least a total stranger hadn't walked in on her.

She peeked over the blanket. "Why are you back so soon?"

"Pitts closed the store and headed to his cabin. I didn't want to keep him company any longer. He doesn't have much to say." He took off his coat, scarf, and hat, hanging them on the peg by the door, and walked toward her. "Want me to help you rinse your hair?"

Clara swallowed the lump in her throat and waited for her pounding heart to stop. What should she say? She shivered from the cold air that swirled into the cabin when Jeremy entered.

"That soap's going to dry if you don't rinse, not to mention you're shivering." Jeremy held the blanket as she lowered into the water, then placed it across the tub blocking her from his vision.

"Lean your head back."

She ignored the voice telling her she shouldn't

be naked, even if under a blanket barrier, in front of a man she wasn't married to. However, she trusted Jeremy with her life and her body. She gripped the blanket to the sides of the tub and slid down.

Jeremy placed one hand under her neck supporting her and with his other hand worked water through her hair.

His massaging fingers and hand cupped under her neck relaxed Clara. She closed her eyes and enjoyed being pampered. The last time someone washed her hair she was a young girl. His gentleness added another patch to her heart with Jeremy's name on it.

Chapter Twenty-Six

Jeremy clenched his teeth and willed his desire to go away. Clara leaning back with her eyes closed, allowing him to wash her hair was more arousing than holding her in his arms. He rinsed her hair and cleared his throat.

"Time to get out before you start shivering." He stood and walked to the stove, keeping his back to the tub and the sound of sloshing water.

"Are you covered?" he asked, picking up a boiling bucket of water.

"Yes."

He turned to the tub and nearly doubled in-two. The sight of her shiny wet hair hanging over one bare shoulder and the blanket pulled about her small frame, she gave the appearance of a mermaid he once saw in a book.

"How am I to dress if you're…?" Her gaze dipped to the tub.

He dumped the bucket of water in the tub and moved to the bed. He'd noticed a twine strung about a foot down from the ceiling by the bed earlier. Grabbing the cover off the bed, he hung it over the string. Her knees and below would show, but he wouldn't be able to see the rest.

"There. You can stay behind there while I bathe."

She blushed and ducked behind the blanket.

Jeremy hurried to the stove, poured the second heated bucket into the tub, and shucked off his clothes. Stepping into the warm water, he groaned with delight.

"Are you all right?" Clara's soft voice echoed through the room.

Knowing she was only on the other side of a blanket set his blood pounding in his ears. She could walk around, see him… And what? She wouldn't sink to her knees by the tub and wash his hair. She wasn't that bold.

He spread his fingers and ran his hands back and forth through the water. The silkiness of the water felt like her hair slipping through his fingers when he washed her golden locks. The thought brought his shaft to life. He slid down in the tub, wetting his hair.

Raising his head out of the water, the sound of humming and fabric rustling reminded him he wasn't alone.

Jeremy peered toward the blanket. Clara's lower legs were encased with a billowy white fabric. He preferred the union suit that clung to her curves.

He quickly finished washing, dried with another blanket Clara had left by the tub, and dressed in clean clothes.

"I'm going to run our cloths to the laundry." He said, donning his coat and hat.

Clara's head popped around the blanket. "Oh! You're done?"

He motioned to his clothed body with his free hand.

"You know, there's no one here but me to impress. You don't have to put on your dress and all the other woman things you need to go with it."

She scrunched her nose. "I'm not out trudging through snow. I'd prefer to dress like a lady."

"I'll only be a few minutes." He pulled the door tight behind him, thinking he should have told her to put the bar across.

Clara stared at the door. She'd let that man wash her hair while she lay naked in a bath tub. Granted, she was covered by a blanket, but still. And he hadn't tried anything even though her thoughts had definitely headed in a very carnal direction.

She waved her hands in front of her face to ease the heat scalding her cheeks. There was a part of her that willed his hands to move lower, to her neck and breasts. To knead her breasts as he had when they slept in the same sleeping bag. She knew these thoughts were wanton, but she longed to feel Jeremy touch her that way again.

Why? I don't want to be tied to him or any man so why would I wish something that can only be if we are married?

Disgusted with her thoughts and reprimand, Clara picked up her corset, wrapping it around her body. She grasped the front and tugged, trying to secure the hooks. She worked on it until her arms couldn't pull any longer. *How come I can't get this on?*

Jeremy knocked on the door and entered. "Are you dressed?" He stood at the door, scanning the interior. She should have been dressed by now.

Clara peeked around the blanket and the sight of her flushed face and wide eyes started his heart racing.

"I have a problem with this corset, again," she said slightly louder than a whisper.

He walked over to where she peeked out from behind the blanket. "I'm pretty sure if I can unhook it I can hook it. Would you like me to help?"

Her cheeks reddened like coals in a fire. "I-I shouldn't have you... Oh bother, maybe I should just leave it off."

"We won't go anywhere, and I haven't run screaming for the hills at the sight of you yet."

She chewed on her bottom lip. "I'll know and feel undressed the whole time." She peered up into his eyes and stepped out from behind the blanket with the corset front clutched in her hands.

The night he helped her out of the contraption, he'd only felt her small, soft breasts. Today the soft creamy mounds were visible, making his pulse quicken and sent his thoughts tumbling over one another.

With shaky hands, he pulled off his gloves and grasped the front of the corset. His knuckles skimmed across the soft fabric of her shift, moving up her body, latching the hooks. He'd be lying to himself if he said he wasn't enjoying the feel of her undergarment under his knuckles. He kept his gaze trained on his fingers.

When they met her silky skin at the top, pressing into her soft breasts, a jolt shot to his toes. He'd touched breasts before. Mostly on women he'd paid to bed. This woman with her wide innocent eyes and sharp tongue should feel the same, but she didn't. Touching her so intimately with the lights on and gazing into her eyes, he was struck with a possessiveness he'd never felt. And didn't like.

Clara sucked in a breath as his hands touched her soft skin.

"Sorry, my hands are cold." He stared down into her eyes. He'd witnessed that longing before. His body responded heating and moving closer to her.

Jeremy tipped her chin up and placed his lips on hers for a brief kiss. "You're welcome." He stepped back and waved to the dress draped over the bed. "You better get that on."

Clara blushed and petticoats swished as she spun back behind the hanging blanket.

Jeremy stared at the blanket a moment before shedding his coat, hat, and scarf and adding more wood to the stove. He couldn't control the way his body reacted to Clara. But he could damn sure control his mind. This woman wasn't what he wanted. *So why does my body keep acting like it is?*

Clara walked out from behind the blanket, her old boots clunking on the wood floor. "The bread needs to come out of the oven and our dinner is ready." She smoothed her skirt and stepped around Jeremy.

He walked over to their pack and pulled out eating utensils. Keeping busy left him less time to contemplate his reaction to the woman. She bent, opening the stove and emitting mouth-watering aromas into the small room. Jeremy licked his lips, watching the sway of her skirt and hips, as she moved about setting things on the table. She removed their dinner from the warming oven and sliced one of the loaves of bread.

Clara did cut a fine figure in her dress. When she wore the men's clothing, she was cute in a child-like way, but dressed in her own clothes, one could see she was a well put-together woman. His thoughts started his blood humming. He moved to the door, heading out to get more wood.

"Where are you going, dinner is ready," Clara asked watching him with narrowed eyes.

"I'm getting more wood." He grasped the door latch.

"Shouldn't you put on a coat?"

"I'll only be a minute." He ducked out the door and head straight for the wood pile in the lean-to. Cold air was best for his affliction.

Clara shook her head and smiled. Why would Jeremy go out to get wood when he could have brought a load in when he came from the store? She shrugged and continued preparing the table for their meal. She enjoyed doing little things like preparing a meal or helping Jeremy with the dogs. The need to help had nothing to do with him helping her find Randy. It was because it made her feel good to assist him in any way. This meal was one small way she could show him how much he meant to her.

Humming as she put the meal on the table, Clara realized this was an event she'd never witnessed her mother do. Mother hadn't prepared the meals. That had been Mrs. Ladimer's job. Mother had sat at the table for hours after the children had eaten waiting to eat until Father came home. And most times, he'd already eaten and would grunt and head to bed. In his own room. Her parents hadn't shared a bed since George's birth.

Clara had figured out several years ago her parents' marriage wasn't held together by love. It was fear of not being able to care for her children without a husband that kept her mother in the marriage. Her father stayed because it was a legally binding document he signed when he married. She wanted more than that, she wanted unconditional love. It was out there. Her friend Polly had it, and her aunt Bea had it. How she wished she had those two to consult with right now.

She turned to the table. Her heart did a little skip noticing how Jeremy had neatly set the tin plates and utensils. She enjoyed working beside him.

As if her thoughts conjured him up, Jeremy banged through the door, his arms full of split wood. Clara hurried across to close the door and keep the cold wind out.

Jeremy dropped the wood into the pile by the stove.

"You can wash up using that kettle on the side

of the stove," she said, having a hard time pulling her gaze from his shaggy hair, and unshaven, red face. In Seattle, she'd always shied away from the men who were unkempt, but on Jeremy, it only enhanced his look. The outside, rough-looking man had become very appealing.

Her cheeks heated.

She spun on her heel and stood at the table.

The meat pies and cobbler graced the middle of the table. Jeremy moved to her side, rested a warm hand on her lower back and escorted her to one of the log seats. When he moved to her side while she sat, the loss of his touch surprised her. *Have I become so accustom to his touch that I crave it?*

The conversation tonight was more animated than their usual evening talks over dinner. Jeremy told her about the Harpers, the family that lived in the cabin. He'd met then several times while packing goods in and out of the interior. She enjoyed his stories of people in the area and his thoughts on life in general. That he asked her opinion of things and listened gave her more to think about.

Her father had been a shrewd business man. She'd witnessed the respect he garnered from the men he did business with. But at home, he acted like he didn't know what to do with his wife and children. Now that she'd traveled away from her family, she realized her mother wasn't happy.

Was that why Randy left as soon as he finished school? Are the younger children going to be freer now that Father is gone?

"What's wrong?" Jeremy asked.

She peered into his concerned face. "Have you

ever woke up and discovered perhaps the life you knew wasn't quite what you'd thought?" She refrained from slapping a hand over her mouth, when she realized she'd spoken this out loud.

"Are you speaking about your life?" Jeremy raised a cup of coffee and watched her.

"Tell me more about the Harpers. Why did they send their children to San Francisco for their education?"

Jeremy's frown proved he saw her ploy to change the subject, but he complied and answered her question.

Clara understood the Harpers were preparing their children for life. Something her parents had not prepared her for. Her father had fought her working at the warehouse. At first, she thought it was because she was a woman. But he had women working in his office. In fact, more than she thought he needed. However, she was not allowed in the offices until after his death. Now, she realized he didn't want her working to keep her as naïve as her mother about life.

Your death has slapped me in the face with life, Father.

"Clara, do you want me to do the dishes. You look like you're about to fall asleep." Jeremy touched her arm.

Clara shook off her thoughts and smiled at Jeremy. "I'm sorry. I didn't realize I was so tired."

"I'll do the dishes. Why don't you spread out your sleeping bag and rest?" Jeremy pushed a strand of wayward hair behind her ear.

His simple action brought a lump to her throat,

and tears burned the back of her eyes. She had to be tired. Something so simple should not have caused her to feel so emotional.

She swallowed the lump in her throat. "Thank you, I am more tired than I thought. I'll spread your sleeping bag out, too."

Clara didn't dare look at him. She stood and walked behind the blanket. Sitting at the table she'd had a glimpse of what life could be like with Jeremy. She enjoyed the discussions and appreciated that he asked her questions and listened intently to her answers. She wanted that kind of life. And felt confident she could have it with Jeremy. But she didn't come to Alaska looking for a husband. She came here to help her family.

When she was ready to marry, she wouldn't commit to a man until he'd said the words, she'd never heard uttered between her parents, or to their children…I love you.

Chapter Twenty-Seven

Jeremy quickly brought in more snow to melt to wash the dishes. While he waited for the water to melt, his mind repeated Clara's statement she'd put his sleeping bag next to hers.

They'd slept next to one another many nights in the tent. But this simple act when she could easily ask him to sleep on the floor, told him she enjoyed his company as much as he'd come to enjoy hers.

He tried to stay focused on the dishes, but his mind kept remembering Clara's soft breasts as he hooked her corset.

He finished the dishes long after he'd heard the rustling of her clothes and the creak of the bed as she slid into her sleeping bag. During dinner she'd been miles away a couple of times. He didn't know if she was thinking about them or something else. They'd talked about a lot in the evenings the last few weeks, but she'd said very little about her family, while he told her everything about his. She knew the names of his nieces and nephews. How he'd missed several births, so he'd yet to meet them.

The kerosene lantern on the table didn't penetrate the blanket still hanging by the bed. Clara would like privacy in the morning to dress, but the fabric hindered the heat from getting to that corner of the room. Jeremy quickly undressed, blew out the lantern, and headed to the bed. He tugged on the blanket pulling it from the twine line.

The creak of the ropes under the mattress came from the bed.

The best thing for him to do would be to slip into his sleeping bag and not disturb Clara. This trip had to be the hardest thing that had ever happened to her in her life so far.

The bed squeaked as he sat, then slipped his legs and feet into his sleeping bag and rolled to his back. Twisting his neck, he looked toward the wall. Moonlight spilled just enough light through the window he could see Clara's eyes were closed. He listened to her even breathing. She was sleeping. He'd best do the same.

Clara snuggled into the supple wall at her back. *Jeremy held her tight. She peered into his silver eyes and saw love and commitment. She laughed and threw her arms around his neck, kissing him with abandon. Randy stood next to them, his eyes hidden beneath the low brim of a hat. Why wasn't Randy happy for her?*

"What did I do wrong?" Her voice startled her awake. Clara blinked her eyes. It was dark. She shivered and snuggled deeper into the sleeping bag but couldn't find a warm spot. The air outside the sleeping bag was cold, tingling her face.

Her body didn't ache like when she slept on the hard ground. She rolled and remembered they were sleeping in their bags on a bed. Shivers of cold rippled through her. Clara shoved the bag down, exposing her body to more cold.

Grasping the top of Jeremy's bag, she slid her stocking clad feet in and slipped down between him and the bag. Her night dress caught on the bag opening, she struggled to hold it down as she slid deeper into the sleeping bag with Jeremy, seeking his heat.

Strong arms wrapped around her, and Jeremy's hard body pressed against her back.

I should close my eyes and drift back to sleep. But she was awake, and her curiosity overruled her good sense.

Clara squirmed tighter against his body. The hardness she'd come to know wasn't as big as she remembered. Reaching behind with her hand, she just about had his appendage in her grasp when Jeremy flipped her to her back and loomed over her.

"What are you doing?" His husky voice started her body humming.

Once the initial surprise resided, she said, "I wanted to get warm."

He held her arms up above her head, and his body covered hers.

"Clara, crawling in my sleeping bag to get warm is one thing, but touching certain parts of me will only make us both want what we can't have."

His statement sounded like a dare.

"W-what can't we have?" The thought of his hands roaming about her body and eliciting the heat and sensations his hands did earlier while fastening her corset, started the throb between her legs.

"Making love." He released her hands and sat up.

She stared up into the dark, not wanting to leave the warmth of the sleeping bag. "If I keep my hands to myself will you come back in here and keep me warm?"

He groaned. "Clara, what you're asking is nearly impossible. I'm not a saint. I can't guarantee if I slide back in there my hands and thoughts won't roam where they shouldn't."

Jeremy pushed with his feet to leave the bag. "I'll add more wood to the stove and it will warm things up. I'll sleep in your bag. Being by the wall probably makes it colder."

Clara reached up, grasping his hand, holding him still. "Add more wood, but come back to this bag." She knew her actions were bold and wanton, but sleeping in his arms made her feel loved and secure. She'd rarely experienced either in her life.

He squeezed her hand, released it, and padded across to the stove. The glow of the embers in the firebox cast a red hue over his body that was enhanced by his union suit. He shoved the wood in and slammed the door shut.

Clara watched him walk slowly back to the bed.

He crawled over her and reached for her sleeping bag. That was her answer, he wasn't willing to sleep with her if she wasn't dying. She rolled with her back toward him and tried to hide her sniffling and tears as the hurt in her chest felt like someone had dropped a heavy crate on her chest.

"Are you crying?" his hand settled on her head, stroking.

"No." She sniffed and tried to ignore the ache. Why did his not wanting her hurt so bad?

His fingers walked down her face. "Yes, you are." The bed creaked and shook. He slid into the sleeping bag with her.

"Shhh…why are you crying?" He wiped at the tears with his thumbs as he cradled her head in his hands.

She tried to get her weeping under control before she said anything that would give away the feelings she had for him.

"Clara, you always have something to say. Why are you crying?" Jeremy's calm, whispered question was her undoing.

"I don't understand you." She hiccupped and wiped her nose on the shoulder of her nightgown.

"What don't you understand?" He rested her head on his shoulder.

"You kiss me and touch me, but you back away. It feels like you're teasing me."

"No, you are the one doing the teasing. I want you more than I should." His voice held a husky quality she hadn't noticed before.

"I don't understand?" His reasoning confused her.

"From the first time I met you, you were like a burr under my saddle…"

She tried to shove away from him, but he held her tight.

"A burr in a good way. I couldn't get you out of my thoughts, then you came asking me to be your guide. I didn't want to get involved, but when I heard you were going into saloons looking for a guide, I couldn't let you end up hurt or killed. But you do so many foolish and rash things, I can't believe you lived this long."

She slugged his arm. "I don't usually do so many fool hardy things. I've been given the task of saving my family and I'll do anything to do that."

He chuckled. "That's the other thing that makes me like you. You have conviction when it comes to family."

Her body warmed on the inside at his words.

"And that's the problem. I like and respect you too much to treat you like a woman I'd pay for."

The words sunk in. He did think she was acting like a soiled dove. That was why he climbed into her sleeping bag. Hot tears stung the backs of her eyes. *How have I stooped so low to be thought of as a soiled dove when all I want is what I have at this very moment?*

"Are those tears dripping on my arm?"

She couldn't nod or do anything. The realization of her actions stung her mind and her heart.

"Shh… Sweetheart, don't cry."

Jeremy's soft lips found hers. The kiss started soft and sweet, but seconds in, she registered the change. His tongue swept past her lips, and soon they were both panting. Her hands moved across his muscular back and his hands, slid up and down her body, cupping her backside and pressing her body closer.

His lips moved down her throat, kissing and tasting. A calloused hand ran up her leg pushing her nightgown up her body. She froze. *He only thinks of me as a soiled dove.*

She grabbed his wrist with both of her hands. "Stop. I'm not a soiled dove."

Jeremy kissed her into a dizzy state and drew away. She followed wanting more.

"Clara, I don't kiss soiled doves, and I don't explore their bodies, like I'm going to do yours. A soiled dove is for release. You, are for loving."

The soft flannel of her nightgown skimmed up her body. The fabric had never felt so seductive before. She raised her arms, and the garment whisked over her head.

Her naked body quivered with anticipation. *What would he do next?* She wanted a kiss but refused to beg for one.

His hands cupped her breasts, squeezed, and molded them to his palms. She'd never known this part of her body was so sensitive. She squirmed under his weight and marveled at the tightening of her nipples and the heat careening from her breasts to her throbbing center.

Jeremy leaned forward. She parted her lips waiting for the kiss. A moan slipped through her lips when he took her nipple in his mouth and suckled and nipped. Her body quaked, and her legs clamped together as if trying to hold her together.

"H-how?" She could barely speak for the dryness in her mouth from breathing rapidly.

Jeremy released her nipple. The cold air across the moistness he left was another enticing sensation.

"How what?" His voice purred above her.

She blinked and peered into his silver eyes. "How do you know what makes my body ache?"

"Is it a good ache?"

"Yes and no." She wiggled, trying to subdue the throb and ache at the junction of her legs. "It sends good chills through my body, but at the same time I want…more." Wanting more made her feel like a shameless woman.

"Clara, that ache is good. I'll make it feel even better soon. But first I want you to learn my touch." He kissed her hard, demanding, and pulled back. "I want to be the only man who ever touches you this way."

After the hard kiss, he nibbled her lips and kissed her soft and sweet. His hands slid up, capturing her head and holding her mouth to his as he took her body on a dizzying ride with his kiss.

Her mind in a haze, it took several seconds to realize his mouth had moved back to her breasts. Suckling and nipping, his actions started her body vibrating with an ache she couldn't define.

"Please, do something," she pleaded, her hands clutching his hair.

To her surprise, he moved lower. His tongue lapped at her throbbing area, and her head hit the wall. "What are you doing?"

"You pleaded with me to do something." His mischievous tone did little to stop the sensations now bursting through her body.

He continued teasing her lower regions. Her

body hummed from the attention and the throbbing grew.

"Oh! Oh!" Her body shuddered and bright lights burst in her head.

"That's what I wanted." He slid up her body, dropping wet kisses along the way.

It took her a minute to fully regain her thoughts. "What was that?"

"That was your body experiencing what making love is all about." He kissed her soundly on the mouth and rubbed his union-suited body against her.

"That's making love? But I thought the man had to…" Her face heated. How did one talk about such things with a man? Especially when he'd just done what he had to her body.

"A man putting this," he placed her hand on his hardness, "inside a woman is also love making if it is between two people who love one another. But love making can also be when one person pleasures the other without them coupling."

She thought about that. If this was love making, did he truly love her? And did she want that? She cared for him more than any man she'd ever met, but love led to marriage and she wasn't ready for that.

He twined his fingers with hers. "I'd like to experience coupling with you, but that causes a problem I'm not ready to deal with."

"What is that?" What could coupling possible cause that he didn't want?

"Coupling can result in children. I won't get you with child. Neither of us would be happy to be forced to marry." He lowered his head. His nose touched hers.

She didn't want to think about children or marriage. This trip had shown her she had strength she didn't know she possessed. She wasn't ready to have her adventures squashed by a marriage.

Instead, she wiggled under him and experienced his appendage pressing into her belly. "How can I give you pleasure without coupling?"

He groaned. "Let me take care of you. Don't worry about me."

She wiggled some more, and when he released her hands to shift off of her, she rolled him to his back and toppled over on him. The appendage that fascinated her was rigid and long under his union suit.

Clara started unbuttoning his suit. "I think it's only fair that if I'm to be naked, you should be, too." She unfastened yet another button, and the end of his shaft poked out the opening.

Moonlight filtered into the room giving her a surreal glimpse of this fascinating part of his body. She ran her fingers over the silky head before unfastening the remaining buttons. Once the suit was open, she slid her hands over his shoulders and down his arms, slipping the garment from his upper body. Grasping the suit in her hands, she pulled it down over his hips and off his legs.

Straddling his legs, she took hold of his appendage, running her hands up and down this rigid, yet soft-skinned part of him. Her body began to throb, again. She leaned forward touching the silky tip to her lips. Moving it back and forth across her lips, she tingled to her toes. Jeremy moaned deep and throaty.

"You like that?" she asked.

"Yes," he hissed as she ran her thumb across the top.

"It's so soft and silky. I would have never guessed a man could have such a part on his body." Clara gripped Jeremy in her hand and slid her fist up and down the length. It was such a contradiction—the skin so soft and silky and the form so firm and rigid.

"Move your hand faster." Jeremy's voice was strained.

Clara peered at his face through the dim light. His eyes shimmered as they stared at her. She quickened her movements and he groaned.

"Is that hurting you?"

"No. Keep moving your hand."

She continued, and soon she couldn't believe it possible, but the girth of the shaft expanded and pulsed. He cupped a hand over the top. Something warm and gooey oozed over her hand.

"What is this?" She smelled the substance and rubbed it between her fingers.

"That is my seed. The ingredient that when placed in a woman's body makes babies." He raised up on his elbows. "Is there a rag to clean this up?"

Clara slipped off Jeremy and the bed and found the washcloth he'd used to wash the dishes. She carried it back to the bed after cleaning her hand. Jeremy held out his hand, but she waved it away and went to work cleaning him up. The hard rigid part of him was no longer large or firm.

She glanced up his body and asked, "What

happened?" The incredulous look on his face spoke to her innocence.

"That is the way a man looks most of the time. We only get hard when a pretty woman like you touches or shows us attention, or we think about a pretty woman, or get an urge to mate." He pulled her up beside him and tossed the washcloth. "Didn't your mother tell you about men and women?"

Her mind was still back on all the things that make a man hard. "That's a lot of things. Isn't it painful to walk around like that?"

Jeremy laughed. He liked that Clara spoke what she thought. "Yes, you could say men, especially those that aren't married and don't receive good lovin' from a woman all the time, do have to work hard at keeping their bodies in control." He stroked his hand down the curves of her body and felt his cock coming to life.

Better get that under control. He'd given her pleasure, and she had returned the favor. Now they needed to sleep. *Naked.* He groaned.

"What's wrong?" Clara raised her head from his shoulder.

He peered into her worried face and his frustrations vanished. "Nothing. Everything is fine." Jeremy hugged Clara. "Go to sleep. We'll be moving on in the morning. The sooner we get to your brother, the better."

"I agree, but I'll miss this, being held in your arms." She snuggled deeper into his embrace.

Jeremy smiled. He also enjoyed holding her in his arms. *Perhaps too much.* He should have stayed in the other sleeping bag, but he'd always been a sucker for female tears. He knew he'd caused the tears and couldn't let her think whatever sad thoughts she'd had. Now that he'd tasted even more of her and discovered the passion that he'd expected, he was going to have a hard time walking away from her when they found her brother.

Chapter Twenty-Eight

The following morning, Jeremy waited by the sleds while Clara said good-bye to Pitts. Thinking about the wonderful meal she made last evening along with the fresh soda bread they now had in the provisions and watching her make breakfast he'd witnessed the kind of woman he'd like for a wife. Before their domestic stay at the Harpers' cabin he wouldn't have believed Clara wanted to be a wife.

Having grown up with only Darcy, and then watching her be a good mother and having all the other Halsey wives around, he knew he wanted children. And he wanted a wife who loved them as much as he would. The hours spent with Clara gave him a good idea of who she was, but from her comments at the dinner table, he was struggling to figure out the family she grew up with. Why would a first born son not stick around to help his father run the family business? He hadn't thought much about it before, but now he wondered.

"I'm ready." Clara walked up to him dressed in her traveling clothes of several layers of clothing plus the parka, a scarf, and her new fur boots. When he visited Pitts, while Clara bathed, Jeremy had purchased a pair of the Native fur boots for Clara. The price had been high, but if the boots kept Clara's feet warm he would have paid five times that.

Jeremy couldn't take his eyes off Clara's glowing face. *This was a good stop.* He knew their exploration of one another the night before shouldn't have happened, but he was damn glad it had. Not only did he feel closer to Clara, he felt he understood her a little better. When she stood at the back of her dog team, Jeremy called out for his dogs to move.

They continued running on the ice at the river's edge. As long as the ice remained thick on the edge they could continue riding the sleds and let the dogs pull them.

Jeremy stopped mid-day giving the dogs and Clara a break. Her cheeks were red from the cold, stinging wind.

"Tie your hood tighter making only a small hole to see out of." He pulled on the string drawing her hood tighter around her face.

"I like being able to see around me. I don't want to always be staring at the dogs and your back."

He opened the hood and dipped in for a kiss. Her lips were cold and chapped. Jeremy kept the kiss light and short. "Finish your jerky."

Pitts had also sold him several items to add to

his pack of medical supplies. One item was cream to put on their lips. He went to the sled carrying his personal supplies and grabbed the small jar.

Returning to Clara, he slipped it in her pocket. "When you finish eating, dab that on your lips. Every time we stop add some more. It's something the natives use. I keep my face covered, but I've seen others who have nasty cracks in their lips from the cold and wind."

"Are you going to eat?" Clara held a piece of jerky out to him.

Jeremy took the offered meat. "Thank you."

He watched as Clara fished the jar out of her pocket and removed the lid. She smelled the contents and made a face.

"This smells like the dogs." She waved a hand in front of her nose.

"It's probably bear fat."

She made a face. "Why would I put bear fat on my lips?"

"If you have cracks, I won't kiss you for fear of hurting you." He shrugged, shoved the last of the jerky in his mouth and walked to his dog team.

He lashed the tarpaulin back over the sled with the food supplies and glanced back. Clara had the grease spread across her lips and was on her sled ready to go. Jeremy smiled. He'd figured withholding kisses would be incentive after discovering her hunger for closeness.

The rest of the day flew by, and he prepared camp on the river bank under a copse of cottonwood trees. The leafless limbs didn't keep the weather out, but the dead limbs on the ground made easy access to firewood. The moon barely shed a glimmer of light, but the light from two lanterns he hung from tree limbs aided them as they unloaded the tent and supplies needed for the night.

Jeremy set up the tent while Clara started a fire and dinner. They'd been on the trail long enough she'd learned the nightly routine and now did the cooking. The rations were the same every night. Canned beans and fruit, left-over biscuits, or in the case of tonight, some of the soda bread she'd baked at the Harpers', and whatever meat Jeremy managed to shoot along the way. Today he'd shot and cleaned a rabbit.

The rabbit roasted over the fire. Clara handed Jeremy a cup of coffee when he sat down on a log she'd dragged over to the fire.

"Thank you. You're getting good at this." He motioned around the fire with his cup of coffee. Her coffee also tasted ten times better than what he made.

"Thank you. I've never camped before, but I find I like it. There's something freeing about being out here without anyone around and fending for yourself." She spun the rabbit and went back to opening a can of peaches. An open can of beans sat at the edge of the fire warming.

"I take it your pa didn't take you camping?" He asked the question innocently, but he was curious about her family.

"No. He had very little time for any of us. Mother took care of us and was in charge of the ser-vants. She didn't even know a thing about Father's business." She shook her head. "When Father died and the lawyer arrived with the will and the accountant arrived with the business accounts, she was completely lost. I had to step in and explain things to her and then tell her what to do."

Jeremy scowled. "Didn't your father talk to your mother about business?"

She stared down into the fire, avoiding his gaze. Clara stirred the beans. He knew stall tactics when he saw them. But he had patience. If he waited quietly long enough, she would answer. He'd learned that about her on this trip.

"Father didn't talk to mother, or anyone, about the business, except the people he did business with. He seemed to think a woman was only good for making babies and then taking care of them." She frowned.

"What's bothering you?" He scooted to the end of the log to be closer to her. The expression on her face made him want to take her into his arms and hold her.

"He treated Mother, my sisters, and me like we were too dimwitted to understand things, but he had three women who worked in the office. He was always laughing and talking to them when I would walk in the office to hand in the day's tabulations." Her eyes narrowed. "And he would sometimes have his hand on their back or shoulder." She tipped her head and peered into his eyes. "I never saw him touch Mother."

Jeremy tamped down the disgust he felt toward the dead man. Clara's father sounded a lot like the uncle he and Darcy ran away from. Her story gave him a clearer idea of what Clara's life had been like and perhaps the reason her brother was in Alaska. He'd met many men who came up here to disappear.

This time he didn't hold back. The more he learned about her family the more he understood about Clara. Jeremy grasped Clara's hands and stood, pulling her up into his arms. "I've known men like your father. They treat the people dependent on them with less respect than they treat prostitutes and criminals."

She stiffened in his arms.

"I know speaking of a deceased person like this isn't kind." Jeremy kept his hands locked when she pushed against him with her arms. "But you have to see, what your parents had isn't a usual marriage. I've seen many like you've talked about, I've also seen many that are loving friendships."

He thought of Darcy and Gil and all the Halsey brothers' marriages. That was what he wanted. Clara had stopped struggling and peered up at him. *Are we building that same friendship?* Before he could question any farther, his body overrode his thoughts.

He lowered his head and kissed her bear grease covered lips. The greasy substance didn't take anything away from the way he felt when kissing her. With each kiss it was becoming clear, the struggle between his mind and his body was weakening. Clara was showing there was more to her than foolishness and rash behavior.

Jeremy drew out of the kiss, watching Clara. The dreamy expression on her face and slight smile on her lips, made his chest puff. *Yep, I'm slowly falling for this woman.*

"I think by that kiss, you might just think of me as more than a passing fancy," Clara said, her gaze lingering on his lips before searching his eyes.

"You just might be right." He dipped his head for another kiss. He couldn't get enough of this softer, loving side of Clara.

Her arms slipped around his waist. She clung tight. The salty taste of tears entered the kiss. He softened the kiss and cradled her head in his hands. Drawing back, he kept his gaze on her face. Her eyelids fluttered open, her lashes tipped with ice crystals from her tears and the cold.

"Why the tears? Did I do something wrong?" Jeremy's gut ached thinking he'd said or done something to make her sad.

"I'm happy. I've never known another person as intimately as I know you and that you feel the same…" She wiped her tears on his jacket. "I'm just overcome."

Clara's heart raced in her chest. She'd never felt so alive. Jeremy had strong feelings for her. As much as she didn't want to admit it, even to herself, she was falling hard for him. Watching him head for home while she and Randy headed to Seattle would not be easy. But she wouldn't stop him from going home. It was his plan before she came along.

Jeremy made her feel stronger, smarter than she'd ever believed herself to be. She'd spent the last twenty years believing she was only as good as her father told her she was. But this trip had proved to her she was better and stronger. She'd argued with her mother for a week before she'd given in and allowed Clara to make the plans.

The acrid scent of burnt meat stung her nostrils. "Oh! Dinner!" She pushed out of Jeremy's embrace and pulled the rabbit from the spit above the fire. One side was black, but they could eat the rest of the meat. She hadn't cooked a meal in her life until Father died. Then Mrs. Ladimer had shown her, Grace, and Mabel how to cook, knowing she would soon be leaving if they didn't get the business finances taken care of.

Jeremy took the rabbit from her and starting carving meat onto the tin plate she'd set out for that purpose. When he was finished carving, he tossed the rabbit carcass out onto the icy river.

Clara pulled the beans from the fire and stuck a spoon in the can. She spooned the peaches onto two plates and handed one to Jeremy. They added meat and beans to their plates and sat on the log side by side. She chewed and thought about the last two months while listening to the crackle of the fire and the dogs chewing on their meal. She shot a sideways glance at Jeremy. He was eating and staring into the fire. *Is he thinking about me as I think about him*? Her cheeks heated and she stared back down at her plate.

Last night, she'd learned a lot about herself. She never thought of herself as needing anyone or anything, but she had wanted everything Jeremy gave her. Thinking of the warmth and security she found in Jeremy's arms, her mind wandered to tonight's sleeping arrangements. Her cheeks heated. She could suggest they share a sleeping bag to keep them warmer. Sleeping in Jeremy's arms had become the best part of this trip. Until experiencing the contentment she found in his arms, she hadn't longed for it or known it was missing in her life.

She searched her childhood and could remember when her mother was happy, carefree, and anticipated her husband coming home. It had been since the birth of George, ten years ago, that her mother became fearful and Clara noticed less tolerance from her father.

"You want to share about the storm traveling across your face?" Jeremy asked, not looking at her and shoving a spoonful of peaches in his mouth.

Telling him all about her life just made her see how lacking it had been. And made her feel sorry for herself. Clara scanned Jeremy's profile. This man made her happy. Happier than she'd been in years. There was no way she'd burden him with her sorry life.

"No. Tell me more about your family." She took a bite of the rabbit to show she wasn't talking.

By the time they finished eating, Clara had a good picture of the warm family Jeremy's sister married into and the extended members who had joined through other marriages.

"When everyone gets together that must be a large group of people." She couldn't imagine the chaos Jeremy talked about with such pride.

"Yep. I'm really looking forward to seeing everyone after we find your brother." He smiled then his lips lost their curve and his gaze went dull.

"What's wrong? Is there someone you don't want to see?" she asked, noticing he put his plate down with unfinished food on it.

He stared at her over the brim of his coffee cup. The intense gaze made her fidget.

"No, I'm anxious to see everyone." His gaze flicked to the fire. "Just not looking forward to saying good-bye to you."

The statement caught her by surprise and sent a flock of pigeons loose in her chest. "You can always visit." She hoped the breathiness of her reply didn't reveal how she hoped he did come see her after the business was running. Maybe he'd even ask her to—no! She didn't want to be a wife. Not yet. She had too much to do before marriage stifled her.

He put his cup down and studied her face. A smile slowly crept from his lips to the corners of his silver eyes. "That's a darn good idea. I'll head home, say my howdy-do's, settle in, and come see how you're faring with the family and the business."

The twinkle in his eye and tone started the pigeons flapping in her chest again. Her father had run her life, telling her what she would and wouldn't do. She liked how Jeremy suggested things and complemented her on her ideas.

"That would be fun. I can't leave Seattle until the business is settled and Randy understands the day to day dealings. I don't know how long it will take to get the customers who left back once Randy dismisses the manager." She stabbed her spoon forcefully into her beans, splashing them into the fire. "Something I tried to do." The flames spit and the beans sizzled. Thinking of all the men who had put a stop to her trying to keep the business from going under lit her anger.

"I'll not have another man telling me what I can and can't do."

Jeremy snorted, and a belly laugh echoed through the dark of the night.

He thinks it's funny I can make my own decisions. Clara stood, slammed her plate into the pot of steaming water, and marched to the tent. Now that she knew life could be different than her mother experienced, there was no way she'd get tied to a man who thought her inferior.

In the tent, she plopped onto her sleeping bag and tugged at her boots, pulling them off her feet. She liked the fur boots Jeremy bought her. They were warmer and drier, and she could take them on and off easier because she only wore two pairs of socks. Taking off her parka, she heard the dishes twang and Jeremy muttering. She wiggled out of all her clothes but the union suit while lying on the sleeping bag. The tent they used kept the weather off but wasn't tall enough to stand in. Their personal packs stood against the wall on the other side of her sleeping bag, putting her in the middle. Jeremy's sleeping area was only a foot away from her. He didn't have any protection from the cold tent wall but didn't complain.

She slipped into her bag, her teeth chattering, and pulled the heavy bag up around her face. She loved the cushion of the sheep's wool that was between the canvas exterior and linen interior. The hard ground had a little give with the wool cushion.

The lantern light outside blinked off. The smell of the whale oil invaded the tent when Jeremy entered carrying one of the doused lanterns. He placed it to the side of the opening and crawled to his sleeping bag.

She turned, placing her back to him. A hand landed on her shoulder and she jumped.

"Sorry. Didn't mean to scare you." Jeremy rolled her to face him.

She couldn't see his face in the dark interior of the tent, but his hand remained on her shoulder. His uncertainty was revealed through his light touch.

He cleared his throat. "I'm not sure why you stomped off. I'm guessing you thought I was laughing at you. I wasn't. Honest. I was laughing because every one of the women the Halsey brothers married are outspoken, strong, and don't need a man." He squeezed her shoulder. "In a lot of ways you're like them. When you meet my sister you'll see I learned a long time ago you don't tell a woman what to do. I got knocked on my backside more than once learning that the hard way."

Clara wished she could see his eyes. He sounded sincere. "You really weren't laughing at me?"

"No. You might be small and look fragile as a porcelain doll, but I'd put my money on you in any situation."

He wasn't laughing at me. Joy circled in her heart.

"I'm sorry I stomped off. I was thinking about how my father treated the women in our family, and when I voiced my thought out loud and you laughed…" She sighed heavily. "I didn't realize how sheltered I've been or how tyrannical my father had been until his death and this trip."

Jeremy scooted over and pulled her into his

arms, sleeping bag and all. "I noticed you always ask about my family when I try to learn more about you."

Clara snuggled her head against his shoulder. He shivered.

"You're cold. Either get in your sleeping bag or get in mine," she ordered.

He released her, and Clara rolled onto her back, expecting him to slip in with her. He surprised her by shuffling his bag next to hers. Disappointment washed away some of her earlier joy, but when he placed his head next to hers, she turned toward him.

"Tell me about you as a child," he asked quietly, like they were swapping secrets.

At first Clara had a hard time bringing up memories of her childhood, but the longer she talked, the easier it became. Jeremy listened intently only asking questions that helped her see she had been strong and independent all along. This trip hadn't brought it out, only gave her a chance to see for herself.

"I've never had anyone listen to me and ask me my opinion like you did last night." Clara peered into the darkness trying to see Jeremy. "That was why I was so quiet and went to bed. I was comparing what I'd lived and what I was experiencing."

A soft flutter of a finger caressing her cheek proved Jeremy was still awake and listening. "What you experienced last night is what it should be like between two people who care about one another. At least all the ones I've ever been around."

She rubbed her cheek against his hand and recognized it was Jeremy's knuckles and not a finger.

"Last night I realized my mother hadn't been happy since George's birth ten years ago. It was after that Father became stricter and Mother fearful." She continued to rub against Jeremy's knuckles. The contact nudged away her sadness. "If I were home right now I'd ask her what happened."

"George made how many children in your family?" Jeremy's soft voice whispered.

"Six."

"From what you have said about your father, I would guess, perhaps your mother was not able to have any more children." Jeremy's hand opened, and he cupped the back of her head.

"But why would that change things between them?" Clara's mind raced to try and remember the days following George's birth. Her mother was kept to bed for two months.

Jeremy raised her head. His breath puffed against her lips. "From what you have said of your father, I would suspect he felt your mother lost much of her worth when she could no longer give him children."

Clara started to protest, but his lips pressed to hers. The dizzying kiss, spun her thoughts to the night before. She pulled back. "Why are you in your sleeping bag when you could be in mine?"

His lips rubbed hers and curved into a smile. "We need to sleep not keep each other up half the night."

He kissed her, again, short and sweet and disappeared into the darkness.

She groaned and Jeremy chuckled.

"Goodnight, Clara. Sweet dreams."

Clara smiled. The man always knew how to bring out the best and worst in her. The problem with that, she liked it too much.

Chapter Twenty-Nine

Bitter cold winds and snow storms slowed their progress for a week. If battling Mother Nature wasn't enough, Jeremy still heard the cries of the dog a wolf pack attacked one night. He ran out into the night in his union suit, shooting his rifle into the air. In the end, he'd had to shoot the dog. The pack had torn the animal up too much to save. The next day they moved items around lightening the load for the smaller string of dogs.

Six days later than he'd figured, they straggled into Dawson. Jeremy had never been so happy to see the military post that housed the Northwest Mounted Police and behind that, the nearly three hundred log buildings of various sizes and shapes. He usually only stopped long enough to drop off his freight, get paid, eat a good meal, and bathe. But this trip he had Clara to think about. And they had to decide the best way to find her brother. There was a good chance he'd been in Dawson a time or two since coming north looking for gold. If they checked around they might get a lead that would catch them up to Randy sooner.

He headed straight to Brightly's Saloon to drop off the sleds with the saloon owner's goods. The town was twice the size it had been the last time he'd been here. More wooden buildings stood and more tents scattered around the edges. Even for the amount of snow on the ground people were on a continuous prowl.

"You got supplies!" a man shouted and people swarmed the sleds.

Jeremy pulled out his rifle and fired it into the air. "Get back! I have merchandise for Brightly at the Saloon, nothing more." He stared into gaunt faces. Were they running short on supplies?

A Northwest Mountie stepped through the group still circled around the sleds. "Move on. Let the man go about his business. If he had food supplies he wouldn't be taking them to the likes of Brightly."

"Thank you," Jeremy said, and as soon as the crowd parted headed his team down the street, making sure Clara was right behind him.

Jeremy stopped the dogs in front of the saloon. Music from a hurdy gurdy machine whined as a man stepped out of the establishment.

"What is that noise?" Clara asked, drawing her sleds to a stop beside his.

"It's a hurdy gurdy. A musical instrument. I brought it in with freight last fall." Jeremy glanced up and down the busy street. He didn't want to leave their supplies on the street unguarded after the scene moments ago. The supply boats must not have made it up river before the water froze over.

Leaving Clara unguarded wasn't in his plan either. Her appearance was that of a small man or young man, but if she talked or anyone came close they would know she was a woman.

Several men came down the street and turned toward the saloon.

"Could I speak to one of you?" Jeremy called out, then turned to Clara. "Keep your head down and don't speak."

She nodded and fidgeted with a rope on the sled.

"Yeah? What do you want?" The largest man in the group approached.

"When you go in there could you tell Brightly that Jeremy Duncan is here with his freight?" Jeremy stood between the man and Clara.

The man's gaze roamed over the dogs and sleds and shrugged. "If I see him, I'll tell him." He rejoined his friends. They all laughed and walked into the saloon.

The hair on Jeremy's neck tingled. That man wouldn't say a word to Brightly. Scanning the street, he caught sight of a boy. Jeremy whistled and waved the boy over.

"What you want?" the boy asked, wiping his snotty nose on his ragged coat sleeve.

"I'll give you a dollar if you go in there and bring Brightly out to me," Jeremy held up a silver dollar.

"Money won't buy nothin' in this town. You

got flour?" The boy nodded toward the sleds.

"You bring Brightly out, and I'll give you five pounds of flour, but you can't tell anyone."

The boy stuck out his hand. "Deal."

They shook and he jogged up to the saloon door, disappearing inside.

"He's a better choice than that man," Clara said, stepping up next to Jeremy.

"Yeah, I didn't think about the trouble I'd have just dropping off the freight." Jeremy peered down into Clara's face. Her eyelids were half closed, her lips covered with bear grease, and her cheeks red from the wind. She deserved a week's rest.

"Once we get this unloaded and find a secure place for our supplies, we'll find a nice hotel and rest," he promised. Heavy footsteps behind, spun him to the saloon.

"Duncan! I heard there was quite a storm your way. I didn't expect you to get here before my deadline." Brightly walked forward, his hand extended. The boy trotted by the big man's side.

Brightly was a head taller than Jeremy and three times as wide. He was a formidable looking man with bushy blonde hair and deep blue eyes. But he always treated Jeremy fairly and had a good sense of humor.

Jeremy shook the man's hand. "I set out as soon as there was a lull in the storm. This is my last haul, and I wanted to finish on time." He turned his attention to the boy. "Stay with my friend, and we'll take care of you when we finish with Brightly."

The boy nodded and stood beside Clara.

Jeremy motioned to the three sleds carrying the

saloon's freight. "These are all yours."

"Fine, bring the sleds around back and we'll settle up." Brightly glanced at Clara before he turned back to the saloon.

"Follow me," Jeremy said to Clara and led his dogs and sleds down the alley between the saloon and the building next door.

They stood in the alley behind the building for five minutes before the back door opened and Brightly's saloon manager, Tag Arnold, stepped out with a paper in his hand.

"I'll check off the goods as you two carry it in." Arnold motioned to Clara.

Anger seared Jeremy's gut. "No. Go hire a couple of the men inside to haul it in for you. My job was to deliver, not haul it into the saloon."

The man chomped down on a cigar and glared.

Jeremy stood his ground. After several minutes of silent glaring, Arnold spun on his heel and stomped into the building.

"He looked angry," Clara said at his side.

"I've never had to unload the merchandise before, and I'm not making you haul it. You need a bath and a bed to rest." Jeremy wrapped an arm around Clara's shoulders and waited.

The boy cleared his throat.

"Let's settle up with this young man before they come back." Jeremy and Clara dug into the food supply pack and dug out a five pound sack of flour.

"Don't tell anyone but your folks where you got it from. We don't need every hungry person in Dawson trying to steal from us. We're just passing through." Jeremy handed the sack to the boy, who nodded and headed down the back alleys. He had the good sense to not carry the sack out where many could see it.

Jeremy recovered the supply sled and uncovered the sleds with Brightly's goods. He was ready to leave the sleds and find a hotel when the manager returned with two men.

Jeremy made sure the men took the items off the sleds without damaging them. Glancing up, he noticed Clara stood just behind Arnold and to the side, watching him tally the merchandise.

The men picked up the last two items, carrying them into the saloon.

Arnold tapped his pencil on the paper. "You're missing two boxes."

Jeremy strode over to the man, tamping down a wave of rage. "Are you accusing me of stealing?"

"No. He isn't." Clara stepped forward. "Mr. ..."

"Arnold." The manager stared at Clara and took a step back. "Who are you?"

"She's with me." Jeremy put his body between Clara and Arnold.

Clara put a hand on Jeremy's arm, gently moving him to the side. "Mr. Arnold, that paper has twenty five boxes and crates listed. If you go inside you will see that twenty-five were unloaded. You are the one who lost track."

Jeremy couldn't stop the smile stretching the corners of his lips from cheek to cheek. He had no doubt she was good at her job in the warehouse.

"My payment, please." Jeremy held out his hand, waiting.

The man shook his head, but placed a leather pouch in Jeremy's glove.

Jeremy opened the pouch, saw the gold dust, and then hefted it in his hand. Over the years he'd learned the weight for certain sums, and this felt close enough to the double rate.

"Thank you." He took Clara's hand and led her to the team of empty sleds. "Follow me."

He took control of the sleds with their supplies, leading the dogs back out into the street. The livery where he usually kept his horses was the best place to keep the dogs and the supplies until they were ready to leave.

Clara grasped the lead dog's leather, patted his head, and led him down the alley behind Jeremy. She hoped they found a hotel soon. Her legs grew heavier with each step, and her eyelids harder to keep open. The last two nights she'd slept little because of the howling wind and worrying about the arrival of her monthly time. The first time had been light, but she was running out of petticoats to tear up and use for rags. They never stopped long enough anywhere during her time for her to wash them. Rather than try and hide them from Jeremy, she'd discarded the used ones along the trail.

She always had a lack of energy during this time, but adding that onto her lack of sleep and added activity, she had little energy.

They finally stopped at a large, well-maintained livery. Clara found an upturned crate and sat on that while watching Jeremy deal with the man wearing a smithy's apron over several layers of clothes.

She leaned her head against a post and watched

the men move about unharnessing the dogs, stack-
ing the empty sleds near other sleds, and then placing the loaded sleds in a stall. The scene played out
like a dream. The visions drifted in and out of her
mind along with spaces of white.

"Clara? Sweetheart?"

Someone shook her shoulder, and her head
slipped off the post, toppling her over.

"Whoa." Strong hands caught her. "Clara, wake
up. We're going to the hotel now."

She struggled to gain consciousness. Fighting
against her heavy eyelids, she lifted one, then the
other and peered into Jeremy's intense gaze.

"Are you well?" he asked, pushing wayward
strands of her hair off her face.

"I'm just worn out." She licked her lips. The
nasty taste of the bear grease registered. The oint-
ment was smelly and tasted worse, but it did keep
her lips from cracking and chapping.

"What's the closest nice hotel?" Jeremy directed his comment to the man who stood behind him.

"The Westminster. About a block down on the
right." The smithy was flat-out staring at her, but
she didn't care.

"I'll settle Clara then come back for this pack."

Clara tilted her head and saw the canvas pack
with her clothing sat beside Jeremy.

She shook her head and whispered. "Don't
leave it."

Jeremy leaned closer and whispered back,
"Why?"

"It has your payment in it," she replied only for
Jeremy's ears.

"It's fine." Jeremy kissed her cheek, helped her to her feet, and walked toward the door with one of his arms wrapped around her waist. "I'll be back. Don't let anyone near that pack, Clara's afraid they might take her corset."

She smiled at his joke and wrapped an arm around his waist. Once they were settled in the hotel room, she'd take a nap then get cleaned up. Jeremy would take care of their belongings. She could get used to having him around to take care of things.

Clara woke with a start. The lantern light seemed overly bright. She blinked and turned her head. The room had a heavy dark wood wardrobe and log walls.

She sat up. Heat and wet between her legs shot her off the bed.

"How long have I been sleeping," she croaked and scanned the room for her pack. Her parka draped over a chair and her boots stood alongside. She walked over to the wardrobe and flung the doors open. Her clothes were folded and hung in the massive piece of furniture. A smile tipped her lips.

Jeremy was so thoughtful. She spotted the last of her torn petticoat neatly stacked and grabbed two of the folded rectangles, shoving them inside her shirt. Next—find a lavatory. She opened the door to the hallway and peered out. There were numbered doors up and down the hall. *Surely, there was a lavatory on one end?*

She shuffled down the hall worrying about the soiled wad of rags between her legs falling out. The good thing about wearing men's clothes—they held the rags in place better than her open-crotched drawers. At home, she usually stayed home from work the first two days of her monthly. It was too hard to deal with while moving about as she did for her job.

The last two doors on either side of the hall had signs. One had a sign with lovely gold lettering: LAVATORY. The door across the hall: BATH. She opened the door to the bath to take a peek. It was a long, deep, metal tub with faucets. Who would have thought she'd find such luxury in the middle of the Yukon?

Closing the door, she heard a noise down the hall. She glanced up and spotted Jeremy walking to her room. *Dare I call to him?*

He knocked on the door, then entered. Clara didn't even have time to turn the knob on the lavatory before he rushed back out into the hallway.

"Jeremy!" she called, only loud enough he would hear.

His silvery gaze found her, and his long legs carried him to her in quick order.

"I wondered where you went." He laid a palm against her cheek. "How are you feeling?"

"Better. I need to use this room, then I'd love to take a bath." She peered into his worried eyes and smiled. "I'll be fine after a couple night's sleep in a bed."

"I'll start the water and get your clothes."

"You don't have to do that. Besides you don't know what I want to wear."

"You'll want all your women clothes." His left eyebrow rose.

A laugh burst from her chest. "Yes. I'm in civilization, I'd like to dress like a woman." She opened the lavatory door. "I'll be in the room in a minute to get my things."

She closed the door on his concerned face and tended to business.

Back in the room, she gathered up her under-garments and the wool dress. If she had another clean union suit she'd wear it under the dress…

Jeremy entered the room. "I hope you don't mind, I put us down as husband and wife again. I don't like the idea of you alone and so many men around."

Clara glanced over her shoulder. His stance and set to his chin weren't apologetic. Whether she liked it or not, he wasn't letting her out of his sight. She smiled. "That's fine. I've become used to your snoring and slovenly ways."

She burst out laughing when his expression slackened and his eyes lit for a rebuttal.

"I don't snore, and you can't say I'm slovenly. You're the one that leaves your clothes all over the place."

With her garments hanging over one arm, she walked up to him and grabbed the beard he'd let grow rather than try and keep it shaved on the trail. "I'd like to look at your face and not this beast now that you have the facilities to shave."

He grabbed her up in his arms, dangling her feet off the floor. "I'll show you what a beast is like." Jeremy rubbed his wiry beard against her cheeks.

"Put me down!" She kicked and shoved with

her arms.

He eventually slid her down his front.

"Go get that bath, you smell worse than the dogs. Makes me wonder how you can come off calling me a beast." He winked.

If the wink hadn't told her he was kidding, the tone of his voice and sparkle in his eyes would have.

"Could you do me a favor while I'm bathing?"

"I can try."

"Would you purchase two more sets of men's small union suits for me? They are warmer than my undergarments, I'd like to wear one under my dress." She blushed at the way he watched her.

"I'm not sure I like the idea of you wearing men's undergarments all the time." He smiled slyly. "I like the feel of some of your undergarments."

"Oh!" She slapped his arm and left the room. His chuckle followed her down the hall and into the bathing room.

She locked the door and turned to the steaming tub of water. She usually didn't soak in a tub when on her monthly, but she couldn't wait to slip into the warm water and soak the weeks of sweat off. Even though they'd traveled through storms and bitter cold winds, she found the exertions and layers of clothes quite often left her sweating. She reeked. Each layer she took off added more foul odors to the room.

"I wish I had some lovely smelling salts to add to the water." She stepped out of the union suit and into the water, grabbing up her bar of soap.

"Ohh…" She leaned back, wetting her hair.

Just the silken feel of the water sloughing the sweat away was heavenly. Lathering her hands, she set to work cleaning her hair. Once all the strands were slick with soap, she dunked her head and rinsed.

Dallying hadn't been on her mind when she stepped in the tub, but as her body warmed and kinks and knots loosened, she lingered, enjoying the heat and warmth.

Three sharp raps shot her to a sitting position.

"Whose there?" she asked.

"Jeremy. I have the item you asked for."

"Just a minute." Clara stood and noticed the water was tinged pink. Embarrassed, she pulled the plug and stepped out. A shelf had several folded linens. She grabbed one and wrapped it around her body before taking the two steps to the door. The lock clicked free under her trembling fingers. Jeremy's head appeared through the opening of the door.

"You okay?"

"I'm fine." She held out her hand to take the union suit, but his gaze searched the room.

"Why is there a dark spot on the floor?" He pushed into the room.

Clara shoved the door shut, mortified that he'd…that she…Her face heated, and she spun around to find him staring at the soiled rags with her clothing.

Chapter Thirty

Jeremy studied the bloody rag a moment and it all made sense. Why Clara had been so slow and drained of energy. Having been on the move at a young age with his older sister, he knew all about women's monthlies. In fact, more than most men cared to ever know, or did know after years of marriage.

He also knew women could be touchier about what a man said at this time. Keeping his face calm, he turned to Clara. Her usually pale complexion shone a bright red. Her eyes were downcast.

"Why didn't you tell me about your condition?"

Her head popped up, and her wide eyes stared at him. Her mouth hung open just enough to make him wish he had her in his arms to kiss.

"H-how? I'm not…"

"I grew up with an older sister dragging me all over the place. She never kept anything from me and taught me what I know about men…and women." Jeremy took her by the shoulders. "Get dressed while I clean this up."

She dropped to her knees beside him. "No, you don't have to clean up after me. Go to the room. I'll be along shortly."

He heard the conviction in her voice. One of these days she'd understand he didn't mind helping her. But he also knew women tended to think the reason they were able to have babies was a mystery only they could share.

Jeremy kissed the top of her head. "I'll go. But if you take too long, I'm coming back."

"I won't be long, I promise." Clara stared into his eyes.

"Good. Because I have a wonderful dinner planned for you." He stood and walked to the door. "Lock this behind me."

She rose to move to the door and he exited.

In the hall, he leaned against the wall, waiting until he heard the lock click and Clara moving around inside before he pushed away and headed to the stairs. This new discovery changed his dinner plans. He grabbed his coat from the room and took the stairs two at a time to the lobby.

While purchasing the union suits, he'd found a small restaurant and had bargained for a good meal by giving the owner some of their supplies. Rather than bring Clara down to the restaurant, he'd see if they would deliver to the room.

"You're early," said Mrs. Warren the restaurant proprietor. "I haven't started the preparations."

"I'd like to ask another favor." Jeremy pulled

out the sack of gold he earned for delivering Brightly's goods. "Is there a chance I could get you to
deliver our dinner to the Westminster Hotel room
two-oh-six?"

The woman nodded. "I'll deliver it at seven."

"I appreciate your extra effort." Jeremy poured
a small mound of gold in the woman's palm and left
the establishment, whistling.

At the hotel, Jeremy jogged back up the stairs
and entered their room. Clara wasn't back yet. He
glanced around the room and set about moving the
small table by the bed to a corner where he could
put the chair on one side of the table. *I need another
chair.*

There were chairs placed along the wall in the
hallway. He ducked out of the room and grabbed the
nearest one. Tonight they would eat at a table and
enjoy food that they didn't have to prepare. Dawson City was a growing town because of the gold
seekers, but for all the gold, it seemed they were
poor when it came to food supplies. He'd learned
from Mrs. Warren that most of the restaurants were
barely able to feed the hordes spending the winter
in town. They were down to meager supplies and
worried they weren't going to make it until the river
thawed and the boats could make it upstream. It
was worth giving the woman some of their supplies,
so they could eat something other than beans, biscuits, and canned fruit.

The door opened. Clara stepped into the room,
her dirty clothes in a bundle in one arm.

"Toss that over there with my dirty clothes. I'll
have someone take them to be laundered."

"What are you doing?" She placed her clothes on his and stood by the door watching him move furniture.

"I ordered dinner be delivered to the room. We can stay here, eat, and go to bed early." Jeremy picked up a pad of paper and pencil he'd bought while getting the union suits. "Rather than run around asking all over the place about your brother, I thought we could write up a query to put in the newspaper, asking anyone who has met Randy Bixbee to come by the Westminster and ask for me."

Clara sat on one of the chairs. "How do you know the right people will read the announcement?"

"We'll give it a couple of days and if no one comes forward, then we'll start asking around. One thing I've noticed, unless a man is illiterate, everyone up here reads whatever they can get their hands on. They'll read a year-old newspaper over and over again. Granted the information is months old, but everyone here craves news from home."

Jeremy sat down across the table from her and started writing. "Where all has your brother been?"

Her brow scrunched and her nose crinkled as she thought. "He was at Circle City first, then Forty Mile." She traced the pattern on the table cloth with her finger. "Where he is now, I don't know." Clara raised her scared eyes to his. "Do you think he's dead?"

He didn't want to lie, but he also didn't want to dash her hopes. "It's hard to say. Since you haven't heard from him in some time that could be a possibility."

Tears glistened in her eyes.

"But he could also have staked a claim far from any of the settlements, got a partner, and doesn't travel to the settlements."

Jeremy reached across the table and captured her hand in his. "We'll find the truth and proceed with the information." He spun the paper on the table. "Read this and make any additions or changes you want."

Clara released his hand and picked up the paper. She read through it, then picked up the pencil, bowed her head over the paper, and began changing and adding.

He smiled watching her think then change a sentence here and there. He'd intentionally written the announcement fast and without much thought. The hasty missive gave Clara something to focus on while they waited for dinner.

Knocking on the door drew him out of his own thoughts of what could have happened to Randy.

Jeremy answered the door and was pleased to see Mrs. Warren. She had a basket over one arm.

"I've brought your dinner as you asked. Just return the dishes and basket to me tomorrow." She stared past his head and smiled.

"Thank you," Clara called out.

"Thank you," Jeremy said, taking the basket from the woman. "Could you tell me the closest laundry?"

"The closest will be the most expensive. If you don't mind walking to the end of Main Street, my friend Mrs. Burly does laundry better and for less money." Mrs. Warren nodded and left.

Jeremy closed the door and crossed the room.

Clara whisked the paper out of the way, and he placed the basket on the table.

She raised the towel over the top and sniffed. "This smells delicious. How did you get that woman to deliver food?" She set the food out and then napkins, utensils, glasses, and a jar of milk.

"Oh! Look, Jeremy, milk!" Clara clapped her hands. "And roast, carrots and potatoes, and leavened bread!"

She peered into the basket and grinned. "And apple cake!"

Jeremy's mouth watered at the sight and hearty aromas. "Mrs. Warren out did herself. I gave her flour, sugar, powdered milk, and butter. She made the wonderful dishes."

"I wondered how she could make such a wonderful meal when the crowd in the street were starving." Clara stared at her plate. "This almost makes me feel guilty."

Jeremy took her hand. "Don't feel guilty. You and I had the forethought to purchase supplies you'll need to find your brother and get to St. Michael. It's not your fault others didn't bring in the right amount of supplies, or that the boats didn't make the last run."

He stared at the food. How long since he'd had a meal like this? Eight months? Ten? The last time he was in Dawson City. Once he returned to Sumpter he would never eat another biscuit or hunk of jerky.

Clara clasped her hands and bowed her head. Jeremy did likewise. He and Darcy hadn't been much for praying over their meals. They had prayed before, hoping they had a next meal. But as an adult he liked the idea. Especially now that he could thank God for keeping him safe to return home.

Prayers done, they both stabbed a carrot and started in on the dinner. Jeremy didn't say a word as he slowly worked his way through the food on the plate in front of him. He was pretty sure he'd never tasted anything as wonderful. Not even his sister-in-laws' cooking.

He shoved the empty plate to the side and set the cake plate in front of him. His mouth watered thinking about sinking his teeth into the dense, moist dessert.

"I'm full. Do you want to finish this before you eat the cake?" Clara shoved her plate to him. She'd eaten two slices of moose roast, half the potatoes, and two slices of bread. "I ate too much bread to finish. I'll eat the cake later."

"Once I eat my cake I'm done." He stuck his fork into the dessert.

"It seems a waste to let this go uneaten…" She stared at the food on her plate.

"You don't have to eat it all if you're full." He slipped the bite in his mouth and closed his eyes. This was almost as good as kissing Clara.

"I could wrap the food up and save it for tomorrow or find someone who is hungry." She wrapped the bread in her napkin.

"Clara. Don't. We'll be here several days and take our meals at Mrs. Warren's. She'll keep us fed if we pay and give her supplies." Jeremy would have thought coming from her lifestyle she wouldn't think twice about leftovers.

"Meals that I'll have to pay for." Her eyes remained downcast as she again traced the pattern on the table cloth with a finger. "The only money I have left is yours. What I owe you for guiding me. I can't afford meals like this until we find Randy."

"Look at me." He waited, hoping she didn't take what he had to say wrong. Otherwise, she'd balk, thinking he saw her as charity.

Gradually, her chin raised and her gaze met his.

"You stopped being a job to me the second day on the trail when I saw you weren't going to be a burden and you took on some of the chores. At that point, I considered you a partner and not an employer." He put down the fork and grasped her hands. "As far as I'm concerned, you earned half the money from Brightly. So enjoy the meals while you can because we don't know where we'll have to travel to find your brother."

A tear slipped down her cheek. "Thank you," she whispered.

"Aw, hell, don't cry." Jeremy stood, scooped her into his arms, and kissed the tears from her face.

Her small hands grasped his face, and she drew out of the kiss. "I like you better without a beard."

"I didn't see you refusing any kisses while I had a beard." He raised an eyebrow and moved to capture her lips.

She held him back. Her green eyes sparkled. "I was willing to overlook the beard and the smell to kiss you."

He frowned. "Smell? Woman, you weren't smelling too sweet either."

Her eyelids drifted half closed. "I know. I can't

imagine how you tolerated me.”

"I held my breath.”

Clara shoved him backwards. He let her fall from his arms, but made sure she landed on her feet.

"That wasn't nice!" Clara plopped down on the edge of the bed.

He smiled back. This was a side to her that intrigued him. She'd shown fire before but this was different. She wasn't just angry, she acted like she wanted to fight with him to make up. He'd never had a love interest before and the idea set his mind to all kinds of images.

"I'd like privacy to change into my nightclothes." She sat primly on the side of the bed, glaring.

"You just got dressed not an hour ago. Why didn't you put your nightclothes on after the bath?" He leaned back against the door, crossing his arms and ankles.

 Indignation lit her eyes. "It wouldn't be proper to eat my dinner in my nightclothes.”

Jeremy had all kinds of improper things he wanted to do to her. However, he was rational enough to know they shouldn't happen. "No one would have known.”

A large sigh fluttered her pink lips. "The woman who delivered the dinner would have seen me sitting in my nightclothes.”

"And thought we were married and that I'd been a wonderful husband by having your dinner brought to you." He was starting to believe they were married. Starting to think she might fit in with the Halsey women.

"But we aren't married." She sighed. "And while we've gone beyond what is proper while on the trail, I'd like to have a semblance of normalcy tonight."

That snapped his control. "Do you want me to get another room?" He would if she insisted, but he didn't want to change the charade. As much as it shocked him to realize it, he could see a future with this woman at his side.

She shook her head. "No. I don't think I could sleep if I were in this room alone." Longing flickered in her eyes. "You can stay here an-and sleep in this bed." Her hand moved back and forth across the coverlet. "But, please, can you give me some time to change, alone?"

He couldn't ignore the longing or the heartfelt plea. Jeremy shoved away from the door and walked over to the table where the announcement lay.

"Have you finished this?"

"Yes."

"I'll take it to the newspaper office." He grabbed his coat and hat. "I'll be back in an hour."

"Thank you."

The relief and softening of her face drew him back across the room. He cupped her chin and tilted her face upwards. Leaning down, he placed a chaste kiss on her sweet mouth.

"I'm glad you don't want me to move to another room." He kissed her again, just as soft, and left the room. In the hall, he leaned against the door and took in several deep breaths.

This could be our last night together.

He wasn't sure when it happened or how, but the thought of sending her off with her brother was causing an ache in his chest that was completely unexpected.

Chapter Thirty-One

Clara quickly undressed. She left the union suit on under her nightgown to help hold the rags in place. Noise outside the window caught her attention. She pushed aside the lace curtain and peered into the street. Boisterous voices carried on the cold night air along with the music she'd heard coming from saloons.

She put her clothes away and pulled back the covers on the bed. "Should I leave the lantern on?" Without light Jeremy would be noisy when he returned.

Her thoughts turned to the man. He had taken her bleeding and the mess it entailed without blinking, running, or deriding her. Mother had always talked of this time in a woman's life like a curse. She'd hidden herself away from her husband and had little contact with the children. Other than the inconvenience, her mother had been the driving force that insisted Clara not go to work the days she was bleeding. And had kept both Clara and her sisters, as they each came of the age, from attending social functions while their monthlies visited.

What an unusual relationship Jeremy and his sister had. That she allowed him to know so much of a woman's world intrigued Clara. She wanted to meet this person. Wanted to meet all the family members Jeremy spoke so openly and lovingly about.

She loved her family but not with the same intensity that Jeremy bestowed on his family. What would it be like to live in a family that so openly adored one another?

Her eyelids grew heavier.

Clara slipped under the covers and snuggled into the soft mattress. It was heavenly compared to the hard ground they'd been sleeping on. She missed the sound of Jeremy's breathing. But he'd soon join her. The knowledge fluttered her insides. In the nearly three months they'd been traveling together, she'd fallen in love with him. Knowing her need to be in Seattle and his desire to get home, she didn't see a future for them and that caused the fluttering to turn to pricks of pain.

She curled into a ball and squeezed her eyes shut. Thinking about parting hurt too much. She'd rather think about him joining her in the bed. Her monthly made her more emotional and shyer about having his hands roaming about her body.

Clara snuggled under the covers, listened to the outside noise and the steam radiator heating the room, and waited for sleep to overtake her.

The click of the door lock and the thud of boots hitting the floor, pulled Clara from her fitful slumber. She remained still, listening to Jeremy's movements. The rustle of clothing told her he was undressing. A creak registered his approach to the bed. The light blinked off. The mattress dipped and groaned on his side.

Clara remained curled, facing away from Jeremy's side of the bed. She evened her breathing and waited. The bed wiggled. Jeremy's body curled around hers along with the spicy scent of his shave cream, making her feel safe and cared for.

Jeremy kissed her neck and settled behind her.

She grasped his hand, lacing her fingers with his and held their hands against her chest before falling asleep.

The next time Clara woke she was alone in the bed. She listened. The only sound was activity in the street below and the heat register. The gray dawn of a new day gave enough light in the room for her to know it was mid-morning. Why had Jeremy let her sleep so long?

She slipped out of bed and glanced at the chairs. That was where it sounded like he'd undressed the night before. His clothes were gone. In three strides, she stood at the wardrobe. She donned her clothing, combed her hair, braiding it into one plait, and pulled on her button shoes.

A trip to the lavatory was due then she'd look for Jeremy in the lobby.

She finished her business, went back to the room and collected a shawl and her pocketbook. Clara closed the door to their room, wrapped the shawl around her shoulders, and headed to the stairs. The hallway had proven colder than the room. She found the lobby even colder. The door opened and closed three times by the time she'd crossed the area to the desk.

"Did Mr. Duncan leave a message for me?" she asked the clerk behind the counter.

"Yes. He paid for your breakfast in the restaurant at the back corner of the hotel. You're to go in and eat. He will be back by eleven." The clerk smiled and motioned to the back of the building.

She peered down the dark hall. "That will take me to the restaurant?"

"Yes. There is a door from the hallway into the restaurant."

"Did he say where he was going?" She didn't like asking. And the way the clerk's eyebrow rose made her even more uncomfortable.

"He was headed to the livery to take care of the dogs."

She smiled at the clerk. "I guess if I hadn't been so tired, I would have remembered him telling me that last night. Thank you."

He smiled back seeming to take that as a good excuse for not knowing what her husband was up to.

Clara marched down the dark hallway, took a deep breath, and pushed the door open to the restaurant. A round woman with a dirty apron and big smile met her.

"Are you here for breakfast?"

"Yes. My husband, Jeremy Duncan, already paid for it."

The woman giggled. "Oh my, yes! He is a charmer that one." The woman spun on her tiny feet. "I have a nice table away from the drafty door."

Clara fell in step behind her and sat at a small table near the kitchen door.

The woman snatched a pot of coffee off a potbelly stove warming the room. "Here's some warm water. I'll bring you some tea and your food."

Clara nodded and scanned the other customers in the restaurant. Three men in red uniforms caught her attention. They had to be Northwest Mounted Police. One man was older, in his forties perhaps, the other two appeared to be closer to her age. A blush heated her cheeks when the two younger men caught her staring at them.

They both smiled and tipped their heads her direction.

Clara snapped her gaze from them to the small window looking out on the street. The woman returned with a soft boiled egg, toast, jelly, and tea leaves.

"This looks wonderful! I haven't had an egg since leaving Seattle."

"I've been able to keep a few chickens. But not many are willing to pay what I ask for an egg." The woman smiled warmly. "You are a lucky woman. Your husband told me he'd pay my price to give you an egg."

Clara blushed. Knowing the egg was expensive

made her fearful of eating it. *But if Jeremy did pay a ridiculous price for the egg, I should eat it.* She dipped her spoon into the yolk, put the bite in her mouth, and closed her eyes, savoring the flavor. If she'd been told how much she would miss certain foods, she wouldn't have believed it. Now, she would never take anything for granted having spent the past two months living off the same rations and sleeping in the cold on the hard ground.

She had one slice of toast to eat when she looked up. The two younger officers stood at her table. Clara took a sip of tea to wash the food down and smiled at them.

"We couldn't help but notice you're sitting alone. Would you mind if we kept you company?" the darker of the two asked, grabbing the back of a chair and pulling it away from the table.

Before she could answer, a hand rested on her shoulder and a kiss buzzed her cheek.

"My wife and I would be honored to visit with you." Jeremy took the seat next to her and motioned for the men to be seated.

"We should get back to the station," the blonde one said, tugging on the other officer's sleeve.

"Yes, we should go."

The two spun on their heels and strode out the door.

Clara turned to Jeremy, he was staring after them with a dark expression on his face.

"I haven't finished eating. Do you want anything?" she asked, smiling behind her tea cup. It appeared Jeremy was jealous.

"Why did those two think you needed company?" He turned his silver gaze on her.

She swept her hand to encompass the room. "Do you see any other females? Perhaps they thought I looked lonely." Placing her hand on his arm, she leaned close. "I woke to an empty bed and felt forgotten until I discovered you had my comforts arranged for me." She kissed his cheek. "Thank you."

Clara's innocent kiss twisted Jeremy's thoughts from anger and jealousy to flaring desire. The clatter of dishes stopped him from cupping her head and kissing her with abandon. He'd held her close all night, enjoying her soft curves tucked against him. Waking, he'd decided a walk in the frigid Dawson City dawn would cool his ardor. And it had, until he walked into the restaurant and saw the two officers hovering at Clara's table.

"You're welcome. Finish eating." He leaned back in his chair and pulled a newspaper out of his pocket and began reading.

Clara squeezed his arm. "Did they put our announcement in there?"

"Yes. They even featured it on the inside page." Jeremy pointed his gaze at her plate. "Eat."

He waited until she picked up the toast and spread jelly on it before he went back to reading the paper.

The woman he'd visited with earlier while bartering for Clara's breakfast walked up to the table. "Coffee for me, please."

"I'm sorry but all we have is tea." She smiled pleasantly, no doubt, hoping he'd offer that up from his supplies, as he had a pound of butter.

"Tea will be fine." If he kept handing out their supplies, Clara and her brother wouldn't have enough to make it to St. Michael.

He placed the paper on the table with the advertisement face up.

Clara picked the paper up and read. "It reads well," she said, her brow furrowed. "Why did you take out the section mentioning his family is looking for him?"

"Most would read that to mean there's an inheritance. We don't want someone getting the idea either of us, or Randy, are worth a lot of money. This way it looks like we want information to discover what happened to him and nothing more."

She nodded her head. "I see. That's a good idea." Placing the paper back on the table she peered into his face. "Do you think we'll learn anything from this?"

"If he's been in town at all, someone will have some information."

The woman returned with a cup and a pot of tea.

"Thank you." Jeremy replenished Clara's cup then poured a cup for himself. He leaned back in the chair and studied the people in the restaurant. He and Clara were the only couple. Several of the well-dressed men in the room gave them curious glances and lingered their gazes on Clara.

The men who had stood at this table when he arrived and the glances by the other men in the room clenched the fact he wasn't letting Clara out of his sight when out in the public. He didn't believe for a minute she would go with another man, but he knew there were some men who didn't take no for an answer.

"Jeremy, what's wrong? You've got a dark look on your face like when the police officers were standing at the table." Clara set her cup down and placed both hands on his arm. "You've nothing to be jealous about. I don't care for advances from men."

He patted her hands. "I know. But there are some men who don't listen when a woman says no."

"I promise I won't go anywhere with anyone but you." She smiled.

His mood lightened. He bathed in the glow of her smile and raised her hand to his lips. "That's good to hear. Would you like to look around Dawson while we wait for someone to respond to the advertisement?"

"I would love to see Dawson with you. But I'll need my coat."

She started to stand. He shot to his feet to draw back her chair. Jeremy extended his crooked arm, and she slid her hand through his arm. They left the restaurant, walked through the hall and lobby, and up the stairs to their room.

Inside, she blushed and moved to the wardrobe. "I need to freshen up before we go outside."

Jeremy took a seat in the chair. "I'll be right here when you're ready." He saw she clutched a handbag as she dropped her shawl on the bed and headed for the door. A smile crept across his face. He'd noticed when Darcy married, she did similar things when on her monthly. It was a natural thing, or so Darcy told him all those years ago, so why did women make it so mysterious?

Five minutes passed when he began to wonder if he should check on Clara. The door knob turned and she entered. She crossed to the wardrobe and blocked his view of the interior as she rummaged around inside the piece of furniture, before closing the door and facing him.

Jeremy took her coat down from the peg by the door and held it out.

Clara slid her arms in and drew the strings tight on the hood.

He pulled on his coat and opened the door. With his hand on Clara's back, he directed her to the stairs, through the lobby, and out into the busy street.

He'd planned to take her to First Street where he'd noticed several sweet shops and a jewelry store. But Clara started down the street the opposite direction. He held tight to her arm linked through his as they weaved in and out of the people surging along the board walks and snow-packed paths.

"This is a big city," Clara said, standing in front of the Alaska Commercial Co. "I can't believe all the restaurants. And look there's a milliner, there's a dressmaker, and that street of saloons." She shook her head. "Other than all the saloons this is like walking around Seattle, only the streets are more primitive."

"I know a street that I think you'll appreciate." Jeremy led her off Front Street and over two blocks to First Street. They were close to the river with the bitter cold wind blowing in off the half-frozen water.

"What could possibly be any different here than any other street?" Clara pushed tighter against his side.

Jeremy pulled open a door and ushered her into the warm interior. The store was run by a Tagish elder.

"Clara, I'd like you to meet Charlie. He's a Tagish Indian who started this trading post when the first Whiteman arrived in the area." Jeremy put his hand out to Charlie.

The old man's round face crinkled as he smiled, showing he had several teeth missing.

"Welcome, old friend, new friend." Charlie motioned with his other hand. "See you like, I make deal."

Jeremy talked about the weather and Charlie's family while watching Clara move about the store, looking, touching, and admiring.

"Anything you like?" Charlie called to her.

Clara sent Charlie a warm smile. "There is much I like, but I still have a long way to go before I reach home and don't wish to squander my money."

She ran her hand over a fur muff. "My sisters would love one of these and my brothers would like the hand-carved antler knives. And mother could use these herbal teas." Clara looked up. "How much for the items I described?"

Jeremy could see her mind working behind that furrowed brow. He'd already determined he would buy the items and have Charlie send them to the hotel.

Charlie walked over to where she stood. He picked up each muff until he found two nice ones, then walked over to the knives. "Which?"

Clara followed him, pointing to two of the smaller knives.

"And these?" Charlie moved to the jars of teas.

"One to help her sleep." Clara glanced over her shoulder at Jeremy.

He nodded and smiled, hoping she would also pick out something for herself.

Charlie returned to the counter with the items. "Seven dollar for all. Good deal. Less than I charge others."

Jeremy held his breath to see if she would purchase the items.

She ran her hand over a muff and fingered the etching on one of the knives. "I shouldn't, but it would be a shame for me to not take something back to the others."

"I agree." Jeremy captured her hand closest to him. "And did you see something in the store you would like?"

"I don't need anything. I've had the experience of the trip to take home with me." Clara pulled out her pocketbook and placed money on the counter.

Jeremy turned to Charlie. "Do you have any jewelry?"

The man smiled broadly. "Yes. Daughter just made nice necklace of red stones." He turned to a cupboard behind the counter and pulled out a small wooden tray. Placing the tray on the counter he beamed up at Clara. "My daughter find pretty stones and say they need worn."

Chapter Thirty-Two

Clara had never seen anything so red and shiny as the stone nestled in a filigree of fine gold. "It's beautiful!"

Charlie held it out to her. "You see you like."

Her fingers trembled as she held the fine chain in one hand and the stone in the other. She'd never owned a necklace or any piece of jewelry other than her father's watch.

"Let me put it on for you." Jeremy took the necklace from her fingers and wrapped the chain around her neck. His fingers tickled the hairs at the nape of her neck as he hooked the ends.

"Let me see." His gaze moved from her face down her neck to the spot at the top of her bosom where the shiny stone hung.

"It's so beautiful, but I don't need it." Clara put her hands up to unclasp the chain.

Jeremy's hands stopped her upward motion.

"But I need to see it on you. Charlie, I'm buying the necklace."

"It's too much, I shouldn't…"

"It's my gift to you." Jeremy turned from her and paid Charlie.

She didn't see how much the necklace was worth, but she had a feeling more than he should have spent.

Charlie had her gifts wrapped in brown paper. Jeremy scooped them up and offered her his arm.

"We should head back to the hotel and see if our announcement brought any visitors." Jeremy opened the door, and then stepped to her left, keeping her toward the buildings as they made their way back to the center of town and the hotel.

"You shouldn't have spent so much on this necklace," she again tried to convey such an extravagant gift wasn't necessary.

"Honestly, I can't wait to see it next to your skin." He winked.

Her face heated and her heart raced. His comment was bawdy. And worse, it sent her insides squiggling and her mind to conjuring up exactly how much skin he wanted to see.

She refrained from any more comments about the necklace. Instead, she took in the sight of the bustling city. The muddy streets didn't deter the population from being out in force. Each block had a restaurant or two, saloons, and the stores had signs saying what they had. It was a shame the boats hadn't made it here with supplies. Most of the population had to be eating game and very little else.

Jeremy tugged on her arm, hurrying by a

gambling hall. Men milled about in front of it. She didn't want to tarry either.

Brushing past a group of men, she heard someone utter the name "Bixbee".

"Stop." She dug her heels in and slipped her arm from Jeremy's.

"What are you doing? This isn't a place for you to stop." Jeremy now faced her, his expression showing he wasn't happy with her actions.

"I heard a man say, 'Bixbee.'" She looked over her shoulder and pointed. "There. Those four were the ones talking when I heard it."

Jeremy grabbed her hand with his free one and walked over to the group. "Excuse me. As my wife and I were passing, she overheard one of you say, 'Bixbee.' Is he someone you know?"

Clara watched the four men as each one studied first Jeremy and then her. Finally, the red-faced, red-bearded man nodded his head. "What's the name Bixbee mean to you?"

Clara started to say he was her brother.

Jeremy squeezed her hand. "We told his family we'd look for him while we were here."

"If you want to see the bloke, he runs the gambling hall on Sixth Street. If I was you, I'd forget you heard his name. He's no one you'd want to tell his family about," said the tall blonde man, standing next to the red head.

"Why?" Clara couldn't believe her brother was at a gambling hall and these men thought so little of him.

"He's not the sort you'd want to have your woman around." The man stared at her, but his words were directed at Jeremy.

Clara could hardly breathe as her chest constricted. What was he talking about? It had to be a different Bixbee. Randy would never be a threat to her or any woman.

"Thank you." Jeremy drew her away from the men and continued down the street. "Breathe, Clara. There's no proof yet that the man they're talking about is your brother."

"I'm sorry. It's…the men were so adamant about him being…" She swiped at the tears trickling down her cheeks. "It has to be someone else. It can't be Randy."

"I'll take you and your packages to the hotel then go over and see if I can learn if it is your brother." Jeremy propelled her down the street at a faster clip.

"I'm going with you." She wanted to be there when Randy found out she was looking for him.

"No. You're staying in the hotel. A gambling hall isn't a place for respectable women. I promise, if it is your brother, I'll come get you before I talk to him." Jeremy squeezed her hand and looked down at her.

She'd trusted this man with her life on so many occasions, but having him order her to stay away when her brother might be so close, her stubborn, independent nature was digging its heels in.

She wanted to trust Jeremy would tell her the truth about Randy. But she also knew he would withhold information he thought might hurt her.

They stopped in front of the hotel.

Clara rammed her hands on her hips. "The only

way I'll stay here is if you promise you will tell me everything you find out about the man and come get me as soon as you know if he is my brother." After her trek into Soapy Smith's parlor, she wasn't going into a gambling hall, especially with Jeremy who would believe it was his duty to save her honor.

Jeremy smiled, not the eye sparkling, take-her-breath-away smile, but the wry smile he bestowed on her when he knew she wouldn't budge from her stand.

"I promise. As soon as I know if he is Randy, or if he isn't Randy, I will come straight back here and tell you. But you have to stay in the room and wait for me." He opened the hotel door, ushering her in and up the stairs.

"I'm hungry." Her stomach had started to rumble right before they walked past the gambling hall.

"You can nibble on the bread from last night. We'll go to Mrs. Warren's when I get back." Jeremy unlocked their room and walk inside with her. He placed the wrapped packages on the table. Facing her, he grasped both her upper arms and leaned down, his face only inches from hers. "Stay in the room. Don't follow me. I promise, I'll be back soon."

His mouth covered hers in a deep, tongue-tangling, body-heating kiss. He drew back as she gasped for air and equilibrium.

"I mean it. Stay here. A gambling house is no place for a lady."

Clara watched him slip out the door and smiled. As a rule she didn't like to be bossed around by anyone, but Jeremy's kisses lessened the sting of the orders he gave. *And he called me a lady.*

Jeremy stood in front of the third gambling hall on Sixth Street. The other two didn't have anyone by the name of Bixbee but the second one had sent him here. He turned down his coat collar and shoved through the large wooden door.

Men and scantily clad women swarmed the floor like horn flies on a dead carcass. He'd never taken to gambling, seemed like a waste of hard earned money. He stood at the door several minutes taking in the lay of the room and searching for someone dressed fancy and holding court. That would be the owner of the establishment.

A table in the back had three women hovering around four well-dressed men drinking and playing cards. The end of the bar stood ten feet away from the table. He sauntered through the crowd, stopping now and then to watch action at the tables.

At the bar, he put a foot up on the rail and twisted his body to see the room and the table where he presumed the owner sat. One of the half-dressed women sashayed up to him. She smelled of too much perfume and had colored stuff packed on her face.

"Honey, want to buy me a drink?" She smiled, stretching her painted lips wide across prominent teeth.

"I'll buy you a drink if you tell me who owns this place." Jeremy slid a dollar across the counter to the bartender who arrived at the same time as the woman.

"Bixbee. That man at the table there. The one

with wavy brown hair and green eyes." She pointed a long thin finger at the man sitting directly behind the table.

Jeremy studied the man. He didn't have any physical features that reminded him of Clara other than green eyes. "What's his first name?"

The bartender placed the drinks on the counter. Jeremy slid one toward the woman.

She scrunched her face in concentration. The expression did nothing to help her looks.

"I don't think I've ever heard his first name. All I've ever heard him called is Bixbee."

"Do you think you can ask the other girls and see if they know?" He held a silver dollar up for her to see.

Her gaze dropped to the coin. "Sure. I could do that. But why don't you go ask him yourself?"

"I want to make sure he's the man I'm looking for before I talk to him."

Her eyes narrowed. "You aren't here to cause trouble are you?"

"No, just looking for a man for a friend." He dropped the silver dollar into her cleavage. "Go ask around for me, and I'll have another one of those for you."

Her eyes lit up, and she sashayed over to a table and whispered in a girl's ear.

Jeremy drew his attention from the woman and watched the men at the table. If the man was Clara's brother, why hadn't he sent his family a letter? Owning a gambling hall wasn't the most respectable occupation, but he could have at least let the family know he was alive. And if he was Randy, having received other letters from his family, one would have thought he'd have someone fetch his mail from Forty Mile.

It didn't make sense, but as Jeremy watched the man, he noticed a mannerism that was similar to Clara's.

The painted up woman returned. "Velvet thinks his first name is Randolph, but she wasn't sure. No one else has ever heard him called anything but Bixbee."

"What hours are the hall closed?" He would bring Clara here and have her take a look at the man. But not while the business was running.

"This place never closes. But the slowest hours are early morning." She put a hand on his arm and leaned in close, giving him a look at her goods pushing up over her low neckline.

"The boss has to sleep. When is he not down here on the floor and where does he live?"

"You sure ask a lot of questions. You could come up to a room with me, and I could answer your questions in private."

Jeremy didn't want anything to do this woman, or any, other than Clara. "Answer my questions here. I'll pay you, and you can move on to someone else who would pay for your company."

She pouted a moment before answering him. "Bixbee leaves the floor about three in the morning and doesn't come back until five the next night. He lives in the back half of the second floor. You can get there up the stairs in the back."

Jeremy put another coin on the counter. "Thanks."

Without looking back, he strode to the door and out into the dark. Tonight, he planned to take Clara to dinner and a play he saw on a poster tacked to the opera house door. She'd need the distraction until they could visit Bixbee tomorrow at a reasonable hour.

Chapter Thirty-Three

Clara stood behind Jeremy on a small landing at the top of the stairs behind the gambling house Bixbee owned. In a few minutes she could be face to face with Randy. Her emotions had been up and down since Jeremy returned yesterday saying he couldn't confirm the man running this gambling house was Randy or not. Trying to take her mind off the possibility, Jeremy had escorted her to a nice dinner and then a play. But her mind kept wandering to why. Why hadn't Randy contacted them? Why was he running a gambling house? Did she want to find him? Down deep, she had to admit she'd hope they didn't find Randy, and she could go back and say he was dead. She'd then run the business in Russell's stead until he was of age to take over the business.

Her skin felt too tight and her head pounded with guilt and anxiousness.

Jeremy knocked again, louder.

She clutched the back of his coat, soaking up his strength.

"Coming!"

Was that Randy's voice? It had been so long since she'd heard it she couldn't be sure.

The door opened. "I'm not hiring."

The gruff tone reminded her of her father's stern reprimands. Clara peeked around Jeremy.

"Are you Randy Bixbee?" Jeremy asked, putting his arm out to keep her behind him.

"Why do you want to know?" The man's brows scrunched together.

Clara stepped around Jeremy. "He's asking for me. Clara Bixbee, your sister."

The man's eyes widened. His gazed drifted from the top of her parka to her fur boots. "Take off the hood."

Clara pushed the parka hood back. Bixbee's eyes widened.

I found Randy!

Elation that she'd accomplished her mission was short lived by the fact she didn't care for his attitude. She'd come a long way to find him, and he acted as if she were a salesman trying to sell him pots and pans.

"What are you doing here?" His voice dropped to barely above a whisper.

"Let us in, and she can tell you." Jeremy put his hand on her back, guiding her toward the door.

"Who are you?" Randy's face reddened. He crossed his arms, blocking the way into the building.

"Randy, this man, Jeremy Duncan, has helped me travel to Dawson to find you. You can trust him. He's saved my life several times." Clara put a hand on Jeremy's arm that had wrapped around her middle when Randy blocked their entry.

Her brother's gaze traveled over Jeremy and then came to rest on his protective arm around Clara. Randy scanned the alley and stepped aside, letting them enter what appeared to be a small parlor.

"Hazel. Hazel!" Randy roared, making Clara jump.

A robust woman with dark curls stuck her head out of a door to the right. "What are you yellin' about?" Her sleepy brown eyes spotted them and she smiled. "I didn't know we had company. Be right there."

Clara glanced at Jeremy. His brow was wrinkled in a frown.

"Have a seat. Hazel will get us some coffee." Randy took a heavy arm chair and motioned to a velvet covered settee.

Clara grasped Jeremy's hand and led him over to the dainty-looking piece of furniture. She sat, pulling Jeremy down beside her. He shifted, and sat on the edge of the cushion.

"Why did you stop writing?" Clara asked, peering into eyes the same color and shape as her own. Something they had both inherited from their grandmother.

"I didn't want Father to find me. He sent some detective to Forty Mile trying to bring me home. Thought I'd come if he dangled the business in my face." Randy sat back in his chair, pulled a cigar from a box and clipped the end.

"Father's dead. That's why Mother sent me to find you." Clara watched his reaction.

His expression didn't change.

"About time the old bastard died."

"Randy! How dare you speak about our father like that!" Clara would have bolted off the settee if not for Jeremy squeezing the hand he held.

"Mother should be happier with him gone. At least she doesn't have to pretend anymore."

Clara stared at her brother. "What are you talking about? Mother was devastated. And now the new manager is stealing, and we can't do anything about it. The attorney says the business is in your name and as females, mother and I can't run the business. That's why I'm here. You need to come help get the business back running properly."

"Oh no! I didn't want that business when he was alive, why would I want it when he's dead." Randy lit the cigar.

"How can you be so callous? Mother and the children will be out in the streets soon if you don't do something. Do you want that for your family?" Anger boiled in her gut and rose slowly.

"Of course I don't want them out in the street. I'll send some money down to help out."

"That's not what they need. Some money now and then won't keep the house and won't be steady income. We need you to take over the business. They won't listen to Mother or I, we need a male. Russell is too young."

"Hire someone you trust." Randy waved the lit

cigar at Jeremy. "Like this man you seem to think so highly of."

Clara stared at Randy. How could he so nonchalantly offer up a man he didn't even know to run the family business?

"Why won't you come back?"

Randy peered at her over his steepled fingers as he puffed on the cigar. "How old are you?"

"Twenty-two. Why?"

"Then you're old enough to know our father was a womanizer."

"No! I won't have you—"

Jeremy's voice cut in. "Clara, listen to your brother. Think about the things you were telling me about him."

She spun her head to peer into Jeremy's solemn face.

"Remember you said he had too many women in the office and he touched them?" Jeremy's eyes held sympathy.

Her mind tried to focus on the words and the images she remembered. Her mother crying late at night. Her father supposedly working. The women in the office hovering around her father, him smiling, something he never did at home.

Hazel emerged from the room. "I have a pot of coffee all made. I'll get some cups."

Clara stared at the make-up, the low-cut dress, and the way the woman swayed when she walked. Her gaze flew to Randy. He was unabashedly ogling Hazel. She swung her gaze to Jeremy. His gaze was on her. The worry on his face stopped her thoughts.

He squeezed her hand and leaned close. "We'll

figure out something."

She nodded even though her world was crashing around her. *Mother sent me to bring Randy back. I've failed.*

She shot a glance at her brother. *He's no better than Father. Why would mother want him around anyway? She was just as adamant as the attorney that I couldn't run the business. I've never wished to be a man, but today, if I were, I'd punch Randy for his disrespect and tell my mother and the attorney to go fly.*

Hazel placed a tray with four cups and saucers and a pot of coffee on the table next to Randy. She poured the cups and handed them to Clara and Jeremy.

Clara tried to smile at the woman who was working hard at being civil. With all that she'd learned since crossing Randy's threshold, Clara had thoughts bouncing in her head so fast she couldn't fully concentrate.

"I'm Hazel, Bixbee's fiancée." She handed Randy a cup. He smiled up at her and grinned around his cigar. "Of course he had another fiancée before I threw her out." She laughed heartily, and Randy joined her.

Clara squirmed in the settee. This wasn't the quiet, gentleman she remembered her brother to be. Did living up here for four years do that to a man? She glanced at Jeremy. He'd been here longer, and he still had manners and treated her with respect.

"I guess there's nothing I can say to make you come home?" Clara searched her brother's face for any sign he sympathized with his family's plight.

Growing up she wouldn't have thought him to be so callous.

"I like it here. Up here I can be who I want to be without reprimand and casting a bad reputation." Randy slurped down his coffee. He set the cup down, and then really studied her. "How did you make it to Dawson? The rivers haven't thawed enough for boats from St. Michael."

"I came through Skagway. Over White Pass with dog sleds." She smiled as his jaw dropped. "I told you, Jeremy saved me several times. If not for him guiding me, I wouldn't have made it this far." She sobered. "I only regret, I won't be bringing you back to Seattle. Mother is going to be devastated. She and the children were counting on you to come save the warehouse."

"This is your sister?" Hazel stared at her in awe. "Blazes, Bixbee, you won't even go out in a dogsled on a good day."

"Yeah, well, I nearly froze to death once and I don't care to do it again." Randy scowled at Clara.

"Is there anything I can say that will make you come home?" Clara had to give one last effort to sway him. Even though her mind was already planning how she could save her family.

"Nothing. I'm happy here. Happier than I was the twenty years I lived at home." Randy puffed on the cigar and blew smoke toward the ceiling.

Clara stood. "Then I have nothing more to say. When you do feel like visiting, I hope Mother is still in our house."

Jeremy stood. "I have something to say. Or ask. Since you are the oldest living male relative to

Clara, I'd like to ask for her hand in marriage."

Clara stared at Jeremy. His request stunned her. She knew he liked her and they got along well enough, but to ask for her hand? The earnest expression and firm set to his mouth made her heart race in her chest and her head scramble to understand. Was Jeremy only asking because he felt sorry for her? Or because he felt even more protective now that her brother wouldn't be traveling back to Seattle with her?

She turned her attention to her brother unsure whether to say something or keep quiet.

Randy stood. He once again ran his gaze up and down Jeremy. "If my sister wants you, I don't see any reason for me to not allow a marriage." He winked at Clara. "Besides, if Mother finds out you've been traveling alone with this man, she'll make you marry him. After all, appearances are all that matter."

Now Clara's jaw dropped, and her insides twisted. Her mother would have forced a wedding between she and Jeremy had she known the two had shared a sleeping bag more than once. But as Jeremy had said, it was just between the two of them. Having her brother shove proprieties in her face when it was blatant that he was keeping house with a harlot…

Clara shoved her hands on her hips.

"Your lack of respect toward our parents and your family gives you no voice to cast stones." She spun her gaze to Jeremy. "And while I'm flattered you asked for my hand, I'll not be a charity case. I'm pretty sure I can find my way back to Seattle on my own."

Jeremy couldn't stop the smile creeping onto his face. He'd feared Clara would think his request for her hand dealt only with his need to protect her.

"With those flashing eyes and your stern demeanor there's no way I'd call you a charity case." Jeremy took hold of her arm, forcefully escorting her toward the door

They needed to talk, and he didn't want to do it in front of her callous brother.

"We'll contact you before we leave town," Jeremy said to Randy and pulled Clara out onto the landing and down the stairs.

"What are you doing? I don't want to talk to you. I don't want to talk to anyone right now." Defeat had taken over the bravado of Clara's words.

He hadn't arrived at Randy's expecting to ask to marry Clara. But seeing how heartless her brother was toward her and their family, he couldn't let her travel home or save her family alone. She'd worked her way into his senses, and he didn't want her battling on her own.

He grasped Clara's hand and led her out to the street. He didn't stop until they stood in front of the hotel.

"Hurry in out of the cold." He nudged her through the doorway and up the stairs to their room.

Inside their room, he helped her take off her coat. When he turned back around from taking off his coat, Clara was pacing.

He planted his feet blocking her movement. "Talk to me."

"I failed." Her round eyes glistened with

unshed tears. "Mother wanted me to bring Randy back. She will be disappointed in me because for the first time, I didn't obey."

"This has nothing to do with obeying. Your brother refused. There is nothing you can do about it." Jeremy stepped forward, pulling her into his arms. He wanted to take all her pain away.

She hiccupped. "It's my fault."

"Why is it your fault?" He cradled her head between his hands and studied her face. Over the past couple of months he'd grown to love this face. Seeing the agony in her expression, he kissed her cheek.

Her eyelashes fluttered to her cheeks. "I was hoping I wouldn't find him."

Her barely whispered words shook him. "Why?"

Raising her lashes, her dark green eyes blazed. "Because I wanted to go home and prove to every-one a woman can run the business."

"Now it can happen. Marry me. You'll go home with a husband, who can be the man you need to dismiss the thieving manager, and then you can run the business." He dropped a soft, quick kiss on her lips.

Panic widened her eyes. "But you're headed home. I can't keep you from your family. You'll resent me."

When he'd asked for her hand, he hadn't had a chance to think it all through. But the anguish in her voice tugged at his heart. He knew the only answer he could live with.

"I can postpone going home as long as you'll

be with me when I do. How old did you say Russell is?"

"He's twelve. It would be eight to ten years before he's ready to run the business. That's too long to keep you away from your family." She grasped his hand in hers.

The way she clung to his hand and was adamant he see his family gave his heart hope. She might be tossing out all the reasons not to marry but she cared for him.

"Then we'll find a manager we trust and take long trips to see my family until Russell is old enough to run the business." He tipped her chin up and peered into her eyes. "Say you'll marry me."

"Are you sure you want me and all the trouble with my family?"

Jeremy stared into her eyes. "You have more grit than your brother, and I've seen your business sense. I think between the two of us, we can make things right." He did believe in her business sense and faith in family. The more he thought about it, while she wasn't the type of woman he'd thought he'd marry, she had grown in his heart.

Her eyelids lowered, and her voice dropped to a whisper. "What if I stray to other men, like my father and brother seem to stray to lots of women?"

Jeremy laughed, garnering him a scowl from Clara. "I've watched you around other men. If you were tempted by other men, you would have invited those two Mounties to sit at your table. And you wouldn't have pointed a gun at Walter at Bennett Lake." He drew her face closer to his.

"You're a one man woman, and I believe I'm

the man." He poured his feelings for her into the kiss and came up as breathless as Clara.

"Say you'll marry me." He kissed the tip of her nose. "I promise, I'm not asking out of charity, I'm asking because I don't like the prospect of not seeing you every day."

A smile crept onto Clara's face, putting a glow in her eyes. Her arms wrapped around his middle. "You truly want to marry me?"

"If I didn't I wouldn't have asked."

"Yes. Yes, I'll marry you."

Jeremy didn't think he'd ever been as happy as hearing those words made him. He hollered, picked Clara up, and swung her around once before placing her feet on the floor. Grabbing their coats, he handed Clara hers.

"Where are we going?" She asked, donning the coat.

"To find a preacher to marry us. Then we'll take stock of our supplies. We're headed to St. Michael tomorrow. There's no sense in hanging around here now that we know Randy doesn't want to go home."

Chapter Thirty-Four

Clara stood in the small church staring into Jeremy's eyes. He'd insisted on buying her a new dress to wear for the ceremony. It was a beautiful green velvet with satin trim around the cuffs and high neckline. Randy and Hazel were present as well as the preacher's wife and daughter.

She barely heard the words spoken by the preacher.

Jeremy's voice rang loud and strong as he answered, "I do."

She tried to be as strong and confident when it was her turn, but she could barely squeak the words out.

Jeremy squeezed her hands. His confident smile and crinkles beside his eyes eased some of her tension. She didn't come to Alaska to get married. She came to save her family. Now she was starting a new family with Jeremy. While the idea of marrying Jeremy thrilled her, it also frightened her. She needed him for the male influence at the warehouse but would he take over? And once they were around more women, would he discover, maybe he'd made a mistake marrying her?

"I now pronounce you husband and wife." The preacher smiled at her and winked. "You may now kiss your bride."

Jeremy scooped her in his arms. The moment their lips touched, all thoughts vanished, and she plunged into the heady sense of being wanted and desired. Heat started at her toes and flashed up her body, starting the throb between her legs that only Jeremy could start and stop.

Her knees buckled and Jeremy caught her.

"I think you need to take your wife to bed," Hazel said, bumping Jeremy's arm.

The words doused the ardor that had swept over Clara.

Her spine straightened, and her legs found new footing. "I believe we had a dinner planned with the two of you," Clara said, standing on her own and linking arms with Jeremy.

"I'll get your coats," the preacher's wife said, hurrying to the pew where they had all piled their coats when they arrived.

Jeremy took Clara's coat from the woman and helped Clara don the parka. "Don't let Hazel's lack of manners spoil our night," Jeremy whispered in her ear.

She shook her head and followed Randy and Hazel out of the church.

On the church stoop, Randy turned to her. "I

need to get back to the gambling hall."

"We planned to have dinner with you." Even as she protested, she realized Randy had never intended to join them. He no longer cared about family. She sighed. "Will I see you again?"

Randy stared down the street. "I don't know. I might show up some day to see how everyone turned out."

"You'll be welcome whenever you visit." Jeremy put out his hand.

The two men shook. Clara couldn't help the feeling she'd never see her big brother again. She flung herself against him, hugging him. "Please come visit," she whispered and backed away.

Randy nodded slightly and started walking down the street.

Hazel gave her a brief hug. "I'll see what I can do to get him to visit. But Bixbee's got a mind of his own."

"Thank you, Hazel." Clara watched as Hazel ran to catch up with Randy. The two walked side by side down the street and turned a corner.

"What will I tell Mother?"

"The truth."

Clara jumped at Jeremy's answer. She didn't realize she'd spoken out loud until he answered her. "Yes, of course. The truth. I think there have been too many secrets kept in my family."

Jeremy offered his arm, and she slipped her hand through the crook at his elbow.

"It looks like it's just the two of us for dinner. How about we have it brought to the room?"

Tremors of excitement sent delicious sensations

racing through her body. Tonight they would consummate the marriage. She stared at her husband's profile. Her heart expanded and ached with happiness. *He genuinely seems pleased with being married to me.* It seemed fitting after all the time they'd spent just the two of them that tonight's dinner would be the same.

"That sounds like a very good idea."

Jeremy squeezed her arm against his side. "I'm glad you agree." The twinkle in his silver eyes hinted at his happiness.

They arrived at the hotel in the gray dusk of the long night. Jeremy escorted her up to their room and left her alone while he went to the little restaurant in the back of the hotel to request dinner.

The time alone gave her a chance to get out of her parka and boots, and loosen her hair. Clara combed the strands until they glistened in the lantern light. She stood in front of the wardrobe contemplating whether to change into her night clothes or stay in the lovely dress.

The door opened and closed. Instead of turning to see who had entered, she continued to stare into the wardrobe, now nervous and shy about being alone with Jeremy. The idea was ludicrous, since she had been alone with him since the first day they set out for the interior, but now he was her husband.

A husband had no one to answer to, but a wife had to answer to her husband. Her brow wrinkled. Jeremy had shown he didn't believe a woman to be inferior to a man, and he spoke of allowing her to run the business. Had her father told her mother she would be allowed privileges before the marriage and then changed his mind?

Images of her mother and father flashed through her mind and she shivered.

"Are you cold?" Jeremy's hands grasped her upper arms, sliding up and down.

She spun out of his grasp. *What have I done?* Clara moved to the far side of the room as thoughts poured through her mind. I'm now legally bound to do what this man tells me to do. He is in charge of everything I need to survive. *Just like he was all the way here.*

Glancing at his face, she found confusion and hurt. *He would never hurt me or use me.*

"I'm sorry." Clara walked up to him and wrapped her arms around his middle. Hugging his strong, warm body, she shook off her fears. Jeremy was always truthful and always there for her. He wasn't like her father and brother.

"What are you sorry for?" Jeremy tipped her face up.

She peered into his questioning gaze. Her heart ached with the love she had for this man. "For letting my doubts and fears get the better of me."

"You know I would never do anything to hurt you or let anyone else hurt you." His eyes peered deep into hers.

"Yes. That's why I feel so foolish to have these fears. You aren't my father or my brother. You would never let me down or make me feel of no value." She raised up on her tiptoes, and he dipped his head, meeting her halfway.

"I'm sorry," she said before touching his lips.

His arms embraced her to his chest, lifting her

feet off the ground as he deepened the kiss, taking her on a dizzying ride. When he broke the kiss, his forehead rested against hers.

"You have my promise I will never do anything to make you doubt me."

She still found it hard to believe this strong, handsome man who could have any woman he wanted, married her.

Knuckles rapping on the door interrupted their embrace. Jeremy set her down beside the bed and walked over to the door. A woman from the restaurant held out a basket.

"We'll bring the basket back in the morning," Jeremy said, handing the woman a coin.

She nodded and left the room. Jeremy closed and locked the door before he returned to Clara's side.

"Do you want to eat or do you want me to prove how I feel about you?"

The desire in his eyes and fingers playing with the buttons on the front of her dress started her body humming. *If he looks at me with this intensity every day of my life, I will be a happy woman.*

"I'm not very hungry." She tipped her head back as Jeremy kissed her behind the ear, and down her neck as his fingers began unbuttoning her dress.

The soft kisses, his fingers gliding down her front exposing her to his touch, heated her body. He captured her mouth while his hands worked her dress over her shoulders and hips. Gasping for air, she drew out of the kiss and glanced down her body. Her corset had her breasts bulging over the top. Green velvet pooled around her petticoats. The sight added to the desires raging in her.

Clara ran her hands under the suit jacket Jeremy had on, shoving it to the ground behind him. Her fingers quickly unbuttoned his white shirt, revealing he wasn't wearing his usual union suit. Her hand skimmed over the taut skin and sprinkling of dark hair covering his muscular chest. She wanted to touch all of him, not just his chest. Shoving the shirt off his shoulders, she dropped kisses down his front, moving lower with each kiss.

On her knees in front of Jeremy, she worked the trousers loose and slid them down his muscular legs clad in tight-fitting flannel drawers. She gasped at the sight of the bulge in the front of the drawers. Savoring the anticipation, Clara molded her hand over the bulge, memorizing the length, breadth and firmness.

"Come here."

Jeremy pulled her to her feet and unhooked the corset. The garment thunked to the floor behind her.

"I want to touch you as intimately as you touched me." Jeremy cupped a breast and teased the nipple through her cotton shift with his tongue.

The sensation tingled to her toes. Her fingers gripped his sides like talons on a hawk.

"You like that?" he asked, stopping to look up at her.

"Y-yes-s," she hissed trying to control the waves of sensations rolling inside of her.

"I think you'd like it even better undressed."

She nodded, and in quick order, Clara found herself unclothed and lying on the bed, with Jeremy beside her.

"You still have your drawers on." She pouted and tucked her fingers in the waistband of his clothing.

"I can remedy that."

The clothing flew through the air, and his naked body hovered above hers. His intense gaze stole her breath. "Clara, the first time for a woman can be painful. Tell me if I hurt you."

Clara nodded and bit her bottom lip. He was big, and she still didn't understand how it would fit, but she trusted Jeremy. The yearnings she'd felt when they slept together and his hands roamed her body, she felt there had to be more. This was the more. She wanted to experience it with him.

Jeremy kissed her deep and long, swirling her tongue with his, escalating the sensations. He slid down, nipping, sucking, and teasing her nipples, one then the other. She squirmed under him, rubbing her woman curls against his belly and sifting her fingers through his hair, holding him to her breasts.

The throb between her legs now pounded in her head, she wanted… "Jeremy?" she begged. "Now, please, something…"

"Not yet, Sweetheart."

His mouth continued to give her breasts attention, but one of his hands rubbed her woman parts and her body jerked.

"Easy," Jeremy's whispered words, barely registered as his finger slid between her legs and inside her body.

The throbbing grew. Panting, she moved against Jeremy's hand trying to draw him deeper. She needed more.

"Please, more," she begged and squirmed.

He pulled out, and she cried out in dismay.

Jeremy slid up, drawing her into a mind-numbing kiss.

She shook her head. She didn't want a kiss she wanted…

He spread her legs with his and pressed his shaft against her opening.

Yes! Finally, he would appease the ache inside her.

His length slowly entered. She opened, felt the stretch, his easing in, a twinge of pain…, and bliss.

He pushed once, filling her completely, and she gasped.

"Does it hurt?" He kissed the side of her face.

"No. It's wonderful."

Jeremy grinned and started a slow rhythm entering and retreating. Gradually, his movements thrust quicker and deeper.

The throb pounded in her head, pulsed in her body, and she exploded in shards of light and tingling sensations. Jeremy continued to move, driving deeper, faster. The explosion hit Clara again and at the same time Jeremy pulsed inside of her and collapsed.

His body covered her completely and smashed the air out of her.

Gasping, she beat on his arm. Just as she thought she'd pass out from lack of air, he rolled to his side, dragging her with him. He clutched her to his chest, breathing hard, and kissed her forehead.

"Clara, that was worth waiting for." He pushed her hair out of her face and kissed her lips.

"Is it always like that?" she asked, running her hands over his chest. They were married. She could run her hands over him all she wanted in the confines of their home. *Home*. Where would they live? She didn't want to live with her mother and siblings.

"With you, yes, it will always be like that." His hands roamed down her body, cupping her bottom and drawing her hips tight to his.

He was still inside her. After the throbbing and explosions, she was surprised to feel his length twitch and grow as he continued to knead her bottom and nuzzle her breasts.

She ground her hips against his, and the throbbing started again. Now that she knew what to expect, Clara experimented, lifting a leg, resting it on Jeremy's hip. This brought her humming parts even closer to his body, adding to the sensations.

Jeremy rolled her to her back, and she wrapped both legs around his waist. This drove him deeper into her. The dizzying sensation of him driving hard, fast, and deeper, shook her body from their joining out to her finger tips and dropped her off a black abyss.

Clara came around wrapped in Jeremy's arms, her back to his front, in the middle of the bed.

"What happened?" Her body still vibrated but her mind was empty.

"You scared me. One minute you're panting and begging me for more and the next you called out my name and went limp." Jeremy kissed the top of her head. "Did I hurt you?"

"No, you didn't hurt me. The sensations were

wonderful and terrifying at the same time. My body trembled, tingled, and everything went black." She wiggled against him. "And now my body is vibrating. Can you feel it?"

"No." He kissed her again. "If I didn't hurt you, that's all that matters."

"I don't understand. If making love is this wonderful, why do some women sleep apart from their husbands?" She glanced over her shoulder at Jeremy. "I didn't want to sleep a night without your arms around me even before you made love to me. How can they sleep alone?"

He kissed her lips. "I'm not sure." Jeremy spun her in his arms. "You really don't want to sleep a night without me?"

For the first time she saw vulnerability on Jeremy's face.

"Never." Clara wrapped her arms around his neck and kissed him to the dizzying heights he usually took her. She drew back gasping for air.

Her stomach growled. "Now, I'm hungry."

Jeremy's body was sated and his heart full. Clara had wanted him to stay with her even before he'd asked her to marry him. His doubts about this marriage were one by one being put to rest.

He used his feet and one arm to pull them to a sitting position at the head of the bed.

"I'll get the food. Stay put." He gave Clara a quick kiss and left the bed.

He'd never heard of a woman passing out when making love. It worried him that he may have been too rough. At this moment, he wished he were back in Sumpter where he could ask Gil or one of the other Halsey men about it. Or even Rachel, as a doctor she would have an answer.

He picked up the basket and placed in on the bed next to Clara. "We'll eat in bed. That way we won't feel like we need to get dressed."

Clara fluttered her eyelashes. "Does this mean you'll make love to me again?"

"Only if you aren't too sore." The red tinge he'd noticed on himself would be her maiden's blood and possibly remnants from her monthly. He'd quickly slipped into bed before she saw it.

Worry he might have damaged her soured his stomach, making it hard for him to enjoy their last good meal until they reached St. Michael.

Chapter Thirty-Five

Jeremy smiled and wearily walked behind the dogs and sled as they entered the outskirts of St. Michael. He'd kept the dogs at a rigorous pace the past month. Clara could keep up when she was refreshed in the morning but by afternoon she'd started riding on the sled. They were both anxious to get out of Alaska and back home.

As they used up the rations, the empty sleds were left along the trail. The stranded gold seekers along the trail waiting for the rivers to thaw would find a use for them. He sold three dogs to men along the river cutting wood for the steam ships. Several of the spots where the steamers stopped to take on fuel had grown into small communities.

He halted the eight dogs pulling the largest sled at the first hotel he saw. Hundreds of tents lined the shoreline and south side of the St. Michael. The tents had to be new arrivals waiting for the rivers to thaw and take them inland to the gold.

"I hope we can find a hotel that isn't full," he said to Clara as she stood and stretched.

"If not, I guess we'll be living in a tent until a ship leaves." She smiled up at him.

Her optimism on the trip and all the hardships she'd endured while still remaining happy gave him even more reasons to be thankful he'd married her. He still couldn't believe she was his wife. He kissed her cold cheek and placed her hand in the crook of his arm as they walked to the hotel door.

"Aren't you worried about our things?' she asked, glancing over her shoulder at the sled and dogs.

"People here aren't as desperate as they were in the interior." He opened the hotel door and was met by a blast of warm air and the smell of baking bread.

A cheerful woman stood behind the counter. "May I help you?"

"We're looking for a room until the next ship heads south." Jeremy stepped up to the counter.

Clara pushed her parka back.

"We have one room that isn't heated very well at the end of the hall upstairs." The woman spoke to Clara.

"That's fine. As long as I don't have to sleep on the ground, I'll be happy." Clara smiled at the woman.

"Then the room is yours…" The woman turned a book around and handed Jeremy a quill pen.

"Mr. and Mrs. Jeremy Duncan," he said, signing the book.

Clara turned the book and added, Clara, behind his writing.

The woman smiled. "Mr. and Mrs. Duncan, here is your key. I'd guess you'll be with us about a week. Word has it that there should be a ship arriving on the eighteenth. That would be your ride south."

"Thank you Mrs…?" Clara asked.

"Mrs. Reid. My husband Herschel helps in the boatyard."

"Thank you, Mrs. Reid." Jeremy handed the key to Clara. "Go on up to the room. I'll get our things and bring them up."

Clara nodded. He watched her until she was out of sight then turned to Mrs. Reid. "What is the best restaurant in town?"

She smiled. "Newlyweds aren't you?"

"Yes." He couldn't stop the smile that spread across his face.

"Gretchen Kemp has a nice place down about two blocks north and over one to the east."

"Thank you." Jeremy returned to the sled, untying the ropes and retrieving their canvas pack. For all his doubts and nay-saying to keep from falling for Clara, he couldn't be happier. With a week until the ship arrived, they had time to purchase a trunk for their belongings and some new traveling clothes. Clara would be happy to get out of the men's clothing.

He scanned the street and spotted two boys hanging out in front of a mercantile. One shrill whistle had them looking his way. Jeremy waved the two over. They jogged across the street.

"You want us, mister?" the taller one asked.

"Yes. I'll give you each two bits if you take my dogs to the livery, unharness them, and feed them. Tell the owner I'll be down in an hour to make him a deal."

Their faces lit up. "You bet!" they said in unison.

"Thank you." Jeremy picked up his pack and headed into the hotel. He'd found making love to Clara while sleeping on the hard ground had its difficulties. But he enjoyed sharing a sleeping bag. Tonight, he had plans for his wife.

The smile grew with each step he climbed. At the end of the hall, he knocked on the door.

"Who's there?" called a female voice.

He grinned. "Your husband."

The door flung open and a female body wrapped around him, arms and legs clinging to him like a berry bush. The woman's scent and hair wasn't right.

"Jeremy! What are you doing?"

Clara's horrified exclamation behind Jeremy squeezed his heart. He dropped the pack and peeled the woman off him, holding her at arm's length. He stared into the terrified face of a woman with brown hair.

"Ma'am, leave me be," he said forcefully.

The door behind him slammed shut.

"Billy, I'm so glad you came back." The woman grabbed his hand and started kissing him.

"Ma'am, I'm not Billy. Go back to your room." He pushed the woman in the room and shut the door.

Spinning, he tried the door Clara had opened. It was locked. He rattled the knob. "Clara, let me in. I can explain."

The door didn't open. Pressing his ear to the wood, he heard her pacing.

Damn! She only paced when she was angry.

He took the stairs two at a time and found Mrs. Reid in the kitchen in the back of the downstairs. "Ma'am, do you have another key. Some crazy woman jumped me in the hall when my wife opened the door and now she won't let me in."

Mrs. Reid's face flushed a deep red. "I forgot Mrs. Durfee was at the end of the hall. I'll come with you and explain things to your wife." The woman flounced past Jeremy and up the stairs.

He followed. If Clara didn't believe Mrs. Reid or believe in him, he may have made a mistake marrying her. All the women who married Halsey men, including his sister, stood by their men with the fierceness of a she-bear before marriage.

Clara stomped back and forth across the small room, anger burned her cheeks. *How could he*! He knows the kind of men that are in my family. He knows I won't condone that kind of behavior. We talked about it several nights after Dawson.

The knob of the door shook again. She backed against the bed, not ready for a confrontation. Unsure what she would say or do.

The door opened, and Mrs. Reid peeked in.

"Mrs. Duncan. I'm sorry I didn't warn you and your husband." The woman stepped into the room. "I'm afraid Mrs. Durfee has gone a bit mad since her husband was killed in an accident. She calls every man she sees Billy and clings to them."

Clara shook her head. She wasn't sure she could erase the sight of the woman in Jeremy's arms.

He entered the room, his hat in one hand, their pack in the other. "Clara, that woman flew out of the room at me."

She wanted to believe the sincerity dulling his eyes. *I want to believe he loves me.*

Mrs. Reid walked over and squeezed Clara's hand. "He didn't do anything wrong. It was all Mrs. Durfee. She's not right in the head since her husband died." She cleared her throat. "I'll leave you two alone."

The woman left, closing the door quietly behind her. Clara jumped at the click of the latch.

"Clara, I know how you feel about wandering men. I would never do that to jeopardize our marriage. I swear, I knocked on the door thinking it was ours. She came out so fast and stuck to me I couldn't even see who she was. But I knew she wasn't you. She didn't feel right in my arms."

He took two steps closer and dropped the pack.

Clara continued to stare into his eyes. His words were laced with sincerity. Remorse etched his face. She wanted to believe in him. Lately her emotions were too close to the surface. She couldn't control them like before.

Jeremy closed the space between them and opened his arms.

She teetered. Her body leaned toward him, her heart ached with want for him, but her mind…her mind kept seeing the woman wrapped around him.

He grasped her hand and led her to the bed. "I have plans to take you to a nice dinner and bring you back here and show you, you are the only woman I ever want."

She wanted that. Needed to feel his love, for he'd yet to tell her he loved her. The scene in the hall pecked at her fear he only married her out of honor. She wanted more.

Lacing his fingers with hers, he leaned close and kissed her cheek. "How does a warm bath and putting on one of your dresses sound?"

A bath. One thing she'd learned to appreciate on this trip was a bath. "I'd like the bath very much." She peeked up at him through her eyelashes. "Will you be joining me?"

He laughed. "Sweetheart, if Mrs. Reid doesn't bar me from joining you, I will scrub your back and put even more of a glow on your cheeks."

With that proclamation, he kissed her long, deep, and dizzying, leaning her back onto the bed until he was looming over the top of her. He drew away, and her eyelids slowly fluttered up. His caring gaze peered down at her.

"Clara, you never have to worry about me straying. You have my heart and my body." He leaned down and kissed her dizzy, again.

Her heart skittered around like a rock on a frozen river. *He said I have his heart!*

Jeremy ended the kiss, breathing heavy above her. He gradually stood and moved about the room.

Clara remained on the bed, enjoying the softness under her and lingering over the effects of the kiss and the realization he may not have married her out of charity. If they hadn't been traveling for five weeks with only the occasional pitcher of water to wash with, she'd be willing to have Jeremy make love to her this minute. He couldn't have thoughts of other women when he kissed her so thoroughly.

"Come on, sleepy head, I have your clothes and mine. Let's go find Mrs. Reid and get a bath."

She leaned up on her forearms. Jeremy stood by the door with his set of wedding clothes and hers draped over his arm. Clara clambered off the bed and checked the clothing he had for her and blushed.

"You forgot my drawers, and you only have one petticoat." She held up the dress. "And you didn't get my corset."

His eyes sparkled, and his mouth curved in a devilish grin. "That way I can get you undressed faster when we get back from dinner."

She slapped his arm. "I can't go out in public without the drawers or corset; that would be wanton."

"I like you wanton." He raised an eyebrow.

Clara bent over the pack and dug inside for the items her husband conveniently neglected to dig out. Dizziness caught her unaware, and she stumbled to the side.

"Whoa! What's wrong?" Jeremy's strong arms circled her waist, holding her against him.

She waited for the dizziness to pass, her undergarments dangling in her hand. "I'm fine. I think I need a big dinner tonight is all."

Jeremy turned her in his arms and peered down at her. The worry etched on his face tugged her heart.

Clara traced the lines with her fingers. "I'm fine. I need a good meal and your loving. That's all."

"You're sure all you need is a good meal?"

"Yes. Let's get that bath."

Jeremy bent and picked up the clothes he'd dropped on the floor. He added the items in her hands to the pile in his arms and motioned for her to head out the door.

They found Mrs. Reid in the back of the building.

"We'd like a bath," Clara said, not allowing the lustful thoughts of bathing with her husband to show on her face.

Mrs. Reid smiled. "I figured as much. Everyone who comes in from the interior wants a bath. I have the hot water already in the tub. Add cold to make it a temperature you can tolerate." She opened the door to a small room with a metal tub half full of steaming water. "You'll find towels up on the shelf."

"Thank you." Clara walked into the room.

Jeremy followed and piled their clothes on the only chair in the room.

"Mr. Duncan, you can wait in the lobby. I'll come get you when your wife is finished," Mrs. Reid said from the hall.

Clara didn't know what to say or do. Jeremy was pleading with his eyes for her to say something. "Mrs. Reid. I prefer he stay with me. I had a bad encounter in another hotel where a man walked in on me."

"Oh my! That would never happen here. I keep

a strict eye on the hall when I know a woman is bathing." Mrs. Reid stood in the doorway, her body puffing up in outrage.

"I'm sure you do, but I'd prefer Jeremy stay with me." Clara walked to the door and gently moved the woman out of the threshold. "Thank you for your understanding." She closed and locked the door.

Jeremy captured her hand and pulled her deeper into the room. "Thank you," he whispered and began unbuttoning her wool shirt.

Chapter Thirty-Six

Clara couldn't feel more loved and desired than the week that passed in St. Michael. Every night she fell asleep exhausted from their love making. Every day she learned more about the man she married. When she refused to allow him to buy her clothes, he informed her that he enjoyed buying her things, and he was only using the gold they made hauling the items to Dawson. His sister had his savings, and money to invest in a business, sitting in a bank in Sumpter.

Today, they would board the *Excelsior* for the nine-day trip back to Seattle. Clara shook out the brown wool skirt and ran her hands down the ivory buttons of the cream-colored sateen shirt waist. She'd insisted percale was a fine fabric, but both Jeremy and the dressmaker insisted on the sateen. Jeremy also insisted on a long double-breasted jacket to keep her warm while strolling on the deck of the ship.

Jeremy entered the room and stopped. His gaze moved from her new hat to the new pointed-toe oxfords. "Have I told you how honored I am to be your husband?" He crossed the room, gathering her in his arms.

"No. You've only told me you desire me." She kissed his chin.

"I also can't believe you married me. Thank you." He tilted his head and their lips met.

The kiss wasn't a mating of tongues and longing of bodies. The meeting of their lips was a merging of their growing infatuation with one another.

Jeremy eased out of the kiss and loosened his embrace but kept her circled in his arms. "The trunk is loaded, and the passengers can start boarding."

"We better head to the ship, so we aren't left behind." Clara slipped from his embrace and picked up her coat.

Jeremy held the garment while she slipped her arms in the sleeves.

"You, Mrs. Duncan, are glowing today." Jeremy kissed her lightly on the lips before he buttoned her coat.

"Thank you. I'm excited to get home and introduce you to my mother. And I have so many ideas on how to set the business to rights."

He opened the door and offered his arm. Clara slipped her hand through the crook of his elbow. She enjoyed this habit he'd started when they first met. They left the hotel, walking briskly toward the dock and the ship that would take them home.

Clara stared up at the ship. It was larger and

more sophisticated than the ship that carried her from Seattle to Skagway.

"How did such a large ship get so close to shore?" She stared in awe as they neared the long walkway people ascended to reach the deck of the ship.

"This port is deeper than the one in Skagway. That's why they are building ships here to take goods inland. Now that so many people are coming to Alaska, they have started using the larger ships to haul the passengers and goods." Jeremy squeezed her hand. "But the trip back won't be crowded. Fewer people are headed home than are heading for gold."

Clara raised her skirt and started up the plank ahead of Jeremy. It was comforting to know he was behind her ready to catch her if she should topple backward.

Jeremy had made all their arrangements once the ship had docked, making him familiar with the captain. On deck, after Clara caught her breath, he introduced her to Captain Andrews. His ready smile and gray beard endeared him to her. The captain reminded her of Uncle Dean. She missed her uncle who had worn a beard since she was small. After the greeting, Jeremy led Clara to their cabin where the trunk sat at the end of the bed in a room twice the size of the one she'd traveled to Alaska in.

"This trip had to cost a lot of money." Clara walked to the small window giving her a clear view of the ocean and the sun slowly descending toward the horizon. She turned from the spectacular sight and caught Jeremy watching her. The happiness shining in his eyes caused her heart to skip in her chest.

"We're still using the gold from Brightly." He crossed the room in three strides, gathering her into his arms. "Sweetheart, you don't have to worry about money. I have enough to take care of the both of us until I decide what work I want to do and your family business is making a profit."

"I don't want you using up all your money on frivolous things."

"Our money. When I married you that made everything I own yours as well." Jeremy leaned down.

She could tell he was about to steal a kiss. She turned her face to keep from being distracted from the conversation. "The government doesn't feel that way. It is still all yours."

Jeremy took her hint and while keeping his arms locked around her, he did give her more space. "There are ladies who are trying to change the laws." He peered into her face. "You should join them."

"Really? You wouldn't mind if I marched with the suffragettes for the right to vote?" This was one more layer of Jeremy she enjoyed learning about.

"Heck, if you can run a business, you have enough sense to make the right choice for a candidate. Most women I know have more sense than most men." He glared at her. "But I'll deny I said it if you bring it up around other men folk."

Clara laughed. "You are such a fake."

"What do you mean?"

"You talk all nice and tell me what I want to hear, but then say not to tell anyone you said it for fear they'll think you're weak." Her heart continued to do flips watching his cheeks redden. "It's all right. I won't tell anyone you give in to me."

Relief softened his face. "Thanks. I do have a reputation to uphold."

Clara laughed again and hugged him tight. The notion she went all the way to Alaska and found the man to make her heart and soul happy *and* allow her independence still befuddled her.

"Do you want to be on deck when we pull out of the harbor?" Jeremy asked, holding her tight.

"Yes, I'd like to wave good-bye to Alaska."

Jeremy led her out of the room and up the flight of stairs to the main deck. He kept an arm around her waist while they watched the shoreline fade into the distance. The crew scrambled about as the captain shouted orders. Soon the noise and chaos lessened and the other passengers began leaving the deck.

"What are we going to do for the next nine days?" Clara asked, hoping her husband suggested they spend time in the small bed in the cabin.

"I don't know, what did you do on the way to Skagway?" Jeremy tightened his hold on her, drawing her closer for more warmth as the ship picked up speed in the growing dark and the wind grew colder.

"I spent a good deal of my time in the cabin reading. I didn't like the gambling and rowdiness of the people. When I went outside my room men would put their hands on me."

His embrace tightened. "No one will bother you this trip. I'll see to it."

She rested her head against his side. "I know I'm safe this trip. I wouldn't mind walking around and watching how things work."

Jeremy grasped her hand, leading her toward the center of the ship. "I can make that happen."

They toured the ship until darkness drove them into their cabin. When a bell rang out, Jeremy escorted her down the hall from their cabin and entered a large open room with chairs around beautifully set long tables.

Jeremy led her over to a table already occupied by two other couples. One older, close to the age of her parents, and a couple a little older than she and Jeremy.

"Mr. and Mrs. Sandville, this is my wife, Clara." Jeremy held Clara's chair and seated her next to the older woman, Mrs. Sandville.

"Pleased to meet you, dear. Our husband's met when they brought our trunks to the ship."

Clara nodded to the woman. Mrs. Sandville sat tall in the chair. Her dark hair was streaked with silver. The woman raised a hand to pick up her cup of coffee, jangling silver bangles on her bony wrist.

"Jeremy and Clara Duncan, these are our new friends, Alfred and Missy Thomas."

Clara nodded to the younger couple as Jeremy and Alfred shook hands. She didn't miss the long appraisal Missy gave Jeremy.

"It's nice to be on a ship that isn't full of rowdies and gambling." Clara placed her napkin in her lap, thankful she, Jeremy, and Mrs. Sandville sat on one side of the table while Mr. Sandville and the other couple sat across from them.

"You must have arrived in Alaska on one of the ships carrying the fortune hunters," Mr. Sandville said, picking up a fork and jabbing at the salad on the small plate in front of him.

"I did." Clara studied the man. He was as lean as his wife. His gray hair had streaks of red. His fading blue eyes shone with kindness and reflected high intelligence. She liked this couple very much.

She glanced at Jeremy to see if she should tell more. He smiled and nodded.

"I came to Alaska to find my older brother and ask him to come back and run our family business." Clara forked a bite of salad in her mouth. It had been months since she'd had fresh vegetables. Her eyes closed slightly as she enjoyed the taste and texture.

"Why would he need to come home and run the business?" Mr. Sandville asked, forking more salad into his mouth.

"Our father passed away—"

"Oh dear! I'm so sorry!" Mrs. Sandville placed a hand over Clara's laying in her lap.

"That must have been dreadful on your family," Missy said, staring at Jeremy.

Clara had trouble swallowing the lettuce and set her fork down. *The woman has a husband, why is she ogling mine?*

Mrs. Sandville squeezed Clara's hand, and she tried to shake off the jealousy making her nauseous.

Clara peered into Mrs. Sandville's eyes. "Thank you. When he passed, my mother didn't have any sense of the business. I discovered, while working in the warehouse, our manager was stealing and cheating our customers. I couldn't do anything about it. So we decided since Randy hadn't answered our letters I would come find him and bring him home."

"Is your brother on the ship?" Mrs. Sandville asked.

The lump of jealousy keeping her from eating turned to fretfulness and started to rise in Clara's throat.

A waiter arrived, removing their salad plates and filling the empty spot with a china plate holding roast, mashed potatoes, beets, and rolls.

Clara stared at the food. Her stomach pitched. "I—" She shoved her chair back and hurried from the room. The ladies toilet was a distance from the dining room, but she made it before her stomach heaved.

Standing at the sink, tears trickling down her cheeks, she gulped great gasps of air and willed her stomach to settle.

"Clara? Are you in there?" Jeremy's voice penetrated the pounding in her head.

"Yes." The reply sounded weak to her ears.

"Can I come in?" His wistful plea tugged at the corners of her lips.

"I don't know. I think they frown on men entering this area." She did want to be in his arms, but her legs felt too weak to carry her the steps to the door.

She heard voices in the hall moments before the door opened.

"I've had a bit of experience with these things." Mrs. Sandville put an arm around Clara's shoulders and helped her to a stool at the side of the room. She returned to the sink, wet a cloth and brought it back, mopping at Clara's face. "You have a worried husband out there."

"I know. I don't know what happened. The food, the motion of the ship, and…the conversation all got to me." Clara peeked under her lashes at the woman. She'd expected to see censure but all she saw was sympathy.

"When I was in your condition there were days I couldn't get out of bed." Mrs. Sandville returned to the sink.

"My condition? What do you mean? Newly married?" Confusion swirled in Clara's mind. What was the woman talking about?

Mrs. Sandville faced her. Surprise arched her eyebrows and her mouth formed an "o". "Landsakes, you don't know you're with child?" Then she answered herself. "Of course you didn't, otherwise you would have known the motion of the ship could cause you to be nauseous."

I'm going to have a baby? The notion frightened her. *I can't have a baby. What about the business? Mother and the children? Jeremy said he didn't want children.* Panic overshadowed the queasiness.

"Since you didn't know, I can conclude neither does your husband." Mrs. Sandville came over and put an arm under Clara's and helped her stand. "You and your husband need to go to your cabin where it's private—"

Clara wrapped her hand around the woman's arm. "Don't tell him, please."

Mrs. Sandville stared at her long and hard for a moment. "I assumed this baby is your husband's." Her tone stung with recrimination.

"It is! I-I just need time to adjust to the news before I can tell him. I'm not ready to have children. There's so much I have to do when I get home." She pleaded with her eyes as well as her words.

"I see this is a shock. I'll not say a word, but the longer you wait, he's going to think the worst."

Clara nodded and followed Mrs. Sandville to the door.

Chapter Thirty-Seven

Jeremy paced in front of the ladies toilet. What could be wrong? She didn't say traveling to Alaska made her sick. Did the topic of the conversation make her ill? He thought they'd discussed how they didn't need Randy to run the business.

He started for the door and stopped one stride short when the door opened and Mrs. Sandville stepped out followed by Clara. Jeremy studied his wife. Her pale face and downcast eyes, twisted his guts.

"What can I do?" he asked, moving to her side and wrapping an arm around Clara.

"Help me to the cabin, then return to the dining room and finish your dinner."

He leaned close to hear her.

"I'm not leaving you alone." He tightened his grip around her shoulders.

"I can sit with her while you eat," Mrs. Sandville said, drawing his attention to the older woman who followed them down the hall.

"It's not right to pull you away from your husband and meal." Jeremy knew the couple were kind, but he couldn't prevail on them this early in the trip. If Clara proved sick the whole trip, he would need some relief at some point.

He stopped at the cabin door.

"Oscar will understand." Mrs. Sandville pushed past him, opening the door and moving inside.

Jeremy glanced down at Clara, surprised she hadn't told Mrs. Sandville they could manage. Was she more ill that he thought? His arm still around Clara, he led her to the bed and she sat. He knelt in front of her, holding her hands.

"Sweetheart, is there more to this than the rocking of the boat?" He peered into her eyes.

She flicked a quick glance at Mrs. Sandville then shook her head slightly. "I'm tired and the boat motion is bothering me." She put a hand on his face. "Go eat your dinner and enjoy the conversation. I'll be fine with Mrs. Sandville. By tomorrow, I'll be better. You'll see."

He kissed her palm and then her forehead. She didn't feel warm.

"I'll go, but I'll return as soon as I finish eating."

She smiled weakly and he stood. Facing Mrs. Sandville, he searched her face. She smiled and waved him toward the door.

"We'll be fine. Finish your meal and come back when you're ready. I don't have anything else to do while Oscar smokes in the smoking parlor."

"Thank you." Jeremy glanced over his shoulder at Clara. She smiled and nodded. He left the cabin, pulling the door closed quietly.

He didn't like Clara's paleness or how quiet she'd become. Something was wrong. He wouldn't get it out of her with Mrs. Sandville around, and they both urged him to eat. He'd finish his meal, but he'd be back shortly.

Jeremy strode down the hall to the dining room. Mrs. Thomas was the only one still seated at the table. His plate remained as he'd left it. He nodded to the woman and took his seat.

Mrs. Thomas' hand reached across the table and grasped his arm. "Is everything all right?"

He frowned at her hand and shook it off. "I don't know. Clara is awful pale."

"Some women just aren't strong enough to handle the rocking of the ship." Her superior tone raked across Jeremy's nerves.

"Clara is a strong woman. She didn't have this problem traveling to Alaska." He began shoveling in the food and sinking into his own thoughts.

He sat back to drink the wine served with dinner and noticed Mrs. Thomas wasn't sitting in her chair. His body relaxed even more knowing he was alone. He closed his eyes to settle his thoughts. Arms looped around his neck, and he came up out of his chair, sending it sprawling. He spun, backing against the table.

Mrs. Thomas stood in front of him a wicked smile on her face. "I was just comforting you, there was no need to cause a scene."

"Ma'am, I don't need comfort from you. Excuse me, my wife needs me." Jeremy strode past her, out the door, and down the hall without looking back. *What was wrong with that woman? She's married and so am I.* He'd witnessed a few women in his time that weren't content with one man, but never so boldly. *What was wrong with the women around here? First the crazy lady at the hotel jumped him and now this woman blatantly throwing herself at him.*

At the cabin, he knocked softly and entered. Mrs. Sandville met him just inside the door.

"She fell asleep about five minutes ago. Let her rest. It's the best thing for her. If she's still sleeping in the morning when you hear the breakfast bell, let her sleep and bring her back tea and toast." Mrs. Sandville reached for the latch on the door and hesitated. "Be calm with her. She's got a lot on her mind."

The woman slipped out the door, leaving him wondering at her comments. Jeremy faced the bed. He stood for several minutes watching Clara's serene face. *At least she isn't plagued by an upset stomach while sleeping.* That must have been why Mrs. Sandville said to let her sleep.

Jeremy undressed, blew out the lantern, and slipped in beside his wife on the small bed. The only way he could get comfortable was by pulling Clara up against him and spooning his body around hers. It was a position they'd slept in many nights while sharing a sleeping bag.

Clara woke the next morning and found herself alone in the bed. A quick peek at her watch told her it was mid-morning. *I rarely sleep this late.* A piece of paper sat on the table by the bed.

I'm eating breakfast, will return with tea and toast for you soon. Love Jeremy

It was past breakfast. What could be keeping him? Her stomach growled. *That's a good sign.*

Now that she was awake, she needed to use the facilities and she wanted something to eat. Thankfully, Mrs. Sandville had put away her fancy wool skirt and sateen shirt waist and set out an everyday dress along with one petticoat and her new corset that was easier to don. By the time she was dressed, the urge to use the facilities was even more pressing. She glanced at the chamber pot but preferred to not use that unless it was an extreme necessity.

Clara opened the door and headed for the ladies toilet. She made it into the room and took care of business. Standing at the sink, she drew in gulps of air trying to appease the nausea making her skin sticky with perspiration.

Missy Thomas walked in.

"Oh my, you don't look well. I can go get your husband, he and I were just on the deck walking."

Before Clara could take in all the woman said, Missy disappeared out the door. Surely, she meant Jeremy was walking with Missy and her husband.

A knock sounded on the door and Jeremy's voice called, "Clara, do you need me to come in?"

How had the woman found him so fast? Jealousy added to her queasiness.

"Please, I'm the only one in here," she called as loud as she could.

The door burst open, and Jeremy scooped her

up in his arms. "I brought your tea and toast and found you gone. I saw Mrs. Thomas in the hall and asked if she'd seen you."

"The room please." Clara thought over all that had transpired. She wanted to ask Jeremy if he had been on the deck with Missy. But didn't know how to ask without sounding jealous.

Jeremy carried her down the hall and into their cabin, placing her gently on the made bed. She ran her hands over the top cover. "Who made the bed? I wasn't gone that long.

Jeremy kissed her forehead. "I did. I told the woman who came by earlier that we'd let her know when the room needed cleaned, otherwise to leave it be." His concerned gaze swept over her face. "I didn't want anyone to disturb you."

Tears burned the back of her eyes. His concern for her and all the little things he did swelled her heart, making her chest ache. She circled her arms around his neck and pulled him down on the bed with her. "You are too good to me."

"You deserve only the best, Clara." His lips rubbed softly back and forth against hers before he deepened the kiss.

The languid kiss pulled her away from her worries. She snuggled against him and returned the soft nips and sensual licks.

Jeremy eased out of the kiss, dropping soft kisses all over her face. "You should eat the toast and drink the tea before they get too cold." He sat up, hanging his legs over the edge of the bed.

Clara shoved her body up to sit with her back against the cabin wall. Reaching for the toast, Jeremy offered on a plate, her stomach rumbled.

"Good timing." He smiled.

She nibbled on the toast and took sips of the tea, praying it stayed down and her nausea would ease. After the last bite, her body wasn't as shaky. Jeremy's hand on her leg reminded her of how supportive he was. *He wouldn't make me stay home with the baby.* At first she'd tried to deny that she was with child. But last night, she and Mrs. Sandville figured out she was over a month along. Her monthly hadn't happened since Dawson.

Pushing the thoughts and words around in her head, she opened her mouth to reveal the news.

"Are you feeling up to a walk on the deck? The fresh air would be good for you."

Jeremy was so eager to please, she nodded. And she had felt better up on the deck before they came down to dinner last evening.

He fetched her jacket and helped her put it on. They left the cabin arm in arm and proceeded up to the main deck. The sun peeked through nasty-looking gray clouds.

"The captain says we're heading into a storm."

Clara clutched his arm tighter. "Will there be complications?"

"No, this ship has ridden out lots of storms, but the ride will become bumpier." He grimaced. "Which won't help you getting over your seasickness."

"It's going to take a while before I get over my sickness."

Jeremy studied her.

She opened her mouth, again, to tell him when

someone called out his name.

They both turned. Mr. and Mrs. Sandville sat on chairs along the wall of the ship. The couple waved them over.

"It's good to see you looking well, Mrs. Duncan," Mr. Sandville said.

"Thank you. I'm feeling better today." She took the seat Mrs. Sandville motioned to next to her.

The men began talking about the coming storm and Mrs. Sandville leaned toward Clara.

"Have you told him?"

"I've tried twice and both times I was interrupted." She glanced at Jeremy and smiled when he winked at her. "He's a good man. He'll let me work and not stay home with the baby."

The older woman squinted. "Work? What kind of work?"

"Getting my family's business out of trouble. Mostly office work." She leaned back in the chair, closed her eyes and thought about the first order of business when they returned to Seattle. Jeremy dismissing the manager. "I need to dismiss the manager, with Jeremy's help, then find one we can trust."

Mrs. Sandville touched her arm. Clara opened her eyes and studied the woman.

"You need to take care of that stuff as early as you can when you return. The last few months it isn't proper for you to be out in public while in your condition."

Clara stared at the woman. Was that why her mother always stayed home at the end of her pregnancies? *I thought it was just mother being vain.* She would have to find a good manager and one that wouldn't be bothered by her coming into the office a few times a week even if she was showing.

She shook her head. "I won't hide. And I'm pretty sure Jeremy won't mind."

"What won't I mind?" Jeremy sat down on the chair on her other side.

"That I spend a good deal of time at the warehouse making sure the business is running smoothly," she narrowed her eyes at Mrs. Sandville, and then turned and smiled at her husband.

"I told you, you know the business, I don't. I'm just there as the man to make the others listen to you." Jeremy captured her hand and kissed the back before settling their clasped hands in her lap.

They sat for another half hour visiting amicably with the older couple.

"I would like to freshen up before lunch," Clara said, hoping to get Jeremy back to the privacy of their cabin where she could tell him about the baby.

Jeremy stood, helped her up, and they excused themselves. On the way to their cabin, they were stopped by Captain Andrews. He asked Jeremy to come see him after escorting Clara to the cabin.

There goes my chance. Clara smiled and said, "That's fine. If the captain wants to visit with you, I can lie down for a bit before lunch."

"You're sure? I can stay if you want."

Jeremy said the right things, but she could see he was excited to join the captain.

She kissed him on the cheek and pushed him out the door. "Go enjoy your visit. Come get me when the meal bell tolls."

He leaned in and kissed her lips. "I will." He

grinned and loped down the hall to the stairs leading to the top deck.

She smiled and closed the door. Removing her jacket, she draped it over the chair. To not wrinkle her dress, she slipped it off and set her boots on the floor by the bed. Perhaps, dressed in her undergarments, she could finally get Jeremy's undivided attention.

Chapter Thirty-Eight

Jeremy couldn't believe his luck. Captain Andrews had a nephew looking for work in the Seattle area, and he had experience with warehouses and shipping. *Wait until I tell Clara, we might just have a new manager already.*

He took the stairs down to the lower deck two at a time and bumped into Mrs. Thomas as she turned a corner at the beginning of the hallway.

"Sorry." He grasped her upper arms to steady her as her body teetered from the impact.

Her hands splayed across his chest. "You're so big and strong." Her voice purred.

The hair on his arms spiked to attention just like when he was a kid and someone scraped their nails on a chalk board.

He set her away from him. "Excuse me. I have to get to my wife."

"I'm a woman in need, too," she called down

the hall after him.

Her comment only made his legs move faster. *That woman has a problem.*

He stopped at the cabin door and slowly opened it. His breath sucked out of his lungs and his body heated. Clara stood beside the bed in her corset, shift, and petticoat looking like a woman ready to be bedded.

Three quick strides had him scooping her up in his arms and pressing her onto the mattress.

"Sweetheart, If I could walk into our house every day and see you like this I would never tire of it."

Her eyes flashed with heat. He lowered his head to kiss Clara into the burning inferno that coursed through his body at the sight of her. She returned the kiss with the same passion. While he enjoyed the view of her breasts bulging over the corset, he preferred having his hands on the soft handfuls.

He grasped the top to unhook the first hook and the mid-day meal bell rang through the ship. Ignoring the call appealed to him until he heard Clara's stomach rumble.

Jeremy used his arms to raise up away from Clara. "Let's go eat. We can continue this after you've been fed."

"I don't want food. I want you." She wrapped her arm around his neck and instead of pulling him down, she rose up to capture his mouth in a kiss.

He gave in long enough to loosen her hold and stand up. "No. We'll eat first. You didn't have any dinner last night and only that piece of toast this morning. You'll need your strength for what I have planned for you." He raised one eyebrow, causing her to giggle.

"As long as you promise to return to the cabin with me and not wander off to talk with the captain."

He helped her stand. "I knew you didn't really want me to go, but I may have found you a manager."

She stopped with her dress pulled up to her waist. "A manager? Where? On the ship?"

Jeremy stepped forward, helped her put her arms in the sleeves and buttoned the front of her dress. "No. The captain has a nephew who lives in Seattle, has worked in a warehouse before, and knows shipping. Captain Andrews guarantees he's a hard worker and someone you can trust."

He kissed her nose and maneuvered her to the chair. Jeremy handed Clara the hair brush he bought her in St. Michael. "Fix your hair while I put your shoes on. Wouldn't want people getting the wrong idea when we show up late for a meal." He winked and slid her feet into the oxfords he'd talked her into purchasing.

Standing, he couldn't stop himself from leaning down and kissing her lips while he sifted his fingers through her soft, golden hair. He straightened. "Leave it down. I like the way it glistens in the light."

Clara's cheeks reddened, but she ran the brush through her hair two more times, pulled the sides up with whale bone combs and stood. "I'm ready."

Jeremy opened the door, and they stepped out

in to the hall as Mr. and Mrs. Thomas came strolling by.

Clara tugged on Jeremy's arm. He leaned down.

"Try not to sit with those two," she said.

He didn't ask why because he had no intention of sitting at the same table as Mrs. Thomas.

Inside the dining area, Jeremy stopped and scanned the available seats. Pride squeezed his chest as several of the men seated around the room scanned Clara and gave him an acknowledging nod. *The prettiest woman in the room was his.*

Captain Andrew raised his hand and pointed to two empty seats at his table. Jeremy cringed when he spotted the Thomases at the same table.

"Did you see the captain motion to us?" he asked Clara.

"Yes." She frowned.

"You also see who else is at the table."

"Yes, but they are at the far end and the open seats are near the captain. I'd like to ask him about his nephew."

Jeremy smiled and nodded to the captain. That her business side overruled her discomfort around the other couple didn't surprise him.

At the table, Jeremy seated Clara closest to the captain so she would be able to discuss business with him easily. That left Jeremy to visit with a gentleman he had yet to meet.

He tried to keep an ear on what Clara and the captain said and be a considerate listener in the nearly one-sided conversation with the gentleman on his right. Turning to give the gentleman his attention, Jeremy's gaze drifted over Mrs. Thomas who smiled brightly and winked.

His gut clenched. Jeremy sought Mr. Thomas whose attention was focused on the man next to him. He started to relax, but felt a presence behind him. Turning his head, he caught Clara glaring at Mrs. Thomas. That glare moved to his face as he came into view. He wanted to assure Clara she didn't have to worry about the other woman, but she returned her attention to the captain.

The rest of the meal Jeremy spent his time trying to avoid any eye contact with Mrs. Thomas, keeping in the conversation with the gentleman to his right, and giving Clara attention. By the time the meal was over, a caged feeling nudged at his mind and tightened his muscles.

"Want to go for a walk on the deck?" he asked Clara, needing an outlet for his tension.

"I'd like to go to the room and lie down for a bit. The food tasted wonderful but now that I'm no longer deep in conversation, I'm feeling queasy." She stood as he pulled her chair back, but she didn't meet his gaze.

He tucked her hand in his arm and led her out of the room. Clara's touch remained light. She walked alongside him in silence, adding to a guilt he didn't deserve. Once they were in their cabin, he faced her.

"Clara, I know you saw Mrs. Thomas wink at me. I swear, I didn't do anything to make her think I'd succumb to her advances."

"What do you mean her advances?" Clara frowned and stared at him with the same distrust she'd given him the first time they met in Skagway.

"I won't lie to you. This woman puts her hands on me when there isn't anyone else around. I always walk away." He grasped her hands. "Clara, you are the only woman I want touching me."

He pulled her into his embrace and kissed her, until she sagged against him. He eased out of the kiss. "I believe we had a date to make love after the mid-day meal…"

Jeremy lowered his lips to meet hers.

Clara put her delicate fingers between their lips. "I need to rest."

He didn't like the dull sound of the words, but he wouldn't push his attention. "I'll be back in two hours." He peered into her eyes. "Unless you want me to stay with you."

She shook her head. "No. I really do need to lie down and let my food settle."

Jeremy's gut clenched again. Was it her stomach, or her heart, that was pushing him away?

"All right." He kissed her forehead. "Want me to help you with your shoes before I go?"

"I'm fine. Enjoy a walk on the deck." She sat on the bed, leaned back, and left her oxfords dangling over the edge of the bed.

Ignoring her comment, he leaned down and removed her shoes. He lifted her feet, placing them on the bed, and covered her with a throw that was draped over the chair. He bent, kissed her lightly on the lips, and left.

Agitated, he took the stairs to the main deck two at a time and strode forcefully around the deck three times. *Why doesn't Clara believe me? A wife believes in her husband. I married her, what other proof does she need I love her?* His chest squeezed. Was this marriage a mistake? He thought about waking each morning without Clara by his side. It only made him more upset.

"My goodness, Mr. Duncan, what has you so pent up?" Mrs. Sandville asked. She and her husband stood at the railing.

Jeremy stopped, scratched at the back of his head tipping his hat forward, and studied the two.

They were the only people on the ship he felt like confiding in besides Clara, and she was the cause of his anguish.

"I don't know how to get through to Clara that Mrs. Thomas is throwing herself at me and not the other way around." There he said it to someone other than his wife.

Mrs. Sandville smiled. "Is that all that's bothering you?"

The woman had a glint in her eye and the mention of the other woman hadn't elicited a frown.

"Should there be something else?" he asked.

Now her face lost some of its light. "Not for me to tell." She patted her husband's arm. "I'm going to go see Mrs. Duncan and let her in on the fact Mrs. Thomas throws herself at any man she finds alone. She has a problem, and that's why they are uprooting and moving all the time."

Jeremy turned to Mr. Sandville. "I had a feeling she was that type of woman, but you'd think her husband would keep a tighter rein on her."

Clara couldn't go to sleep. It was more than the

food irritating her stomach. It was trying to decide if she should tell Jeremy about the baby since he seemed to be giving Mrs. Thomas the time of day. She wouldn't be married to a man like her father or brother. And she wouldn't bring up a child in that atmosphere. She wanted her child to have two loving, doting parents not one.

Soft rapping on the door pulled her from her reveries.

"Come in." She wasn't ready to face Jeremy, but she couldn't make him stay out because she didn't have the courage to outright tell him what was going on in her head.

Relief relaxed her hands clenching the throw as Mrs. Sandville walked through the door.

"How are you feeling?" she asked, approaching the bed.

"I kept down the tea and toast this morning and the mid-day meal has stayed down so far, but my stomach is a little queasy."

Mrs. Sandville pulled the only chair in the room up to the bed. "The upset stomach usually only lasts the first three months."

A sly expression took form on the woman's face. "This little upset wouldn't have anything to do with the way Mrs. Thomas has been carrying on around your husband?"

Mortification struck Clara like a cold snowball to the face. Shivers started at her neck and squiggled down her spine. "What do you mean?"

"Clara, that woman has been trying to get the attention of every man on this ship but her husband. She even cornered poor Oscar in the hallway outside our cabin."

Clara stared at the woman. Jeremy had been telling the truth. The woman was throwing herself at him. Jeremy *was* the chivalrous type and wouldn't be mean or crass to a woman or child. The nausea eased as she came to see the truth.

She may not have come to Alaska to "lay claim" but she was going to lay claim to the "gold mine" she'd found in Jeremy Duncan.

Telling that woman off would show Jeremy she wanted him, and then she'd tell him about the baby. That was the problem, she'd let her experiences with her family make her judge Jeremy when he wasn't like the men of her family. He was better.

"Mrs. Sandville, if you'll excuse me. I think I'll go for a walk and find my husband."

The older woman smiled and opened the door. "I'll see you at dinner."

Clara nodded and swung her feet over the edge of the bed. The sight of her shoes sitting side by side started her heart racing. Everything Jeremy did for her showed his love. *Why have I been so blind?* He may not say he loves me but everything he does shows his love.

She donned her shoes, slipped her arms into her jacket, and stepped to the door. Grabbing the latch to open the door, she heard raised voices. One of them was Jeremy's. She opened the door and peeked out.

Chapter Thirty-Nine

Jeremy had never come so close to hitting a woman. Even thinking it made his gut tense.

"Mrs. Thomas, back away from me. I love my wife and want nothing to do with you."

"Mr. Duncan, your wife will never know." She pressed her body against his.

Shudders of disgust washed through him. Jeremy grabbed her arms and forcefully shoved her backwards. "I'll know. I would never do anything to hurt Clara or taint our love. Go back to your husband."

He spun on his heels, striding toward the cabin and safety.

A body hit him from behind. Arms wrapped around his neck.

"Get off!" He grabbed her arms, ripping them from his neck and lunged forward.

The door of their cabin opened, and Clara

stepped into the hall.

Panic seized him, spreading pain through his chest.

"Clara it isn't—"

She held up a hand, walked past him, and stood in front of Mrs. Thomas. Clara's hands sat firmly on her hips. Seeing that stance washed away his fear.

"Mrs. Thomas, take your sorry self back to your husband." Clara pointed a finger in his direction. "This man is mine, and he will be until I can't take another breath of air. He's the father of my child, and I'll not have you chasing after him like some harlot."

Jeremy stood behind Clara enjoying the raking she was giving the woman.

My child? He stared at the back of Clara's head. *Why did she say my child like she had one*?

Mrs. Thomas shook a finger at Clara. "I'm going to tell my husband how your husband attacked me."

Clara laughed. "Is that the same thing you tell him every time you throw yourself at another man?"

Mrs. Thomas glared at Clara and hurried down the hall.

Clara spun around, facing him.

Her fierce statement he was her man had wiped away all Jeremy's doubts. She was a woman who would fit in with the Halsey family, and she fit perfectly in his heart.

Jeremy embraced her to his chest and kissed her. She snuggled into his embrace and kissed him back.

He eased away, holding her at arm's length.

"Thank you! I couldn't get rid of that woman."

"You're welcome." Her eyes glistened with tears.

"Why are you crying? And what did you mean by your child? Do you have one you haven't told me about?" He knew she was a virgin, or was she? The first time had been right after her monthly…

Clara laced her fingers with his and tugged him toward their cabin. "I have something to tell you." She glanced up and down the hall. "But not here. In our cabin where I can fully enjoy your reaction."

He followed, mulling that over. If she was looking forward to his reaction…

Once inside the cabin, Clara pushed him into the chair then sat on his lap. She cleared her throat. "There's a reason I've been upset this trip. I didn't realize it until Mrs. Sandville disclosed all my symptoms."

Clara put her hands on either side of his face and smiled. Her green eyes sparkled with excitement. "I know you once told me you didn't want to make a baby. But that was back before we were married." She took a deep breath. "I'm hoping you're feeling a little kinder to the idea now that we're married, because… We're going to have a baby."

Jeremy stared into her eyes. *We're*. His mind grasped what she said. His gaze dropped to her tiny middle. "You're with child?"

"Yes. But I won't be one of those women who stays in bed the whole time. I have to be at the warehouse to make sure we don't lose any more customers and it can support two families. My mother's and ours."

"Jumpin' jingles!" Jeremy hugged her tight then let her go. "Oh, did that hurt?"

Clara laughed. "No silly, I'm not that far along. But Mrs. Sandville says that I'll have the uneasy stomach for the first three months."

"A baby." The idea filled his heart with even more love. "We're going to have a baby."

"Yes." Clara laughed.

"Sweetheart, you have made me the happiest man. I promise to love you and all the babies you give me with all my heart."

"I know. And I wouldn't have it any other way."

Jeremy embraced her to his heart and kissed her with the undying love he felt for her and their child. One by one, he unfastened her buttons and made slow, lingering love with his wife.

Chapter Forty

Clara couldn't believe they would soon be on land again. Her stomach was ready for solid ground and no more swaying. Though she'd discovered her queasiness went away when Jeremy made love to her. She'd told him so, and they spent the remainder of the trip spending most of the hours in their cabin.

"Captain Andrews will meet us tomorrow at the warehouse with his nephew," Jeremy said, joining her at the railing.

Worry gnawed at her insides. "I hope we still have a warehouse." She scanned the crowd on the dock, even though she knew no one would be there to meet them. She'd sent a letter by dog sled from Dawson after she married Jeremy to let her mother know Randy wasn't returning and she was bringing a husband. But her family had no idea when they'd arrive.

Jeremy put his arm around her shoulders and

squeezed. "Don't worry, I sent a letter to my sister when we were in Dawson. I told her to bring money and see that your family was taken care of."

Clara stared into the pale blue eyes she adored. "You didn't need to do that."

"Your family is now my family. I'm sure Darcy has taken care of what needed to be done in our absence." He kissed her temple and waved.

"Who are you waving to?" She spotted a small, dark-haired woman and tall, good-looking man waving and smiling.

"Darcy and Gil."

The love and pride in his voice brought tears to her eyes. She blinked them away and stared. "Mother!" She exclaimed seeing her mother next to Darcy. "They brought Mother with them!"

Clara moved along the railing until they stood first in line to exit the ship.

"Mrs. Duncan, it has been a pleasure to visit with you. I'll bring my nephew around to your warehouse at one tomorrow." Captain Andrews shook her hand and then Jeremy's.

"Thank you, Captain." She gave the man only half her attention as she studied her mother. She looked well. More rested and her face less etched with lines then when she put Clara on the ship for Skagway.

Jeremy held her arm, running alongside Clara, as she ran down the plank and into her mother's arms.

"Mother!" Clara exclaimed and hugged her mother. So much had happened to her since they last held one another.

"Clara." Mother held her away scanning her face. "You are glowing. This young man of yours must be the cause."

"Mother…" Clara tugged on Jeremy's hand she still clutched, pulling him out of his sister's arms. "This is Jeremy Duncan, my husband."

"Mrs. Bixbee, I'm pleased to meet you. Clara has been worried about you and her brothers and sisters." Jeremy gave her mother a one-armed hug, and then pulled her into the hug.

"My, you are a tall, handsome man." Mrs. Bixbee blushed. "Having met your sister I was expecting someone not so…"

"Tall and good looking. Yeah, Darcy isn't all that purdy." Jeremy joked and received a slug in the arm from Darcy.

"You would have thought spending so many years in the wilds of Alaska would have changed you, but you're still as immature as ever," Darcy said, hugging Jeremy around the waist with one arm.

Clara liked Darcy already.

"I have a buggy waiting for us," Gil said, herding everyone away from the dock.

"What about our trunk?" Clara looked back toward the ship.

"The captain will make sure it gets to us," Jeremy said, winking at Gil.

Clara studied the two men. There was an age difference, but if she didn't know they weren't blood related, it would be easy to believe they were.

Gil helped her mother and Darcy into the front seat of the buggy, while Jeremy helped Clara into the back and climbed up beside her.

"I can't wait to see the children. I bet they've all grown so much." Clara clutched Jeremy's hand and watched the familiar stores and streets pass by.

"Hey, Darcy, where's your brood?" Jeremy asked.

"Mabel and Russell are watching them." Darcy smiled over her shoulder at Clara. "Your sisters and brothers have been a big help with our children while Gil and I cleaned up the warehouse."

"Cleaned up the warehouse?" Clara stared at the backs of Gil and Darcy's heads.

"These two dismissed that nasty manager and talked several of our clients who had left into coming back." Mother turned slightly in the front seat and smiled at her, and then Jeremy.

Clara looked into her husband's face. "What all did you write in that letter you sent?"

"You'll see tomorrow when we go to the warehouse." Jeremy squeezed her hand and stared ahead.

The house came into view.

Clara sighed. There had been a couple times on her trip when she wondered if she would see the Gingerbread trim and inviting door again.

Gil reined the horse to turn up the small drive between their house and the neighbors, stopping the buggy in front of the small, shared stable. The kitchen door flew open. Russell, Mabel, and George ran down the steps. Grace walked behind them, a large smile on her face.

Tears ran down Clara's face. Happiness wrapped around her, and she couldn't stop smiling as Jeremy lifted her out of the buggy and set her on the ground in front of him.

Arms encircled her and the questions bunched all together until she couldn't understand what anyone said. She returned the hugs and kissed cheeks.

"Why are you crying?" George asked when they all stood watching her.

"Because I'm so happy to see everyone." She linked her arm through Jeremy's. "There were several times on this trip when I didn't think I'd make it back here to see each of you." Clara peered up into Jeremy's thoughtful face. "But Jeremy was always there, taking care of me."

"Everyone, this is my husband, Jeremy Duncan. Jeremy, this is Grace." She put her hand out to take one of Grace's. "Mabel." Her sister smiled shyly. "Russell." Her brother held out his hand and shook with Jeremy. "And George." Jeremy ruffled her youngest brother's hair.

George grabbed her hand. "Come on. There's more people to meet."

Clara glanced at Jeremy who shrugged, but he had the mischievous smile she'd learned meant he was hiding something.

Jeremy followed Clara and her brothers and sisters into the house. He didn't know what was up, but knowing Darcy, she planned a party to celebrate their wedding.

They walked through a large kitchen and down a short hall and turned into a parlor.

"Surprise!" The shout made both Clara and himself take a step back.

Jeremy scanned the room and his smile grew. Hank and Kelda stepped forward to embrace him and Clara. He introduced them and was swallowed up in a hug from Ethan and Aileen.

"Zeke and Maeve couldn't make it, but they send their love and will see you soon," Ethan said, releasing Jeremy and pulling Clara into a hug.

No sooner did Jeremy break loose, than Clay and Rachel wrapped him in a welcome-home hug. Small children, some who looked familiar, and those he'd never seen called him Uncle Jeremy and hugged his legs and waist. Little Shayla wasn't so little any more. She smiled shyly and hugged him. His eyes burned from tears building behind his eyes. He'd never dreamed of a homecoming like this.

Jeremy found Clara, hugging Lily and surrounded by the Halsey females. He walked over, captured Clara's hand and led her to a spot in the middle of the room. He cleared his throat and when that didn't quiet the room he whistled.

Quiet descended.

He looked each Halsey adult in the eyes and said, "When I left Sumpter five years ago, it was to prove to myself that I could make a living on my own. It wasn't that I didn't think of all of you as family, I just wanted to prove something to myself." He swallowed and stared into Clara's loving eyes. "I'm back, for a while here in Seattle while Clara takes care of her family's business, but when we can leave it to one of the other family members, we'll be spending our time between here and Sumpter."

Returning his gaze to the room full of family, he added, "Seeing all these children, it's a good thing we're going to be adding a cousin to the mix."

The woman all gasped and moved forward

in one wave to sweep Clara away from him. He couldn't stop smiling with the pride he felt.

Gil slapped him on the back. "I never figured you'd come back with a wife, let alone a baby on the way, but little brother, you have become the man I saw in the boy."

"Hear, hear!" said the other Halsey men.

Jeremy stared in the eyes of his family, but it was when he caught Clara's gaze and the love shimmering there, that he knew he was truly, and finally, home.

About the Author

All my work whether it's my romance or my mysteries have Western or Native American elements in them along with hints of humor and engaging characters. My husband and I raise alfalfa hay in rural eastern Oregon. Riding horses and battling rattlesnakes, I not only write the western lifestyle, I live it.

I love to hear from fans. You can find or contact me at:
patyjag@gmail.com
or my website – www.patyjager.net

Historical Western Romance
Gambling on an Angel
Improper Pinkerton
For a Sister's Love
Christmas Redemption

Halsey Brother Series
Marshal in Petticoats – Gil's story
Outlaw in Petticoats – Zeke's story
Miner in Petticoats – Ethan's story
Doctor in Petticoats – Clay's story
Logger in Petticoats – Hank's story

Halsey Homecoming Trilogy
Laying Claim – Jeremy's Story
Staking Claim – Colin's Story
Claiming a Heart – Donny's Story
A Husband for Christmas - Shayla's Story

Letters of Fate Trilogy
Davis
Brody
Isaac

Silver Dollar Saloon
Savannah
Lottie Mae
Freedom

Contemporary Western Romance
Perfectly Good Nanny
Bridled Heart

Historical Paranormal Romance
Spirit of the Mountain
Spirit of the Lake
Spirit of the Sky

Thank you for purchasing this Windtree Press publication. For other books of the heart, please visit our website at www.windtreepress.com.

For questions or more information contact us at info@windtreepress.com.

Windtree Press
Hillsboro, OR

www.ingramcontent.com/pod-product-compliance
Lightning Source LLC
Chambersburg PA
CBHW061216190726
48288CB00001B/206